BETT[...]

THE ULTIMATE COLLECTION

Betty Neels's novels are loved
by millions of readers around the world,
and this very special *12-volume collection*
offers a unique chance to recapture the pleasure
of some of her most popular stories.

Each month we're bringing you a new volume
containing two timeless classics—irresistible love
stories that belong together, whether they share the
same colourful setting, romantic theme, or follow the
same characters in their continuing lives...

As a special treat, each volume also includes an
introductory letter by a different author. Some of the
most popular names in romance fiction are delighted
to pay tribute to Betty Neels; we hope you enjoy
reading their personal thoughts and memories.

We're proud and privileged
to bring you this very special collection,
and hope you enjoy reading—and keeping—
these twelve wonderful volumes!

Volume Twelve

*—with an introduction from
international bestselling author*

Anne Weale

**In this very special collection
you are invited to share Betty Neels's first ever book
and her last, in one unique volume!**

*SISTER PETERS IN AMSTERDAM
EMMA'S WEDDING*

We'd like to take this opportunity to pay tribute to **Betty Neels**, who sadly passed away last year. Betty was one of our best-loved authors. As well as being a wonderfully warm and thoroughly charming individual, Betty led a fascinating life even before becoming a writer, and her publishing record was impressive.

Betty spent her childhood and youth in Devonshire before training as a nurse and midwife. She was an army nursing sister during the war, married a Dutchman and subsequently lived in Holland for fourteen years. On retirement from nursing Betty started to write, inspired by a lady in a library bemoaning the lack of romantic novels.

Over her thirty-year writing career Betty wrote more than 134 novels and was published in more than one hundred international markets. She continued to write into her ninetieth year, remaining as passionate about her characters and stories then as she was with her very first book.

Betty will be greatly missed, both by her friends at Harlequin Mills & Boon® and by her legions of loyal readers around the world. Betty was a prolific writer and has left a lasting legacy through her heartwarming novels. She will always be remembered as a truly delightful person who brought great happiness to many.

THE ULTIMATE COLLECTION

Volume Twelve

SISTER PETERS
IN AMSTERDAM

&

EMMA'S WEDDING

Two full-length novels

Harlequin Mills & Boon Limited,
Eton House, 18-24 Paradise Road, Richmond, Surrey TW9 1SR

This compilation: THE ULTIMATE COLLECTION
© Harlequin Enterprises II B.V., 2003

First published in Great Britain as:

SISTER PETERS IN AMSTERDAM © Betty Neels 1969

EMMA'S WEDDING © Betty Neels 2001

ISBN 0 263 83654 1

Set in Times Roman 11 on 13 pt.
141-0503-103842

Printed and bound in Spain
by Litografia Rosés, S.A., Barcelona

Dear Reader

Whenever I go to a secondhand bookshop or garage sale, I always hope to find a copy of *Sister Peters in Amsterdam*, the first title on Betty Neels's long backlist. Published in 1969, it was followed the same year by three more romances, and by 1978 she had published forty—a prolific output she maintained to the end of her long life.

But the regularity of her new books was by no means the only reason for this much-loved author's success. It was her distinctive 'voice' and her unswerving values that drew readers to her. Regardless of trends, she followed her own star and—the wife of a Dutchman herself—created scores of delightful Dutch heroes with the perspicacity to fall in love with young women who often lacked the beauty and self-confidence of conventional heroines.

Some years ago, I had the pleasure of meeting Betty and we exchanged many letters about our books and our lives. She was as delightful in person as her stories suggest. One of the most unassuming *grandes dames* of romantic fiction, Betty Neels seems likely to be one of the most enduring.

Anne Weale

SISTER PETERS
IN AMSTERDAM

by

Betty Neels

CHAPTER ONE

IT was one o'clock, the corridor leading from the main hospital to the Children's Unit was very quiet. As Matron accompanied the professor to the ward, her thoughts were busy. She knew that the morning clinics were over; Sister Peters would be back from lunch and the children should be quiet enough for him to have a talk with her, before making his decision.

When the exchange plan had first been suggested by the Grotehof Hospital in Amsterdam, her own hospital committee had had no hesitation in recommending Sister Peters, who was in charge of Children's Casualty and Out-Patients as well as the ward. However, she had hardly expected matters to have gone forward as rapidly as they had. The professor had arrived within a few hours of his conversation with her, and she had had no time to speak to Sister Peters. She hoped that everything would go smoothly. As they reached the glass doors of the ward, she looked at the tall man beside her; he seemed very pleasant; rather quiet perhaps, but he had a charming voice and spoke excellent English. He did not open the doors but stood watching the girl sitting on a low chair with her back to them. She wore a shapeless white gown over her uniform, but the frilled cap—a dainty affair of spotted muslin—perched on top of a coil of vivid red hair, showed her rank. She had just put down a feeding bottle on the table before her, as she hoisted a fat baby on to her shoulder. She patted his back while he glared at them through the door. Presently he gave a loud burp and was rewarded by a light kiss on the top of his head as he was neatly tucked under her arm while she stooped to lift a fallen toddler to its feet again. As she stood up, two small children ran over to her and caught hold of her apron and toddled beside her as she went over to the cots. The doors squeaked as the professor opened them, but she didn't look around.

'I'm all behind, Nurse.' She spoke in a clear, unworried voice. 'Johnny's been sick again. I popped him into a bath and put him back to bed. He'd better be seen as soon as I can get someone.' She tucked the baby expertly into his cot, picked up one of the toddlers and looked over her shoulder. She was surprised to see Matron, but remained unruffled. Still holding the child, she went across the ward to her. She was a pretty girl, with large brown eyes, extravagantly fringed with black lashes, a small straight nose and a wide mouth, nicely turned up at the corners. She was smiling as she spoke to Matron.

'Good afternoon, Matron. I'm sorry, I didn't hear you come in.' Matron returned her smile.

'Good afternoon, Sister. Have you no nurses on duty?'

'The clinics were late this morning, Matron. Nurses are all at second dinner; they'll be back any minute now.'

She glanced at the man standing so quietly at Matron's side. She supposed he was a visiting doctor looking around the hospital, and wondered why he chose to come at such an awkward time. Matron's next words cut across her thoughts.

'Sister, this is Professor van Essen, senior consultant pediatrician at the Grotehof Hospital in Amsterdam.' She paused. 'He is just taking a look round.' She tuned to him. 'Professor, this is Sister Peters.'

The girl put out her hand. 'How do you do, sir?' She smiled at him in a friendly way, and thought how handsome he was in a dark, beaky-nosed fashion.

The professor shook hands and returned her smile, saying only, 'How do you do' in a rather formal way. He caught Matron's eye.

'May I go round with Sister, Matron? That is, if she can spare the time.'

He waited patiently while Sister Peters took off her gown, handed the toddlers over to a nurse who had just come in, and put on her cuffs. Having adjusted these to a nicety, she indicated her readiness to conduct him around the ward. His tour was a thorough one, his questions searching and numerous. Sister Peters began to think that he would never go, and blushed guiltily when he said at length:

'Forgive me for taking up so much of your time, Sister. I do have an excellent reason for doing so, and that must be my excuse.' He hesitated, and she thought he was going to say more; instead he smiled at her so charmingly that she felt a distinct stab of regret when he left the ward.

She wondered about him once or twice during the rest of the day and so far forgot herself as to day-dream about him—something quite alien to her nature, for she was a sensible young woman who accepted her life cheerfully and made the most of it. Only persistent cries of 'Adelaide, it's your turn to make the tea' from the other occupants of the Sisters' sitting room brought her back to reality, and as she jumped to her feet to put the kettle on, she told herself not to waste her time on such senseless mooning. This sensible attitude of mind, however, did not last very long, and her last thoughts before she slept that night were of the professor from Holland.

Coenraad van Essen, walking back with Matron to her office, assured her that he considered Sister Peters would be most suitable for the post in his hospital. Matron nodded her agreement.

'Sister is a first-class nurse,' she said. 'She's young, I know, barely twenty-five, but she has had several years' experience and is especially good with children in Out-Patients and Casualty, and I understand that she will be working for you in those departments at your clinic.'

'Will she object to living in Holland for a year? Has she family ties or—er—is she engaged to be married?'

Matron reassured him. 'Sister is the daughter of a country parson, she has twin brothers younger than herself—still at school, I believe. They are a devoted family, but I see no reason why she should not go to Holland, for to the best of my knowledge she is not engaged. She's a very popular girl, but shy, and makes no effort to attract attention.'

'There could hardly be any need to do so,' murmured the professor, 'with that hair.'

Matron looked rather taken aback. 'It is rather striking,' she conceded, 'but I can assure you that whatever the colour of her hair, Sister Peters is ideally suited for the post.'

They parted on the friendliest of terms, arranging to meet in Matron's office in the morning, as the professor had expressed a wish to be present when Sister Peters was offered the job. It was almost nine o'clock the next morning when the phone rang, and Adelaide, who had been half expecting a summons, answered it. It was Matron. 'Sister Peters, would you come to my office at once, please?' She answered with a meek 'Yes, Matron,' and thought uneasily of the noisy toddlers and untidy ward yesterday afternoon, which Matron would not have failed to observe. Perhaps the professor had remarked on it, although he had appeared oblivious of the chaos and noise around him. 'And so he should,' thought Adelaide. 'If he runs a children's clinic he must know that they shout and yell and vomit and wet their nappies, irrespective of Matron or doctors' rounds.' She smoothed her apron, put on her cuffs and patted the cap on her astonishing hair, told the staff nurse where she was going, and set off for the office.

When she knocked and went in, the professor rose from the arm of the chair where he had been sitting, and she returned his greeting with a rather startled good morning as she went across the room to Matron's desk. She eyed that lady warily. She appeared to be in a good humour, but with Matron that didn't always signify; she could deliver a telling set-down in the friendliest possible way. Adelaide stole a look at the professor, lounging against the mantelpiece, with his hands in his pockets. He was looking at her and smiling almost as though he read her thoughts. She bit her lip and went a little pink as she dutifully gave Matron her full attention.

'You have doubtless heard of the exchange scheme between this hospital and the Grotehof Hospital in Amsterdam, Sister.' Matron looked at Adelaide, but gave her no time to reply. 'As you know, an arrangement has been made for our two hospitals to exchange a member of our staff for a period of one year. The hospital committee has decided to nominate you, and I must say that much as we shall miss you, I must endorse their choice. Professor Van Essen feels that you will be most satisfactory for the post of Out-Patients and Casualty sister in his clinic—it only remains for you to decide if you will accept the offer.'

Matron rounded off this speech with an encouraging smile and nod. Adelaide, who had been listening with growing surprise and excitement, was still trying to find her voice when the professor spoke.

'Before you say anything, Sister Peters, I should like you to know that I and my staff will be very happy to welcome you at the clinic, and will do our best to make you happy as well as keep you busy while you are with us,' he smiled down at her. 'Please say that you will come.'

Adelaide looked up at him. She liked his quiet, unhurried voice, she liked his face. He was very good-looking, she decided, but good looks didn't count with her. His nose was certainly very beaky; she wondered why he wore glasses. His eyes were twinkling now, and she saw his lips twitch, and realised that she had been staring. She bit her lip. 'I'm sorry,' she stammered. 'Quite understandable, Sister,' he smiled. Adelaide made up her mind. She liked the professor, and rather to her own surprise, for she was not a hasty girl, found herself accepting his offer without further preamble.

'Good, Sister Peters. I will leave Matron to make all the necessary arrangements, and shall hope to see you in due course.'

'Well, that's settled.' Matron sounded pleased. 'You will want to go back to your ward now, Sister. Perhaps you will come and see me this afternoon, and I will tell you all the details then.'

Adelaide thanked her, and repeated her thanks rather shyly to the professor as he held the door open for her. He said nothing further, however, only smiled briefly.

Her mind was in a whirl as she walked back to the Children's Unit. Perhaps she should have taken more time to decide, but the professor had seemed so sure of her acceptance that it had seemed quite natural to say yes immediately. She felt a thrill of excitement. She hoped that Dutch wasn't too difficult a language, for she supposed that she would have to learn it if she was to make a success of her new job. It suddenly seemed most important that she should do well and please the professor.

CHAPTER TWO

As Adelaide walked towards the Children's Clinic at eight o'clock on the morning of her first day in Amsterdam, the professor was coming down the staircase of his lovely old house on the Heerengracht. Below him he could see Castor and Pollux, his two labrador dogs, sitting side by side, waiting for him to take them for their morning walk. As he crossed the black and white tiled hall he gave a cheerful good morning to his butler, Tweedle, who looked up from the coat he was brushing.

'Good morning, Mr Coenraad.' He looked at his master over his old-fashioned spectacles. 'You'll need to wear a coat.' He spoke in English, with the respectful familiarity of the old family servant and friend. The professor, born the Baron Coenraad Blankenaar van Essen, and possessed of a considerable fortune, would always be 'Mr Coenraad' to Tweedle and his wife, who acted as the professor's housekeeper. The butler's earliest recollections of Coenraad had been the conversations they had held with each other as he opened the great front door to allow the small boy and his even smaller sisters to go through on their way to the park or to school. The professor stood waiting patiently for his coat. He was polishing his glasses and looked quite different without them, and considerably younger. His eyes, bright and searching, were blue-grey.

'Any news?' he asked, as he put on his coat. Tweedle eased it over the broad shoulders.

'Freule Keizer telephoned and asked me to remind you that she expects you to take her to the Concertgebouw this evening.'

The professor frowned. 'I suppose I must have said I would take her. Oh, well, I can't disappoint an old friend.'

He had known Margriet Keizer since childhood. She was now a handsome young woman, and there had been some speculation among their friends as to whether they intended to marry. She was suitable in every way and would make an admirable wife for the professor, as she had been at some pains to let him realise, but so far he had remained a good friend and nothing more. All the same, Tweedle, who disliked her, was very much afraid that he would marry her sooner or later, even if only for the sake of an heir.

Coenraad, threading the Volvo through the early morning traffic, was not thinking of Margriet, however. Today, the English Sister would be at the clinic for the first time. He hoped that he had made a wise choice—she had seemed exactly the type of girl they had been hoping for, but there was always the language difficulty. Even with lessons it would be a few weeks before she could make herself understood. It would be interesting to see how she would make out.

He parked the car and strode rapidly through the Vondelpark, the two dogs careering ahead, making the most of their half hour's run. Back home, the professor read his post and glanced at the papers as he ate his breakfast. At precisely ten minutes to nine he left his home for the hospital. There he left his coat and gloves in the changing room, and walked down the familiar corridor. His registrar, Piet Beekman, came out of Casualty as he passed. They were friends of long standing. Piet was the professor's junior by five years and married to a nurse. They had a baby son, and Coenraad was the little boy's godfather, and a frequent visitor to their flat. They said '*Dag*' briefly and Piet fell into step beside his chief.

'She's here, the English girl—I've not seen her, but Staff Nurse Wilsma says she's nice, but has the most frightful red hair.'

The professor nodded, only half listening, his thoughts already busy with the day's work. They went through the door Piet had opened, into his office. Adelaide and the staff nurse had their backs to him as he entered. She looked very small and slight beside the sturdy Dutch girl. The two girls turned round as Piet closed the door, and came towards the doctors. Adelaide gave an inward sigh of relief; the professor was exactly as she had remembered him—no, that wasn't true; he was even better. They smiled at each other and shook hands, and Piet Beekman was introduced.

'You'll find the routine here very similar to your hospital in London, Sister Peters. Dr Beekman and I will speak English with you until your Dutch is adequate. I understand lessons are already arranged?'

As he himself had sought out an old friend of his father and persuaded him to give Adelaide lessons, the question was an unnecessary one, but Adelaide, who was feeling shy in her strange surroundings, was glad to be able to talk about the arrangements which had been made for her.

She had enjoyed the hour before the professor had arrived. Staff Nurse had taken her over the clinic and she had opened and shut drawers and peered into cupboards and examined trolleys, and drawn the conclusion that Casualty at least was almost identical with its English counterpart. She thought that, even with the language barrier, she would be able to manage quite well. She liked the nurses. Zuster Wilsma was a little younger than herself, a big jolly girl, blonde and blue-eyed. She had been at the clinic for a year now, and although her English was fragmental, Adelaide guessed that she was going to be a great help to her. Nurse Eisink was the senior student nurse, as dark as Zuster Wilsma was fair, and only half her size. She had enormous pale blue eyes and a very attractive smile. The third nurse, Zuster Steensma, was the junior, a thick-set, stolid girl with black boot-button eyes and blonde hair that she obviously didn't bother about a great deal. She beamed at Adelaide, who beamed back. She was quite undeterred by their inability to communicate excepting on the most basic terms. It seemed to her that she was very lucky; they all seemed so anxious to be friendly and helpful.

The desk in the professor's office was, however, a different matter. The forms upon it were not in the least like those to which she had been used, and the printing on them was quite incomprehensible to her. She determined to stay on that evening and study them. They were of various colours; if she was very careful to watch during the clinics, she should be able to identify them later, and learn their various uses. The Dutch she had heard so far had been quite beyond her; indeed, by nine o'clock, a dozen small worries and doubts had assailed her, but somehow the sight of the professor's placid face and his firm handshake had done much to put her fears at rest. She liked Dr Beekman too, he looked good-natured and cheerful. He was nearly as tall as the professor, but of a burlier build, with very fair hair and blue eyes. He spoke English with fluency, but with a terrible accent.

The professor asked her gravely if she could say '*Ja*' and '*Neen*', and everyone laughed, and she felt quite at ease. He noted this as he was putting on his white coat; it seemed the right moment to start work; he signed to Zuster Wilsma to bring in the first little patient, and work started.

The clinics finished for the day at five o'clock, and the doctors left together. The professor was very well satisfied with the day's work; Adelaide, despite her difficulties with the language, had managed well. She had not been easily flustered or put out. As he took off his coat he congratulated her on getting through the day so competently, and told her to go and enjoy her evening, for she had earned it. Adelaide wished them both a cheerful goodbye, and they went on their way; Piet Beekman to his home, the professor to do a round of his private patients in the town.

Adelaide stood where they had left her, thinking about the professor. She liked him, very much. The thought that she would be working with him every day for a whole year was an extremely pleasant one. She finished clearing up and went along to Casualty. Staff Nurse had just come on duty, and would be there until the night staff arrived. Adelaide said goodnight and went back along the corridor to the office, went inside, and shut the door. She was off duty, no one need know that she was there. She was determined to study the forms and papers lying on the desk; she had had to be told a dozen times during the day which was needed. She wondered how the doctors had managed to keep their patience with her. It wasn't going to happen again. She sat down on the professor's chair, got out her dictionary and notebook, and set to work. It was far worse than she had anticipated—it meant looking up every word, one at a time, and she hadn't known that the Dutch liked their verbs at the end of their sentences, and not in the middle. By the end of an hour she had sorted out the forms and had learnt what they were for, but she had no idea how to pronounce the words she had so carefully learned to write. Someone had told her—in England before she left—that if she pronounced every letter in a Dutch word, she would be understood, but had omitted to tell her that the Dutch alphabet didn't sound the same as the English one anyway; so she sat, happily and painstakingly mispronouncing every word.

She was heard by the professor, on his way back from seeing an urgent case in the children's ward. As he passed his office he saw the light beneath the door and wondered idly who was there. He decided to have a look, and it was his rather startled gaze which met Adelaide's eye as she looked up from his desk. She was trying to say *Geneeskundige Dienst*, and getting in an appalling muddle.

The professor shut the door. 'That's rather a difficult word for you to cut your teeth on, you know.'

Adelaide jumped up. She looked surprised, but not in the least disconcerted. In reply to the professor's enquiry as to whether she wasn't off duty, she said:

'Yes, I am, sir, but I want to learn these forms before tomorrow. I was a great hindrance to you today.'

She watched the professor take off his topcoat and draw up a chair, waving her back into his at the same time.

'I don't think you have the pronunciation quite right,' he remarked mildly. 'Do you know what all these are?' He waved at the mass of papers on the desk.

'Oh, yes, sir. I've got them all written down, and when I have a lesson with Mijnheer de Wit, tomorrow, I shall ask him to teach me how to say them correctly.'

The professor took out his pipe. 'Do you mind if I smoke?'

She looked surprised and shook her head.

'It occurs to me that it would be to the advantage of all of us if you learn the pronunciation now, Sister Peters.'

Adelaide gathered her books together and started to get up. In this she was thwarted by the professor's hand, and was forced to sit down again, protesting, 'I really cannot let you waste your time like this, sir.' She sounded rather prim. She had never met a member of the consultant staff who behaved quite as he was, and she wasn't quite sure what to do. He did not appear to have heard her, but reached for the phone and told the operator to get his home. When Tweedle answered, he looked at the clock. He had almost forgotten Margriet.

'Tweedle? Will you ring Freule Keizer and tell her that I'm unavoidably detained. I'll pick her up at the end of the concert and take her home.'

He grinned at Tweedle's sigh of satisfaction; he was well aware of the old man's feelings about Margriet. Adelaide, watching him, wondered why he smiled, and started to protest at his spoilt evening.

'I didn't want to go anyway,' he said. 'It was a Bach concert, I should have gone to sleep.'

Adelaide laughed, and he asked briskly:

'When do you have supper? Eight o'clock? Good, we have three-quarters of an hour. We will take one form at a time.'

He worked her hard, with a merciless criticism which made her blush and stammer, but at the end of the allotted time she had mastered the medical terms well enough to be understood. As she collected her books together, she thanked him, and added:

'I hope you will have a very pleasant evening, sir,' to which he made no reply, merely holding the door politely for her to pass through. When she reached her room she got out her dictionary once more and looked up 'Freule'. It said 'an unmarried female member of the nobility.' She would be tall and blonde, Adelaide decided, and very beautiful. Her clothes would be exquisite. Adelaide hated her. Doubtless the professor admired blondes. She tugged at her own red mane as she tidied herself for supper, and

jabbed the pins in with a complete disregard for the pain she was
giving herself.

She longed to ask some questions at supper, but conversation,
although friendly, was of necessity limited. She sat, listened to
the unintelligible chatter around her, and wondered what the professor was doing. He was still in his office, having been delayed
by a phone call from Tweedle reminding him that he still hadn't
had his dinner. He lighted his pipe and reached for his coat, and
went in search of his car. It had been a long day; he yawned, and
hoped that Margriet wasn't going to be too maddeningly boring
about Bach.

Adelaide loved Amsterdam. On her second evening at the hospital, Zuster Zijlstra had walked with her to the Spui, where
Mijnheer de Wit lived. They went through the Kalverstraat, and
had found time to take a quick look at the shops, gay with pretty
clothes and jewellery and silverware. Zuster Zijlstra rang the bell
of the small gabled house and, when the door opened, waved
Adelaide a cheerful goodbye. Adelaide, left to herself, pushed the
door wider and heard a voice telling her to come upstairs. She
climbed several steep flights before she saw who had spoken to
her. An elderly white-haired man was standing on the tiny landing. He introduced himself and led her into his flat. Here, he
wasted no time, but took her hat and coat, sat her down at the
table, and plunged into her first lesson. Rather to her dismay, he
spoke Dutch, only using English when he saw that she was completely befogged. At the end of an hour he wished her a polite
good night, and sent her back with a great deal of homework. He
seemed pleased with her, but Adelaide thought that she would
have to work very hard indeed to keep him so.

Zuster Zijlstra and Zuster Boot, from Men's Surgical, both
spoke a little English. They took Adelaide shopping as often as
possible during the next few days; the feast of St Nicolaas was
only a few weeks away. They explained that she should give small
gifts to the doctors and nurses she was working with, and also
explained the enormous numbers of chocolate letters displayed in

the confectioners' and *banketbakker*. It seemed that it was cus-
tomary to exchange them with friends and relations. Zuster Boot,
a practical young woman, volunteered to supply the christian
names of the clinic nurses so that Adelaide could buy the appro-
priate letters for them; she already knew that she must get a C
for the professor, and a P for Piet Beekman. They roamed from
shop to shop in their off-duty, choosing scarves and stockings and
fancy soap, and admiring the lovely things on display. When they
were off duty in the afternoons they went to Formosa in the Kalverstraat, where Adelaide sampled *thé complet*; she was enchanted
with the tray of savoury tit-bits and cream cakes and chocolates,
with its accompanying pot of tea.

Just before St Nicolaas, she and Staff Nurse Wilsma spent an
hour choosing presents for the two doctors. Dr Beekman was easy;
he never had a pen of his own. They chose a vivid green one he
couldn't possibly mislay. The professor was rather more difficult;
he seemed to have everything. In the end they settled for a leather
wallet. Wilsma was sure that he had several already, but observed
that he could always put it away and use it later.

There was no clinic on the morning of St Nicolaas. Instead the
nurses and porters set about transforming the Out-Patients' waiting hall. Paper chains and flags hung around the walls, and tables
were set up, covered with gay cloths and loaded with glasses and
plates and great baskets of oranges. The annual party for the hospital's small patients was to be held that afternoon. St Nicolaas
and Black Pete would be coming to distribute the presents. Adelaide, opening tins of biscuits, asked, 'Who gives this party, Zuster
Wilsma?'

Her staff nurse, scooping sweets into countless little bags,
stopped her work to reply. 'Professor Van Essen. He pays for it
all too. He'll be coming, and his aunt and sisters—he's got two,
and his nephews and nieces—and his close friends'—she looked
at Adelaide, and added, 'and Dr Beekman and his wife and baby.'

Adelaide hadn't understood half of what Zuster Wilsma had
said, but there wasn't time for explanations, anyway. They still
had to fill several sacks with presents.

At two o'clock the first guests arrived; most of them had mothers or big sisters with them. Adelaide sat the children in rows on the floor; the grown-ups lined the walls. Presently Zuster Zijlstra arrived, opened the piano, and started to play the first of the traditional tunes, and everyone began to sing. Adelaide didn't understand a word, but when St Nicolaas appeared with his black slave, she laughed and clapped with everyone else, and carried the smallest toddlers up to receive their presents. She was enjoying herself enormously. At length the Saint made his stately exit, sent on his way by enthusiastic and rather shrill singing. Adelaide dumped the baby she was holding into the nearest nurse's lap and went over to the tables to pour lemonade and hand out biscuits.

There was no lack of helpers; she piled the oranges in baskets ready for the nurses to take round, talking all the while to Zuster Zijlstra in her mixture of Dutch and English. It was at this moment that the professor, with his aunt and sisters, chose to join them. They all seemed to know Zuster Zijlstra, and greeted her like an old friend. Adelaide, started to move quietly away, but the professor, who had been expecting her to do just that, put out a detaining hand and turned her smartly round, and performed his introductions in English.

She found herself the centre of an animated group. His two sisters were very like him, with dark hair and blue eyes; they wore their elegant clothes with a careless grace. His aunt was small and slim and just as elegant as her nieces. She eyed Adelaide with bright black eyes and talked to her in a gentle voice. They were all charming to her and chattered and laughed until they were presently joined by several children, who addressed the professor as Uncle, and smiled shyly at Adelaide as he introduced them. When, after a little while, they all bade her goodbye. Adelaide watched them go with regret; it seemed unlikely that she would meet them again.

The professor made no attempt to go with them. Adelaide hesitated.

'I must go and help the others; I'm not doing my share. It was delightful meeting your family, Professor.'

She was about to turn away when an attractive young woman put her hand on the professor's arm. Adelaide looked at her. This must be Margriet. At once, and irrationally, she disliked her. Freule Keizer was extremely good-looking, with blonde hair and blue eyes and a magnificent figure; she was dressed with the simplicity of wealth with a sparkling bandbox finish that caused Adelaide to put an involuntary hand up to tidy away the curly wisps escaping from her cap. She was suddenly aware of the lemonade stains on her apron and its deplorably creased condition.

Margriet spoke. 'There you are, Coenraad. I wondered where you had got to.' She gave Adelaide a cursory glance. 'Are you coming?'

The professor had apparently not heard her.

'Sister Peters, I should like you to meet Freule Keizer.' He turned to the girl beside him. 'Margriet, Sister works with me in the clinic.'

The young women shook hands and smiled politely. Margriet's smile didn't quite reach her eyes.

'How awful for you, having to work.' She made it sound like an insult.

'But I enjoy it, you know,' Adelaide protested. She was struggling to overcome her dislike of Margriet, who looked astonished and turned to the professor.

'You don't know how lucky you are. You've at last got a nurse who is wedded to her work.' Her tone made it clear that work was all that Adelaide could hope to wed. Her glance rested on Adelaide's hair and she allowed her beautiful eyebrows to arch slightly. She smiled. 'Such unusual hair! You must find it a great drawback.' The professor, listening idly, heard Margriet's last remark.

'How bad your English has become, Margriet. I don't think that drawback is the word you mean.' He sounded reproving.

Margriet laughed—she had a charming laugh.

'Do forgive me, Sister—there, I have forgotten your name already. It's quite true, my English is shocking; that's because I dislike speaking it, I suppose.' She turned to the professor. 'I must go and say goodbye to Lisette and Paula. Shall I wait for you in the car?' She didn't wait for him to reply, but said goodbye to Adelaide with cold charm, and slipped away.

'I must go too, Professor.' Adelaide looked pink and was breathing rather quickly, struggling to regain her temper.

The professor said, 'Of course, Sister, but don't forget that we shall all be meeting in my office in an hour's time to open our presents.'

When Adelaide got to the office it was just striking six o'clock. She was the last one to arrive and found Zuster Wilsma and the other nurses grouped around the desk, laughing and talking with the doctors.

The professor looked up as she came in. 'Good, now we can begin,' he cried, and pushed a pile of gaily coloured parcels in front of the youngest nurse. 'You first, Nurse Eisink.'

They all watched as she undid each parcel and admired the contents in turn. Zuster Steensma followed, her homely face alight with pleasure, and then Zuster Wilsma, and lastly Adelaide. As she unwrapped the first package she asked:

'But how can I thank the givers if I don't know who they are?'

Dr Beekman laughed. 'That's the whole idea, Sister. You mustn't know. Remember St Nicolaas gave them to you, and thank him.'

She did this, piling up the pretty trifles in front of her. The last two parcels were elegantly wrapped and tied with ribbons. She opened the flat box first, and gazed with delight at the fur-lined suede gloves inside.

'They're beautiful!' she exclaimed, and tried them on. They fitted perfectly. She looked around at the faces of the others watching her; it was impossible to tell from their expressions which of them had given her the gloves. 'Thank you, St Nicolaas,' she said, and added, 'I can't think who they are from.'

She opened the last parcel. It was quite small, and she almost dropped it when she saw what it was, wondering who could possibly afford to give her Madame Rochas perfume. Perhaps all the staff had put together. She took a blissful sniff, and thanked the

Saint with a fervour which left her audience in no doubt as to her delight.

The two men opened their parcels together amidst a good deal of laughing and joking from the nurses, and by the time they had finished it was almost seven o'clock. The doctors got ready to leave, Dr Beekman reminding Zuster Wilsma, who was on duty until the night staff came on, that he was on call. No sooner had they gone than Adelaide sent the two junior nurses off duty. They lived in Amsterdam, and were looking forward to an evening at home with their families, and more presents. Zuster Wilsma rammed the last of the paper and string into the wastepaper basket; she looked forlorn. Adelaide remembered that she lived in Amsterdam too.

'You live in Amsterdam, don't you, Staff Nurse? You go home too. I've nothing to do for the rest of the evening.' Her Dutch was clumsy, but Zuster Wilsma understood her and grinned with delight. She shook hands with Adelaide and tore off as fast as she could go. It seemed very quiet when she had gone. Adelaide sat down and looked at her presents again, wondering who had given them.

It was almost eight o'clock when she heard the ambulance bell. She went quickly to Casualty, switching on the powerful light over the couch and opening the door for the ambulance men. The blue flasher shone on the man hurrying towards her with a blanketed bundle in his arms. He laid his burden gently on the couch and took the blanket away. The little girl looked about two years old; she was unconscious, her little face the colour of skimmed milk. Even as Adelaide reached for the oxygen mask the blue tinge deepened, and the harsh breathing became more agonisingly difficult. Adelaide pushed an airway gently between the tiny teeth and slipped the catheter attached to the sucker down it. She switched on the motor, which made a reassuring purr. While she had been working, she had been aware of the mother standing close by. Now, with the essentials done, she turned to her. 'Bronchitis?' she asked. The woman nodded.

Adelaide beckoned to the ambulance man, glad he was one she had met several times before.

'You'll stay?' She pointed to the sucker and oxygen mask. He nodded and she went quickly to the phone on the desk and asked for Dr Beekman urgently. When she heard the voice on the other end of the line, she said in her quiet efficient voice:

'Dr Beekman? There's a small girl just in—bronchitis and laryngeal stridor. She's unconscious and her respirations are very difficult. Will you come, please?' The voice said 'Yes' as she put down the phone and went back to the child, who looked worse. She cleared the sucker, put it carefully down the little throat again and gave it to the man to hold again, then sat about laying up a trolley. The tracheotomy instruments were always kept ready; there wasn't much for her to do. She drew up a local anaesthetic into a syringe and was putting a sandbag under the small shoulders when she heard a car draw up outside. The ambulance man glanced at her—he wanted to be on his way; she thanked him as he hurried away, and said over her shoulder:

'The doctor is here. Everything's all right,' and smiled reassuringly at the mother, sitting quietly in a corner. She turned back to the child, who gave a strangled breath as the professor came in.

He dropped his coat on the floor and stood for a moment looking at the small convulsed face, his fingers on the flaccid wrist.

Adelaide went to the head of the couch and steadied the child's head between her hands.

'Everything's ready,' she said quietly. 'The local is on the lower shelf.'

The child hadn't drawn another breath. The professor didn't stop to scrub, but quickly injected the local anaesthetic, picked up a scalpel, and made a cut—quite a small one—in the little throat, securing it with a small hook. He spoke softly to the mother—Adelaide thought it sounded comforting, although she couldn't understand what he had said—and the woman murmured a reply. He slit the trachea neatly, holding it open with the knife handle while he inserted the dilators. He mopped unhurriedly, and slipped

in the tube with an unerring hand. He waited a moment, pushed
the inner tube in and tied it securely. The operation had only taken
a minute or two. They stood watching while a faint pink colour
slowly started to blot out the blueness. The little girl's breath
rasped in and out of the tube, but it was regular again. The professor dabbed at a tiny spot of blood on his cuff.

'Close call,' he observed. Adelaide's brown eyes smiled at him
over her mask, and he smiled back. 'Nice work, Sister.'

He went to the phone and asked Zuster Zijlstra to come to
Casualty as soon as she could. A moment later she came in quietly. She was a tall girl, with merry blue eyes; she and Adelaide
got on well together. She winked at her now, and asked 'Busy?'

Adelaide, doing neat things with gauze and strapping, smiled.

'No, but you will be!'

The professor, who had been talking to the mother, turned
round.

'Ah, my good Zuster Zijlstra, I want a cot, and oxygen tent,
and a nurse to special this child. Will you fix them up for me,
please?'

Zuster Zijlstra tossed her head. 'You always want something,'
she complained. 'I'll do it at once, sir,' and disappeared again.

The professor walked over to the couch.

'I expect you've got some writing to do. I'll stay here.'

He stood by the patient, listening to Adelaide asking the mother
the routine questions which had to be asked before the child could
be admitted. She managed rather well, using a minimum of words
and being very wary of the grammar. Her pronunciation was peculiar at times, but on the whole he thought that she must have
worked quite hard during the month she had been in Holland.

Zuster Zijlstra came back. She scooped up the small figure on
the couch very carefully and went to the door, which the professor
held open for her.

'I'll come with you. I'd better write up some sedation and an-
tibiotics for her.'

Adelaide finished what she was doing and showed the mother
how to get to the ward, then began to clear up; there wasn't a

great deal for her to do. She made up a fresh tracheotomy pack and put it in the autoclave, then stripped the linen off the couch and made it up anew. She was washing her hands at the sink when the professor returned.

'The child's fine. Zuster Zijlstra's a wonderful nurse.' He looked round. 'Where's Staff Nurse?'

Adelaide dried her hands carefully. 'At home. She lives in Amsterdam.'

'You took over her duty.' It was more of a statement than a question.

'Yes, sir. I don't mind in the least. I wasn't going anywhere.' She sounded quite cheerful about it.

'You should have taken your off-duty,' he said evenly.

She threw the paper towel in the bin, and went to turn off the autoclave.

'I rang Dr Beekman.' Her voice held a question, politely put.

The professor was getting into his coat.

'*Touché*, Sister Peters. I have taken Beekman's duty over until midnight; his people have come down from Drente for St Nicolaas.' He grinned at her, called good-night, and was gone.

CHAPTER THREE

CARDBOARD Father Christmases had taken the place of St Nicolaas in the shops. Adelaide bought presents for her family and sent them home. She might have felt homesick, but the friends she had made among the hospital sisters took care to include her as much as possible in their own activities, so that she had little time for moping.

Mijnheer de Wit spent a whole lesson describing the Dutch annual holidays to her. It seemed that Christmas was strictly for the family and more sober than the English version. The giving of presents was usual in the larger towns; in the country the day was marked by a splendid meal and plenty to drink. Turkey and Christmas pudding hadn't gained much of a foothold, but many homes in Holland had a Christmas tree. New Year—now, that was different. The old man waxed eloquent in his beautiful Dutch—New Year was for everyone to enjoy. He made it sound exciting.

Adelaide had been rather puzzled by the amount of unwelcome attention her red hair had caused. Small boys called out after her in the street, mothers bringing their children to the clinic remarked on it, often with a laugh or pitying look. She was aware that her hair was rather unusual, but it had seldom been commented upon. One evening, at the end of a tedious lesson on the complexities of the Dutch verb, she mentioned it to her teacher. He broke into a rumbling laugh.

'My dear young lady, the Dutch, as a nation, dislike red hair, and your hair, if I may say so, is very red. You must expect comment upon it, at least when you are in public. I must add that this is the general opinion. Many people admire it,' he twinkled at her. 'I do myself.'

Dr Beekman was early the following day; he had some notes

to write up, and sat doing this while Adelaide sorted the X-rays. They had become good friends and Adelaide had spent pleasant evenings with his wife Leen; the girls had liked each other at once. Adelaide put the last X-ray on the desk and turned to the doctor.

'Is my hair an awful colour?' she asked.

His blue eyes opened wide. 'Well, it is rather red,' he replied cautiously. 'Why do you ask?'

She started to tell him. She hadn't heard the professor come in; he leaned against the door, listening, as she explained about the small boys. 'Oh, well,' she said in a matter-of-fact voice, 'we're all afflicted with something, I suppose. Red hair is no worse than a squint or jug handle ears, or a large beaky n…' she stopped, because of the expression on Dr Beekman's face. He was looking over her shoulder, at someone behind her, and trying not to laugh.

The professor advanced into the room; his 'good morning' was quiet and uttered in a bland voice.

Adelaide felt herself blushing hotly, but she faced him bravely and said, 'I do beg your pardon, sir. I wasn't speaking of your nose…' she stopped and tried again. 'Yours is quite a nice sort…' She encountered the professor's eye. It was fixed steadily upon her; there was absolutely no expression on his face. She had a horrid suspicion that he might be laughing at her, and lifted her chin and looked down her own pretty little nose.

'I like beaky noses,' she said, and was relieved to see him smile.

'Thank you, Sister Peters. Your good opinion will do much towards enabling me to bear my affliction with equanimity.' He added thoughtfully, 'How thankful we should be that we do not have the squint.'

Adelaide smiled uncertainly. She still wasn't sure if he was amused or merely polite—as was his wont. She minded very much if he were to be angry; just lately she had found herself going to a great deal of trouble to please him…

The professor, however, did not seem to share her feelings. He was running through the X-rays on his desk, and said briskly:

'Shall we get started?' He glanced at her, smiling faintly, and that was the only crumb of comfort she had.

Out-Patients closed for the two days of Christmas, but of course Casualty stayed open. Adelaide arranged to go on duty at one o'clock on Christmas Day, so that the nurses could go to their homes for the remainder of the day. She had been to the English Church in the Groenburgwal and sung carols, and felt a little homesick. There had been a dinner for the nurses on Christmas Eve; Matron had sat at the head of the long table, lighted by candles, and they had sung Dutch carols before they had started their meal. It had been pleasant and homely and she would write a long letter home about it.

It was very quiet in the clinic; Casualty was empty. She went along to her little office; she might as well start her letters, it would give her something to do. There was a parcel on her desk, wrapped in red paper patterned with robins, and tied with tinsel ribbon. Her name was on the label, written in the professor's deplorable writing. Inside were three books: she looked at the authors—Jan de Hartog, Johan Fabricius, and Charles Dickens. She was relieved to see that they were all in English as she laid them on the desk before her. It was nice to be remembered; probably the professor had thought that she would miss the presents she would have had had she been in England. He was, she noticed, very considerate towards his staff. She had read quite a lot of *A Christmas Carol* when the phone rang. She picked up the receiver quickly, expecting a casualty call; instead, she heard the professor's voice, sounding remote, wishing her a happy Christmas. She wished him one in return, and thanked him shyly for the books. She could hear a background of children laughing and shouting, and the steady murmur of voices, and pictured the family party gathered at his home; she supposed Freule Keizer was there too. Quite unbidden, a large lump came into her throat; she swallowed it desperately back and said in a steady voice: 'I'm wanted on the other phone, sir. Goodbye.'

After a minute or two she pulled herself together, chided herself for being such a spiritless goose, and went into the tiny clinic kitchen to make herself a cup of tea.

Two days after Christmas, the clinic opened again, and as was to be expected, it was packed. The waiting room was full to overflowing by nine o'clock, and Adelaide, feverishly hunting for notes and X-rays, hoped that they would get finished by first dinner. Punctual to the minute, the professor, accompanied by Piet Beekman, stalked in. He wished her good morning briskly and added briefly in a deceptively mild voice: 'As fast as you like, Sister. I hope all the notes and X-rays are here; we have a full morning's work.'

Adelaide stiffened with resentment at the unfairness of his remark. She wasn't a conceited girl, but she was aware that she did her work well. She shot him a cross look, wasted on his downbent head.

Staff Nurse Wilsma, back from a well-earned coffee break, had brought Adelaide's post with her. She took it gratefully, glancing at the envelopes before stuffing them behind her apron bib. One of them had an Amsterdam postmark. She wondered what it could be, but there was no time to look. Zuster Steensma was struggling in with a small boy who was screaming and kicking and hitting at her with his small fists. His mother scuttled in after them; she looked frightened as she dodged round them and took the chair in front of the desk. The professor looked up from his notes and smiled at her, but forbore to speak; he would not have been heard in the din.

Adelaide handed Piet the examination tray she was holding and sailed across the room like a pocket battleship, plucked the small tyrant from the wilting nurse, and whisked him on to a couch. Admonishing him soundly for being such a bad boy, she removed his shoes and top clothes with the ease of long practice, evading his arms and legs with skill. He was so astonished that he stopped crying, and when he opened his mouth to start again, Adelaide pulled such a face that he burst out laughing instead.

'Now be quiet,' said Adelaide. She had discovered that the children responded just as well to English as Dutch; it was the tone of voice that mattered. There was quiet in the room. The professor murmured something to Dr Beekman, who laughed. They came over to the couch together, and Piet smiled at her and patted her on the shoulder.

'It must be that hair of yours, Adelaide!'

While they were drinking their coffee, she remembered her letters; there was no time to read them all, but she glanced at the two from England, then opened the Dutch one. The envelope was large and of very thick paper. There was an invitation inside from the professor's aunt, for Old Year's Night. She couldn't understand quite all of it, and took it over to the professor.

'My aunt,' he said. 'She has a party every year, and always invites my clinic Sister.' He frowned at Piet's astonished face, and not giving him the chance to speak, said, 'You and Leen are going, aren't you, Piet? You could take Sister along with you, couldn't you?'

'Yes, of course.' He turned to Adelaide. 'You'll love it, it's like Christmas and St Nicolaas rolled into one.'

That evening, he told Leen about it. 'There's never been a clinic Sister invited to his aunt's house before.'

His wife laughed. 'But, Piet, remember that Adelaide is a stranger here—I expect Coenraad thinks she deserves some fun while she's in Holland.'

Adelaide was ready and waiting when the Beekmans called for her. She had taken great care with her hair, the chestnut brown bow she wore in it exactly matched her velvet dress. It was last year's, but it suited her anyway. She hadn't been able to afford a new one. It was a bitter cold night, and they were thankful for the fragrant warmth which enveloped them as Bundle, the butler, ushered them into the hall of the Baroness's house. A maid took the girls upstairs while Bundle took Piet's coat and went in search of the professor, who followed him back into the hall.

'Piet, before we begin the festivities, that case we admitted today…' the two men became absorbed. Adelaide, coming downstairs with Leen, had ample opportunity of studying the professor in the hall below. She hadn't seen him in a dinner jacket before;

he looked very handsome. Her heart began to beat faster; he had never seen her out of uniform. The two men turned round, and the professor's eyes swept over her and on to Leen. She doubted if he had even noticed that she wasn't wearing her cap and apron. She said good evening in a small voice, and they all went into the salon where his aunt was standing. She greeted Adelaide pleasantly, and beckoned to Mijnheer de Wit, who was standing nearby, and asked him to take her round and introduce her to everyone. Adelaide went with him from group to group, murmuring her name as she had been taught, and trying to remember the names murmured back to her. Her hand was shaken so many times her arm began to ache. The old gentleman drew her on one side.

'Now you know everyone, Miss Peters.'

Adelaide shook her head. 'I can't remember a single face or name.'

He laughed, and patted her arm. 'Never mind, here's someone you know anyway.' He nodded towards the professor, who was crossing the room. Margriet Keizer was with him; she had an arm in his, and was chattering gaily. She looked charming, her green dress making Adelaide very aware of her own slightly out-of-date model. The head-to-heels glance Margriet gave her as they shook hands did nothing to improve Adelaide's feelings, and she suddenly wished with all her heart that she had never come. She glanced around her; she just didn't belong, these people were so obviously well-to-do and leisured and beautifully gowned. The thought that they might be pitying her, as Margriet was, pinkened her cheeks. She hated the professor's aunt for inviting her; she hated him too, just because he was there, carelessly friendly and not in the least interested in her.

They stood together in a small group, while she matched Margriet's gaiety with a wholly false vivacity of her own. This put a strain on her usually retiring nature, and when a young man in a brocade waistcoat joined the group and asked her to dance, she accepted with pleasure. She didn't much care for the owner of the waistcoat, who was, she suspected, younger than herself, but at least he wanted to dance with her. The professor had had ample opportunity to do the same if he had wished. She sensibly decided to enjoy herself. Her partner danced well, their steps suited, they circled the large room, and she took care to turn a smiling face in the professor's direction. It was a pity that he wasn't looking. He was dancing with Margriet.

During the next hour or so she had frequent glimpses of him; she noted that he danced with a great number of the women guests, and several times with Margriet. She was agreeably surprised to find that she did not lack for partners, and danced every dance, telling herself sensibly that she might as well forget the professor. Having come to this conclusion, she went off to the supper room with Jan Hein, the youthful owner of the brocade waistcoat, and lingered over the delicacies provided until almost midnight. When they went back to the salon everyone was standing, glasses in hands, waiting for the clock to strike. Its silvery chimes were drowned by the outburst of sirens and hooters and fireworks from all over the city. Glasses were raised and a round of hand-shaking and kissing began.

Adelaide, unused to the tonic effects of champagne, was enjoying herself; she had even forgotten the professor, standing talking to his aunt, just behind her. She watched Jan pushing his way towards her through the crowd, and realised that he was rather drunk. She decided to evade him, and stepped backwards into the professor's arms. She felt herself turned neatly round to face him, to be kissed squarely on her mouth.

'A Happy New Year, Miss Peters.' The band had just started to play again, a Strauss waltz, and before she realised what was happening, they were half way round the room.

'How very high-handed,' she remarked coldly.

He reversed neatly into a corner. 'Don't you like dancing with me, Miss Peters?'

She looked up at him, and said with an incurable honestly. 'Yes, I do, very much.'

They went on dancing; she hoped that the band would forget to stop and tried to think of something clever to say. Her mind was blank, but luckily the professor didn't appear to be much of a conversationalist while he danced. She stopped worrying and gave herself up to the pleasure of dancing; the professor danced very well indeed, but she had known he would. The music stopped and someone tapped her on the arm. It was Piet Beekman.

'We must go, Adelaide. The baby-sitter said one o'clock, and not a moment later. Are you coming?'

Before she could reply the professor said in his easy way:

'Why not let Sister stay? I am sure she will have no lack of offers to see her home, and in the unlikelihood of her being on her own, one of us will see her back later.'

'Thank you, professor, but I should like to go now; I'm on duty in the morning.' She spoke quietly in a stiff little voice and turned away with a brief good night to find the Baroness, who rather surprisingly kissed her and urged her to come and see her again. Adelaide made a vague reply to this, thinking it very unlikely that she would see her hostess again. She intended to concentrate on her Dutch lessons and her own small circle of friends in the hospital. She watched the professor and Margriet going towards the balcony. She wasn't sure what she had expected from this evening—perhaps that if he saw her out of uniform, he would realise that she was a girl as well as a highly trained cog in the hospital machinery. As she went upstairs with Leen to get her coat, she allowed herself to remember that he had kissed her, but then so had a great many other people; she derived little comfort from the thought.

She said goodbye to Leen and Piet at the door of the Sisters' home, and went upstairs to her room, where, despite the lateness of the hour, she sat on her bed thinking about the evening. One fact emerged very clearly—she was in love with the professor.

She had a whole day to get over the party. Casualty was slack; there was no clinic. She sat in her office, scowling over her Dutch grammar. After a while she shut her books and wrote a letter home. She gave a colourful and gay account of the party; it was slightly exaggerated, as she wanted her family to know what a

good time she was having. She carefully made out a money order
to go with the letter. The boys' school fees would be due again
soon. They were clever, and deserved the best education that
could be managed. Her thoughts played truant again, and she wondered if Professor Van Essen was rich. She had no idea where he
lived, but she supposed he had a good practice in Amsterdam. It
was natural that she should think about Margriet Keizer too, for
she was obviously a close friend of his.

Adelaide opened her book again; she was behaving like a silly
schoolgirl. She reminded herself what she was doing and who she
was. She resolved to think no more of the professor, but work for
him to the best of her ability and be pleasant and friendly and
take no interest at all in his private life. She was well aware that
this high-minded resolve, if put to the test, might well prove
worthless; in the meantime, she told herself sternly, she would
apply herself to her Dutch grammar.

The day seemed endless—Wilsma took over Casualty duty at
two o'clock, and Adelaide went out into the grey cold day and
walked until she was tired. The streets were almost empty; she
supposed that everyone was within doors, visiting or receiving
visits from family. She began to feel lonely, but told herself resolutely not to give way to self-pity, and when she found a small
café open went in and had a cup of coffee, and walked back to
the hospital again. Most of the Sisters were out, and supper was
quickly eaten by the few who remained. She went to her room
and busied herself washing her hair, until Zuster Zijlastra came
in to tell her about her visit to her home. It was late when she
finally put out the light, to lie awake in the dark, remembering
the professor's kiss and their dance together. Common sense reminded her that nearly everyone in the room had kissed her too—
he had only done what was obviously the custom. No amount of
wishful thinking on her part could make it otherwise. She went
to sleep on the hopeless thought.

She felt nervous at the idea of seeing the professor again, but
she need not have worried. There was no time for talk beyond a
hurried good morning. Casualty was full with children who had

burnt themselves with fireworks, eaten too much, or, taking advantage of the relaxing of parental discipline over the holidays, had found the matches and got burned, or sampled the contents of aspirin bottles. Adelaide stayed in Casualty, while Zuster Wilsma took the clinic, and the professor and Dr Beekman went back and forth as they were needed. By midday Casualty was empty again, and they all sighed with relief. It was fortunate that the morning clinic had been a small one. Refreshed by their one o'clock dinner, the staff assembled once more for the afternoon session, which Adelaide knew would run far over the scheduled time. There was little leisure for private thought, which was perhaps why she was able to work cheerfully with the professor for the rest of the busy day without any feeling of awkwardness or embarrassment. By the end of the afternoon she had slipped back into their usual professional friendliness—casual and matter-of-fact, and quite impersonal. It had been easier than she had expected.

A few days later the professor mentioned that he had some beds at another hospital in Amsterdam. 'Only four,' he explained, 'to take the overflow if we get a run on the beds here. I'll arrange for you to be taken there one day, so that you can look around.'

Adelaide was packing dressing drums with a practised hand.

'I should like that, sir, thank you. If you could give me two or three days' notice so that I can arrange the duty rota.'

She snapped a lid shut, opened the perforated strip around the drum, and put it on to the loaded trolley.

The professor scrawled his signature, put away his pen, and got up to go.

'Very well, Sister. I'll let you know. Good night.' He walked to the door, but stopped halfway and said over his shoulder: 'Are you quite happy here, Sister Peters?'

Adelaide folded a dressing towel, flattened it with a thump, and laid it with its fellows.

'Yes, sir, I am, very.'

He gave a non-committal grunt and went out, leaving her standing staring at the closed door, wondering wistfully if he minded in the least if she was happy or not.

The promised visit to the hospital took place at the end of the week, but not, as she had hoped, in the professor's company. Dr Beekman took her in his Volkswagen. It was a bitterly cold day, with low grey clouds, turning yellow at the corners.

'Snow,' said Piet Beekman. 'A good thing we arranged to come today.'

Adelaide braced herself against the seat as he raced round a corner, much too fast.

'Doesn't the professor come to see his patients?'

Dr Beekman cut a swathe through a bunch of dignified cyclists, miraculously missing them all.

'Yes, more often than not—but he's going to some reception or other at the Amstel Hotel early this evening, so he wanted to get away in time.'

He drew up with a squeal of brakes, wrenched the wheel round, and shot up a side street, to stop with devastating suddenness before a large gloomy door.

'Here we are,' he said cheerfully, and leant over and opened the door for her to get out. Adelaide took stock of her surroundings. The hospital was on a corner, and looked bleak. Once inside, however, she discovered that the bleakness outside had not been allowed to penetrate its walls. The wards were bright with coloured paint and gay with flowering plants; the children in them looked happy. The place sounded like a parrot house. Half way round, Dr Beekman was called to the phone. She guessed what it was before he told her. He had to go back to the clinic.

'I don't suppose I shall be long,' he said. 'One of the Sisters will take you round the rest of the wards and I'll come back for you later.'

'No, don't come back, Dr Beekman, I'm sure I can find my way back. Just tell me the number of the tram I have to catch, and I can't go wrong. And if I do, I'll get a taxi.'

He was uncertain. 'Are you sure?' He thought for a moment. 'You'll need a twenty-four tram.'

Adelaide nodded. 'I'm off duty at five o'clock, anyway. I'll go straight to the Home.'

He looked relieved. 'All right, then. See you in the morning. *Tot ziens.*'

Another hour sped by. Theatre Sister, who had taken Piet Beekman's place, insisted on Adelaide having a cup of tea before she left. They sat sipping the weak, milkless beverage, carrying on a halting but entirely satisfactory conversation. It was nearly six o'clock when she got up to go. Assuring her kind hostess that she could get back to her own hospital quite easily, she went down to the entrance hall. There was no one about, so she opened the heavy door and stepped out into the street. It clanged shut behind her, a second before she made an instinctive movement to push it open again. She was standing in a blizzard; she had never been in one before, but this blinding curtain of snow couldn't be anything else.

Adelaide stood hesitating, glad that she had worn a raincoat and boots. She looked around as well as she was able; there was no one to be seen, and no traffic either, but she guessed it would start again as soon as the snow stopped. She decided against going back into the hospital. She would walk in the direction of the trams, and wait until they started again, or even take a taxi. She began to walk along the street, taking the right-hand fork as Dr Beekman had said. The snow was already thick under her feet, but by keeping to the wall by the side of the street, she made quite good progress. The bridge was a surprise—she didn't remember it—it looked a temporary affair, and she walked carefully over it and followed the wall curving to the right. Through the snow she caught the glint of water, and stood still, trying to remember where she was. It didn't take long for her to realise that she was, for the moment at least, lost.

Luckily she hadn't come far; she decided to retrace her steps to the hospital and shelter there until the weather cleared or someone could take her back. Halfway over the bridge, she glimpsed a large brick building looming ahead; it looked like a brewery or factory of some sort. It had been on her left as she approached the first time. At least, she thought so. She realised, suddenly, that she didn't know any more. She stopped, clutching the flimsy handrail, swallowing panic, and forcing herself to look carefully in all directions. The snow, beating into her face, half blinded her, nevertheless, she decided, with a sudden lifting of her spirits, that there were lights on her left, and not too far away. Where there were lights, there would probably be people. She walked slowly towards them, terrified that she would lose them. She picked her way through the snow, the lights becoming blessedly stronger with each step. They came from a large building, streaming from glass doors at the top of a flight of steps.

Adelaide climbed, aware of the icy wetness of her feet in her sodden boots. There was a uniformed man at the door, who opened it for her, and she stood on the doormat in front of him, oblivious of his startled look, brushing the snow from her face so that she could see where she was. She was in a large, luxurious foyer, lights from half a dozen chandeliers shone on gleaming tables and mirrors and massed flowers. A group of men, immaculate in white ties and tails, were talking some yards from her. Adelaide had time to recognise the professor before he looked round and saw her, and walked across the thick-piled carpet towards her. He looked distinguished and elegant and very angry.

'What in thunder are you doing here, Miss Peters?' His habitual calm seemed to have deserted him completely.

If she hadn't been so cold, she would have burst into tears; as it was, she said as clearly as her chattering teeth would allow:

'I'm lost. I came in to ask the way.' She frowned as fiercely as her snow-stiffened eyebrows would allow. 'I had no idea you were here,' she added with a monumental dignity rendered pathetic by her grotesque appearance. 'Please don't let me keep you from your friends. The doorman will explain how I can get back.'

The professor, with a resigned air, said nothing, but unbuttoned her raincoat and took it off. He said something briefly to the doorman, who disappeared and returned within the minute with a pair of slippers, which he substituted for Adelaide's useless boots.

'Won't you take off your hood, Miss Peters?' The professor

spoke with excessive politeness. She obeyed wordlessly, and watched her clothes borne away out of sight.

'They'll be dried,' he explained briefly. 'There's a writing room here, you can wait there. It will be empty at this time of day.'

She scuffled after him in the too large slippers. As they passed his friends he murmured something, and they smiled at her and nodded with kindly faces, so that she smiled shyly back at them. The writing room was small and cosy, with a small fire burning cheerfully. The professor indicated a chair which he had drawn up to its warmth. 'I'll get someone to bring you some coffee.' He gave her a nod and disappeared.

The coffee was hot, and tasted rather peculiar but nice. Adelaide drank one cup quickly, and poured a second cup from the elegant pot. There was a small plate of tiny sandwiches on the tray; she tried one. She hadn't tasted anything like it before and she didn't know what it was, but found it delicious. She drank the rest of her coffee and felt a pleasant warm glow spreading over her; she supposed it was the warmth of the little room which made her feel so sleepy. She ate another sandwich, then closed her eyes. When she opened them again, the professor, looking remote, was sitting in a chair opposite hers. She sat up at once, and said in her matter-of-fact voice:

'I went to sleep, it was so warm in here. If my coat's dry, I'd like to go, please. I expect the snow has stopped by now.' She got up, very conscious of her untidy hair and crumpled skirt. The professor got up too.

'I'll ask them for your things and arrange for you to go back.' He walked to the door, but before he could open it, it was flung wide, and Margriet Keizer came in. She looked magnificent, in a low-cut gown that showed off her figure to perfection. She ignored Adelaide and spoke rapidly and angrily in Dutch to the professor. He chose to ignore her ill-humour, and answered placidly in English.

'Ah, Margriet, you had my message. Miss Peters got lost in the snow on her way back to hospital. Fortunately she came here for help. I'm just going to arrange for her to go back. Perhaps you'll keep her company while I'm gone.'

He left them together, standing in hostile silence. Margriet rustled to a chair.

'How stupid of you to go out in such a bad snow-storm, Miss Peters. I suppose it was chance that brought you here?'

Adelaide looked surprised. 'Yes, of course it was chance, Juffrouw Keizer. I had no reason to come here otherwise.'

'Well, it was an unfortunate chance for us. Do you realise that we are guests at a reception here and that I have been left alone without an escort while Coen—Professor Van Essen wastes what should have been a pleasant evening?'

Adelaide flushed hotly. 'If your evening has been spoiled, I'm sorry.' She paused and looked at her watch, surprised to see that it was after seven. 'It is still early, and you have the evening before you.' She spoke quietly, genuinely sorry for the other girl's disappointment. But her sympathy was wasted.

'It's not much use being sorry, is it, now that the harm's done. You don't seem a very sensible young woman. It seems to me that you can't be very suitable for your job.'

Margriet broke off as the professor came back into the room with Adelaide's things. She thanked him for them in a tight little voice and put them on quickly, evading his helping hand. She said good night to Margriet, who made no reply, and went across the foyer, not noticing the people in it. The professor caught her up at the door.

'Not so fast, Miss Peters. I need my coat.'

Adelaide was pulling on her gloves, her nice warm gloves St Nicolaas had given her.

'I am perfectly able to go home, sir. Thank you for your help, and I'm sorry if I've spoilt your evening.'

The words came out in a rush, rather louder than she had intended. He looked at her reprovingly.

'I shall take you back to the hospital, Miss Peters. You are one of my staff and I am responsible for you. Kindly say no more.'

He shrugged himself into his coat and took his gloves from the doorman. They went outside together, the snow had stopped fall-ing—it had already been swept away from the hotel steps. The Volvo crunched with gentle disdain for the soft, treacherous stuff through the quiet streets. There wasn't much traffic about, but the tramlines were already being cleared. The professor turned the car and headed it towards the centre of the city.

'Forgive my curiosity, but why did you allow yourself to get caught in the bad weather? It must have been snowing…?'

She explained. It sounded rather silly.

'I should have gone back inside and waited. It was foolish of me. I've given you a great deal of trouble…'

'Yes, indeed you have,' agreed the professor. After that, she could think of nothing further to say. When he stopped outside the Sisters' Home, he said merely: 'Stay where you are,' and got out and walked round the car and opened the door. The snow had piled up; he didn't seem to notice that it was covering his thin evening shoes. He leaned down and whisked her out of her seat and over the drift, on to the doorstep, and set her gently on her feet. He rang the bell.

'You are a goose, aren't you?'

His voice was the calm one he used on his more contrary pa-tients. Adelaide blinked, her eyes suspiciously bright. He wasn't angry, he wasn't even annoyed. He had not, in fact, wasted any feelings on her at all. She said good night in a subdued voice and went inside, where she met Zuster Zijlstra coming out of the sit-ting room. The big girl looked at her with astonishment.

'Adelaide, where have you been?' Her big blue eyes explored her friend's deplorable state.

'I got caught in the snow-storm.' Adelaide spoke gaily. 'I want a bath and a huge meal.'

They went laughing upstairs together, and at supper Adelaide, using the mixture of English and Dutch the other Sisters managed to understand, gave them all an amusing and not quite accurate account of her evening.

It didn't seem so funny when she was in bed. She looked at her watch. For the professor the night would still be young. She pictured him at the Amstel Hotel, dancing, she supposed, with Freule Keizer. She remembered his thin shoes in the snow, and went suddenly to sleep half way through an improbably day-dream in which he had contracted pneumonia from wet feet, and she had saved his life by her devoted nursing.

The professor showed no signs of pneumonia the following morn-ing, however. He came into the clinic, looking in the best of health, at exactly nine o'clock. There was a nurse off sick, and he had to wait until Adelaide and Nurse Eisink fetched the first two children. Adelaide settled a tired-looking woman into the chair by the professor's desk, and started to peel off the numerous woolly garments of the very young baby she had brought in. The professor put down the out-patient card he was reading.

'Someone off sick, Sister?'

She paused in the process of unbuttoning. 'Zuster Steensma, sir. She caught cold yesterday.'

He put the card down.

'Zuster Steensma does not appear to enjoy your iron constitu-tion, Sister Peters.'

Adelaide disentangled the rest of the baby from its clothes, rolled it neatly in a blanket and gave it back to its mother. She glanced towards the desk, and he gave her a friendly smile.

'And an iron constitution is one of the least of your many attributes.'

She blushed. He must have overhead Margriet on the previous evening. The day, which had begun rather badly, suddenly took a turn for the better.

CHAPTER FOUR

TOWARDS the end of January the weather became very cold. Frost sparkled everywhere and the canals were covered with ice. Within three days, the first skaters appeared. The nurses hurried off duty in anoraks and slacks, their skates slung around their necks, making for the nearest canal. The skating went on until after dark when lights shone across the ice, hot chestnut and potato chip stalls sprang up like magic and did a roaring trade. The Dutch were enjoying one of their favourite sports.

Casualty became crowded with children with cracked collar bones and wrists and ankles. The nurses recounted tales of their prowess on the ice to Adelaide; they were all anxious that she should learn to skate. It was so easy, they explained; all you needed was a strong skater to hold you up while you found your feet and got your balance. They suggested several people who might teach her, but warned her jokingly not to accept any offer of help from Professor Van Essen; he was an expert on skates who, while tolerant of beginners, didn't care to waste his time on them. Dr Beekman, who had come in while they were chattering, agreed that the professor was very good indeed, and he couldn't imagine him wanting to teach anyone.

Adelaide could think of nothing she would like better than to be taught to skate by the professor, but it was obvious that if she were to wait for him to offer to do so, she was unlikely to set foot on the ice at all. It was unfortunate that the professor should choose that morning to ask her if she had been on the ice yet. She replied, 'No, sir,' in a most uncompromising manner, and when he further suggested that she should join him with Piet and Leen on the ice that evening, she put down the tray of instruments she was carrying with a quite unnecessary clatter.

'It's very kind of you to ask me, sir, but I...' she hesitated, for the professor was staring at her thoughtfully, and searched desperately for an excuse, wishing at the same time that she could stop blushing like a silly girl whenever he spoke to her. Her sigh of relief was quite audible when at length he said:

'Another time, perhaps, Sister Peters?'

He said no more, and she went along to Casualty with her tray. When she returned shortly afterwards, he had gone to do a ward round.

She wished that she had told him that she was unable to skate; but if she had done so, she reflected, he was too kind a man to do other than offer to teach her, and that, as the nurses had said, would never do. The sight of a group of rosy-cheeked nurses, on the way to the canals, and glowing with well-being, did nothing to improve her mood, so that when she met two of the housemen from the main hospital on her way over to lunch, and they invited her to skate with them that evening, she accepted with alacrity. She didn't know them well; she wasn't even sure she liked them, but she wanted to skate. The thought that once she had learned she could accept any further invitation from the professor overcame any doubts she had as to whether she really wanted to go out with Dr Visser and Dr Monck. They promised to bring some skates for her, and arranged to meet her after eight o'clock that evening. She ate a hurried lunch, worrying about what she would wear. She finally decided to go shopping, and came back with blue slacks and an anorak which fastened tightly under her chin. She went back on duty quite excited, longing for the evening.

Adelaide enjoyed her first lesson on the ice. She found it exhilarating, and her vague feeling of dislike for Doctors Visser and Monck was lessened by the delight of finding herself on skates. They held her up while she got her balance, and then went slowly up and down the canal with her between them. She was awkward at first, but by the time they had gone the length of the canal three or four times she was beginning to find her feet, although she had to keep her eyes on her skates, which had a habit of going the wrong way if she didn't. Doctors Visser and Monck carried on a conversation over her down-bent head, pausing from time to time to beg her to keep her feet straight, strike out strongly with the left foot, and above all, keep her head up.

Adelaide obediently lifted her eyes from her all-important feet, clutched her companions firmly and looked around her. The Singel was crowded; the children had gone, their places taken by older girls and boys, married couples skating arm-in-arm, courting couples with arms entwined around waists, and elderly gentlemen showing a surprising turn of speed. The Singel was well lighted, and she saw the professor while he was still some distance away. She realised that he had seen them too, for he was making an apparently leisurely progress towards them. He had his hands clasped behind his back, and looked, just as most of the men she had seen that evening, very much at home on his skates. He came to a quiet halt and gave her a cold stare.

'Good evening, Miss Peters. Enjoying yourself, I trust?'

Adelaide smiled at him. 'Yes, thank you, very much.'

He nodded casually to her companions. 'Your—friends are giving you a good time?'

'Oh, but they're not my friends,' she spoke with devastating candour. 'I've said hallo to them in hospital, of course, but I met them this afternoon and they said they would teach me to skate.' She smiled at them in turn and then at the professor, who, however, did not smile back. She remembered guiltily and very clearly then how she had refused his invitation to join his skating party that evening. How ill-mannered and rude he must think her—her pink cheeks grew scarlet and she opened her mouth to explain just as Piet and Leen, closely followed by Margriet, joined them. Leen asked her if she was all right and she said, 'Yes, thank you. I'm doing awfully well—I hope.'

Margriet laughed softly. 'How clever of you to find two men to teach you, Sister, and don't you feel foolish learning to do something you would normally learn as a child?'

Adelaide was unable to think of anything to say to this remark. She turned to Dr Visser.

'Please may we go on skating? I don't want to miss a minute.' She smiled at everyone, taking care to include Margriet, who said at once: 'Don't let us keep you. Go and enjoy yourself—I'm sure you will with these two young men.'

There was a sly note of amusement in her voice which made Adelaide uneasy. She forgot it a moment later, however, as they left the others behind and continued on their way. She was doing better now, striking out boldly and much too intent on keeping her balance to do more than wonder what Doctors Visser and Monck were arguing about. They turned and went back along the other side of the canal. Half way down they passed Piet and Leen who waved, and then the professor and Margriet, who did not. Adelaide, watching them skim past, had to admit to herself that although she liked skating, she didn't much like being with her two companions.

'I'd like to go back,' she said suddenly, and was surprised when they agreed to do so without demur. They all climbed the bank and took off their skates and set off in the direction of the hospital. They walked together, arm-in-arm, and Adelaide, grateful for their kindness, kept up a steady flow of conversation in her halting Dutch. They had been walking for ten minutes or more before she realised that they weren't going in the direction of the hospital.

'You've taken the wrong turning, I'm sure; the hospital's over that way.' She pointed over her shoulder. Dr Monck laughed, and gave her arm a tug.

'This is another way back—besides, there's a club here, just down the street. We'll have a drink and a bit of fun.'

Adelaide frowned in the dark. 'I don't want a drink, thank you. You both go to your club and I'll go back.'

She had no idea where she was now, but that didn't matter. Dr Monck held her arm a little tighter.

'Don't be a silly girl, of course you'll have a drink—several drinks.'

Adelaide didn't like the way he laughed. She stood still, planting her feet firmly on the icy road, and disengaged her arms from their too friendly grasp. She sought vainly for the right words in Dutch, but could think of none. She would have to use English and hope that they understood.

'I'm not being unfriendly,' she said crisply, 'but I don't want a drink. Thank you,' she added politely. 'I'm going back to the hospital.' She once more removed their arms; they were laughing again, standing close on either side. She drew a deep steadying breath.

'If you don't leave me alone I—I shall plant you a facer!'

The professor's quiet voice, suggesting that the two young men should take themselves off, while he saw Sister Peters back to the hospital, fell into the ensuing silence like drops of icy water. Doctors Visser and Monck stood looking sheepish and foolish. Adelaide gave the professor a relieved smile and then turned to the two young men.

'Thank you very much for teaching me to skate, and I hope you have a pleasant evening at your club.'

They mumbled a reply as she turned away and started to walk back the way she had come, this time with the professor at her side. After a while he broke the silence.

'Do you know what a facer is, Miss Peters?'

Adelaide was surprised at such a silly question; she had two young brothers at home.

'Yes, of course I do, sir.'

'And would you have—er—planted them?'

She nodded. 'Don't you think I could?'

'On the contrary, Miss Peters,' his voice was dry, 'I'm sure that you are capable of anything.'

They walked on in silence until they arrived at the hospital gates, where they paused.

'I must explain something.' Adelaide spoke in a determined voice. The professor eyed her.

'Don't bother,' he advised. But she was not to be put off, and started to speak, the words tumbling over each other.

'I was told that you were a very good skater, and hadn't much patience with beginners, so I couldn't go with you, could I? But I didn't want to tell you—I was going to learn first, so that if you asked me again... And then I met those doctors. I don't know them very well, and I don't think I like them very much either, but they said they would teach me to skate.' She looked at him shyly, and added with her usual candour: 'I'd much rather have been with you, but you do see that I had to learn to skate first, don't you?'

She was standing under the lamp at the hospital gates; it shone on her hair, which had escaped from her hood. It glowed like bronze in the light. She looked about fifteen years old, and very pretty.

'Didn't anyone tell you that those two young men were rather wild?' She shook her head. 'No, I don't think so, but my Dutch isn't very good yet, someone may have told me and perhaps I didn't understand.' She looked apologetic.

'I shouldn't go out with them again, if I were you,' advised the professor. 'Wait until you can hold your own in our language.'

'That's a very good idea, sir. I'll take your advice. It was kind of you to bring me home,' she continued. 'How fortunate that you happened to be coming down that street just then.'

The professor agreed.

'I wasn't frightened, you know, but it was rather unpleasant. Thank you very much, and good night, sir.'

She went indoors and up to her room to undress and lie in bed and remember every word the professor had said; and that, she decided, as she prepared to sleep, was easily done, for he had said very few. On his way home, the professor called in at the Beekmans' flat. They had just got in, and Leen was making coffee. He took off his coat and accepted the cup she offered him, then told then what had happened.

'Are you skating tomorrow evening? You are? Good, Piet, will you invite Adelaide to go with you, and I'll meet you on the Koningsgracht about seven. Between us we should be able to turn her into a passable skater, but don't tell her that I'm coming too; she has a bee in her bonnet about attaining perfection before accepting any invitation to skate with me. The silly girl,' he added.

Leen poured out another cup of coffee.

'Let's all come back here afterwards; though I haven't anyone to sit with little Piet.' She frowned.

Coenraad got up and put on his coat.

'Mrs Tweedle will love to come; I'll ask her.' He thanked Leen for the coffee, wished them both good night, and went home.

Adelaide was delighted when Piet asked her to go skating with them that evening.

'I'd love to, if you're sure I won't be a nuisance?' she asked anxiously. 'I'm not awfully good yet.'

'You're doing very well,' Piet said stoutly. 'Another few hours and you'll be as good as any of us—well, almost as good.'

She found Leen and Piet waiting for her. It was already dark, but the ice on the canals glistened in the lights. There were more skaters than ever. They started off, Adelaide in the middle, still rather uncertain of her feet. They had not gone far when Leen cried:

'Look who's here! Coenraad, how nice to see you!'

He came to a halt beside them. He was wearing a sheepskin jacket and his dark hair was uncovered; he was going grey at the temples and it showed up under the lights. He slapped Piet on the shoulder and kissed Leen's cheek. The little nod he gave Adelaide was friendly, she wondered why he looked so pleased with himself. She looked around, but there was no sign of Margriet.

'I'll get between you two girls,' he said, and crossed his arms and took Adelaide's hand in his gloved one.

'Which foot?' she asked anxiously, and they all laughed, and he gave her hand an encouraging squeeze.

'The left.'

Two hours later they all sat down on the bank and took off their skates. It had been wonderful. Adelaide had stopped looking at her feet once she had realised that the professor would not let her fall. It was a great deal more fun now that she was able to look around her. She told him so, turning her glowing face to his. She looked very happy. They were all panting and very hungry; their breath wreathed around them in little clouds; it would be very cold later on in the night. She sat down and let the professor untie the knots she had made in her straps. Their faces were very close, her dark eyes sparkled as she said:

'I could have gone on for ever. I felt so safe with you.'

The professor took off her skates and tied them together. 'Your skating does you credit, Miss Peters, you will soon be safe on your own, won't she, Piet?'

He took off his own skates, picked up Adelaide's, and they all set out, in the best of spirits, for Piet's home.

The flat was warm and cosy when they reached it. A nice-looking elderly woman was putting on her hat and coat as they came in. Leen introduced her as Mrs Tweedle who had been minding the baby. She gave Adelaide a bright bird-like glance as the professor escorted her politely from the room. While they were waiting for the taxi, he said:

'Thank you, Mrs Tweedle, I'll be back in a couple of hours. Don't wait up.'

'All right, Mr Coenraad.' She got into the taxi and settled herself comfortably while he gave his address to the driver. He stood back, and she put her head out of the window.

'That's a nice young lady, that new nurse of yours, sir. Nice manner too,' she breathed.

He agreed. 'And an excellent addition to our staff, Mrs Tweedle, a pity that she will only be with us for a year.'

They had an uproarious supper. Leen thought it would be a good idea if Adelaide spoke Dutch. This she was very willing to do; she had quite a large stock of words by now and had learnt a great deal of grammar. Her efforts at conversation, however, though determined, provoked so much laughter that they decided that it might be better to speak English. After supper the girls cleared away the dishes and washed up in the tiny, well-equipped kitchen, and Leen went to fetch little Piet for his bottle. She gave him to Adelaide to hold while she went to get it ready. He was a big placid baby, and sat on her lap, his head pressed against her shoulder. Adelaide stroked the soft blonde down on top of his head; she had quite forgotten the two men sitting on either side of the stove, talking quietly; little Piet smelled nice and gurgled

sleepily and chuckled when she tickled him. It must be nice to
have a baby, she thought wistfully.

The professor took her back to the hospital soon afterwards.
The roads were ice-covered and slippery. He took her arm and
walked with a rocklike steadiness down the middle of the street,
hoisting her gently back on to her feet each time she slipped. For
most of the way they walked in a companionable silence. When
they did talk it was about the next day's clinic, and the hospital
and the chance of the ice holding for a few more days. When
they reached the hospital gates Adelaide said in her friendly voice:
'Wasn't it a lovely evening? I'm so glad I can skate. Thank you
for teaching me.' She wished him good night and watched him
go back through the swing doors into the quiet streets. She still
had no idea where he lived, and wondered if she would ever know
him well enough to ask. She thought it unlikely.

Adelaide was late off duty. Now that she was thoroughly settled
into the clinics she scrubbed for theatre if there were emergency
ops. There had been three that day, all within an hour or two of
each other. There had been a prodigious clearing-up to do afterwards. She changed quickly, wrapped herself well against the raw
cold of the evening, and walked quickly to Mijnheer de Wit's flat
in the Spui. She was beginning to enjoy her Dutch lessons; she
could understand a fair amount of what was being said by now,
although she was still hesitant about talking. However, her teacher
seemed pleased enough with her, to judge by the amount of homework he gave her. He was waiting for her now in his untidy little
sitting room and she hastened to make her apologies. He listened
gravely, correcting her accent as she spoke, and making her repeat
her words again, until she was perfect. She took off her outdoor
clothes and spread her books on the table.

'You are a good pupil, Miss Peters,' he said in his dry old
voice.

Adelaide was surprised. 'Am I? How kind of you to say so,'
and she added with candour: 'It's a terrible language.'

The old gentleman laughed. 'Now you know why so many of

us speak English and French and German, even if only a few words. But you have tried very hard, and I will reward you a little. We will shut the grammar and we will talk. You may ask questions of me—in Dutch, of course—and I will answer them.'

Adelaide, who hated grammar in any language, shut her books and settled back in her chair. She looked charming, her hair gleamed like copper in the light, she was wearing a dark green dress, which was the envy of her colleagues, who had not got the advantages of Marks and Spencer. There were a great many things she wanted to know, and one thing in particular.

'Why does Professor Van Essen wear glasses?'

Mijnheer de Wit took off his own spectacles and looked at her sharply.

'Miss Peters, I find that a most peculiar question.'

'Yes, I know, but I don't mean to be impertinent. You see, it isn't just curiosity. I've noticed he doesn't use one of his eyes…' She added apologetically, 'I work with him every day, and I look at him quite often.' She went a little pink.

Mijnheer de Wit put his glasses back on. 'You are a perceptive young lady. Coenraad van Essen is practically blind in one eye, but it is never mentioned, you understand?'

Adelaide sat forward. 'Please tell me about it; you must know that I like and admire him…'

Her teacher nodded vaguely. 'It's quite a story—we will have a cup of coffee before I begin.'

Their cup of coffee had become a small ritual which Adelaide knew better than to ignore. She got the cups and saucers and silver rat-tail spoons and put them on the table, while the old man fetched the coffee. He poured it carefully, put some Speculaas on a plate of Pynacher Delft at Adelaide's elbow, then settled himself in his chair.

'Coenraad's father was a great friend of mine. He was an excellent and well-known doctor, not a children's specialist, as his son is, but a physician. When the Occupation took place in 1940, he was left alone by the Moffen and allowed to carry on with his work. Coenraad and his two sisters were small children, you understand, and I don't suppose the war meant a great deal to them at that time. Not until their father was arrested for helping his Jewish patients to escape. He was shot, his house and possessions confiscated, and his wife sent to a camp. Coenraad's mother died there. You have perhaps heard of the Tweedles, who look after Coenraad?' Adelaide nodded. 'They went into hiding when the doctor was shot and his wife arrested and took Coenraad and the two little girls with them. They cared for the children until the Bevrijding, and later went back to the house on the Heerengracht with them. They are devoted to Coenraad, and he to them. It was a considerable time after the children were back in their old home when Coenraad confessed that he was gradually losing the sight of one eye. He had been knocked about quite considerably when his parents were arrested and the house searched; a blow from a rifle butt had damaged his eye; by the time he could be taken to a specialist, there was nothing more to be done about it.' The old man looked across the table to Adelaide. 'You haven't drunk my excellent coffee.'

She had forgotten all about her coffee. She was still seeing a small boy—nine, ten years old?—being ill-treated by brutish adults. She raised enormous brown eyes, suspiciously bright, to her teacher.

'He is always so kind and patient with the children. That's why, of course.'

Mijnheer de Wit made no comment, but said again:

'Drink your coffee, and we will have a second cup.'

She drank, swallowing the chilly liquid without tasting it. He filled their cups and she took a sip and went on speaking her thoughts out loud.

'He seems so…self-sufficient. Doesn't he want to marry?'

He didn't seem surprised at her question.

'When Coenraad decides to marry, I think it unlikely that he will tell anyone about it beforehand.' He paused, and added slowly:

'There are always rumours, of course.'

Adelaide blushed. 'I didn't mean to be inquisitive—he's such a nice person, I would like him to be happy. He deserves it.'

Her teacher sucked the last of the sugar from his cup, making a regrettable noise in doing so.

'He will be...he will be. Now, my dear young lady, let us discuss your homework. You still have great difficulty with the conditional; supposing you study it well before your next lesson, and we will try and overcome your reluctance to speak in any tense but the present.'

Adelaide gave a little laugh. 'I'll do my best, Mijnheer de Wit. You are so kind and patient, I only hope that when I am back in England I'll have an opportunity to speak Dutch. It won't be very likely.'

She got up, took the cups out to the tiny kitchen, and put on her coat. She had said good night, and was half way down the precipitous little staircase to the floor below when the front door bell jangled through the house. She heard the click of the lock as it was opened by the kind of remote control commonly used in the older houses. Someone was coming upstairs, two at a time, and very fast. She had time to clutch the narrow hand rail firmly before the professor was upon her; he filled the staircase completely.

'Don't knock me down,' she cried, and then, 'Good evening, sir.'

He had stopped on the stair below her. 'Good evening, Miss Peters.' He cocked a black eyebrow at her books. 'Lessons?' He didn't wait for her to nod. 'Will you wait for me? I want to talk to you. I have to give this to De Wit.' He indicated the pile of papers under one arm. 'I'll only be a moment.' He edged past her and went on up, not waiting for her reply.

She continued on her way, and sat down on the bottom step to wait for him. He was back again, empty-handed, after only a few minutes, and opened the door and ushered her outside. There was an icy wind blowing down the Spui as they turned into the Kalverstraat, walking briskly. When they reached the narrow steeg which was the accepted short cut to the hospital, he kept straight on. Adelaide hesitated, not sure if she was supposed to turn down its familiar gloom, but he took her arm and steered her past and across the street to the warm, well lighted lounge of the Hotel Polen. Adelaide sat down on the chair he had pulled out for her, trying to think of something to say. She very much wanted to ask him about that awful time when his parents were arrested, but was fairly certain that if she did so, he would simply not answer, but get up and go away and leave her alone. So instead she made a banal remark about the weather, which he ignored. He ordered coffee, and at last broke the silence.

'I won't keep you long, Adelaide, but it's too cold to stand talking in the street.' He unfastened his coat and told her to do the same. It was richly warm in the café; she hoped that he would put her heightened colour down to the fact that she was feeling the change of temperature. The coffee arrived, and he sat back in his chair, looking away from her out of the window, so that she could watch him unobserved. She jumped when he spoke.

'What is your opinion of Nurse Wilsma?'

Adelaide took her eyes off his face and thought.

'May I ask why you want to know before I tell you, sir?'

'You may. When you go back to England, we shall have to appoint a new Sister in your place. Nurse Wilsma seems an obvious choice, but I—we don't see every aspect of a nurse's work, you know. She's good, but she is also...' he frowned, trying to find the exact word he wanted '...slapdash, though not always.'

Adelaide put down her cup; she didn't really want it, it was a good excuse not to have to drink it.

'She's very good, especially in an emergency—and sweet with the children, and that's important to you, isn't it? Perhaps she is a little slapdash, but she is young, isn't she? Give her a few months as a *Hoofdzuster*, and you will find she is everything you could wish for.' She pushed her cup away, and in a quite different voice said:

'I don't go back to England until October. It's still only March...unless you wanted me to go back sooner?'

He was thunderstruck.

'Good heavens, no, Miss Peters. The thought never entered our heads. We are more than pleased with you.' He shot her a sharp glance. 'I thought you knew that.' He smiled at her, and looked all at once ten years younger. 'Did you think that I was giving you the sack?' he asked mildly.

She smiled back at him. 'No, not really, but you did sound as if you couldn't wait for me to leave.'

'Forgive me, that wasn't my intention. Now, about Nurse Wilsma, could you prepare a monthly report—I do not need to say an honest one, to you. That will give us several months to assess her before we offer her the post.'

Adelaide started to do up her coat.

'Yes, of course I will, Professor, and I'm sure that they will be excellent ones, too. And now you won't mind if I go?' She got up, and he got up with her. 'I've kept you, I'm sorry.' They were at the door. 'I'll say good night, sir.'

'Say whatever you like, Adelaide, but perhaps you will bear my company as far as the hospital? I want to look in on that fractured pelvis you had in theatre this afternoon.'

They crossed the street and started to walk down the *steeg*. It had begun to rain.

'A pity it won't freeze any more now,' the professor remarked. 'I enjoyed our skating party, didn't you?'

'Yes, very much.' Adelaide smiled up at him, thinking for the hundredth time what a nice person he was to be with, and they fell to arguing in friendly fashion about the Dutch weather. The walk to the hospital had never been so short for her as it was that evening.

CHAPTER FIVE

ADELAIDE was standing, hot and rather tired, drying instruments. It had been a very busy day. Casualty had been more than usually active. Only swift action had saved the life of a two-year-old toddler with extensive scalds, and that had meant delays in dealing with all the many and various injuries that came in. Adelaide had somehow managed to be in two places at once, helping in Casualty and supervising Out-Patients for Dr Beekman, but the professor had become more and more demanding, so that in the end she had had to stay with him. They worked together over the child, setting up a transfusion of blood plasma, going swiftly through the whole routine of shock treatment, meeting each emergency with the seemingly unhurried movements of experts. When at last the small patient was carried carefully to the ward, the professor had followed it, leaving her to deal with the minor ailments still waiting.

The last one dealt with, she looked at the clock. Out-Patients would have finished some time ago. Adelaide started cleaning up. She had had no tea, and only a snatched dinner, so that when the professor strolled through the door, looking cool and immaculate and presumably without a care in the world, she threw him a look over the mask she had not bothered to take off which caused him to raise an enquiring eyebrow.

'You've had no tea, Sister,' he stated sapiently.

She gave a little snort behind her mask, and went on stringing forceps with the ease of long practice. He came nearer.

'You look like an enraged bundle of calico,' he remarked cheerfully, eyeing the enveloping theatre gown. Only her muslin cap, perched on top of her rather untidy hair, looked fresh and dainty. He leaned across the trolley and twitched the mask down under her chin. She gave an exasperated gasp, but he took no notice, removed the forceps from her grasp and continued stringing them. He handed her the completed bunch.

'You put them away, you know where they go far better than I.' He cast an eye over the trolley. 'You've done the needles and knives? Good, we shall be ready in ten minutes or so.' He handed her another bunch. 'I've not had any tea either,' he said, in such a plaintive voice that she burst out laughing.

'But the Dutch don't mind missing their tea in the afternoons, it's only the English who can't bear to go without it.'

The professor nodded. 'I know, I had an English grandmother and an English nanny. Between them they taught me a proper respect for afternoon tea.'

Adelaide shut the cupboard door and locked it. 'So that is why your English is so good, Professor?'

'Thank you. I imagine your Dutch will be equally good if you continue to make the progress Mijnheer de Wit tells me about.' Adelaide looked surprised, and he went on to explain. 'He was a friend of my father's, and naturally he assumed that as you are working at the clinic, I should want to know how you are getting on.'

Adelaide undid her gown and put it with the pile of sheets and dressing towels ready for the laundry. She glanced up at his words, to find him staring at her intently. She felt a quick glow of excitement, instantly dispelled by his next remark.

'You look hot and tired,' he observed.

Adelaide sighed.

'Yes,' she agreed, 'I am.' What he really means, she thought, is that I'm bedraggled and bad-tempered; and I am. She stripped off her frills, rolled down her sleeves, and put on her cuffs.

The professor looked at her watch. 'Since I have been the cause of you missing your tea, perhaps you will come and have a meal with me in—shall we say—forty minutes? I'll be at the hospital entrance.'

Adelaide, half way through the door, stood with her mouth open, looking at him. Her eyes looked enormous, her lipstick worn off hours ago, the end of her nose shone, and she was quite unaware of how pretty she looked despite it all. She shut her mouth with a snap.

'It's very kind of you, Professor Van Essen, but I have other plans for the evening.' She spoke stiffly; she was a poor liar and avoided looking at him.

'What plans?' he persisted. She searched feverishly for a genuine excuse, failed, and looked at him helplessly. He met her embarrassed gaze blandly.

'Just so, Sister. You don't consider it quite—suitable for a member of the nursing staff to accept an invitation from a consultant; but I must really point out to you that you have been with us for some time now, and I have had no opportunity of talking to you about your job and reactions to working here in Amsterdam. Since we're both hungry, surely we can—how do they say it?—kill two birds with one stone?'

Adelaide, listening to him skilfully cutting the ground from beneath her feet, wished most unreasonably that he had asked her for any other reason than that of convenience. She remembered what Mijnheer de Wit had said about her hair. Perhaps the professor wouldn't care to go out with someone as conspicuous as she was.

'What about my hair?' she said gruffly, and watched him look her over, rather taken aback.

'I imagine you will run a comb through it,' he suggested mildly.

'I don't mean that.' She stopped and swallowed. 'You don't mind going out with it?'

The professor suppressed a smile. 'No, I don't mind. Should I?'

'The Dutch don't like red hair, and—and people stare at me sometimes. Mijnheer de Wit told me. You heard me telling Piet Beekman about it.' She went rather pink.

'I remember. We discussed ears and noses too, didn't we?' He spoke seriously enough, but she cast him a suspicious look.

'Yes, well, you know what I mean. Do you mind?'

'No, I don't mind. You forget that I had an English grandmother, perhaps that accounts for the fact that I quite like it.'

Adelaide felt relieved. 'Then I should like to come, thank you. I'll be at the front door in about half an hour.'

She whisked away, all her splendid resolves forgotten in the excitement of going out with the professor.

She looked very nice as she came down the hospital steps, thirty minutes later. Her green coat was well cut, and the little green hat matched it exactly; she was wearing the gloves that St Nicolaas had given her. She greeted the professor rather shyly, but with great composure. She had taken herself to task while she changed. The professor was a kind and considerate man for whom she worked and as such it was perfectly natural that he should take an interest in her work. It was all very simple. Just the same, when she had taken a final look in her mirror she had turned away quickly, suddenly pierced with a longing to be blonde and Dutch and beautifully dressed, and, above all, admired by Coenraad van Essen.

She looked about her with naïve pleasure as she got into the professor's dark green car, and remarked with a disarming frankness:

'How beautifully it's polished. Whenever do you find the time to keep it all so?'

The professor made a little choked sound and thought of Henk, his elderly chauffeur, who cherished the car like a baby, not to mention the Rolls-Royce in the garage behind his house. He tried to imagine Henk's face if ever he found his master cleaning the car.

'I have some help,' he said briefly. 'Do you drive, Miss Peters?'

'Oh, yes,' said Adelaide cheerfully. 'My father's got an old Austin, but I'm a bad driver, and as we can't afford a car for a good many years yet, I only drive when there's no one else.'

They turned into the Leidsestraat and, after a minute or so, pulled up. 'Here we are,' said the professor. 'I thought at first we would go the Five Flies, but I think you'll like it better here.'

She looked at the sign over the door. Dikker and Thijs. She had never heard of them. They went inside to a quiet, elegant opulence that took her breath. There was music somewhere in the background as the head waiter came forward to greet them.

'*Goeden Avond, Juffrouw,*' he bowed smilingly to Adelaide.

'*Goeden Avond*, Mijnheer de Baron.' He led them to a table and settled her in a chair. She looked across the table, frowning quite fiercely at the professor, who waved aside the proffered menu, and sat back comfortably, waiting for the question he knew was coming.

'Why did he call you Baron?'

'I am.'

'You mean that you're a baron as well as a professor? I didn't know.' She sounded disapproving.

'Yes,' he answered coolly. 'I saw no reason to tell you.'

She looked like a little girl who had been unexpectedly slapped.

'I'm sorry, Adelaide, I didn't mean that. I inherited one and worked for the other. It doesn't make any difference, you know. I'm the same man I was ten minutes ago.' He beckoned the hovering waiter. 'Would you like to choose, or will you leave it to me?'

She looked at the menu; it was large and listed an impressive array of dishes. It was written in Dutch too. She might choose something fearfully expensive.

'Please will you choose for me? Something simple,' she added, mindful of his pocket. The professor chose carefully, ordering dishes which would have cost her a week's pay. The waiter went away. Adelaide clasped her hands in her lap, and said in a little rush:

'I'm sorry, Professor.' She sounded rather stiff, but eyed him honestly. 'I was very rude. Of course it's none of my business. It's just that I was surprised.'

She had no idea what a peculiar effect she was creating on her companion, but privately and fervently wished that she could stop blushing.

'Thank you, Miss Peters. Tell me, don't you approve of titles?'

She opened her eyes wide. 'Well, of course I do. Only I'm not used—that is, I don't know anyone with one. I—I don't come from that sort of background. My father's a country parson.' She said it with pride.

He smiled charmingly. 'Yes, I know, your Matron told me. Tell me about your family.'

She didn't realise how skilfully he was putting her at her ease. It wasn't until they were sitting over their coffee that she said suddenly:

'You wanted to ask me questions about my work, and I've talked and talked.' She looked at him anxiously. 'Did I bore you?'

'Indeed no, I've enjoyed every minute. We can talk about work some other time.'

'I think I should go back now,' she said. She hadn't realised that they had been sitting there for so long. He didn't try to stop her.

'Supposing we drive back round the canals?' he suggested. 'It's a lovely evening. Amsterdam is at her best on these spring nights.'

The professor knew his own city well, pointing out the picturesque houses and telling her small fragments of history which he thought might interest her. Half way down the heerengracht he stopped the car. 'Shall we get out for a minute? You'll see it all so much better, and it's very lovely here.'

It was indeed lovely; the canal lay smooth and cold in the moonlight, and on either side the beautiful gabled houses stood as they had stood for centuries. Adelaide had a strange feeling of timelessness. She sighed and shivered. The professor put an avuncular arm around her and pulled her close into the comfort of his tweed coat.

'You're cold. I shouldn't have suggested that we got out of the car.'

'I'm not cold; it's just that this is all so beautiful and peaceful and ageless. I shall miss it very much when I go back to England.' She pointed across the canal. 'What a lovely house that is, opposite. I wonder who lives there, and if they love it and look after it. I expect it's beautiful inside.'

'Yes, it is.'

'Have you been inside?' she asked.

'I live there.'

Adelaide turned to look up into his face.

'You mean you live there...it's your home?'

'Yes. It's rather large for me, you know.' He smiled down at her. 'The ancestor who built it had a wife and children; I shall have to follow his example.'

Adelaide didn't reply. The idea of the professor having a wife and children and living happily with them in his lovely house, while she went back to England and never saw him again, was very lowering to her spirits. She wanted this moment to last for ever; his arm felt very solid and comforting around her, and she would have liked to have buried her face in his shoulder and had a good cry. Instead, she took a few steadying breaths.

'It really is time I went back.' Her voice didn't sound quite right, but she persevered. 'Thank you for a delightful evening. I did enjoy it.'

She moved, but instead of releasing her, his arm tightened and pulled her round to face him. He put a finger under her chin and tilted her face up to study it intently. She looked white in the moonlight, and forlorn. She stood passive in his arms while he bent his head and kissed her; she returned his kiss with an innocent passion, forgetful of everything but that moment. When they drew apart she whispered:

'Please don't say anything.'

They got into the car, and drove without speaking to the hospital. The professor helped her out and went and pulled the old-fashioned bell outside the nurses' home, then stood waiting beside her on the doorstep. He was as calm and self-possessed as usual. She stole a look at his face; it was impossible to read his thoughts. He turned his head and looked at her in a detached, faintly amused way. She thought wearily, 'He was just being kind.' She said in her soft little voice:

'Thank you for comforting me just now—I suppose I was feeling homesick. I'll not think of it again, and I know you won't wish to either.' The door opened then, and she slipped inside with a murmured good night.

* * *

The days slipped by; it was the end of spring, although the weather was still cold, with rain and wind and low-flying clouds. Adelaide did some sight-seeing. She went to Alkmaar—the cheese market wasn't open, it was too early in the year, but she loved the quaint little town. She explored Delft, and wandered round its magnificent churches and longed for enough money to buy some of its exquisite pottery. She spent a day with one of the Sisters whose home was in Medemblik. It was like living in the sixteenth century again, only the inhabitants spoilt it by wearing modern clothes. She whiled away several hours in the old castle; it was cold and draughty and grim, but it had a lovely view over the Ijsselmeer.

The clinic was as busy as always; in Casualty, burns and scalds and injuries from skating gave place to broken arms and legs from falling off bicycles, and limp little people who had fallen into the canals, fishing or sailing boats.

That particular Saturday there had only been a small clinic in the morning. Dr Beekman had taken it as the professor was away. Casualty was slack too. Adelaide sat in her office and worked at her books and thought about him. She supposed he was somewhere with that odious Freule Keizer. She got out a sheet of paper and applied herself to making out the off-duty for the following week. She sat and looked at it for a few minutes, then tossed it aside rather pettishly and began to draw rows of beaky noses on her blotting pad. She wondered what Zuster Boot had meant when she said that the professor came from a patrician family. She would look it up when she went off duty. On second thoughts, she decided that she wouldn't look anything up; she was getting far too interested in the man. She tore up the beaky noses and started once more on the off-duty. She decided, once again, that she would be pleasant and friendly in a cool way; she was a sensible young woman, not a silly girl, it should be quite easy to keep to her resolution. She drew a splendid beaky nose, with eyes beside it adorned with glasses. She looked at it longingly, then tore the paper up savagely.

That evening she went for a long walk with two of the Sisters.

They got back to the home tired out, and she went to bed and slept at once. She was awakened by one of the night Sisters, and sat up in bed to find the light on. She looked at her clock. She had only been asleep for half an hour; it was barely eleven. Night Sister came from Friesland, and spoke a Dutch Adelaide found difficult to understand, but she was able to make out that there had been a bad accident—a bus full of children coming home from a school outing. There were, according to first reports, a lot of casualties; she was wanted on duty at once.

Adelaide dressed fast, screwed her hair up anyhow, and pinned her cap on to the deplorable result. She fastened her blue buckled belt as she ran: she had forgotten her cuffs. All the lights were on in Casualty and the clinic; one of the nurses was already laying out extra equipment. Adelaide swept instruments off shelves, collected receivers and trays, and put them in the autoclave. She told the nurse to lay up trolleys wherever she could find the room, and asked her to get the salines and blood plasma bottles out, then she went to the cupboard and got out the two satchels which were kept for emergencies; she was collecting the pethidine and morphia ampoules from the DDA cupboard when Piet Beekman came in. He saw the satchels.

'Good girl, we'll go straight there. They can manage here for the time being. There'll be plenty for us to do.'

They caught up their satchels and ran outside to the waiting ambulance. It raced through the city, along the Rokin, across the Dam Square and into Damrak, and turned off into one of the small streets close to the station. It halted on the edge of a large crowd, which made way for them to reach the space cleared by the police. The small victims were lying and sitting around the wreckage from which the police and ambulance men were still passing children. The bus in which the children had been travelling had gone into the back of a lorry-load of scrap-iron, and an oil tanker behind it, unable to stop in time, had hit the bus with such force that the back had been lifted high into the air. It now rested at a sharp angle, its nose buried in the piles of scrap-iron on the wrecked lorry, its back wheels in the air.

They wasted no time: Dr Beekman marshalled his helpers into a team, and started going from one child to the next, Adelaide with him, giving the necessary injections and first aid so that the children could be moved as soon as possible back to the hospital. Two ambulances had already moved off; Adelaide and Piet were bending over a small boy when a policeman made his way over to them. He looked worried. 'There's a child still in there,' he said. 'She's jammed on the steering wheel and none of us can reach her. We're waiting for the acetylene cutters and the other equipment; the fire brigade are bringing them, but it will take a bit of time to clear the nose of the bus from the wreck of the lorry, before we can use any of it. The child's injured for sure, and terrified. We're afraid she might fall before we can get her out, and there's nothing but broken glass and iron below her.'

Piet said, without pausing in his work: 'Isn't there enough room for a man to get through, or are you afraid of his weight tipping the bus?'

'Both,' said the policeman. 'We've had several attempts.'

Adelaide finished a neat bandage on the boy's leg and got up from her knees.

'Let me go,' she said. 'I'm small and light enough to crawl down the bus, and I'll stay with the child until you can get us out.'

Piet looked doubtful, but she gave him no time to say anything, and walked quickly across to the wrecked bus with the policeman. He picked her up and lifted her until she could reach the ruined door, get a hold on it, and wriggle inside. She was appalled at the mess; it was a shambles. She kept very still and looked round her, deciding what to do. She would have to make her way down the steeply inclined bus to where she could hear the child crying. She began to edge through the mass of broken seats and wood-work. As she got nearer, her torch picked out the terrifying barrier of broken glass between her and the child. Great spears of it stood rooted in the floor, hideous icicles of it hung from the crazy ceiling. Adelaide crawled nearer; she could see the little girl now, covered in dust and filth, and frantic with fear. She was on her back, her body wedged in the spokes of the wheel, her head hanging and small legs dangling. Adelaide went as near as she dared, slid an arm carefully between two jagged pieces of glass, and put it under the child's head. Then she eased the other arm through a splintered hole and under the thin small knees. She drew a sighing breath and took stock of the situation. The child, as far as she could see, was covered in scratches and abrasions, but there did not appear to be any large wound. She was light in Adelaide's arms, but they were already starting to ache, and she wondered how long she would be able to support the small body, crouching awkwardly, not daring to move. She was conscious of a fine dust creeping up her nostrils; her clothes were covered in it. She had lost her cap; her hair hung in a red tangle around her shoulders, her apron was hopelessly torn, and so was the sleeve of her dress. She supposed that help would come soon. The little girl looked at her with enormous eyes; she had stopped crying. Adelaide smiled.

'Hullo, what's your name?'

She could barely hear the whisper: 'I'm Miep.'

'What a lovely name,' said Adelaide chattily. 'Well, Miep, I'm going to sit here with you for a minute or two until someone comes to get us out. Shall I tell you a story?'

She embarked on a story of The Three bears. It was a jumbled mixture of Dutch and English; she wondered if Miep had any idea what it was about—she wasn't sure herself after a minute or two, but it seemed to soothe the child, for she didn't cry again. Only when a piece of wreckage came tumbling wildly down the bus, to slide away into the dark around them, did she cry out. Adelaide's voice faltered as the torch beside her toppled over and rolled away, its light doused. She cried in a frightened little voice, 'Oh, Coenraad, please come.' Saying his name had made her feel better; she suddenly knew that he would, and told Miep so in such a cheerful voice that the little girl stopped crying again and listened quietly to Adelaide's story.

Coenraad van Essen sat beside his aunt in the stalls of the Concertgebouw; the programme of classical music was almost over, but to the professor the strains of Beethoven's fifth symphony merely provided a dimly heard background music to his thoughts. His mind was wholly engaged with the problematic treatment of the acute interssusception which he had admitted that afternoon. He was annoyed to be disturbed by a tap on the shoulder. He listened to the whispered message given to him by an attendant, spoke briefly to his aunt, and went to the manager's office to take Dr Beekman's call. He listened without interrupting while Piet spoke, said briefly that he would be along at once, and went to get his car.

He drove fast through the city, passing ambulances with lights flashing, on their way back to the hospital. Obviously the rescue work was well under way. He parked the car in a side street, and pushed his way through the crowd. He saw Piet immediately kneeling beside a little girl. Coenraad looked round. There weren't many children left, those that were didn't appear to be badly hurt. A fire tender drew up beside the wrecked bus, and several men began to unload equipment. He'd got to Piet by then, and without more ado held the small skinny arm flexed while Piet arranged a sling and gave him a short and concise account of the children's injuries and what had been done for them. An ambulance man arrived and carried the small patient away and they moved on to a boy, sitting propped up against a pile of coats. Blood trickled sluggishly down his face from a scalp wound, it had dyed his shirt a dark, sticky red. Coenraad laid him down with the observation that surely everyone knew that head cases lay flat. His skilful fingers were probing the long cut hidden under the blonde hair. 'He's a concussion all right. Get him back to the clinic, Piet, as soon as possible.' He was busy with a pad and bandage, and frowned suddenly.

'I thought you said Adelaide was with you? Has she gone back?'

Piet looked up. 'No. There's a child trapped in the nose of the bus, she's in there with her.'

The professor said nothing, but looked at the upended bus and turned to Piet with raised eyebrows.

'There wasn't anyone small or light enough to get to the child.'

Coenraad nodded. 'I see. But I think it's time I got them out.' He went over to the men standing round the fire tender and stood talking for a minute, then took off his dinner jacket and hoisted himself through the door Adelaide had entered. It was very dark inside, but he could hear Adelaide's voice. He listened carefully to the queer jumble of words and grinned to himself. It was then that his foot touched a piece of the wreckage, which went slithering down towards the nose of the bus. The child cried out in the sudden silence which followed. He heard Adelaide call too, but it seemed wisest not to answer her.

When he got back to the rescue squad they had already begun to cut a hole through to the driver's cabin; they had moved as much of the scrap-iron as they dared, and now two men stood ready with a metal stretcher from one of the ambulances. As the cut metal fell away they eased it through on to the mass of glass and splintered wood inside. It would make a firm base from which to work. The professor lowered himself to the ground and wormed his way carefully inside the bus.

Adelaide, crouching by the now unconscious child, saw the light from his torch and had a brief shadowy sight of him, and then heard his quiet voice.

'Adelaide? Are you all right?'

'Coenraad! Yes, I'm fine.' She tried hard to stop her voice from shaking. 'I think Miep is unconscious; she hasn't answered me for the last few minutes.'

The professor was quite close to her now, separated by the smashed glass. He glanced at her briefly.

'Keep still for a little longer.'

She watched while he got cautiously to his knees and examined Miep. It was a good thing that the small creature had passed out; he would be able to work much faster. He ran gentle hands over the flaccid arms and legs; he could feel no broken bones, it was more likely that there was an internal injury. The wheel was wrapped around her waist, gripping her fast. He set to work on it, while Adelaide tried to keep her arms from shaking; the strain on them was almost unbearable.

It seemed a long time before Miep was free and he was able to take her in his arms and lower himself on to the stretcher again, to push her carefully out to the waiting hands beyond. He knelt down again and took the glass cutter from his pocket. Adelaide had pulled her arms back, and crouched, resting them on her lap. Their numbness was giving place to a cramp which was almost unbearable, and bringing her near to tears. When the professor after one fleeting glance, asked 'Cramp?' it was all she could do to nod—she would not trust her trembling mouth to form the words.

He spoke bracingly. 'Rub your arms and try and move your fingers; you'll need them in a minute to plait that hair.'

This time she managed a shaky smile and said in a determinedly bright voice: 'Very well, I'll do my best.' He wasn't looking at her now, so she could let the tears trickle down her dirty cheeks; it was surprising how much better she felt for them. She rubbed her arms as she had been bidden to do, the professor was lifting away the first pieces of jagged glass as she started, very clumsily, to gather her hair into a plait. There was very little room; she dared not move too much, it took a long time; by the time she had finished he was easing away the last splintered sheet of glass between them.

He was so close to her that she could see the little beads of sweat on his forehead. The same fine white dust that coated her face was on his; his hair was powdered with it too. She dismissed the frivolous thought that he would be a remarkably handsome old man with the speed it deserved, and worried instead about the long scratch she could see on the back of one of his hands. Her alarming thoughts of tetanus and a possible dreadful death were brought to an abrupt end by the professor's voice, very much alive, its placid tones unaltered by his recent exertions.

'Put your arms around my neck, I'm going to lift you through.' She felt his arms around her waist, and clasped her own round his neck, and was lifted neatly through the hole he had made. His deep, rather pedantic voice was just above her ear.

'You have a saying in English—It's an ill wind that blows nobody any good.'

'Whatever do you mean? I don't see…' They were kneeling on the stretcher now, and she loosened her hands from his neck and looked enquiringly at him in the torchlight. She was quite unprepared for the quick light kiss he gave her. He laughed a little.

'Now do you see? This is my honorarium.' Without another word he pushed her down on to the stretcher and towards the gap where they were waiting to help her out. Piet helped her to her feet and gave her a bear-like hug.

'Adelaide, are you OK?'

'Yes, of course. What about the little girl, is she all right?'

'She's in hospital by now; she looked pretty bad, but at least she's alive.'

He gave her a warm smile and turned to grin delightedly at Coenraad. The glare of a flash lamp made them start; there were several more as they joined the firemen and police, busy clearing up the mess. After a few minutes they said goodbye, and Adelaide found herself between the two doctors, being hurried to the car. They put her between them on the front seat, and the professor turned the car towards the hospital. He spoke briefly to Piet over her head.

'Rub Adelaide's hands, will you, she's going to need them presently.'

It was pleasant to sit back while Piet massaged her tingling hands in his great paws, and watch the professor, as relaxed as though he were returning from an evening's outing, shoot the Volvo between two trams, with a broad grin for the indignation earthily voiced by the drivers. To his enquiry, presently made, as to how she felt, she answered briefly:

'I'm fine, thank you.'

'You're filthy dirty.' He barely glanced at her. She wondered what she looked like, and was glad there was no mirror for her to see. The professor was speaking again in a brisk voice.

'Half an hour for us all to have a bath and change. Sooner, if you can manage it.'

He swung the car through the hospital gates and stopped outside the Sister's Home. Lights were on in Casualty and the theatre wing, the clinic was ablaze with them. Adelaide found herself lifted down and propelled gently to the door, which the professor opened for her. 'Thank you, sir,' she said politely, and was surprised when he took one of her very dirty hands in his and said:

'You're a very brave girl.' His voice sounded kind. He gave her a little push and went on in a different, brisk voice: 'Half an hour, not a minute more.'

It wanted five minutes to the half hour when Adelaide arrived at the clinic. Excepting for her hair, which she hadn't had the time to wash, she looked exactly the same as usual. She put on a gown and tied her hair in a theatre cap, then pushed open the door of the Intensive Care room. Piet was already there and looked up as she went in.

'Hullo, Adelaide. There are three for theatre here. The fractures are already over on Orthopaedic, the rest are warded here. The professor wants you in theatre to scrub up. Dr Van Hoven is operating, they're going to be tricky cases.'

There were plenty of nurses on duty, the hospital hummed with them. The theatre was ready and waiting for the first case. Adelaide scrubbed up and started threading needles and checking swabs. The doors opened and the first patient was wheeled in, the anaesthetist at the trolley's head. The child was put on the theatre table. It was just after one o'clock in the morning.

The last case was wheeled out of theatre at half past four. Dr Van Hoven stripped off his gloves, and he and the anaesthetist, nodding their thanks to Adelaide, went off together. She started to clean the knives and needles while the two nurses washed and sorted instruments and cleaned the theatre. They were all tired, but no one disputed the rule that the theatre had to be left spotless and ready for use as soon as possible. Adelaide had just laid the last of the needles away when Night Sister put her head round the door.

'There are relief nurses coming on now; there's breakfast waiting for you as soon as you like.' They smiled at each other, two young women who had done a good night's work, before Night Sister hurried off.

An hour later, breakfasted, shampooed, and very sleepy, Adelaide climbed into bed. She wasn't on until eleven, so she could sleep for an hour or two.

Punctually she walked into the clinic. The waiting room was as full as usual. She went into the office, where the professor, calm and immaculate, sat at his desk. He looked up briefly to answer her good morning, but Piet greeted her with a sigh of relief.

'Thank heaven you're here! I can't find a thing.' He took a second look at her. 'It's a pity the papers can't photograph you now, instead of printing the ones they took of you last night.'

Adelaide, already restoring order among the notes, gazed across at him.

'What do you mean? Did they take some photos? Whatever for?'

'You're in the morning papers; I expect you're in the English papers too.'

She piled some X-rays beside the professor. 'Well, if they're as bad as all that, no one will recognise me,' she said reasonably. She stopped, struck by the thought that her parents, confronted by a photograph of herself taken by flashlight when she was not at her best, might be alarmed. This awful thought was interrupted by a cough from the professor.

'I—er—took the liberty of telephoning your father early this morning. I thought he might be anxious if there should be some mention of the accident in his paper. There probably is, you're a heroine, you know.' His voice was dry.

Adelaide blushed, and for that reason, frowned heavily.

'Thank you very much, sir. It was kind of you to think of it. But what a lot of fuss to make.'

She was fidgeting with a pile of notes, and getting them into a sad state of untidiness. She dropped them like hot coals as the professor said crisply: 'I shall be wanting those in a minute.'

'I'm sorry, sir,' she said meekly, and then, 'Professor?'

He sat back and said encouragingly, 'Yes, Sister?'

She stood in front of him, trying to be composed and cool, and to forget his kiss amidst the ruins of the bus—his fee, he had called it.

'I must thank you for getting me out last night. I was very frightened, you know. It was so dark. I believe you saved our lives, and I am indeed grateful. Just thanking you doesn't seem enough,' she added worriedly.

'Thanking me is quite enough, Sister Peters. It just so happened that I was there. It could have been anyone else, you know.'

She felt surprised at this. 'But I knew it would be you.'

The professor was studying the papers before him, his pen busy once more, and she didn't expect an answer. She gave a small unconscious sigh.

'Did you and Dr Beekman go to bed? You both look very tired.'

'It was hardly worth it, Sister. We'll go off early if we can.' He glanced up from his work, half smiling. 'Thank you for your solicitude. Now, if you are ready, shall we have the next patient?'

CHAPTER SIX

THE professor was well known and liked in Amsterdam and the publicity about the bus accident was considerable, but he shrugged it off politely. Adelaide, too, came in for a large share of praise and admiration, which tried and embarrassed her. Miep had been admitted to the ward with fractured ribs and a perforated lung, and she went each day to see her.

A few days after the accident, Miep's parents had found Adelaide in the office. It was not yet nine o'clock, and there was no one else there. They had shaken her by the hand and thanked her over and over again for the part she had played in Miep's rescue. The more they talked, the less she understood, and when at length the professor arrived, she had no hesitation in introducing them to him and slipping out of the room. Ten minutes later she walked quietly into the office again and wished the doctors good morning. Piet Beekman greeted her in his usual friendly way, but the professor, already sitting at his desk, gave her a baleful glance.

'How can you wish me a good morning after the shabby way you treated me just now? I am surprised at you, Sister. You ran away.'

Adelaide felt indignation swell inside her and began a hot denial, caught the professor's eye and said rather lamely:

'Well, you didn't need me, sir.'

The professor looked critically at his beautifully kept nails.

'On the contrary, Sister, I find your presence essential,' he said gently. He looked across at Piet. 'Don't we, Piet?'

Dr Beekman agreed cheerfully. 'Can't find a thing when you're off duty, Adelaide.'

She laughed. 'What nonsense you talk! You just don't look.' She turned back to the professor, her starched apron crackling fiercely.

'Are you ready to start, sir?'

She spoke in a bright, professional voice that caused both men to look up at her openmouthed; she had remembered, just in time, her resolve to be pleasantly friendly but cool, and very, very efficient.

The weather turned warm, the clinic seemed more crowded than ever. The shops were full of summer clothes, and holidays were the main topic of conversation.

Miep was nearly well again, and was going home in a day or so. Adelaide had bought her a new dress, ready for the great day, and took it along to the ward on the evening before Miep was to be discharged. The little girl was sitting up in her bed, playing Snakes and Ladders with the professor, who was lounging on the counterpane, thereby breaking a strict rule enforced by Zuster Zijlstra. He was demanding and accepting advice from the children in the nearby cots, and the noise was considerable. Zuster Zijlstra, writing her report as Adelaide went past her office, shrugged her shoulders and waved her on to the ward. She pushed open the door, took one look, and decided to go back later. Miep hadn't seen her, and the professor's head was bowed over the game. However, she had hardly got her hand on the door handle when he bellowed above the din: 'Don't go away, Sister, I want to see you.'

Adelaide advanced towards the bed. The clinic had finished only an hour ago; she wondered what he could want her for, as he had had plenty of time to speak to her during the day. She hesitated when he patted the counterpane. 'Sit down and don't be a goose. If I can break a rule, so can you.'

He spoke in Dutch, to the great delight of the children, who shouted *'Dag Zuster'* in a deafening manner, and urged her to break the rules like the doctor. Outnumbered, she sat down gingerly on the side of the bed, to be immediately enveloped in Miep's excited embrace. The little girl had seen the dress over Adelaide's arm, and bounced wildly around the bed, hugging Adelaide until she cried for mercy.

'The doctor's taking me home,' Miep said importantly. 'In his car.' She beamed at them both.

'Ah, yes.' The professor glanced at Adelaide. 'We thought it would be nice if you came too. You're off duty tomorrow afternoon, aren't you? Dr Beekman will take the clinic.'

Adelaide wondered how he knew she was off duty, and realised that there was nothing to stop him studying the off-duty rota in her office.

Miep was smiling at her coaxingly. 'You must come, Adelaide.'

Adelaide smiled back at the child. 'Yes, of course I'll come.' Her voice was warm and kind. She turned to the professor. 'What time shall I be ready, and where shall I meet you, sir?' She was friendly and pleasant, but her voice was the voice of a Ward Sister addressing a consultant. Even in her own ears it sounded prim, and when the professor said quietly: 'You're sure you want to come?' she cried. 'Oh, yes, please!' with all the warmth back again, and quite forgetful of the role she had cast for herself.

The following afternoon she fetched Miep, radiant in her new dress, and went to the clinic entrance. They were very punctual, but the Volvo was already there. The professor got out and lifted Miep into the front seat, admired her dress and told her what a pretty girl she was. She threw her arms around his neck and gave him a smacking kiss. Adelaide, standing and watching, was horrified to hear Miep's voice.

'Now kiss Adelaide and tell her she's got a pretty dress too.'

She saw the professor turn an amused face to her, and took an involuntary step backwards.

'No!' As she said it, she thought how silly she was, when she wanted him to kiss her so much.

'No?' He was laughing at her now 'But I may admire your dress, may I not?'

She thought he was being polite. The dress was plain, pale green and last year's. Her arms were bare, and so were her sandalled feet. She was very conscious of the vividness of her hair in the sunshine and the sprinkling of golden freckles across her nose. She got into the car and he shut the door and leaned over it to ask her if Miep always called her Adelaide.

'Yes, you see I told her that that was my name when we were in the bus.'

When he suggested that he should do the same in order not to confuse the little girl, she agreed readily enough; it seemed a sensible enough suggestion.

It didn't take long to get to Velsen, where Miep lived. They drew up in front of a small terraced house and her whole family came to the door; there seemed to be a great many of them. Everyone went inside, and Adelaide and the professor were escorted into the front parlour, an unlived-in little room, obviously used only on important family occasions. The furniture, by no means modern, had been so polished by zeal and love that it glowed; the small window, shut firmly against dust, was almost obscured by a multitude of pot plants. Even the cushions were plumped up to exact squares.

They all sat around the room, drinking milkless tea and eating a very creamy cake. Adelaide sat between a young man and a big blonde girl; they smiled at her and stared at her hair, but didn't say a word. She looked across at the professor and envied him the steady flow of small talk issuing so effortlessly from his lips. After a little while, he caught her eye, and she stood up and shook hands endlessly, gave Miep a final hug, and got into the car.

'What nice people,' she remarked as he eased the Volvo over the brick road towards the main street, 'and so kind and hospitable. I hoped I would see the rest of the house—they didn't all live in it, did they?'

The professor shook his head. 'No, most of them were cousins and aunts and uncles come to welcome Miep back home. He had halted the car, waiting to join in the continuous stream of traffic on the motorway. Adelaide settled herself firmly into the comfort of well-kept leather. 'What a lovely day—the hottest we've had.'

'You're not on duty until five, are you, Adelaide? There's plenty of time, shall we go to the sea first and perhaps have tea somewhere?'

It was very tempting. Adelaide said 'Yes' before she had stopped to think, and even then she stilled the accusing little thought that she was not keeping to her resolution by the sensible one that she was very unlikely ever to go out with the professor again.

Having absolved her conscience, Adelaide prepared to enjoy her outing. The professor proved to be an excellent companion. She remembered wistfully the evening they had spent together in Amsterdam; he had been a delightful host then, but today he seemed younger and bent on amusing her. By the time they arrived at the Grand Hotel, Huis ter Duin, she had forgotten all her scruples about his wealth and title, and all her good resolutions, too. They had tea on the terrace, and afterwards, as they had half an hour to spare, strolled along by the water's edge. The breeze whipped her hair around her face, and after a few minutes she took off her sandals and splashed through the water, the professor strolling placidly beside her, smoking his pipe. She didn't talk a great deal, and the professor hardly at all. She paddled along in a happy companionable silence until he looked at his watch.

'We'll have to be going if you don't want to be late on duty, Adelaide.'

They found an upturned boat near the hotel, and she sat down and dried her feet on his handkerchief, put her sandals back on, and then began an ineffectual attempt to tidy her hair, watched lazily by her companion. 'Leave it alone,' he said. 'It looks very nice.' He knocked out his pipe. 'When are you having your holiday?'

Adelaide thrust a last pin into position and said guardedly:

'I don't know.'

'Are you going to England?'

She made a pattern on the sand with her sandal. 'No, I don't think so. I...I thought I'd have a holiday when I get back home.' She made her voice sound cheerful, and looked carefully away out to sea.

'Won't your family be disappointed?' he queried.

She frowned at his persistence, and resisted a strong desire to tell him that she hadn't enough money for the journey, not if she was going to help with the boys' school fees. But of course she couldn't, especially to someone like the professor who, she suspected, never had to think about money anyway. She frowned fiercely at the horizon, and blinked away threatening tears.

His placid voice came from somewhere behind her shoulder.

'A pity you're not taking a couple of weeks during the summer. I'm going over to Dorset at the end of July, and thought you might like a lift there and back. You live somewhere near Rye, don't you? I practically pass your family's doorstep.'

Adelaide didn't answer at once; she had heard what he had said, but she couldn't believe it. She turned her head and said soberly enough:

'You mean I could go home and come back again in your car?' She looked at him searchingly. 'Wouldn't you rather be by yourself?'

'No, I like a travelling companion on a long journey.'

Adelaide bit her lip. A long journey. Just how long? She was, she knew, extremely old-fashioned in many ways, due no doubt to being the daughter of a country parson who still lived according to the standards of his youth. She asked cautiously:

'How long would it take?'

The professor hid his smile very successfully; perhaps because he was a doctor, he was remarkably good at reading other people's thoughts.

'If we leave early, directly after breakfast, you should be home for tea.' He went on, the twinkle in his eye belying the gravity of his tone: 'I took one of the Sisters over with me a couple of years ago—she came to no harm,' he added wickedly.

Adelaide felt her cheeks grow hot. She said with tremendous dignity:

'But I didn't mean—that is, I never...' she looked at him helplessly. 'I'm rather old-fashioned and I don't know how to change.' She was relieved to see him smile again.

'Yes, you are, aren't you? But don't change, Adelaide, we all like you as you are, and there's no need for you to get flustered.'

He was mocking her gently again. 'It seems to me it's a sensible idea, and I have always thought you to be a sensible person.'

This remark had the same effect as a bucket of cold water upon Adelaide. She told herself that it was just what she needed to chase away the very silly thoughts that had been floating around her head. It was indeed a very sensible arrangement, made, she reminded herself sternly, between two sensible people. She said politely: 'Thank you very much, Professor, I should be very glad to accept our offer...' He cut her off briskly.

'Good. Get your leave fixed up, then. I should like to go on the nineteenth, that will get us back for early August—plenty of casualties then. Now we'd better go back.'

He said no more about it, but maintained a casual conversation to which Adelaide found herself responding quite cheerfully. He got her to the hospital with five minutes to spare; she wasted one of them standing in the doorway of the Sisters' Home, answering his careless wave, and watching the gleaming car disappear into the maze of narrow streets around the hospital.

She had plenty of time for her thoughts that evening. Casualty had never been so slack—bee stings, wasp stings, sunburn—all could be dealt with without the aid of a doctor. She took as long as possible to clear up and get Casualty ready for the night staff, then walked through to her office where she sat down at her desk and allowed herself to think about her afternoon. Margriet Keizer would probably get to hear about it—Adelaide looked at the clock—the professor was doubtless dining with her somewhere at that very moment. She sighed and opened the day book and started to count the entries. Half way down the page she stopped, struck by the thought that it wouldn't matter in the least if Margriet did know. The professor had neither done nor said anything that even the most jealous of girl-friends could have objected to.

Adelaide lost no time in getting her holiday booked. The very next morning she went to Matron's office and arranged it with the Directrice, who agreed pleasantly that it was indeed too good an opportunity to miss. Besides, she pointed out, it would give

Zuster Wilsma a chance to show what she could do. Adelaide hurried back to the clinic, there was still ten minutes before the professor was due to arrive. Should she tell him at once that she could come with him, or wait until their coffee break, or would he mention it first?

The professor didn't come. Piet walked in alone and offered the information that the boss was having a few days off, adding gloomily that it couldn't have been a worse time for him to be away. Adelaide swallowed her disappointment. A few days meant two, three, perhaps four days, so she would have to be patient; in the meantime there was plenty of work to do.

The professor had gone away on the Tuesday, and by Sunday evening there was neither word nor news from him. Adelaide longed to ask, but dared not—Piet was a dear, but a great tease, if she showed any but the most casual interest as to the professor's whereabouts, he would be sure to comment upon it. She held her tongue, worked harder than was needful, and went every evening to the swimming pool outside the city with Zuster Zijlstra and her fiancé and Dr Bos, who had a girl-friend in Giethoorn and talked about her all the time. Adelaide was glad she was on duty that evening. It was hot and close in the clinic and a swim would have been wonderful, but not, she decided, if she had to listen to any more of Henk Bos's tales of his Mia. She busied herself changing the pillow slips and couch covers and making sure that everything was ready for the morning clinic. Casualty was always full on a Monday; it was as well to have the clinic ready.

She started to fold a pile of towels, wondering for the hundredth time where the professor was. He hadn't taken a holiday since she had arrived at the hospital. He was going to have two weeks in July, that left a month—perhaps he had changed his plans and wasn't going to England after all?

The sing-song wail of the ambulance interrupted her thoughts, and she hurried through to Casualty. It was a small boy, fallen head first from a fourth floor window in a tenement house close to the hospital. She telephoned Dr Beekman, borrowed a nurse from Zuster Zijlstra's ward, and set to work on the child, who was deeply unconscious. He would be an urgent theatre case by the look of things. She sent the nurse to warn Theatre Sister, and waited while Piet examined the boy.

'I've warned the theatre, shall I get Dr Van Hoven?' He nodded. 'We'll have to start at once if he's to have a chance. Any idea when he last had a meal?' He was thinking of the anaesthetic.

She had already asked the child's mother. 'Six o'clock, nothing since, luckily.'

She slid a triangular bandage under the battered little head and tied it loosely under the dressings; she had already undressed the little boy as far as possible. She watched him being taken to theatre, then started to clear up once more. It was late when she at last reached her room. She had stopped to console the parents as best she could, and then waited to hear the result of the operation—it was a relief to be able to tell them that their small son had a chance to live, slender though it was.

She must have been more tired than she thought, for she overslept. Stopping only for a cup of tea, and catching up a slice of buttered toast in her hand, she dashed over to the clinic, ten minutes late. Casualty was empty, the nurses well ahead with their work in the clinic, she wished them a good morning and went to her office to write up the books and eat her toast. It was already warm, it would be hot later. The day, which had only just begun, seemed to stretch endlessly before her. She flung open the door on a loud sigh. The professor was sitting at her desk, immersed in a pile of notes before him. He looked up, frowning slightly as she banged the door behind her, and said smoothly:

'Good morning, Sister Peters. Forgive me for not getting up; and for appropriating your office—the nurses turned me out of my own room.' He caught sight of the toast, and raised his eyebrows.

Adelaide ignored the eyebrows and said in a formal little voice which effectively concealed her pleasure at seeing him again:

'Good morning, sir. I don't need the office, thank you.' She put the toast down carefully on her desk and picked up the laundry and dispensary books, a box of scalpels for sharpening, and a large bag of mending which the professor had thrown carelessly on the floor. She was at the door when he reminded her gently:

'Don't forget your toast, Adelaide.'

She snatched it up, looking cross, and was half way through the door when he spoke again.

'Will you tell Dr Beekman to come and see me here as soon as he arrives; and you come with him, please.'

Adelaide remembered the casualty of the evening before. Had something gone wrong; had they made some terrible mistake?

'The little boy who was brought in last night—they did a trephine—he's all right, sir?'

He didn't look up. 'In excellent shape, Sister. And now, if you don't mind…'

Adelaide went out, closing the door with an exaggerated care that was far more annoying than the bang she was longing to give. Half an hour later she was back in the office with Piet behind her. This time the professor got up and she sat down in her chair behind the desk, the men one on each side of her. They made the little room seem even smaller. She folded her hands on the starched whiteness of her apron and waited composedly for the professor to speak, her outward serenity covering her true feelings.

'I thought that we would have a picnic,' he began. 'This evening. The clinic staff and Zuster Zijlstra; she'll come, I know. You bring Leen with you, Piet, we'll need your car anyway, I can't get everyone into mine. We'll go to Noordwijk and swim and have supper on the beach.'

Piet grinned. 'A wonderful idea. What do you say, Adelaide?'

She choked back her bitter disappointment. She was on duty that evening and wouldn't be able to go.

'It's a lovely idea,' she said cheerfully.

'Who's the unlucky nurse on duty?' Piet asked.

Adelaide adjusted a cuff to an exact correctness and said ungrammatically: 'Me.' She tried to make her voice sound cheerful. 'Well—er—no, Sister, you're not,' the professor's voice was very smooth. 'I arranged for Zuster Zijlstra's staff nurse to take over at five. That's if you have no objection?'

No, she had no objection. She said so quietly, her heart thumping with happiness, her thoughts racing ahead; arranging the work, contriving how to have the day's work finished on time, regretting the simplicity of her black swim-suit, thankful for the new white bathing cap with that ridiculous fringe. She could press the blue and white striped cotton during the dinner hour... 'Shall we get started, Sister?'

She could tell by the professor's voice that he had already said it once, even twice. She jumped to her feet.

'Of course, sir.' She smiled at him, dazzlingly. 'It's a very heavy clinic too.' Her eyes danced; life, she felt, could be wonderful when you least expected it.

The last little patient left at ten to five, and the entire staff set to with a will to get the clinic tidy. Even the professor stayed behind to help, sitting calmly filing X-rays amidst the ordered chaos of clearing up. Adelaide eyed him lovingly; she thought he looked tired and rather sad. She wondered if Margriet had refused to marry him after all, and her heart leapt at the thought. He lifted his head, and she looked away quickly, ashamed to feel so happy for such a reason.

Zuster Zijlstra was almost ready when Adelaide got to her room.

'Hallo, Adelaide. Hurry!'

Adelaide needed no second bidding. She tore off her uniform, showered and dressed, and then stuffed the despised black swim-suit into her beach bag, she added the new swim-cap and a short towelling coat, gathered up her bag, and pronounced herself ready.

They were the last to arrive. Zuster Wilsma was in Piet's car. Zuster Eisink and Zuster Steensma were sharing the back of the Volvo with the professor's two dogs. He was waiting with the car door open.

'Adelaide, Leen wants to gossip; you'd better go with Piet.'

She slipped obediently into the seat beside Leen, and listened smilingly to Leen's account of little Piet's amazing cleverness without hearing a word of it.

They went through Noordwijk and past the main beach, until

the professor finally stopped at a small secluded arc of sand, empty but for a couple of gaily striped tents, and a handful of the wickerwork hooded chairs so beloved by the Dutch and so coveted by the British. They came to life as the cars stopped. Adelaide recognised the professor's sisters and their children; she supposed the two men with them were their husbands. They were all enveloped in a happy laughing mass and hurried off to change and thence to the water's edge where a ball game was in progress.

She looked around for the professor and saw him in the water, on his back and supporting a small boy on each arm. The little boys were shouting and laughing; the professor appeared to be asleep. The ball game became hectic, with a great deal of splashing and short sharp bursts of swimming. Adelaide, racing to retrieve the ball, saw the diving board moored some distance out from the shore. She was a strong swimmer; it looked very tempting. She didn't think she would be missed if she swam quickly there, had a couple of dives, and then back. She ducked away, and when she was clear of the others, changed to the crawl, tunnelling through the clear water, head well down; so it was that she missed the professor as he passed her, going very fast and quietly. He was waiting for her when she reached the board and heaved her up with a powerfully muscled arm.

They sat side by side, getting their breath and dangling their feet in the water. The sun was still warm on their bodies. Adelaide was trying to think of something to say—she longed to know if the trip to England had been arranged, but perhaps it would sound a little too eager if she asked him. Instead she said:

'What a beautiful evening.'

'Very.'

She tried again:

'And such a beautiful beach.'

'Very beautiful.'

She went bravely on. 'The water's warm too.'

'Yes.'

She was suddenly exasperated. 'Don't you want to talk?'

She quite forgot to say 'sir'.

'Yes, I do, when you've finished discussing the landscape.'

Adelaide went pink. 'I'm making conversation; it's polite,' she snapped. She watched him laughing and almost choked on a childish rage which melted completely at his next words.

'You know about my eye, don't you?'

She turned and looked at him deliberately and said softly:

'Yes, I do. I'm sorry.'

He continued placidly. 'I've been in Vienna; there's a good man there. Sometimes I get impatient—wanting a miracle, I suppose. The only one he gave me was a pair of new glasses.'

Adelaide tried to keep her voice normal. 'And has it helped?'

'Oh, yes,' he said cheerfully. 'The small grey blurs are now large grey blurs.'

She marvelled at the lack of bitterness in his voice.

'How did you find out that I knew?' Surely Mijnheer de Wit hadn't told him, or had she, shameful thought, made herself conspicuous by looking at him too often? She had to know.

'You always stand on my good side when we're at work.' He changed the conversation abruptly. 'I've got the trip to England arranged.'

She gave a sigh of relief. 'I thought that perhaps you had changed your plans, and we weren't going.' She frowned. 'How did you know that I had arranged my holiday for the last two weeks in July?'

'I rang the Directrice.'

There was a great commotion behind them, at least half the picnic party were about to board them. Adelaide felt a large hand between her shoulders. 'In you go,' said the professor, and gave her a push.

They all spent some time diving and swimming around the board, and when they were tired out, swam in a body back to the beach, where the lazier members of the party had set the picnic ready.

Adelaide surveyed the food spread out on the gay cloths with something approaching awe. Lobster patties, golden brown chicken legs, with elegant pink frills, vol-au-vents spilling something delectable over golden pastry, baby sausage rolls, minute pork pies, cheese of every sort, baskets of fruit. It seemed to her unsophisticated eye more like a banquet without its usual background than a picnic on the beach. She sat between a quiet youngish man, whom she identified as a brother-in-law of the professor, and a boy of about ten, who addressed the quiet man as Uncle. They plied her with food, and flattered her subtly by carrying on a conversation in Dutch, helping her unobtrusively when she stumbled over a word. It was, she thought, the nicest picnic she had ever been to. She turned to her companion and asked:

'Do you live here?' She looked round; there was no house to be seen on the dunes.

He waved vaguely inland. 'We have a summer villa; we spend as much time here as we can in the summer. The whole family come—Coenraad is here most weekends. You should come too, Adelaide,' he added kindly.

'You're very kind, but I'm not often off duty at the weekends.' Too late she realized that she had taken it for granted that she would be invited with the professor, and her cheeks flamed. If her companion noticed he made no comment, but said merely:

'A pity, but you must come when you can.'

'Thank you, Mijnheer Tesselaar de Klerk.' She was pleased that she had remembered his name.

'And for heaven's sake call me Cor!'

It was cooler now; the girls had put on their beach coats and the men wore an assortment of sweaters and shirts. They looked like a band of gipsies. Only the smallest of the children were still tearing around in the briefest of garments. They drank the last of the fragrant coffee and started to pack up the remains of the feast. It was a leisurely task, interlarded with a considerable amount of talk; by the time they were ready, it was a deep twilight.

They wandered back to the cars and said protracted good nights while children were caught and stowed away, protesting sleepily. Adelaide started towards Piet's car, but was stopped by a hand on her shoulder. 'Over here, Adelaide.' The professor opened the door of the Volvo; Zuster Steensma and Zuster Eisink were already in the back, the dogs sitting damply at their feet.

'In you get.' She got in, and watched him go round to the other side and slide into the seat beside her. He was wearing a baggy old sweater over his slacks, which made him seem very large in the dim light. He backed the car, and they went back the way they had come, through the quiet evening. The journey to the hospital seemed very short; afterwards she couldn't remember a word of what had been said, only that she had thanked him before they had all got out of the car, and he had cut her short by saying:

'Please don't thank me—it is I who should thank my excellent nursing staff for their unceasing hard work.'

He had said it very pleasantly, but that hadn't prevented her from feeling that now that the picnic was over, she had been put firmly back in her place.

CHAPTER SEVEN

IT was a glorious morning when the Rolls slid away from the hospital. It was still early, but the clinic staff were all there to give Adelaide and the professor a rousing send-off. Adelaide's case had been put in the boot, and the nurses had gathered round her, wishing her a happy holiday rather wistfully. She cheered them up with the news that she would be sure to bring back something for each of them, and got into the car, settled in her seat, and opened the road map the professor had thoughtfully provided for her. They were going via Utrecht and Breda and Bruges and then to Calais, because she didn't know that part of Holland; and although they wouldn't have much time to stop, it would be interesting to see another part of the charming little country.

They turned into the Churchilllaan, and were immediately hailed from the pavement by Margriet Keizer. Coenraad brought the car to a halt, and they sat waiting for her to reach them. She looked cool and crisp and beautifully turned out in a white dress which Adelaide guessed was couture. She put a hand fleetingly on the professor's, as it rested on the wheel, and smilingly greeted them both. Adelaide noticed with satisfaction that the professor gently removed the hand and put his own on his knee.

'Surely this is early for you to be out, Margriet?'

She ignored the edge of sarcasm in his voice. 'Yes, I know, but I have some shopping to do.' She glanced at Adelaide, eyeing her pale blue dress with thinly veiled contempt.

'How fortunate for you, Miss Peters, that Baron Van Essen is going to England, and you had the chance of a lift.' Her mouth curved in a smile that didn't quite reach her lovely eyes. 'I do so admire you nurses, working for a pittance—barely enough to dress on, I should imagine.'

Adelaide was determined to keep her temper, and stated fairly:

'Well, we wear uniform for most of the day, so we don't need many clothes.'

Margriet's eyes flickered over the blue dress. 'Yes, I expect you're able to make your things last for years.'

Adelaide remembered, just in time, that she was a clergyman's daughter. 'Yes, I do,' she replied quite gently. Margriet turned back to Coenraad.

'Why didn't you let me know that you had planned a trip to England? I suppose you thought that I was booked up for the summer. We could have had a wonderful time.' She shot a quick look at Adelaide, sitting so quietly. 'The Baron and I have known each other all our lives.' Her voice was honeyed.

'I've known that for a long time,' Adelaide replied, and before she could say more, the professor said curtly:

'I had always thought that you disliked England?'

Margriet looked put out, and then laughed.

'That's true, but I suppose that I could even like England if I were with you, Coenraad.'

Adelaide was looking steadily ahead of her, apparently engrossed in the passing traffic. She had no intention of allowing Margriet the small triumph of knowing that she had upset her. She went on watching the street in an unruffled calm until Margriet, finding the professor unresponsive, at last made her farewells and, with a final wave, left them. The professor started up the car once more without speaking, and Adelaide busied herself with her map. It was quite two minutes before he broke the silence.

'I must admire your forbearance, Miss Peters. Margriet is sometimes rather tactless, but I imagine that you are far too sensible a young woman to let anything she said annoy you.'

Adelaide closed the map with an unnecessary violence, her brown eyes flashing. To be addressed as a sensible young woman so soon after Margriet's thinly veiled sneers was really too much for her good nature. She sat upright, her hands gripping her handbag as though it were Margriet's throat. She spoke deliberately, between her teeth.

'Pray don't trouble yourself about my feelings, Professor—or should I say Baron?' Despite herself her voice shook a little. She kept her eyes on the road ahead of her, not caring if he answered her or not. They were travelling very fast; the professor seemed bent on overtaking everything in sight. She stole a quick peep at him. He was laughing. He said in gently mocking tones:

'You are in a bad temper, aren't you?' His voice changed, she had never heard it quite so harsh. 'And you are not to call me Baron, now, or at any other time.'

She said stubbornly, 'Why not?'

'Because neither my family nor my friends address me as such.'

She was in a mood to argue. 'You forget, Professor, that I am a nurse, working for you.'

'No, I haven't forgotten,' he smiled briefly, 'but I count you among my friends, you know, and since we are friends I shall call you Adelaide until we get back to work, and then I promise that you shall be Miss Peters again. Could you not call me Coenraad, on the strict understanding, of course, that I become a professor again the moment I walk into the clinic?'

She had to laugh at this. 'Yes, I should like that, and I'm sorry I was cross just now.' Her good temper was quite restored. She was, after all, on holiday. Margriet seemed very far away, and she had the whole day to look forward to. She opened the map again and started picking out their route. The breeze was blowing her hair gently on her downbent head, she put up a hand and brushed a loose strand away from her forehead, with the unself-conscious gesture of a child. She was absorbed in her map reading, and quite unaware of the charming picture she made.

They drove steadily south; the car needed little urging. Adelaide sat quietly, watching Coenraad. She liked the way he drove, with a minimum of movement and fuss. As they approached Breda, they were held up for a few minutes in a small village, where the local band, banners flying, was proceeding down the main street. They were playing *Piet Hein*, and Coenraad took up the refrain, whistling under his breath. Adelaide, who recognised the tune and had been taught to whistle by her brothers, joined in, and they whistled their way through a selection of tunes for the remainder of the road to the border, where the *douane* waved them by with a cheerful salute.

Adelaide abandoned her whistling for questions about the countryside through which they were passing, which the professor patiently answered. She was disappointed in Belgium; it looked untidy and faintly neglected after the neat houses and gardens of Holland.

It was a pity that there was no time to stop at Bruges; it looked delightful, but the professor drove straight through the town without pause. He had had to slow down because of the stretches of cobbled street, it was a relief when they were once more on the main road. They swept through Ostend, and presently, Veurne. It seemed the *douane* here was just as uninterested in them as the first one had been. Adelaide looked around her.

'I've been in three countries in one morning,' she said naïvely.

'Four by tea-time,' he reminded her.

That put her in mind of something, and she said rather shyly:

'Mother would like it if you would stay to tea with us.' She paused. 'That is, unless you have other plans?'

'None,' he replied cheerfully, 'and if you hadn't asked me, I daresay I should have invited myself. I hope you're hungry now, I thought we would have a meal before we go on board.'

They made their way through Calais down to the docks, and watched while the car was loaded aboard, then walked back to the town, where he took her to a small restaurant in a side street. It had red check tablecloths on the few tables scattered on the scrubbed floor; it surprised her to see that the people sitting at them were very smart. Adelaide had no idea that it was famous for its cuisine. She looked at the menu card and put it down again.

'I don't know anything about French food, so please will you choose for me?'

When it came, the food was delicious, and she paid him the

compliment of eating a hearty meal and listening intelligently to his comments upon French cooking.

Afterwards, when Adelaide tried to remember the crossing on the boat, she found it difficult to recall any clear memories of it. She only knew that the professor had been a delightful companion, and that the time had flown so fast that she was amazed to see the cliffs of Dover looming up out of the summer haze.

It was just tea-time when they turned into the short curving drive of the rectory. Adelaide looked round happily. The rectory was a small Regency house, with a square porch and large windows on either side. It was shabby as to paint, but the garden was well tended and a riot of colour. She looked at Coenraad, who said before she could speak: 'It's delightful; I can't think of a better place in which to have tea.'

At that moment one of the windows opened and a grey-haired gentleman looked out. He waved and withdrew, to reappear a moment later at the front door, in time to engulf Adelaide, who had jumped out of the car, in a fatherly hug. She had time to introduce Coenraad before her mother came running out of the house. She was very like her daughter, with the same very red hair, beginning to fade a little, but still an arresting colour. She kissed her daughter and shook the professor warmly by the hand before summoning Adelaide's brothers, clamouring around their sister. They were sixteen years old, and identical twins, big for their age, with fair hair and their father's mild blue eyes. They said 'how do you do' with proper respect, but within a very few minutes were involved in an animated discussion concerning the hidden beauties of the Rolls-Royce engine. The Reverend Mr Peters brought this to an end, however, by telling the boys to let Nellie know that Adelaide had arrived. The two gentlemen then repaired indoors to join the family for tea. As they crossed the hall, a short, stout, elderly woman came through the baize door under the stairs, and stopped when she saw them.

'Tea's ready, Reverend.' She spoke to her master, but looked at the professor, her sharp old eyes raking him from his dark well-brushed hair to his exquisitely polished shoes. He bore her scrutiny with good nature, and when she was introduced as the main-stay and friend of the entire family, remarked that they were indeed fortunate to have her. The two men watched as Adelaide came through the door and flung her arms round Nellie's neck, to be greeted with a 'There, Miss Addy, it'll be nice to have you home for a bit, and now go and eat your tea, there's a nice whole-some cake I made. It'll do you good after all that foreign food.'

Tea was a gay meal, with a great deal of laughter and chatter. Adelaide, sitting by her mother, was able to watch the professor where he sat, discussing the works of Bacon with Mr. Peters. Listening to snatches of their talk, she decided that the professor must be a very clever man to earn her father's approbation on a subject in which he was considered something of an expert. They had eaten all the sandwiches and had cut deep into Nellie's cake, when her mother said, 'I'm going to talk to that nice professor, Addy dear, and send your father to talk to you.'

Mr Peters, his serious talk curtailed firmly by his wife, wan-dered over to sit by his daughter, to question her about her life in Holland. Adelaide answered willingly enough, but as she was listening to her mother's conversation as well as she was able, she was somewhat distraite, a fact which her father put down to her long journey. Her mother had a quiet voice; Adelaide found that she was unable to hear a word. To look at the professor's face was of no use. It bore his usual placid expression. He wasn't saying much, but he smiled, and once looked across the room directly at her in a thoughtful way. She wondered what they were talking about.

They were talking about her; her mother had thanked Coenraad for bringing Addy home. 'We've been longing to see her.' She turned a little pink, and said with the same engaging candour as her daughter, 'She wanted to come home so badly, but the boys are to stay another year at school and she helps.' She raised her brown eyes, so like Addy's, to her companion, who said nothing, but was listening with interest. 'They're very clever, and deserve their chance. In a year or two we shall be able to paint the house and have a new car, and Addy can spend all her money on herself, bless her.' She looked fondly at her daughter.

Adelaide saw the faint, amused smile on the professor's face and wondered what her mother had been saying. She would have liked to have joined them, but her mother was deep in conversation again.

'We've been waiting to thank you for going to Addy's rescue in that bus; she didn't say much about it, although we read about it in the papers. She told us that she owed her escape and perhaps her life to you. We are indeed most grateful to you, Professor.'

He looked embarrassed. 'There were a dozen men waiting to do what I did,' he replied. 'I just happened to be the nearest. Adelaide was the brave one.' He told Mrs. Peters what had happened at some length.

Adelaide, from the other side of the room, wondered what they could be talking about so earnestly. She went over to the tea tray to refill her father's cup, and lingered long enough to hear her mother invite the professor to stay the night, and his regretful refusal. He had, he said, promised to arrive at his destination by ten o'clock that evening. Adelaide gave her father his cup and went and sat by her mother, just in time to hear Coenraad say, in answer to her mother's question:

'Yes, a very old friend. I couldn't disappoint her, she is someone of whom I am very fond.' He didn't add that the old friend was his childhood's nanny, installed as his housekeeper in the small manor house which his English grandmother had left him.

'Then stay on your way back,' said Mrs Peters and Adelaide felt a little thrill of delight when he said yes, he would like that very much. He got up to go shortly afterwards, and made his goodbyes.

Adelaide stood by her father, listening to Coenraad's quiet voice, and realised that she wouldn't hear it again for two weeks. She gave him her hand and thanked him for her lovely day and wished him a pleasant holiday in a subdued voice. His hand felt oddly comforting as she put her own into it. When she looked up into his face she saw that his eyes were dancing with laughter, and thought uneasily that he might be reading her thoughts. She was glad when her mother spoke.

'Why not come to lunch, Professor Van Essen? Nellie will cook you a lovely wholesome English meal, and Addy shall make an apple pie.'

He accepted with alacrity, and released Adelaide's hand without speaking again to her. She stood waving with the others as he drove away without looking at her.

The professor arrived at the rectory about midday, at least an hour earlier than he had said. As he got out of the car at the open front door, Matthew and Mark came dashing out to meet him. They were delighted to see him again, though he suspected that their interest might be more for his car than himself. Mr Peters put his head out of his study window and begged him to come in at once and not to allow the boys to bother him. They all went indoors together and into the study, where Mrs Peters sat knitting and keeping her husband company. They all talked at once, and he thought what a happy family they were. When he apologised for being early, Mrs Peters said cheerfully, 'But we've all been waiting for you to arrive. Addy's in the kitchen, why not go and tell her you're here, for I'm sure she must be finished by now.'

Adelaide stood at the kitchen table, rolling pastry, and taking her time about it. Coenraad wasn't due for another hour, it stretched ahead of her endlessly, but if she was busy the time might go a little faster. The door opened behind her. It would be her mother, come to see if she was ready.

'He might not like apple pie,' she said.

'He loves it.' She was quite unprepared for his voice, and spun round to face him, her heart beating a tattoo against her ribs to shake her. She quelled her desire to fling her floury arms around his neck and tell how glad she was to see him, and instead frowned darkly.

'You're early,' she said. 'Look at me.' And was vexed when, without further words, he did so. She stood in front of him, in a cotton dress almost covered by a large apron, her hair tied back in an untidy pony-tail. She remembered that she hadn't any make-up on. She felt her cheeks grow hot under his gaze, and with a forlorn little gesture turned back to the table and bent over her pastry. She didn't look up when he came and sat on the edge of the table.

'You told me to look at you,' he said reasonably, and ate some pastry. 'I'm sorry I'm early. Shall I go away and come back again when you've had time to put up your hair and turn into the cool and composed Miss Peters?'

Despite herself, Adelaide burst out laughing.

'That's better,' he said. 'I was beginning to think you weren't glad to see me.' He absent-mindedly ate some more pastry. 'You look very nice as you are, Addy.'

She drew the pie dish towards her and gently laid her dough over the apples therein. She didn't look at him, because he would be laughing at her, and she didn't think she could bear that. She was making an edge to her pie, her eyes intent, the black lashes curling on her cheeks.

'Have you had a good holiday, Addy?'

Adelaide raised her brown eyes to his, her smile very sweet; she had quite forgotten her appearance.

'I've had a lovely time!'—her face glowed—'I'll never be able to thank you for letting me come with you. Did you have a good time too?'

'Oh, yes,' said the professor. He sounded rather non-committal. 'I don't suppose it was as much fun as yours.'

She considered this. 'Well, the boys were home.' She smiled warmly at him. She was so happy she wanted to smile all the time. She pushed a long strand of hair out of her eyes, leaving a trail of flour down one cheek. He leaned forward and wiped it away with his handkerchief, then kissed the cheek. Adelaide gasped and turned her head. His face was very close, his eyes full of laughter. Her breath caught in her throat and she seemed, re-grettably, to have lost all control over her breathing.

The kitchen door opened and they drew apart as Nellie, laden with washing from the garden, came in. She tossed it into the big basket by the window and came over to the table, and said in scolding tones: 'Now, Miss Addy, that pie'll never get baked if you don't put it in the oven this instant.'

Adelaide picked up the pie obediently, glad of something to do, took it over to the Aga and spent an unnecessarily long time arranging it in the oven, while her cheeks cooled.

Nellie turned her attention to the professor. 'Good morning, sir, and it's nice to see you again. You've had a fine holiday, I'll be bound. The girls all over you and never a dull moment!'

Adelaide banged the oven door, whirled round, and said in a choking voice: 'Nellie!'

'Well, Miss Addy dear, I'm not meaning to be disrespectful, but the professor's a handsome man—you'll allow that, surely? A real nice gentleman, I call him. Why, you said so yourself!'

Adelaide felt her just cooled cheeks redden once more, and she didn't look at the professor when she spoke.

'You're a flatterer, Nellie. You can't expect Miss Addy to agree with you, she works with me every day and sees only my worst side.'

Adelaide caught his brief glance as she stood at the table, cleaning up. She felt goaded.

'I'm usually far too busy to waste time on your looks or your character, Professor.' She spoke tartly, hating herself for the cheap remark. Her words shocked Nellie, but he only laughed, and laughed again when Nellie said, 'Hoity-toity, Miss Addy, that's no answer.'

Coenraad grinned wickedly. 'She's right, you know, Nellie. I mustn't work her so hard, then she will have more time to study me.'

He cocked an eyebrow at Adelaide, who started to laugh— indeed, she felt that if she did not laugh she would burst into tears. She went meekly over to the sink when Nellie said:

'Miss Addy, you go and wash your hands and face and put up that hair this minute! What the professor thinks of you I do not know.'

Adelaide supposed it must be amusing for him to see how

obediently his efficient clinic Sister obeyed this order. She took off her apron and was washing her hands when he strolled over and stood beside her. 'Nellie wants to know what I think of you, Addy. Don't you want to know, too?'

She didn't dare look up from drying her hands, but shook her head, flung the towel down and ran across the kitchen without looking at him at all and through the door, banging it hard behind her.

As she came into the study twenty minutes later, her father was pouring the sherry. In that time she had contrived to turn herself into a cool and poised young lady, freshly lipsticked, and not a hair out of place. She stood in the doorway and was glad when the professor saw her and came over and handed her a glass.

He looked her over coolly. 'An excellent imitation of Miss Peters, if I may say so, Adelaide.'

She smiled uncertainly, feeling shy, and not quite sure what to say. She was saved from replying by the arrival of Matthew, who looked at her in astonishment and asked:

'Good heavens, Addy, you're not going out, are you? You've put your hair up too.'

She ignored his brotherly candour with icy composure, taking care not to meet Coenraad's gaze, and listened to her companions discussing the little jaunt they had planned for the afternoon. Down the Brighton road was an enjoyable prospect for a sixteen-year-old boy. She envied her brothers with all her heart.

Adelaide spent the afternoon packing. She had been rather silent during luncheon. Her father had remarked upon it, and her mother had looked across the table, smiled at her and said:

'Addy's a little sad because her holiday is almost over, aren't you, darling?' and Adelaide had smiled back and said 'Yes,' and had done her best to believe it herself. However, when she came downstairs at tea-time, she seemed in the best of spirits and greeted the returned motorists with every sign of good humour. The professor had brought a large box of chocolates for Mrs Peters, and sat beside her during tea, listening to her gentle conversation, and afterwards helped carry the tea things back to the kitchen. It was explained to him that Nellie always put her feet up in the afternoons. The boys were left to wash up, and the others strolled back to the drawing room where Adelaide remarked that she should go and finish her packing, and as nobody suggested that she should do otherwise, she presently went upstairs, where she stood at her bedroom window watching her parents, with Coenraad between them, walking off in the direction of the church. They appeared to be enjoying their conversation, and had apparently forgotten all about her.

Supper was a simple meal. When it was over, they clustered around the table in the study and played Monopoly—a game Mr Peters was much addicted to. Being a poor man, the mythical thousands he lost and won afforded him great pleasure. At ten o'clock, however, his wife said firmly that they would not play any more.

'These two have to leave early in the morning, and they have a long journey before them.'

She set off to the kitchen, leaving Adelaide to tidy away the game. The boys had gone to bed, her father and Coenraad were discussing Greek mythology. She looked out of the open window; the garden, patterned in bright moonlight, was beautiful. She put the cards away in a drawer in her father's desk. Both men seemed engrossed in their conversation; that Reverend Mr Peters, happy to have found someone who could quote Greek poetry in the original, certainly had no eyes for the moonlight. Neither, apparently, had the professor. She emptied an ashtray with unnecessary noise, sighed soundlessly, and went to kiss the bald patch on her father's head. She said good night to the top button of Coenraad's waistcoat, and went upstairs to bed.

The morning was glorious. As Adelaide got into the car she thought that the garden had never looked so lovely. She hated saying goodbye; she waved until the little group standing at the Rectory gate was hidden by the curve of the road, and then sat back very quiet. The tears she had been holding back spilled over and ran slowly down her cheeks, and when a large white handkerchief was proffered wordlessly by the professor, she accepted it with a grateful sniff, mopped her eyes, blew her nose in a no-nonsense fashion, and said in a watery voice:

'Thank you. I didn't mean to cry. Father says that a snivelling female is one of the most tiresome afflictions man is called upon to endure.'

He laughed. 'I admire your father. We had a most interesting talk last night.'

'What about?'

'Oh, metaphysics. He was able to tell me a great deal about ontology.' He paused. 'He gave me some excellent advice about other matters, too.'

At the thought of her father, she swallowed another hard lump of tears, and said, determinedly cheerfully:

'That's funny. Father never gives advice unless he's certain that it will be taken.' She wondered what Coenraad could possibly want advice about, but he wasn't going to tell her, saying merely:

'But I have every intention of taking it,' and then changing the conversation so pointedly that she knew she must ask no more questions.

She powdered her small red nose and applied herself to the task of being an agreeable companion. This entailed listening intelligently to the professor's views on coarse fishing, of which she knew nothing. She had the good sense not to ask why it was coarse in the first place, she had in fact only a very sketchy knowledge of the sport, but it was pleasant listening to the professor talking, and thus pleasurably occupied, the journey to the car ferry seemed surprisingly short, and even the long wait in the queue to go aboard went unnoticed.

Once aboard, they walked briskly round the deck until the cliffs of Dover were sufficiently far away for her to be able to look at them without feeling homesick, and it wasn't until later that she realised Coenraad's thoughtfulness in engineering their peram-bulations. By the time they had a cup of coffee, they were docking at Calais, and the slow process of disembarking began. Coenraad had said nothing about lunch. Adelaide wondered about it as they at last emerged from the Customs shed and made slow progress through the town. Now he left the main road and after threading through several narrow streets, stopped outside the restaurant they had visited previously. Obedient to his injunction to remain where she was, she waited quietly until he returned, followed by a waiter carrying a hamper which was stowed carefully in the boot. The professor got back into the car and nursed it carefully over the atrocious cobbles until they joined the N40.

'I thought we'd have a picnic. We'll stop the other side of Ostend, there's a golf course there between the main road and the sea. We'll have lunch there and go over the border at Sluis.'

Adelaide, who would have cheerfully eaten yesterday's bread and a heel of cheese, so long as it was in Coenraad's company, thought this an excellent idea. They bowled along, with only the shortest delay at the French border. An hour later they were going through Ostend. They left the car by the side of the road and scrambled over the dunes until they could see the sea from the shelter of some trees.

Adelaide, unpacking the hamper, thought that the contents, though not as numerous as the dishes served at the clinic picnic, looked just as delicious. She arranged the paper cloth thoughtfully provided and laid the chicken mousse, green salad, thin bread and butter and fruit carefully upon it. She surveyed the result of her work, and said, 'This isn't a picnic. A picnic is sandwiches and thermos flasks. This is a feast!'

Coenraad opened the bottle he had carefully removed before she examined the basket. He filled the glasses and handed her one, and said '*Proost.*' She took a cautious sip, while he watched her smilingly. 'It's quite harmless, Addy.'

Adelaide felt herself grow pink, took a defiant gulp and choked. He had to thump her back while she whooped trying to get her breath. He was nice about it, and didn't laugh until she had enough breath to laugh with him. They ate everything, while she listened to preposterous tales of his student days, only half be-lieving them. When the last crumb had disappeared, she packed everything tidily back in the hamper, while he sat back against a tree, smoking. She was startled when he asked:

'Do you go out much in Amsterdam, Adelaide?'

She sat back on her heels and considered his question.

'No, not a great deal. Once or twice with Dr Bos…'

The professor blew a smoke ring, and remarked quietly:

'He'll miss you while you're away.'

'Good gracious, no. He's gone to Giethoorn; there aren't any roads there,' she explained, airing her knowledge. 'His girl-friend lives there. He told me all about her; no one else wants to listen, you see.'

Coenraad digested this interesting piece of information, and rolled over on to an elbow. 'Who else have you been out with?'

'Well, I went to Haarlem to an organ recital. I enjoyed it, it was a wonderful church too…' she hesitated. 'I went with Dr Vos. He's in the Path Lab,' she added unnecessarily, and felt indignant when the professor laughed.

'Addy! He must be sixty—and a widower.'

'I know, that's why I went.' She saw his raised eyebrows, and hurried on to explain. 'I mean he's almost old, isn't he? I didn't know he was going to…well…' She stopped. 'He was horrid!'

Coenraad sat up leisurely, and asked with interest: 'What did he do?'

She studied her hands. 'He was—unpleasant, and I got annoyed.' She spoke with hauteur, her cheeks pink with temper, her eyes flashing, her beguiling little bosom heaving like a temperamental film star's, just at the remembrance of it. She had for the moment forgotten the professor, who had his eyes closed. She went on:

'Of course, I go to Leen's flat quite often, and I go out with Zuster Zijlstra and Zuster Boot too.'

They fell to discussing the delights of Amsterdam until Coenraad, seeing the time said that they must be off. He helped her to her feet, and they went back to the car.

They reached the outskirts of Amsterdam just before seven o'clock. They had stopped in Delft for tea, and wandered around the charming little town, the professor obligingly bearing her un-complaining company while she inspected a variety of shops. Now he slowed the Rolls down to weave his way through the evening traffic. Adelaide had become rather quiet. Tomorrow would be reality again, and she tried not to think of it. Her gloomy thoughts were interrupted by Coenraad's voice. 'There's a letter in the pocket next to you, Addy. Will you take it out and read it?'

She did as he had asked. 'It's in Dutch,' she said.

'Yes, read it out loud, it will be excellent practice for you.'

She obeyed, reading in her careful Dutch. When she had come to the end, he said: 'I must compliment you on your progress, Adelaide,' and she felt a thrill of pride. She must remember to tell Mijnheer de Wit. She waited for Coenraad to speak, and when he didn't, said:

'How kind of the Baroness, but I think I had better go straight back to the hospital, if you don't mind.'

'I do mind—and my aunt will be very disappointed.'

Adelaide frowned. 'I'm not dressed,' she said stubbornly.

'Nor am I. Besides, you can tidy your hair and all the rest of it at Tante Anneke's.'

She could think of no argument in the fact of his reasonable tones, and he swung the car into the Herengracht and drew up before his aunt's house. The big house door was flung open by a beaming Bundle, who surely had been lying in wait for them. He led them to the small parlour where the Baroness liked to sit. She was there now, erect in her chair, beautifully dressed, and obvi-ously delighted to see them both. She put up her cheek for Coen-raad to kiss and took Adelaide's hand.

'You nice child, to take pity on my curiosity. I want to hear all about England. Ring the bell, Coenraad. Jannie can show Ade-laide where she can freshen up.'

Adelaide went downstairs some ten minutes later to find Coen-raad waiting for her. As they crossed the hall, he said easily:

'I've been telling Tante Anneke about your clever brothers.'

This was a subject near to her heart, and she was drawn so

skilfully into the conversation that by the time they were half way through dinner she had lost her shyness, and was enjoying herself. Nevertheless, when she presently got up to go to the hospital, and was pressed by her hostess to visit her again soon, she accepted with a hidden reluctance.

Only the preceding night, lying in bed listening to the murmur of her father's and the professor's voices, she had resolved to see as little as possible of him once they were back in Holland, and she knew that he was a frequent visitor to his aunt's house. It had seemed simple to make the decision then; now she was not so sure. She had not forgotten Margriet.

They didn't speak on the short journey to the hospital. Coenraad got her case out of the boot and gave it to a night porter to take over to the home, then walked across the courtyard with her. He opened the door, but when she went to pass through she found her way barred by the careless hand he was resting against it. She stood still.

'Remind me to call you Miss Peters tomorrow.'

She laughed. 'You won't forget. I'll be in uniform, you know.'

'The clinics will be packed out. They always are after the summer holiday.'

They stood silently. Adelaide knew that she must make an end to her fairy tale. She gave him her hand. 'It was lovely—today, I mean. Thank you, and thank you for taking me in your car. It's like waking up from a beautiful dream. Good night…Coenraad.'

She slipped through the door.

CHAPTER EIGHT

THE professor had been right; the clinics had never been so busy, and they were booked to capacity for two or three weeks ahead. Adelaide looked through the appointments book the next morning and hoped that Casualty would be slack, though there wasn't much chance of that. Indeed, just before nine o'clock, a woman rushed in with an unconscious child in her arms. Adelaide made out with some difficulty that the little boy had swallowed some pills a short time earlier. She sent the nurse to phone Dr Beekman and set about treatment. She had got the airway in, and succeeded in getting the stomach tube down, when she heard footsteps. She recognised them at once, and spoke without stopping her work. 'Good morning, sir. An overdose—unknown pills taken between seven o'clock and now. Unconscious for about ten minutes, his mother says.' She indicated the woman standing in the doorway with her free hand. She started to syphon carefully, and didn't turn around.

'Keep that up, Sister, I'll see to the injections.' He was already opening the phials and drawing up the contents. He questioned the mother quietly as he pushed in the needle, working quickly and smoothly. Adelaide, still busily syphoning, thought what a nice person he was to work with in an emergency. She couldn't remember seeing him hesitant or anxious, she had never seen him really angry either. She doubted if she ever would.

They worked on the child in a partnership of shared knowledge and skill, not speaking until presently the professor said:

'He'll do.' He turned away and asked Piet, who had just come in, if there were any beds. Piet nodded. The professor walked to the door.

'Good, let's have him in for a day or two. I'll talk to the

mother.' He turned to go, saying over his shoulder: 'Out-Patients in ten minutes, Sister.'

Adelaide looked at the mess around her, and Piet laughed at her expressive face.

'I'll take the child to the ward, it'll give you more time to clear up.'

Adelaide sent the nurse along to warn Staff Wilsma to be ready for the professor, she herself would have to stop and show the nurse, sent to replace Zuster Eisink who was on holiday, and new to the work, what to clear up and what to get ready. It took longer than she had thought it would, and the clinic was well started as she went down the corridor. She could hear the professor's voice as she opened the door; it was quiet but had a distinct edge to it. She found him sitting with his head mirror on, waiting to examine the small boy Zuster Wilsma was vainly trying to hold on her knee. Adelaide imagined from the look on Zuster Wilsma's face that the struggle had been going for some time. She walked over, transferred the tyrant to her own lap, and whispered: 'Go and have your coffee, you must need it.' Then she turned her attention to the child wriggling on her knee. 'Sit still, you bad boy,' she said in a no-nonsense voice. She held him firmly and went on in her careful Dutch. 'The doctor's going to look at my teeth, then I shall have a sweet.' She produced one from her pocket. She had his attention now.

'Then the doctor will look at your teeth, and you can have a sweet too.' She produced another one, and laid it beside the first. 'You hold them.'

He took the sweets, clutching them in his hand, and sat quietly while the professor, with an expressionless face, looked at her teeth. This done, he turned to the child, who looked doubtful.

'You shall have both sweets,' said Adelaide quickly.

When he had gone, the professor looked at her quizzically.

'How do you do it, Sister Peters? Or is it a closely guarded secret? Whatever it is, you lost none of it on holiday, though I can't say the same for your Dutch. There wasn't a single verb in that sentence.'

'I never know where to put them,' she replied airily, 'so I save them up until the end.'

This remark was greeted with roars of laughter from the two men.

'We shouldn't tease you, Sister Peters, your Dutch is really quite good, isn't it, Professor?'

The man at the desk nodded.

'It's so good you shall try your skill on the next patient, Sister. It's that child Lotte Smid. Last time she came she bit Piet!'

The day wore on rapidly; the clinic worked late, and Adelaide stayed to help clear up after the doctors had gone. She listened to the nurses' chatter as she checked dressing packs, and scissors and scalpels, and refurbished the trolleys. It seemed as though she had never been away; her holiday was just a lovely dream. Excepting for the hours spent working together, she saw nothing of the professor during the following weeks. She had quietly refused an invitation to go to his aunt's home with him, and was unreasonably upset when he didn't persist with the invitation.

She persevered with her Dutch lessons, and even the exacting Mijnheer de Wit was pleased with her. It seemed a waste of time to work so hard at something she wouldn't need much longer, but it filled her free time, when she wasn't exploring Amsterdam, or window shopping with the other Sisters. The weather was getting cool, and the wind was chilly. The shops were showing tweeds and pretty clothes for the evening.

One evening at the beginning of October she was going slowly down the Kalverstraat on the way to her lesson. She had plenty of time and was looking rather aimlessly in the shop window. It had been a horrid day in the clinic; Piet had been in a bad temper, and the professor hadn't been there all day. Adelaide stopped at Krause and Vogelzang's to admire a blue velvet dress; very simple, and very expensive. The professor's voice spoke over her shoulder.

'Very charming, Adelaide. Will you buy it tomorrow?'

Her pulses racing, she looked round at him. 'You made me jump, sir.' Her voice was nicely under control, and formal. When-

ever he called her Adelaide, she took refuge in formality. But now
he smiled at her in such a friendly fashion that she forgot to be
stiff.

'Do you see the price?' she asked.

He glanced at the ticket. 'It seems reasonable enough,' he remarked.

'Reasonable!' She made a sound regrettably like a snort. 'Why,
for that money, I could send the boys...' she stopped. 'I could go
home for another holiday,' she added lamely, and looked anxiously at him. He looked reassuringly vague. For one dreadful
moment she had supposed he had heard her thoughtless remark.
She sighed, unconsciously—and very audibly—with relief. If he
had been as poor as she was, she might have confided in him
weeks ago, but to tell a man of his wealth and position would
have been tantamount to begging... She went scarlet, just thinking
about it.

'I'm on my way to my Dutch lesson; I mustn't be late.' She
turned away from the tempting window, and he fell into step
beside her.

'Do you mind if I walk with you as far as the Spui?' He took
her arm. 'I'm going that way myself.'

'If you're going somewhere, you'll be late,' she said idiotically,
very conscious of his arm.

'I?' he queried. 'No, I've plenty of time.'

They reached Mijnheer de Wit's door, and he rang the bell.
She wondered where he was going. The faintly mocking look he
gave her stopped her just in time from asking. The door gave a
faint click, and he pushed it open for her to go in.

'Do you walk back to the hospital alone, Adelaide?'

She paused in the doorway, carefully avoiding his eye. The
temptation to say 'yes' was very great, but good sense and the
resolution she tried so hard to keep stifled it.

'Jan Hein is calling for me—you remember I met him at Baroness Van Essen's party.' She smiled convincingly, and started to
mount the stairs. Appalled at the ease with which she had lied,

she reflected sadly that he was the last man on earth she would wish to deceive.

It was pure coincidence that Adelaide should meet Jan Hein while she was out shopping in the Leidsestraat the following morning. Rather to her surprise, he remembered her, seemed delighted to see her again and carried her off for a cup of coffee at a nearby café, which was not, she thought, the kind of place the professor would have chosen. It was a mean thought, she decided, and tried to make up for it by being extra nice to Jan. She succeeded so well that he asked her rather diffidently if she would go out with him.

'There must be something you want to see. I've a car. What about a trip to Volendam, or Alkmaar—better still, let's go to the Open Air Museum at Arnhem. It'll be cold, but I'm sure you'll like it.'

With almost no hesitation at all, she agreed. She had a free day in two days' time—a Friday. They arranged to meet outside the hospital at half past ten, and parted on excellent terms with each other.

Friday morning was exactly right. The chill of a Dutch autumn was softened by the still warm sunshine. Adelaide wore her tweed suit and carried a head-scarf; it might turn cold during the afternoon, she had learned not to trust the wind since she had lived in Holland.

They took the road to Naarden and stopped for coffee at Jan Tabac, where they sat at one of the big windows overlooking the motorway, and watched the cars stream past. Adelaide, listening to Jan talking about himself, wished it was the professor sitting beside her—not, she thought, that he ever talked about himself. Not to her, at any rate. She gave herself a mental shake and resolved not to think about the professor for the rest of that day. She succeeded in this rather well, so that by the time they had arrived at Arnhem, she was beginning to enjoy herself.

'We'll lunch first, shall we?'

Jan was easing his little Fiat 850 coupé through the centre of the city, looking for an empty parking meter. With unexpected good luck he found one without much trouble, parked, and took Adelaide's arm to steer through a couple of narrow streets into the Nieuwe Plein and the doors of the Riche National. They talked happily through a luncheon they ate with healthy appetites, and Adelaide was surprised to see that it was almost two o'clock when they once more reached the car. She supposed the museum wasn't very large, for the journey back to Amsterdam would take them at least an hour and a half. In this she was mistaken, as she realised when they arrived at the park in which the museum was set up. There were few people about, and they strolled around while she looked her fill at the perfectly arranged farms and cottages, representing every province and age in Holland. By the time she had explored the Zaanse village it was growing chilly, with the sun slipping quickly out of sight behind the evening clouds. She tied her scarf over her bright hair and turned a smiling face to Jan.

'What a lovely day. I have enjoyed it. I might have gone back to England and never seen all this.'

'When do you go?'

They were walking back over the little wooden swing bridge.

'In about a month. The date hasn't been fixed yet.'

'A month's a long time, we must do this again. I've enjoyed it too.' He took her arm. 'Let's get some tea, there's a café at the end of this path.'

It was almost closing time, but a cheerful waiter took their order, and then stood leaning against the door, a model of patience. They were his only customers. The steady flow of foreign visitors had dwindled to a thin trickle by autumn, and no Dutchman was likely to be there at that time of the day—he'd be at home with his life and family, looking forward to the evening meal. The waiter shivered; he would like to be home himself. He watched with well-concealed relief as his customers got up to go, accepted his tip with dignity, and sped them on their way.

It was the rush hour in Arnhem. Jan joined the stream of traffic going out of town, and Adelaide was glad of their slow progress.

Their road ran alongside the woods and the view was magnificent, but she knew better than to distract Jan's attention from the road. He was an impatient driver, and she found herself comparing his testy manner with the professor's placid acceptance of the traffic jams they had encountered when he had taken her to England. He had remained quite unruffled, merely making up time between the delays with some fast driving which had opened her eyes. The traffic thinned out after a time, nevertheless dusk was thickening as they turned off the motorway on to the Amersfoort road. They hadn't gone very far along it when the car gave a lurch. Jan wrenched at the wheel and swung back on to the right side of the road, thankful that there was no other traffic, and came to a halt.

'That's a tyre gone,' he said gloomily.

Adelaide already had her hand on the door. 'I'll help you change it.'

He looked at her gratefully, thankful for her matter-of-fact acceptance of the situation.

'Would you hold the torch?'

He busied himself setting up the red triangle behind the car, and had just got the jack in position when the headlights of an oncoming car, driven fast, picked them out against the emptiness of the surrounding countryside. The lights dipped, and the car stopped without sound within a few yards of them. Adelaide watched the professor, moving much faster than he usually did, get out and cross the road. He came closer to her—so close that she could feel the rough tweed of his jacket against her shoulder. From the gloom above her head he spoke.

'Good evening, Adelaide. Can I help in any way?' He didn't sound very interested.

'We have a puncture, and Jan has to change the wheel.'

He grunted something she couldn't quite hear, and moved away to see what Jan was doing. The two men murmured together, and Adelaide, shining the torch steadily on them, suppressed a shiver. It was getting very chilly, and she wished she had a thicker coat, or even a scarf for her neck. The professor went back to his car

and returned with a lantern, directing its beam on to the tyre, then
he took the torch from Adelaide's cold hand, and switched it off.

'Go and sit in the car. You'll find a rug in the back. We shan't
be long.' He didn't wait to see what she did, but turned away to
help Jan.

Adelaide climbed gratefully into the Rolls. It was warm inside,
and smelled faintly of good tobacco and well-kept leather. She sat
wrapped in the rug, watching the two men working in the pale
light of the lamp. She could hear Jan's quick light voice, and the
professor's slower, deep one, with an occasional rumble of laughter. She relaxed against the comfortable seat, and allowed herself
the luxury of imagining that she was with the professor, and not
Jan. She was so absorbed in this delightful but improbable situation that she was quite startled when the car door was opened.
The professor looked down at her.

'Jan's ready to go.' He helped her out and took the rug from
her and she stood beside the car, feeling awkward, not sure what
to say, and bitterly regretting the lie she had told him the other
evening. He must think that she and Jan were, at the least, very
good friends. She had a wild desire to tell him that this was only
the second time that she had seen Jan since Baroness Van Essen's
party. She opened her mouth, she wanted him to know about it
quite badly. She sneezed.

'You should have worn a warmer coat.' The professor was
faintly admonishing. 'I should join Jan if I were you. He'll give
you a drink at Amersfoort; you don't want to catch a cold.' He
was a stranger, a chance acquaintance giving careless sympathy
and advice.

She sneezed again, and said in a small voice:

'It was warm and sunny when we started out this morning.'

'No doubt.' He sounded maddeningly reasonable about it. 'The
sensible thing would be for you to go back to hospital and go to
bed, but I won't presume to spoil your evening by suggesting it.'

He had walked across the road with her to where Jan was standing, wiping his hands on a piece of rag, and stood looking at them
both, smiling a little.

Adelaide, in her turn, smiled brilliantly at Jan, who delighted her by saying promptly:

'Our evening hasn't even started, has it, Adelaide?'

She tightened the scarf around her bright hair and nerved herself to look at the professor. 'Thanks for your help, sir, we shall be able to enjoy every minute of it.'

She whisked into the car, giving a brilliant performance as a young woman about to enjoy a delightful evening with the man of her choice, and waved airily as Jan started the car. The professor looked lonely standing there on the side of the road, cleaning his hands on Jan's rag. Adelaide longed to stop the car and go back to him and fling herself into his arms, and wondered what he would do if she did. Something tactful, she supposed, with a correctness that would be far worse than a downright snub. She stopped thinking and turned to Jan, to ask with her usual candour:

'Do you really want to take me out this evening, Jan?'

'Yes, of course. How about a meal and then a cinema— No, I've a better idea, I'll phone and see if there are any seats for Snip and Snap at the Carre. You'll like that.'

It sounded fun—it would stop her thinking too. They kept up an unflagging conversation until they reached Amsterdam. Jan stopped the car in a busy street near one of the bridges crossing the Amstel. As she got out of the car, Adelaide could see the bright lights of a restaurant on the opposite corner. Jan took her arm and guided her across to it.

'This is the Fredriksplein,' he explained. 'I thought we'd eat here at the Royaal.' It was warm and pleasant inside in the subdued lighting of the table lamps. They sat in the window, watching the fountain in the centre of the square; it looked cold in the light of the street lamps. Adelaide went off to tidy herself and found that Jan had ordered drinks for them both. Hers looked richly red. She sipped it and it tasted as good as it looked. By the time their meal was ready, she was no longer cold, she even felt full of false cheerfulness which carried her successfully through dinner.

The theatre was full, but they had good seats, and Snip and Snap—Amsterdam's favourite comedians—were on top of their form. Adelaide laughed delightedly at their antics, even when she couldn't understand the jokes.

It was late when the show finished, and she refused Jan's offer of a drink.

'I'm on duty tomorrow at eight, there's a clinic—a special one for measles inoculation. We'll be busy. I think I'd better go back now.'

She thanked Jan charmingly for a delightful day, said good night and went into the Nurses' Home, and immediately forgot him. Her last coherent thought before she went to sleep was of Coenraad, standing in the road by himself.

They were all on duty the next morning. By the time the doctors had arrived Adelaide and the nurses had the children in some sort of order. In theory it was a simple enough business. A steady stream of children trickled through the team's well-organised fingers, submitting with stolid charm or howls of rage to the professor's and Piet's swift and expert jabs. Adelaide, busy with the syringes and needles and the repetitive swabbing of countless small arms, stood beside the professor. It was nice to be close to him, even though he didn't appear to notice her: she didn't count the casual 'Good morning' as he had come in. At ten o'clock, she asked quietly:

'Would you like coffee now, sir?'

He plunged his needle into a very small stoical boy, gave him an encouraging smack on his bottom, and threw the syringe into the bin Adelaide had thoughtfully placed to receive it.

'Sister Peters, you read my thoughts!'

She went quickly and called a halt for ten minutes, while a nurse brought in the coffee ready on the small stove. By tacit consent, the nurses moved away with their mugs and biscuits, leaving Adelaide and the two doctors by the desk.

The professor helped himself abundantly to sugar and selected a biscuit with care.

'You enjoyed your evening, Adelaide?' he enquired blandly.

She composed her face into an expression of delighted remembrance.

'Yes, thank you, Professor. We went to the Royaal.'

'The Royaal?' His brow creased in thought. 'Where's that?'

Piet came to her rescue. 'Nice place. Good food, too. What did you do afterwards, Adelaide?'

'We went to the Carre,' she frowned heavily at Coenraad, 'and I liked it very much indeed,' she added in a challenging tone.

He looked taken aback. 'Er—yes, I'm sure you did. I wasn't aware that I had contradicted you in any way. Everyone likes the Carre. I'm glad you enjoyed your evening, I remember you told me how much you were looking forward to it.' He looked faintly mocking. It was a relief to Adelaide when Piet asked her who she had gone out with.

'Jan Hein.'

'Oh, him!' Piet looked at her in astonishment. 'The fellow with the fancy waistcoats? Lord, Adelaide, couldn't you do better than that?'

Adelaide stared at him angrily, regrettably unable to think of anything to reply to this unfortunate comment. That she shared Piet's opinion of Jan didn't help matters at all.

The professor put down his cup. 'Really, Piet, you must allow Adelaide to choose her own friends. Jan's quite a good sort of fellow—only a boy, of course,' he added in a silky voice that set Adelaide's cup rattling in its saucer.

'Are you ready, sir?' She didn't look at either of the men, but turned her back and piled the crockery on to the tray and carried it away. For the rest of the morning she was silent, excepting when it was necessary to talk about the work in the clinic, and when the last small patient had left, and the doctors were ready to go home, it was Zuster Wilsma who took their white coats and answered their goodbyes, Sister Peters having found it imperative to take the drums over to the sterilising room herself. She banged them down on the bench with undue violence and relieved her feelings by slamming the door violently behind her.

The professor was waiting in the passage outside; she was glad to see him wince at the appalling noise she was making, while her heart leapt to see him there. She wondered what he was going to say. But he said nothing at all, merely nodded unsmiling, and went into the sterilising room on some errand of his own.

CHAPTER NINE

IT was the second week in October, and the hospital ball was to be on the twentieth. There was a good deal of excitement about it, even though work had to go on as usual. It was a Monday morning, cold and blustery and just turned nine o'clock. The professor sat at his desk patiently making illegible notes from the reluctant answers of the young woman he was questioning. She was pale and dirty and uncooperative; he needed a great deal of patience. Adelaide was undressing the young woman's baby; it was pale and dirty like its mother, and very ill. Its puny body was covered in flea-bites. It looked unseeingly at Adelaide out of enormous blue eyes, and wailed continuously in a thin parody of a baby's voice. She pinned on a nappy and rolled it in a baby blanket, and said low-voiced to Zuster Eisink who had just come in:

'Get a lumbar puncture trolley ready, will you, Nurse? We're going to need it in a few minutes.'

She unwrapped the baby again as the professor came over and began to examine the scrap with gentle hands. Without looking up he said:

'What do you think, Sister?'

He had a rather nice habit of asking the nurses their opinion before he diagnosed, and as he never laughed at their sometimes foolish answers, but praised them when they were right, they loved him for it.

'Meningitis,' said Adelaide promptly.

'Then I don't suppose I need to ask for the LP trolley,' he said genially, and went to scrub up.

It didn't take very long. They pulled off their masks and gowns, and the professor told Piet Beekman, who had just come in, to take the baby to the small glass-walled cubicle where Zuster Zijlstra could keep her eye on it. Zuster Eisink took the trolley away, and Adelaide found herself alone with the professor, washing their hands at the double sink. She had avoided him as much as possible since her outing with Jan, although, as she told herself frequently, there was no reason for doing so. All the same, she was glad to see Zuster Wilsma come into the clinic. So, it seemed, was the professor.

'The very girl I want,' he said cheerfully. 'Please go to X-ray and ask for the films I need. I've written the numbers down, they're on my desk.' As the door closed he turned back to Adelaide, and asked, 'Did you say something, Sister?'

Adelaide was puzzled; she knew that all the films that were needed had been fetched.

'Yes, sir. I said—but all the films are there.'

'You're quite right, they are. I wanted to talk to you.'

Adelaide struggled to think of something suitable to say to this, failed, and started to wash her hands for the second time, waiting for him to speak.

'Will you come to the hospital ball with me, Addy?' he went on, and added softly, 'And don't cudgel your brain for a mythical escort this time!'

Adelaide started to blush, and would have washed her hands for the third time if the professor hadn't reached over and taken out the plug. She was wildly happy. There was something else too; her hands dripping before her, she turned to face him.

'You knew that Jan didn't come for me…?'

'Yes, I knew.'

She heaved a great sigh of relief and said, without stopping to think, 'I'm so glad; I wanted to tell you it was a lie, but I couldn't think of anything else to say.' She looked up into his face. 'You must know that you're the last person in the world I'd lie to.'

'Yes, I know that too,' he said quietly. 'Will you come?' He thoughtfully handed her a towel to dry her still wet hands, and went on smoothly. 'You leave at the end of the month, I believe? I think it would be a nice gesture if we went together, don't you?'

Adelaide wondered why they should make a nice gesture, but

put the thought aside. She wanted to go very badly, and she knew she would accept. She was tired of pretending to herself that her feelings for him were purely friendly. Once or twice she had thought that perhaps he was attracted to her, but common sense told her that he had never really given her any reason to believe this. He'd kissed her several times, but that meant nothing when a man took a girl out. She reminded herself that the Dutch *Adel* married into their own circle. Doubtless in his own good time he would marry Margriet. All the same, he must like her a little to have invited her. She heard herself accepting in a cool, friendly voice, and telling him how delighted she would be to go with him, but in an instant she had forgotten her role again.

'Oh, I'll buy a new dress!' she breathed recklessly.

She spent several days looking for the dress. She wanted something really beautiful, and rashly decided to spend some of the money set aside for the boys' school fees. In the end, she found what she wanted, a straight, beautifully cut dress in wild silk; it was in turquoise blue, and cost her far more than she could afford, but Adelaide didn't care.

The days flew by, and she longed for the night of the dance, but dreaded each day as it brought her departure nearer. Her gloom was increased by the professor's brisk cheerfulness. He seemed to take it for granted that she was delighted to be going back to England, and even made passing mention of Christmas in her own home. She was too dispirited to point out that hospital ward Sisters seldom got home for Christmas.

On the day before the ball, Adelaide wasn't on duty until eleven. It was a bright, frosty morning, just the day for a brisk walk. She was standing outside the hospital, waiting for a chance to cross the road, when she became aware that Margriet Keizer was standing beside her. Margriet said good morning so charmingly and in such a friendly manner that Adelaide found herself returning her smile. They crossed the road together, and continued along the pavement, chatting about Adelaide's departure in ten days' time. They turned down the Singel, where it was quieter, and walked briskly along in the chilly wind. Adelaide wasn't sure that she wanted to go walking with Margriet, but she saw no way of avoiding it. She had no idea that Margriet had telephoned the hospital earlier that morning and asked when she was to be off duty that day, or that she had spent a long hour waiting in the hope that Adelaide would come out.

Margriet knew exactly what she was going to say; she had been over it a hundred times since that evening, several weeks ago, when she had asked Coenraad to take her to the dance, and he had told her that he intended taking Adelaide. She had seethed with rage, but by a great effort, concealed it, and said nothing more to him about it. But now... She led the conversation round to the dance.

'It's a marvellous affair,' she said gaily. 'Have you a pretty dress for it?'

Adelaide was surprised. 'How did you know I was going?'

Margriet smiled. 'Why, of course I know. I was the one who suggested you went in the first place. Coenraad always takes me, but I told him that this year, just for once, he should take you. After all, you haven't had a great deal of fun while you've been in Holland.' She stole a look at the girl beside her. Adelaide's feeling had been one of disbelief as she listened to her companion, but she had to admit that it was all true. The professor, after all, had barely mentioned the ball to her since his invitation, save to arrange where they were to meet. She felt the blood drain from her face, but managed to smile quite naturally.

'Poor Professor Van Essen, I had no idea...' she stopped.

'Oh, you mustn't say that,' cried Margriet. 'He has a very high regard for you as a nurse. Neither of us mind in the least, we only want you to have an enjoyable evening.'

Adelaide felt numb, but she supposed that presently she would be able to think what to do; at the moment she must concentrate on walking and talking as naturally as possible. Margriet was the last person who must know how much she had been hurt.

'How kind of you both,' she was surprised to find her voice sounded quite normal. 'It was most thoughtful of you to arrange it.' She looked at her watch. 'Now I really must go, I'm on duty in half an hour. I can take this short cut down this alley, can't I?' She was still smiling. 'I expect I shall see you before I go.' She shook hands with Margriet, unaware of the scornful amusement of the other girl at the ease with which Adelaide had been taken in.

'Just in case you don't, Sister, have a good trip home.' She smiled confidingly at Adelaide. 'I'm longing to tell you a secret— I know I shouldn't, but you'll not say a word, I know. I'm hoping to marry Professor Van Essen quite soon.' She watched Adelaide's face become even whiter than it was already. 'I thought you'd be delighted.' Her blue eyes gleamed with triumph.

Adelaide wondered if she was going to faint, she certainly felt most peculiar; she supposed dully that it was shock. She said quietly, 'I hope you will be very happy, *Juffrouw*. I...I must go, or I shall be late.'

She turned into the alley and walked very fast back to the hospital. She had no idea how she got there, or how she changed her clothes, but punctually at eleven o'clock she walked into the professor's office. Piet gave her a startled look and asked her if she was feeling all right; to her relief, the professor said nothing at all. Only later, as they were leaving to go to lunch, he asked if there was anything the matter. His voice was so kind that she had a tremendous urge to burst into tears, cast herself upon his shoulder, and tell him the whole miserable story—which, her matter-of-fact mind told her, was just about the silliest thing that she could do. Instead she said in an unnaturally bright little voice:

'It's nothing, thank you, sir, only that I have a touch of the toothache.'

Adelaide didn't go to her dinner, but spent the hour in her room. She had to think of something, quickly. She caught sight of herself in the mirror; she looked terrible. She remembered that she had told the professor that she had a toothache. Her teeth had never given her any trouble in her life before, but surely a wisdom tooth could flare up at a moment's notice? She started to weave a pattern of lies, for she could think of no other way out of an impossible situation. She went back on duty, and took care to tell the professor that her toothache was no better.

After the clinic was over for the day, and she was alone on duty, she went along to her little office and carefully composed a little note, regretting her inability to go to the dance with him. It would be natural enough for her to do that if her toothache was bad enough, and there would be plenty of time for him to arrange to take Margriet. This melancholy thought caused her to burst into tears and ruin the note, which she had to re-write, then she put it carefully in her pocket and went to supper. She sat near Home Sister, who commented upon her wan looks, so that she was able to tell her, and everyone else sitting nearby, about the wisdom tooth. Home Sister told her kindly to go to bed with plenty of aspirin and she would send a hot drink up presently.

Adelaide prepared for bed, feeling wretched. She had been brought up to have a healthy horror of lying, and now here she was, having told one, forced to tell more every time she opened her mouth. That she wasn't lying for her own benefit hadn't occurred to her. She lay awake most of the night, deciding what she must do, and in the morning, thanks to her sleeplessness, looked worse than ever. She wished the doctors a subdued good morning when they arrived, and in answer to Piet's sympathetic enquiry as to which tooth it was, said:

'It's a wisdom tooth, I think—the left side. I had no idea they could be so painful,' she added for good measure.

The professor regarded her thoughtfully. 'Why not have it looked at? There may be something that can be done to ease the pain.'

Adelaide busied herself with some charts, her head turned away from him. 'No, thank you, sir,' she said carefully. 'I will probably be much better by this evening.'

The morning seemed very long. She avoided the professor as much as possible, and remembered to wince convincingly when she drank her coffee, and put a hand up to her jaw. The professor noticed her action.

'The right wisdom tooth, I think you said, Sister?'

Adelaide stared back at him. He was looking at her very intently. Which side had she told Piet? He wasn't in the room; she didn't know if that was fortunate or not, she was past caring. She no longer had the least idea which wisdom tooth ached. She said recklessly;

'Yes, the right side, sir.'

At dinner time she sought out Home Sister and reported sick.

'If I could just have the rest of the day in bed, Zuster Groeneveld, I'm sure I'll be all right for duty tomorrow. I'm sorry to miss the ball, but I shouldn't enjoy myself, should I?'

Home Sister agreed, commiserated with her on missing all the fun, gave her a fresh supply of aspirins and a cup of tea, and promised that Adelaide's note should be delivered to the professor at once.

The morning had seemed long; the afternoon and evening stretched everlastingly before her. Most of the Sisters were going to the ball. Adelaide sat in bed, admiring them as they came in turn to show their dresses and sympathise with her. When the last one had gone, she got out of bed and went over to her window and opened it wider, so that she could hear the band playing. She stood there a long time, getting very cold, and not noticing it. She got into bed at last, and lay thinking of what she had to do the next morning. When she had planned everything to her entire satisfaction, she burst into tears and after a little, cried herself to sleep.

At nine o'clock the next morning, Adelaide presented herself at Matron's office. The Directrice was busy at her desk as she went in, but looked up and smiled when she saw who it was. She liked Adelaide, who had proved herself a hardworking, sensible, and popular nurse, and had adapted herself to the hospital routine without tedious comparisons between it and her own training school.

She said graciously, 'Good morning, Sister Peters. I'm sorry to hear that you had to miss the ball. It was a great success. I hope your tooth is better?'

Adelaide was momentarily taken aback. She had forgotten about her toothache in the anxiety of getting her speech, rehearsed during the bitter wakeful hours of the night, clear both as to grammar and meaning. She faltered a little, and said uncertainly: 'My tooth? Thank you, Directrice, but I have no toothache.' She ignored the Matron's look of surprise and plunged into the matter in hand, speaking in her heavily accented but fluent Dutch. 'I should like to leave, Directrice. At once. It is a purely personal matter, nothing at all to do with my work, but it is essential that I go home at once. Will you please allow me to go?' She spoke with a quiet desperation that convinced her hearer of her sincerity.

The Matron looked down at her blotter and asked gently:

'Could you explain a little more fully, Sister? You have been happy here, haven't you?'

Adelaide smiled. It lighted up her tired face.

'I've been very happy,' her smile faded, 'and I'm sorry I have to leave like this, although it is only a short time before I am due to go; and I'm afraid I can't tell you any more than I have done, Directrice.'

'Very well, Sister. I think I know you well enough to understand that you are not making this request lightly. But it would be too late for you to go today, in any case.'

'May I go tomorrow? I can arrange my journey today, and pack this evening.' Adelaide hesitated; she still had one more favour to ask. 'Could I go without anyone knowing about it? I know it sounds extraordinary, Directrice, but I have a good reason for asking.'

The Matron frowned. 'I suppose so, Sister—I shall, of course, have to warn Professor Van Essen.'

Adelaide felt her heart hammer at the name. 'No, please…I mean, may I tell him myself? It isn't inconvenient for me to go… Staff Nurse Wilsma is there, so it won't make any difference.'

If the matron heard the desperate urgency in her voice, she gave no sign, but tidied the already tidy papers on the desk before her, and thought. 'So that's it!' She had known the professor for a great many years; she was very fond of him, now she fought a desire to pick up the phone and tell him to come and cope with a situation she couldn't understand.

Adelaide felt nearer to tears. She took a step nearer the desk and said in a beseeching, carefully controlled little voice:

'Please don't tell Professor Van Essen, Directrice.'

'I promise you I will say nothing, Sister. I am sorry that you are unable to let me help you. I should have liked to have done so. But you know best, my dear.' She smiled with real kindliness. 'Do you want to go on duty? Yes?' She nodded dismissal.

Adelaide went to the door, but turned back when she got to it.

'Thank you for being so kind, Directrice.' She couldn't think of anything else to say.

She went to the Sisters' Home from the office, got her cases and put them in her room, then went to the little telephone box in the hall and rang up a travel agency and booked her ticket for the next day without difficulty. It wasn't a time of year when people travelled for pleasure. It was half past nine when she got to the clinic, which was in confusion. One of the children had been sick on the floor, and a boy in one of the cubicles was in the throes of an epileptic fit. The professor was dealing with it as she went in, but he looked up as she crossed the room.

'Ah, Sister Peters, you seem to have arrived at the right moment. Take over here, will you, while I write him up for something, then if you will give it, we can ward him. We'd better have him on observation.'

Adelaide gave some hasty instructions to the nurse to get the place tidied up, and did as she was asked. It was fortunate, she thought, that they were too busy to have time to talk. Indeed there was no time for conversation for the rest of the morning, nor did they take their usual coffee break. By one o'clock the morning clinic was over, an hour late, and they had to be ready in an hour's time for the afternoon session. Adelaide sent the nurses to dinner and whirled around the clinic, changing couch covers, spanking pillows into shape, putting out paper towels, doing all the small jobs vital to a smooth-running clinic. Piet Beekman had dashed home; the professor sat at his desk, scribbling notes in the morning's case papers. He was a methodical man; the morning's work was never allowed to overlap into the afternoon. Adelaide, checking X-rays with less than her usual brisk efficiency, was very conscious of him. She looked up and caught his eye upon her. She would have to say something about the ball; she sorted half a dozen films into the wrong order, and said in an uncertain voice:

'I'm sorry I couldn't go with you last night, sir. I was very disappointed.'

'So was I,' he answered flatly.

Rather discouraged, she persevered. 'I expect you found someone else to go with?' Despite all her efforts, she was annoyed to hear her voice quiver.

'If you mean did I have a sufficient number of dancing partners, Sister Peters—yes, I did.'

She hadn't meant that at all. She longed to ask him if he had taken Margriet, but didn't dare to do so, and—she glanced swiftly at his downbent head. He was sufficiently out of humour to remind her that it was no business of hers, as indeed, she had to allow, it wasn't.

'Your toothache is better, I hope, Sister? Er—both sides, was it not?'

She dropped the X-rays she was holding, and got down on her knees, scarlet-cheeked, to pick them up. When the professor came quietly from behind his desk and got down on his knees beside her, she dropped them again. He collected them neatly, merely remarking:

'The pain seems to have left you in a highly nervous state, Sister Peters. I think it advisable for you to see a dentist before you suffer a further attack.'

Adelaide jumped to her feet as he uncoiled himself from the floor. She wished he wasn't standing quite so close, he seemed enormous, but when she looked at him his face was as placid as usual. For a brief, terrifying moment she had thought that he might have guessed about the toothache.

'Thank you, sir, but I'll go when I get back to England. My

own dentist—it doesn't hurt any more—remarkable how the pain went...' She realised she was babbling, and stood, for once idle, watching him piling the X-rays neatly into their right order. He put them down on his desk and reached for the telephone. She watched while he dialled a number, but when he said casually: 'This man's a personal friend of mine. You'll like him. I can't allow you to go back to England with even a suspicion of tooth-ache,' she panicked.

'Please don't.' She could hear her voice high and strained. 'I beg you, please don't. I won't go...'

He put the phone back in its cradle, and said in the silky voice she knew so well; 'Just as you wish, Adelaide.' He got up. 'I'm going to have a sandwich. We'll start promptly, please.'

She watched him stalk out of the room, and listened to him going down the corridor. He was whistling, one of the tunes they had whistled together when they had gone to England. She had been very happy then. She stared unseeingly at the notes in her hand, and gave a great sniff. She would have liked to cry, but there wasn't time, nor was it a suitable place in which to give way to her feelings. She finished what she was doing, then went into her office and closed the door. She still had to write a letter to the professor, explaining why she was leaving. She made one or two vain attempts, but it was useless. She would have to do it in the morning. So she busied herself with the off-duty for the next week, and saw to the stores and stationery and linen lists; it was the least she could do. Just before two, she went back to the office in time to help the two doctors on with their white coats, and told Zuster Steensma to bring in the first patient. The after-noon clinic had started.

When she was at last off duty she went to her room, packed her cases and sat down to write some letters. She wondered what her friends would say when they heard that she had gone without a word of farewell; she would write and explain when she was back in England. After supper she went for a walk with Zuster Zijlstra and bade a silent goodbye to the streets as they passed through them. On their way back they walked down the Herengracht, past the professor's red brick mansion. Several of the windows were lighted; she wondered in which room he was sitting, and if Margriet was with him.

She slept badly, and was glad when it was morning and she could go on duty. She went straight to her office; she had to write a letter to Coenraad, and there would be no time once they started work. After half a dozen attempts she achieved a stiff little letter, and was addressing the envelope when there was a knock on the door and the professor looked in. Adelaide jumped up, feeling guilty, wished him rather a breathless good morning, and managed an embarrassed little laugh when he remarked:

'You don't have to look so guilty, Sister; I'm early.'

He showed no disposition to go, so she stuffed the letter and envelope into her pocket and accompanied him down the corridor to his own office, talking to him in a polite voice, as though he were a stranger she had just met for the first time.

The clinic was slack, so Adelaide was able to do what the Matron had suggested and go to first dinner, leaving Zuster Wilsma to finish the clinic with the two doctors. She sat at the table, eating nothing, then went to Matron's office and bade her goodbye. By two o'clock she was at the hospital entrance with her luggage. Here she gave her letter to the porter, with instructions to deliver it to the professor at five o'clock, and not a minute before. To make sure that there was no mistake, she wrote the instructions on the envelope as well, and watched the man put it in the doctors' letter rack by the door, before getting into her taxi. The porter loaded her cases beside the driver, surprised that she was leaving. He shook hands with her and offered to tell the driver where to go.

Adelaide looked at her watch. She had plenty of time, indeed she was far too early, because, she admitted ruefully, she had been afraid of meeting Coenraad again. She made a sudden decision to say goodbye to Baroness Van Essen; she liked the old lady, and would be able to wish her a personal goodbye and give some explanation for her abrupt departure, for which she would stick to her tale of urgent private affairs. She gave the address to the porter, and sat back resolutely looking away from the hospital where she had been so happy.

She rang the bell hesitantly; it was an awkward time to call. The Baroness might not be at home. The door was, however, opened immediately by Bundle, who ushered her inside the house, and in answer to her enquiry as to whether she might see his mistress for a few minutes, asked her to be seated while he went to discover if the Baroness was receiving visitors. She was. Adelaide found herself in the same small parlour as before, where Coenraad's aunt sat comfortably before an open fire. She smiled at Adelaide as she walked across the room.

'How nice to see you, Adelaide. Forgive me if I don't get up. What a long time it is since you were here last. Sit down, my dear. I hope you can spare half an hour for a gossip.'

Adelaide chose a chair facing the door, away from the light.

'Please forgive me for calling like this, but I'm on my way to the station, and I found that I had just enough time to come and wish you goodbye.' She paused, aware of Baroness Van Essen's surprised look, and chose her next words carefully. 'I have to go home unexpectedly...'

'My dear child, no one is ill, I hope?'

'No, *Mevrouw*, just a private matter.'

'Coenraad will be disappointed.'

Adelaide wriggled uneasily in her chair, and said at last:

'I haven't told him yet—at least I thought it best to leave a letter.' She struggled to make her voice matter-of-fact. 'He might not understand...' she began, then stopped, for someone was pealing the front door bell. The door banged shut, footsteps sounded in the hall. Adelaide recognised them; she had been listening to their coming and going in the clinic for the past year. She felt as though she was about to faint, but fainting wouldn't help her now. She half rose from her chair, and looked imploringly at her hostess. The old lady smiled at her.

'I do believe it's Coenraad. Now isn't that nice?'

CHAPTER TEN

THE door opened quickly and violently, and the professor walked in. He shut the door with extreme quietness and stood leaning against it, looking at Adelaide. She had never seen him so angry; his mouth was a thin straight line and there was a vein throbbing at his temple. She deduced, quite rightly, that he was in a towering rage, and waited for the storm to break.

He transferred his gaze to his aunt, and said, in a deceptively mild voice: 'Good afternoon, Tante Anneke—and to you, Miss Peters.'

She caught her breath as he turned narrowed eyes, glinting with rage, on to her once more.

'How fortunate that I find you here. Perhaps you will be good enough to explain this note.'

He waved her letter at her, and she noticed that he was without his overcoat. She looked at the antique wall clock as it chimed the half hour—half past two. She frowned. Why had he got her letter already, when she had been so careful to tell the porter to deliver it at five o'clock? She said in a bewildered voice:

'I thought you had a clinic...'

He stared at her, and she stared back, hiding her agitation as best she might.

'So I have, Miss Peters, none knows that better than you. It just so happened that on this very afternoon I chose to accompany Dr Van Hoven to the front door and collected my post at the same time.'

Adelaide made a small, helpless gesture. 'There's nothing to explain, sir—it's all in my note.'

She picked up her handbag and got up from her chair to take her leave from the Baroness, ignoring him. 'I really must go, *Mevrouw*, or I shall miss my train, and I mustn't keep the taxi waiting any longer.'

The professor didn't move from the door, but said very quietly:

'There is no hurry, Miss Peters. I saw your taxi as I came in, and told Bundle to bring your luggage in and pay off the driver.'

Adelaide found herself shaking with rage at the arrogance of this remark. She stamped her foot into the deep pile of the carpet.

'How dare you?' she asked in a choking voice.

The professor appeared unaffected by this display of temper. Indeed, he looked to her to have recovered his usual good humour. He folded his arms across his chest, and returned her look with one of amused tolerance, which had the effect of inflaming her feelings still further. At this point, the Baroness, until now a silent but interested spectator, got to her feet with a polite murmur and walked over to the door, which her nephew, after dropping a kiss on her cheek, carefully shut behind her. Too late, Adelaide took a few steps across the room, with the vague idea of going through the door too, but the professor put his shoulder against it.

'No,' he said.

She looked at the window, and heard him laugh.

'You'll have to stay and face the music. Won't you sit down?' he continued politely. He left the door and started to walk towards her, and she backed, then blushed furiously as he asked:

'Where are you going? I only want to ask you some questions.'

She knew he was laughing, but carefully avoided his eye and sat down on the extreme edge of a stiff little chair, clasping her shaking hands together.

'Now, Miss Peters, pray help me to understand your note. Are your parents or brothers ill, that you have to return to England so suddenly?'

She hesitated, searching for the right answer, and was almost unnerved when he said, 'The truth, Addy,' in a very gentle voice.

She swallowed the lump in her throat. 'They're all quite well, thank you.'

When he said, 'Do they know you are going home?' she could only shake her head.

'So the "urgent personal matter" concerns yourself?'

She nodded, not trusting herself to speak, her eyes fixed on his waistcoat, while he read the letter through again at his leisure.

'You've written "May I congratulate you and wish you and Freule Keizer every happiness in the future." I wonder why?'

Adelaide swallowed a sob rather noisily and said forlornly: 'You're going to be married.' She looked quickly up at his face, to see him frowning fiercely.

'I can't think how you got to hear of it,' he said carefully.

'Freule Keizer told me the day before the ball,' she gulped. 'She met me as I was going for a walk.'

She was smoothing the fingers of her gloves and heard the professor draw a sharp breath.

'Oh, yes, and what exactly did she tell you?'

Adelaide was past caring what happened next, and repeated Margriet's conversation with her, while he listened in silence.

'She asked me not to tell anyone, but that doesn't mean you, does it?' She spoke to her gloves, not daring to look at him.

He made no reply to this, but said in an understanding way:

'So that explains the toothache.' She nodded. 'So that Margriet and I could go to the ball together,' he continued. She nodded again, and stole a look at him. He was polishing his glasses but looked up and caught her gaze. His eyes were the blue-grey of a Dutch winter sky; she found that she was unable to look away from them.

He said reflectively: 'I do not know why it is so, Adelaide, but you are obsessed with the absurd notion that I should marry Margriet. Oh, I know that it has been common gossip that we should do so, but I have never bothered myself with gossip, nor have I encouraged it. I must make it plain to you that I do not wish to marry her, nor have I ever given her an indication that I intended to do so. It was unfortunate that she told you that she hoped to marry me—it was, how do you say? wishful thinking on her part.' He gave his glasses a final polish and adjusted them carefully. 'What a pity that we should have this—misunderstanding—just as you are on the point of leaving us.'

Adelaide sat silent; there was really nothing to say. She had managed to drag her eyes away from his face, and was once more staring at her gloves. She thought fully how silly she had been; he didn't mind her going in the least. His next words confirmed this.

'I wonder if you would consider coming back for another day or two—until Friday? The clinic is very busy, and you couldn't be replaced until next week. Let me see, it's Tuesday, I shall be taking a day off tomorrow...'

She realised he was expecting an answer. If she had wanted proof that he regarded her only as a useful member of his staff, she now had it. He had come after her because he needed her back in the clinic; that had been the reason for his anger too. She would have liked to have left the house and never see him again, but she had nowhere to go. She forced herself to look at him and answer quietly:

'Provided the Directrice has no objection, I'll stay until Friday, sir.'

'That's a great relief.' He suddenly became very brisk, and went over to the fireplace and pulled the old-fashioned bell rope hanging there. When Bundle answered it, he asked him to get a taxi and put Adelaide's luggage in it.

'I shan't expect you at the clinic this afternoon, Miss Peters; you'll wish to unpack a few things, I expect. May I suggest that you go back now and do so?'

Adelaide got meekly to her feet, and then on her way to the door, said: 'But I must say goodbye to Baroness Van Essen.'

'I'll make your excuses; she'll understand.' He looked at his watch pointedly. 'I really must get back to work.'

She coloured painfully, and went quickly into the hall, where he followed her.

'I'll ring Matron and explain: I'm sure there will be no difficulty.' He ushered her out to the waiting taxi with all possible speed, and Adelaide found herself driving back to the hospital before having the time to voice her protest at not seeing the Baroness. The professor had seemed to be in a great hurry—for him, of course, it had been nothing but a great waste of time.

Adelaide looked miserably out of the window, and tried not to think.

Adelaide was surprised at the Matron's smooth handling of her return to hospital. She went straight to that lady's office upon her return, feeling rather foolish and quite unable to think of anything to say. The Directrice, however, did not seem to expect any explanations, but made some vague remarks about Adelaide's change of plans, told her that her uniform was ready for her in her old room, and hoped she would go on duty at the usual time on the following morning. Adelaide could only suppose that the professor had given her some plausible reason for his clinic Sister's strange behaviour.

The next day seemed endless. The nurses who had heard that she was leaving on Friday greeted her with dismayed surprise; Dr Beekman who was taking the clinic said very little, however, but gave her his usual 'good morning' and talked trivialities. Once or twice she caught him looking at her rather searchingly. She supposed the professor had told him too, and was grateful to him for not enlarging upon the whole sorry business.

The clinics were not as busy as usual, but Casualty was full, with a steady trickle of burns and scalds, cut heads, and small broken arms and legs. The staff were kept busy, and Adelaide went off duty late and rather tired. After supper Zuster Boot asked her to go to the cinema, and she agreed readily, thinking that it would pass the evening hours. She sat through the programme, watching the film with eyes that saw none of it.

She slept very little that night; she longed yet dreaded to see the professor in the morning. She wished with all her heart that she had never agreed to work until Friday. She dropped into a heavy doze just before she was called, and as she wearily pinned up her hair, looked at the hollow-eyed, tired face in the mirror and had to admit that no man, least of all the professor, was going to give her a second glance that morning.

She greeted him in subdued tones, and felt her spirits sink to an even lower level when Coenraad, asked by Piet Beekman if he didn't think that she looked rather off colour, didn't even bother to lift his eyes from his work, merely saying 'probably' in a voice intended to convey his complete lack of interest. Presently, however, he laid aside his charts and asked her cheerfully if she had been able to change her boat reservation for the next day, and expressed the hope that she would have a pleasant crossing. Adelaide, who had now reached the stage when she didn't care if she had to travel by canoe, replied mendaciously that she was looking forward to it immensely. The professor then suggested, with the air of a man who had taken care of the civilities, that they might as well start work, and was soon engrossed in examining a screaming child with a very nasty impetigo. This seemed a suitable time for Adelaide to slip away to her office; Zuster Wilsma was back from her coffee break and could perfectly well take the clinic for an hour or two. Adelaide had known that it would be difficult seeing Coenraad again, but his bland indifference was something from which she had to escape. Halfway to the door, however, she was halted.

'I should like you to stay, Sister.' He spoke in a voice he seldom used; she knew better than to ignore it, and went meekly back to the desk. He had his back to her, looking at a film on the wall screen.

'Have you checked the Out-Patients' list?' His tone implied that she had not. 'There are several difficult children this morning, so we might as well make use of your powers over the juvenile mind while you are still with us.'

He looked over his shoulder at her, but she did not meet his gaze, but looked at the film with an expressionless face, and said in a very professional voice: 'Very well, sir, just as you say.'

It was a tiring morning. The professor was right, as he so often was. One noisy toddler succeeded another till Adelaide's patience was exhausted. Somehow she got through the morning, and during her dinner hour thankfully wrapped herself in her cloak and walked in the hospital grounds. The air was cold and fresh; she went back to the clinic and made herself a cup of coffee and sat and sipped it until the nurses came back from their dinner.

The afternoon clinic was, if anything, worse than the morning. At four o'clock the professor remarked that if he didn't have a cup of tea and five minutes' quiet, he would be a nervous wreck. Adelaide silently agreed, and sent the nurse for the tea tray, then told her to go and have her own. She put the tray on the desk and turned away to go to her own office, but the professor forestalled her.

'Won't you have a cup with us, Sister? Then we can get on again without delay.' She had no choice but to pour out his tea and put it on the desk beside him. He thanked her without looking up from his work, and she was glad when Piet called to her to bring her cup over to the window with his. She had barely sat down to drink it when the phone rang. The professor answered it and said, 'For you, Sister.'

Adelaide put down her cup and went over to the desk and took the phone from him; her hand brushed his as she did so, and the touch set her pulse hurrying, so that her voice shook as she said:

'Sister Peters speaking.' She was surprised to hear the Directrice's voice.

'Sister? I see that you are on duty until noon tomorrow. Professor Van Essen tells me that there will be no clinic in the morning, and I see no need for you to come on duty. I expect you will be glad of a few extra hours before your train leaves. Perhaps you will come and see me in my office between nine and half past tomorrow.'

Adelaide said, 'Yes, Directrice,' and 'Thank you,' and replaced the receiver. The professor had stopped writing and was watching her. She met his bland gaze with a look of enquiry.

'You didn't tell me that there was to be no clinic tomorrow morning, sir.'

'There seemed little point, Sister,' his voice was cool, 'since you will not be here.'

She looked away, and murmured 'Of course, sir' then went back to her cooling tea and Piet, who looked at her unhappy face and plunged into an account of little Piet's efforts to walk. She didn't hear a word of it, but his kindly voice soothed her, so that presently she collected up the tea cups on to the tray and went to call the next patient with her usual quiet composure.

The clinic wound to a close about half past five and the professor got up from his desk as the last small patient was ushered out.

'I am going to the wards,' he said abruptly. He nodded at Piet, who was already taking off his white coat, looked austerely at Adelaide and stalked away. The nurses had already started to clear; she plunged into the untidy mass of papers on his desk, intent on getting cleared up and away before he should return. Piet put on his coat and came and stood beside her.

'We shall miss you, Adelaide.' He produced a small parcel from a pocket and pressed it into her hand. 'This is from Leen and me—just to remember us by.'

She took the little packet and thanked him warmly—she was going to miss Leen and Piet and the baby and Mijnheer de Wit and all the friends she had made in the hospital very much. She held out her hand. 'Goodbye, Piet. I've loved working here.' She added wistfully, 'I hope you or Leen will write to me sometimes and tell me all the news.' She hesitated, then went on: 'Piet, I shall be gone before Professor Van Essen comes back—would you say goodbye to him for me?' She saw the surprised doubt on Piet's face, and hurried on: 'I'll write when I get to England.'

'If that's what you want, Addy,' said Piet slowly. Adelaide watched his burly form go through the door, and began with feverish haste to clear up. Coenraad never hurried his evening rounds, so she should have plenty of time to get away. She took a final look round the now spick-and-span office and went to find Zuster Wilsma. To her surprise, all the clinic nurses were waiting for her. They gave her a parting gift and wished her goodbye with a friendliness which warmed her heart.

Adelaide went to her room on the pretext of finishing her packing, but there was little to do, and she sat idle, trying not to think about never seeing Coenraad again, and when at last she went to bed, she cried herself to sleep.

Her haggard appearance at breakfast was put down to her reluctance to leave the hospital. She was generally liked, and her
friends' goodbyes were sincere. Back in her room, she put on the
green coat and hat, did her face with more care than usual, then
went downstairs to the office. It was already after nine—when she
had said goodbye to the Directrice, she would go for a walk
around the canals.

The Directrice smiled at her kindly and pushing the pile of
papers before her aside, talked agreeably for several minutes before shaking hands and saying goodbye. Adelaide opened the door
and went outside into the corridor. Coenraad was standing there.
He had apparently just come in, for he was wearing a car coat
and was even then pulling off his gloves. She hadn't expected to
see him again and she stood irresolute in the open doorway, doing
nothing. He took a leisurely stride towards her and stretched an
arm to close the door, before taking her arm in a gentle, inescap-
able hold, and started walking down the corridor towards the hospital entrance. Adelaide, unable to do anything else, went with
him. Half-formed sentences came and went in her head, but none
of them made sense. They went through the door and straight to
his car.

'We're going somewhere quiet,' was all he said, and he dumped
her unceremoniously in the seat beside his. Adelaide sat very still.
The situation had got quite out of hand; they had reached the
Munt Toren before she said faintly: 'I'm going for a walk...'

Coenraad eased the car out of a tangle of traffic. 'No, you're
not,' he said placidly.

She tried again. 'I should like to get out...' she began.

'And so you shall,' he agreed. 'We're almost there.'

It was no use; she remained silent until presently he turned into
the Spui and stopped. He got out and walked around to her side,
opened the door and stood wordlessly while she got out too. His
gloved hand took a firm grip of her arm, and he piloted her
through the archway leading to the picturesque square where the
centuries-old Scottish Church stood, surrounded by its close circle
of beautiful friendly little houses. It was very quiet; there was no

one about. Adelaide stood still and attempted to pull free of Coenraad's grip, but he merely tightened it and started to walk away from the church, around the square, taking her with him. He spoke in his mildest voice.

'We can talk here without interruption. I have something to say to you, Adelaide.'

He glanced down at her. She was looking straight ahead, her hair flamed above her white face, she looked pinched and cold.

'You didn't say goodbye,' he observed pleasantly.

Adelaide looked at her shoes as though she had never seen them before. She felt quite unable to deal with the situation, but did her best.

'I'll write to you when I get to England,' she mumbled.

'What will you write about?' He sounded interested. She gave him a startled look, then stared straight ahead again. What would she write about? What was there to say? That she had been foolish and proud and loved him desperately? She gulped. Two tears started to roll down her cheeks, and she put out her tongue and tried ineffectively to catch them. Then she stopped, because the professor, who could read her thoughts like an open book, had stopped. He turned her round to face him and mopped up her tears with his handkerchief, then put his arms around her and pulled her close; they felt very comforting. She saw his smile and the gleam in his eyes as he bent his head and kissed her. He did it slowly and thoroughly and with evident enjoyment. After a while he said:

'Darling Addy, I love you. I loved you the first time we met. I would have told you a dozen times if it hadn't been for your confounded scruples about my money and title. For a year you've driven me to distraction with your cool friendliness and efficiency and starched aprons.' He kissed her again, quite roughly. 'Will you marry me, Addy?'

She had become quite beautiful; her eyes shone, her cheeks were pink. She smiled adorably at him, and reached up and put her arms shyly about his neck. 'Yes...oh, yes, Coenraad!'

They stood together, very close and listened to the chimes telling the hour.

'I love this little church,' said Adelaide.

'Would you like to be married here, Addy?'

The pink in her cheeks deepened.

'Oh, yes, I would! But can we?'

Coenraad kissed her again. 'Of course,' he smiled. 'I'd like to marry you here and now, but I'm afraid our laws don't allow that.' He looked down at her, his eyes twinkling, and pulled her closer.

'But shall we agree to marry just as soon as all the formalities are dealt with, darling?'

Adelaide nodded happily; he tucked her arm under his, and they started walking slowly back towards the archway.

'Where are we going?' asked Adelaide, not really caring.

They stopped, and Coenraad drew her within the circle of his arms again.

The sounds of the bustling city around them barely penetrated the peace of the little place.

'Why, to start this business of getting married,' he said.

'Does it take long? I mean…can we do it all before I catch my train?'

He held her a little way away from him, so that he could see her face.

'Will it matter very much if you don't catch your train?' he asked. 'It's quite a lengthy proceeding. Will you mind staying with Tante Anneke for a few days, do you think—and then I'll take you home.'

Adelaide looked at him with shining eyes.

'I don't mind where I go or what I do as long as I'm with you.'

Coenraad smiled at her very tenderly, then kissed her softly on one pink cheek.

'Darling Addy,' he said, and took her hand as they went back through the archway together.

EMMA'S WEDDING

by

Betty Neels

CHAPTER ONE

THERE were three people in the room: an elderly man with a fringe of white hair surrounding a bald pate and a neat little beard, a lady of uncertain years and once very pretty, her faded good looks marred by a look of unease, and, sitting at the table between them, a girl, a splendid young woman as to shape and size, with carroty hair bunched untidily on top of her head and a face which, while not beautiful or even pretty, was pleasing to look at, with wide grey eyes, a haughty nose and a wide mouth, gently curved.

The elderly man finished speaking, shuffled the papers before him and adjusted his spectacles, and when her mother didn't speak, only sat looking bewildered and helpless, the girl spoke.

'We shall need your advice, Mr Trump. This is a surprise—we had no idea...Father almost never mentioned money matters to either Mother or me, although some weeks before he died...' her voice faltered for a moment '...he told me that he was investing in some scheme which would make a great deal of money, and when I asked him about it he laughed and said it was all rather exciting and I must wait and see.'

Mr Trump said dryly, 'Your father had sufficient funds to live comfortably and leave both your mother and you provided for. He invested a considerable amount of his capital in this new computer company set up by a handful of unscrupulous young men and for a few weeks it made profits, so that your father invested the rest of his capital in it. Inevitably, the whole thing fell apart, and he and a number of the other investors lost every penny. In order to avoid bankruptcy you will need to sell this house, the car, and much of the furniture. You have some good pieces here which should sell well.'

He glanced at her mother and added, 'You do understand what I have told you, Mrs Dawson?'

'We shall be poor.' She gave a little sob. 'There won't be any money. How are we to live?' She looked around her. 'My lovely home—and how am I to go anywhere if we haven't any car? And clothes? I won't be shabby.' She began to cry in real earnest. 'Where shall we live?' And before anyone could speak she added, 'Emma, you must think of something...'

'Try not to get upset, Mother. If this house and everything else sells well enough to pay off what's owing, we can go and live at the cottage in Salcombe. I'll get a job and we shall manage very well.'

Mr Trump nodded his bald head. 'Very sensible. I'm fairly certain that once everything is sold there will be enough to pay everything off and even have a small amount over. I imagine it won't be too hard to find work during the summer season at least, and there might even be some small job which you might undertake, Mrs Dawson.'

'A job? Mr Trump, I have never worked in my life and I have no intention of doing so now.' She dissolved into tears again. 'My dear husband would turn in his grave if he could hear you suggest it.'

Mr Trump put his papers in his briefcase. Mrs Dawson he had always considered to be a charming little lady, rather spoilt by her husband but with a gentle, rather helpless manner which appealed to his old-fashioned notions of the weaker sex, but now, seeing the petulant look on her face, he wondered if he had been mistaken. Emma, of course, was an entirely different kettle of fish, being a sensible young woman, full of energy, kind and friendly—and there was some talk of her marrying. Which might solve their difficulties. He made his goodbyes, assured them that he would start at once on the unravelling of their affairs, then went out to his car and drove away.

Emma went out of the rather grand drawing room and crossed the wide hall to the kitchen. It was a large house, handsomely furnished with every mod con Mrs Dawson had expressed a wish to have. There was a daily housekeeper too, and a cheerful little woman who came twice a week to do the rough work.

Emma put on the kettle, laid a tea tray, found biscuits and, since the housekeeper had gone out for her half-day, looked through the cupboards for the cake tin. She and her mother might have been dealt a bitter blow, but tea and a slice of Mrs Tims's walnut cake would still be welcome. For as long as possible, reflected Emma.

Mrs Dawson was still sitting in her chair, dabbing her wet eyes. She watched Emma pour the tea and hand her a cup. 'How can I possibly eat and drink,' she wanted to know in a tearful voice, 'when our lives are in ruins?'

All the same she accepted a slice of cake.

Emma took a bite. 'We shall have to give Mrs Tims notice. Do you pay her weekly or monthly, Mother?'

Mrs Dawson looked vague. 'I've no idea. Your father never bothered me with that kind of thing. And that woman who comes in to clean—Ethel—what about her?'

'Shall I talk to them both and give them notice? Though they'll expect something extra as Father's death gave them no warning.'

Emma drank some tea and swallowed tears with it. She had loved her father, although they had never been close and the greater part of his paternal affection had been given to her brother James, twenty-three years old and four years her junior. And presently, most unfortunately, backpacking round the world after leaving university with a disappointing degree in science.

They weren't even quite sure where he was at the moment; his last address had been Java, with the prospect of Australia, and even if they had had an address and he'd come home at once she didn't think that he would have been of much help.

He was a dear boy, and she loved him, but her mother and father had spoilt him so that although he was too nice a young man to let it ruin his nature, it had tended to make him easygoing and in no hurry to settle down to a serious career.

He had had a small legacy from their grandmother when she died, and that had been ample to take care of his travels. She thought it unlikely that he would break off his journey, probably arguing that he was on the other side of the world and that Mr

Trump would deal with his father's affairs, still under the impression that he had left his mother and sister in comfortable circumstances.

Emma didn't voice these thoughts to her mother but instead settled that lady for a nap and went back to the kitchen to prepare for their supper. Mrs Tims would have left something ready to be cooked and there was nothing much to do. Emma sat down at the table, found pencil and paper, and wrote down everything which would have to be done.

A great deal! And she couldn't hope to do it all herself. Mr Trump would deal with the complicated financial situation, but what about the actual selling of the house and their possessions? And what would they be allowed to keep of those? Mr Trump had mentioned an overdraft at the bank, and money which had been borrowed from friends with the promise that it would be returned to them with handsome profits.

Emma put her head down on the table and cried. But not for long. She wiped her eyes, blew her nose and picked up her pencil once more.

If they were allowed to keep the cottage at least they would have a rent-free home and one which she had always loved, although her mother found the little town of Salcombe lacking in the kind of social life she liked, but it would be cheaper to live there for that very reason. She would find work; during the summer months there was bound to be a job she could do—waitressing, or working in one of the big hotels or a shop. The winter might not be as easy, the little town sank into peace and quiet, but Kingsbridge was only a bus ride away, and that was a bustling small town with plenty of shops and cafés...

Feeling more cheerful, Emma made a list of their own possessions which surely they would be allowed to keep. Anything saleable they must sell, although she thought it was unlikely that her mother would be prepared to part with her jewellery, but they both had expensive clothes—her father had never grudged them money for those—and they would help to swell the kitty.

She got the supper then, thinking that it was a pity that Derek wouldn't be back in England for three more days. They weren't engaged, but for some time now their future together had become a foregone conclusion. Derek was a serious young man and had given her to understand that once he had gained the promotion in the banking firm for which he worked they would marry.

Emma liked him, indeed she would have fallen in love with him and she expected to do that without much difficulty, but although he was devoted to her she had the idea that he didn't intend to show his proper feelings until he proposed. She had been quite content; life wasn't going to be very exciting, but a kind husband who would cherish one, and any children, and give one a comfortable home should bring her happiness.

She wanted to marry, for she was twenty-seven, but ever since she had left school there had always been a reason why she couldn't leave home, train for something and be independent. She had hoped that when James had left the university she could be free, but when she had put forward her careful plans it had been to discover that he had already arranged to be away for two years at least, and her mother had become quite hysterical at the idea of not having one or other of her children at home with her. And, of course, her father had agreed...

Perhaps her mother would want her to break off with Derek, but she thought not. A son-in-law in comfortable circumstances would solve their difficulties...

During the next three days Emma longed for Derek's return. It seemed that the business of being declared bankrupt entailed a mass of paperwork, with prolonged and bewildering visits from severe-looking men with briefcases. Since her mother declared that she would have nothing to do with any of it, Emma did her best to answer their questions and fill in the forms they offered.

'But I'll not sign anything until Mr Trump has told me that I must,' she told them.

It was all rather unnerving; she would have liked a little time to grieve about her father's death, but there was no chance of that. She went about her household duties while her mother sat staring at nothing and weeping, and Mrs Tims and Ethel worked around the house, grim-faced at the unexpectedness of it all.

Derek came, grave-faced, offered Mrs Dawson quiet condolences and went with Emma to her father's study. But if she had expected a shoulder to cry on she didn't get it. He was gravely concerned for her, and kind, but she knew at once that he would never marry her now. He had an important job in the banking world, and marrying the daughter of a man who had squandered a fortune so recklessly was hardly going to enhance his future.

He listened patiently to her problems, observed that she was fortunate to have a sound man such as Mr Trump to advise her, and told her to be as helpful with 'Authority' as possible.

'I'm afraid there are no mitigating circumstances,' he told her. 'I looked into the whole affair when I got back today. Don't attempt to contest anything, whatever you do. Hopefully there will be enough money to clear your father's debts once everything is sold.'

Emma sat looking at him—a good-looking man in his thirties, rather solemn in demeanour, who had nice manners, was honest in his dealings, and not given to rashness of any sort. She supposed that it was his work which had driven the warmth from his heart and allowed common sense to replace the urge to help her at all costs and, above all, to comfort her.

'Well,' said Emma in a tight little voice, 'how fortunate it is that you didn't give me a ring, for I don't need to give it back.'

He looked faintly surprised. 'I wasn't aware that we had discussed the future,' he told her.

'There is no need, is there? I haven't got one, have I? And yours matters to you.'

He agreed gravely. 'Indeed it does. I'm glad, Emma, that you are sensible enough to realise that, and I hope that you will too always consider me as a friend. If I can help in any way... If I can help financially?'

'Mr Trump is seeing to the money, but thank you for offering. We shall be able to manage very well once everything is sorted out.'

'Good. I'll call round from time to time and see how things are...'

'We shall be busy packing up—there is no need.' She added in a polite hostess voice, 'Would you like a cup of coffee before you go?'

'No—no, thank you. I'm due at the office in the morning and I've work to do first.'

He wished Mrs Dawson goodbye, and as Emma saw him to the door he bent to kiss her cheek. 'If ever you should need help or advice...'

'Thank you, Derek,' said Emma. Perhaps she should make a pleasant little farewell speech, but if she uttered another word she would burst into tears.

'How fortunate that you have Derek,' said Mrs Dawson when Emma joined her. 'I'm sure he'll know what's best to be done. A quiet wedding as soon as possible.'

'Derek isn't going to marry me, Mother. It would interfere with his career.'

A remark which started a flood of tears from her mother.

'Emma, I can't believe it. It isn't as if he were a young man with no money or prospects. There's no reason why you shouldn't marry at once.' She added sharply, 'You didn't break it off, did you? Because if you did you're a very stupid girl.'

'No, Mother, it's what Derek wishes.' Emma felt sorry for her mother. She looked so forlorn and pretty, and so in need of someone to make life easy for her as it always had been. 'I'm sorry, but he has got his career to consider, and marrying me wouldn't help him at all.'

'I cannot think what came over your father...'

'Father did it because he wanted us to have everything we could possibly want,' said Emma steadily. 'He never grudged you anything, Mother.'

Mrs Dawson was weeping again. 'And look how he has left us now. It isn't so bad for you, you're young and can go to work, but what about me? My nerves have never allowed me to do

anything strenuous and all this worrying has given me a continuous headache. I feel that I am going to be ill.'

'I'm going to make you a milky drink and put a warm bottle
in your bed, Mother. Have a bath, and when you're ready I'll
come up and make sure that you are comfortable.'

'I shall never be comfortable again,' moaned Mrs Dawson.

She looked like a small woebegone child and Emma gave her
a hug; the bottom had fallen out of her mother's world and, although life would never be the same again, she would do all that
she could to make the future as happy as possible.

For a moment she allowed her thoughts to dwell on her own
future. Married to Derek she would have had a pleasant, secure
life: a home to run, children to bring up, a loving husband and
as much of a social life as she would wish. But now that must be
forgotten; she must make a happy life for her mother, find work,
make new friends. Beyond that she didn't dare to think. Of course
James would come home eventually, but he would plan his own
future, cheerfully taking it for granted that she would look after
their mother, willing to help if he could but not prepared to let it
interfere with his plans.

The house sold quickly, the best of the furniture was sold, and
the delicate china and glass. Most of the table silver was sold too,
and the house, emptied of its contents, was bleak and unwelcom-
ing. But there was still a great deal to do; even when Emma had
packed the cases of unsaleable objects—the cheap kitchen china,
the saucepans, the bed and table linen that they were allowed to
keep—there were the visits from her parents' friends, come to
commiserate and eager, in a friendly way, for details. Their sympathy was genuine but their offers of help were vague. Emma and
her mother must come and stay as soon as they were settled in;
they would drive down to Salcombe and see them. Such a pretty
place, and how fortunate that they had such a charming home to
go to...

Emma, ruthlessly weeding out their wardrobes, thought it unlikely that any of their offers would bear fruit.

Mr Trump had done his best, and every debt had been paid, leaving a few hundred in the bank. Her mother would receive a widow's pension, but there was nothing else. Thank heaven, reflected Emma, that it was early in April and a job, any kind of job, shouldn't be too hard to find now that the season would be starting at Salcombe.

They left on a chilly damp morning—a day winter had forgotten and left behind. Emma locked the front door, put the key through the letterbox and got into the elderly Rover they had been allowed to keep until, once at Salcombe, it was to be handed over to the receivers. Her father's Bentley had gone, with everything else.

She didn't look back, for if she had she might have cried and driving through London's traffic didn't allow for tears. Mrs Dawson cried. She cried for most of their long journey, pausing only to accuse Emma of being a hard-hearted girl with no feelings when she suggested that they might stop for coffee.

They reached Salcombe in the late afternoon and, as it always did, the sight of the beautiful estuary with the wide sweep of the sea beyond lifted Emma's spirits. They hadn't been to the cottage for some time but nothing had changed; the little house stood at the end of a row of similar houses, their front gardens opening onto a narrow path along the edge of the water, crowded with small boats and yachts, a few minutes' walk from the main street of the little town, yet isolated in its own peace and quiet.

There was nowhere to park the car, of course. Emma stopped in the narrow street close by and they walked along the path, opened the garden gate and unlocked the door. For years there had been a local woman who had kept an eye on the place. Emma had written to her and now, as they went inside, it was to find the place cleaned and dusted and groceries and milk in the small fridge.

Mrs Dawson paused on the doorstep. 'It's so small,' she said in a hopeless kind of voice, but Emma looked around her with pleasure and relief. Here was home: a small sitting room, with the front door and windows overlooking the garden, a smaller kitchen beyond and then a minute back yard, and, up the narrow staircase, two bedrooms with a bathroom between them. The furniture was simple but comfortable, the curtains a pretty chintz and there was a small open fireplace.

She put her arm round her mother. 'We'll have a cup of tea and then I'll get the rest of the luggage and see if the pub will let me put the car in their garage until I can hand it over.'

She was tired when she went to bed that night; she had seen to the luggage and the car, lighted a small log fire and made a light supper before seeing her mother to her bed. It had been a long day, she reflected, curled up in her small bedroom, but they were here at last in the cottage, not owing a farthing to anyone and with a little money in the bank. Mr Trump had been an elderly shoulder to lean on, which was more than she could say for Derek. 'Good riddance to bad rubbish,' said Emma aloud.

All the same she had been hurt.

In the morning she went to the pub and persuaded the landlord to let her leave the car there until she could hand it over, and then went into the main street to do the shopping. Her mother had declared herself exhausted after their long drive on the previous day and Emma had left her listlessly unpacking her clothes. Not a very good start to the day, but it was a fine morning and the little town sparkled in the sunshine.

Almost all the shops were open, hopeful of early visitors, and she didn't hurry with her shopping, stopping to look in the elegant windows of the small boutiques, going to the library to enrol for the pair of them, arranging for milk to be delivered, ordering a paper too, and at the same time studying the advertisements in the shop window. There were several likely jobs on offer. She bought chops from the butcher, who remembered her from previous visits, and crossed the road to the greengrocer. He remembered her too, so that she felt quite light-hearted as she made her last purchase in the baker's.

The delicious smell of newly baked bread made her nose quiver. And there were rolls and pasties, currant buns and doughnuts. She was hesitating as to which to buy when someone else came into the shop. She turned round to look and encountered a stare from pale blue eyes so intent that she blushed, annoyed with herself for doing that just because this large man was staring. He was good-looking too, in a rugged kind of way, with a high-bridged nose and a thin mouth. He was wearing an elderly jersey and cords and his hair needed a good brush...

He stopped staring, leaned over her, took two pasties off the counter and waved them at the baker's wife. And now the thin mouth broke into a smile. 'Put it on the bill, Mrs Trott,' he said, and was gone.

Emma, about to ask who he was, sensed that Mrs Trott wasn't going to tell her and prudently held her tongue. He must live in the town for he had a bill. He didn't look like a fisherman or a farm worker and he wouldn't own a shop, not dressed like that, and besides he didn't look like any of those. He had been rude, staring like that; she had no wish to meet him again but it would be interesting to know just who he was.

She went back to the cottage and found a man waiting impatiently to collect the car and, what with one thing and another, she soon forgot the man at the baker's.

It was imperative to find work but she wasn't going to rush into the first job that was vacant. With a little wangling she thought that she could manage two part-time jobs. They would cease at the end of the summer and even one part-time job might be hard to find after that.

'I must just make hay while the sun shines,' said Emma, and over the next few days scanned the local newspapers. She went from one end of the town to the other, sizing up what was on offer. Waitresses were wanted, an improver was needed at the hairdressers—but what was an improver? Chambermaids at the various hotels, an assistant in an arts and crafts shop, someone to clean holiday cottages between lets, and an educated lady to assist the librarian at the public library on two evenings a week...

It was providential that while out shopping with her mother they were accosted by an elderly lady who greeted them with obvious pleasure.

'Mrs Dawson—and Emma, isn't it? Perhaps you don't remember me. You came to the hotel to play bridge. I live at the hotel now that my husband has died and I'm delighted to see a face I know...' She added eagerly, 'Let's go and have coffee together and a chat. Is your husband with you?'

'I am also a widow—it's Mrs Craig, isn't it? I do remember now; we had some pleasant afternoons at bridge. My husband died very recently, and Emma and I have come to live here.'

'I'm so very sorry. Of course you would want to get away from Richmond for a time. Perhaps we could meet soon and then arrange a game of bridge later?'

Mrs Dawson brightened. 'That would be delightful...'

'Then you must come and have tea with me sometimes at the hotel.' Mrs Craig added kindly, 'You need to have a few distractions, you know.' She smiled at Emma. 'I'm sure you have several young friends from earlier visits?'

Emma said cheerfully, 'Oh, yes, of course,' and added, 'I've one or two calls to make now, while you have coffee. It is so nice to meet you again, Mrs Craig.' She looked at her mother. 'I'll see you at home, Mother.'

She raced away. The rest of the shopping could wait. Here was the opportunity to go to the library...

The library was at the back of the town, and only a handful of people were wandering round the bookshelves. There were two people behind the desk: one a severe-looking lady with a no-nonsense hair style, her companion a girl with a good deal of blonde hair, fashionably tousled, and with too much make-up on her pretty face. She looked up from the pile of books she was arranging and grinned at Emma as she came to a halt and addressed the severe lady.

'Good morning,' said Emma. 'You are advertising for an assistant for two evenings a week. I should like to apply for the job.'

The severe lady eyed her. She said shortly, 'My name is Miss Johnson. Are you experienced?'

'No, Miss Johnson, but I like books. I have A levels in English

Literature, French, Modern Art and Maths. I am twenty-seven years old and I have lived at home since I left school. I have come here to live with my mother and I need a job.'

'Two sessions a week, six hours, at just under five pounds an hour.' Miss Johnson didn't sound encouraging. 'Five o'clock until eight on Tuesdays and Thursdays. Occasionally extra hours, if there is sickness or one of us is on holiday.' She gave what might be called a ladylike sniff. 'You seem sensible. I don't want some giddy girl leaving at the end of a week...'

'I should like to work here if you will have me,' said Emma. 'You will want references...?'

'Of course, and as soon as possible. If they are satisfactory you can come on a week's trial.'

Emma wrote down Mr Trump's address and phone number and then Dr Jakes's who had known her for years. 'Will you let me know or would you prefer me to call back? We aren't on the phone yet. It's being fitted shortly.'

'You're in rooms or a flat?'

'No, we live at Waterside Cottage, the end one along Victoria Quay.'

Miss Johnson looked slightly less severe. 'You are staying there? Renting the cottage for the summer?'

'No, it belongs to my mother.'

The job, Emma could see, was hers.

She bade Miss Johnson a polite goodbye and went back into the main street; she turned into a narrow lane running uphill, lined by small pretty cottages. The last cottage at the top of the hill was larger than the rest and she knocked on the door.

The woman who answered the door was still young, slim and tall and dressed a little too fashionably for Salcombe. Her hair was immaculate and so was her make-up.

She looked Emma up and down and said, 'Yes?'

'You are advertising for someone to clean holiday cottages...'

'Come in.' She led Emma into a well-furnished sitting room. 'I doubt if you'd do. It's hard work—Wednesdays and Saturdays, cleaning up the cottages and getting them ready for the next lot. And a fine mess some of them are in, I can tell you. I need someone for those two days. From ten o'clock in the morning and everything ready by four o'clock when the next lot come.'

She waved Emma to a chair. 'Beds, bathroom, loo, Hoovering. Kitchen spotless—and that means cupboards too. You come here and collect the cleaning stuff and bedlinen and hand in the used stuff before you leave. Six hours work a day, five pounds an hour, and tips if anyone leaves them.'

'For two days?'

'That's what I said. I'll want references. Local, are you? Haven't seen you around. Can't stand the place myself. The cottages belonged to my father and I've taken them over for a year or two. I'm fully booked for the season.'

She crossed one elegantly shod foot over the other. 'Week's notice on either side?'

'I live here,' said Emma, 'and I need a job. I'd like to come if you are satisfied with my references.'

'Please yourself, though I'd be glad to take you on. It isn't a job that appeals to the girls around here.'

It didn't appeal all that much to Emma, but sixty pounds a week did…

She gave her references once more, and was told she'd be told in two days' time. 'If I take you on you'll need to be shown round. There's another girl cleans the other two cottages across the road.'

Emma went home, got the lunch and listened to her mother's account of her morning with Mrs Craig. 'She has asked me to go to the hotel one afternoon for a rubber of bridge.' She hesitated. 'They play for money—quite small stakes…'

'Well,' said Emma, 'you're good at the game, aren't you? I dare say you won't be out of pocket. Nice to have found a friend, and I'm sure you'll make more once the season starts.'

Two days later there was a note in the post. Her references for the cleaning job were satisfactory, she could begin work on the following Saturday and in the meantime call that morning to be shown her work. It was signed Dulcie Brooke-Tigh. Emma considered that the name suited the lady very well.

She went to the library that afternoon and Miss Johnson told her unsmilingly that her references were satisfactory and she could start work on Tuesday. 'A week's notice and you will be paid each Thursday evening.'

Emma, walking on air, laid out rather more money than she should have done at the butchers, and on Sunday went to church with her mother and said her prayers with childlike gratitude.

The cleaning job was going to be hard work. Mrs Brooke-Tigh, for all her languid appearance, was a hard-headed businesswoman, intent on making money. There was enough work for two people in the cottages, but as long as she could get a girl anxious for the job she wasn't bothered. She had led Emma round the two cottages she would be responsible for, told her to start work punctually and then had gone back into her own cottage and shut the door. She didn't like living at Salcombe, but the holiday cottages were money-spinners...

The library was surprisingly full when Emma, punctual to the minute, presented herself at the desk.

Miss Johnson wasted no time on friendly chat. 'Phoebe will show you the shelves, then come back here and I will show you how to stamp the books. If I am busy take that trolley of returned books and put them back on the shelves. And do it carefully; I will not tolerate slovenly work.'

Which wasn't very encouraging, but Phoebe's cheerful wink was friendly. The work wasn't difficult or tiring, and Emma, who loved books, found the three hours had passed almost too quickly. And Miss Johnson, despite her austere goodnight, had not complained.

Emma went back to the cottage to eat a late supper and then sit down to do her sums. Her mother had her pension, of course, and that plus the money from the two jobs would suffice to keep them in tolerable comfort. There wouldn't be much over, but they had the kind of expensive, understated clothes which would last for several years... She explained it all to her mother, who told her rather impatiently to take over their finances. 'I quite realise that I must give up some of my pension, dear, but I suppose I may have enough for the hairdresser and small expenses?'

Emma did some sums in her head and offered a generous slice of the pension—more than she could spare. But her mother's happiness and peace of mind were her first concern; after years of living in comfort, and being used to having everything she wanted within reason, she could hardly be expected to adapt easily to their more frugal way of living.

On Saturday morning she went to the cottages. She had told her mother that she had two jobs, glossing over the cleaning and enlarging on the library, and, since Mrs Dawson was meeting Mrs Craig for coffee, Emma had said that she would do the shopping and that her mother wasn't to wait lunch if she wasn't home.

She had known it was going to be hard work and it was, for the previous week's tenants had made no effort to leave the cottage tidy, let alone clean. Emma cleaned and scoured, then Hoovered and made beds and tidied cupboards, cleaned the cooker and the bath, and at the end of it was rewarded by Mrs Brooke-Tigh's nod of approval and, even better than that, the tip she had found in the bedroom—a small sum, but it swelled the thirty pounds she was paid as she left.

'Wednesday at ten o'clock,' said Mrs Brooke-Tigh.

Emma walked down the lane with the girl who cleaned the other two cottages.

'Mean old bag,' said the girl. 'Doesn't even give us a cup of coffee. Think you'll stay?'

'Oh, yes,' said Emma.

The future, while not rosy, promised security just so long as people like Mrs Brooke-Tigh needed her services.

When she got home her mother told her that Mrs Craig had met a friend while they were having their coffee and they had gone to the little restaurant behind the boutique and had lunch. 'I was a guest, dear, and I must say I enjoyed myself.' She smiled. 'I seem to be making friends. You must do the same, dear.'

Emma said, 'Yes, Mother,' and wondered if she would have time to look for friends. Young women of her own age? Men? The thought crossed her mind that the only person she would like to see again was the man in the baker's shop.

CHAPTER TWO

EMMA welcomed the quiet of Sunday. It had been a busy week, with its doubts and worries and the uncertainty of coping with her jobs. But she had managed. There was money in the household purse and she would soon do even better. She went with her mother to church and was glad to see that one or two of the ladies in the congregation smiled their good mornings to her mother. If her mother could settle down and have the social life she had always enjoyed things would be a lot easier. I might even join some kind of evening classes during the winter, thought Emma, and meet people...

She spent Monday cleaning the cottage, shopping and hanging the wash in the little back yard, while her mother went to the library to choose a book. On the way back she had stopped to look at the shops and found a charming little scarf, just what she needed to cheer up her grey dress. 'It was rather more than I wanted to spend, dear,' she explained, 'but exactly what I like, and I get my pension on Thursday...'

The library was half empty when Emma got there on Tuesday evening.

'WI meeting,' said Miss Johnson. 'There will be a rush after seven o'clock.'

She nodded to a trolley loaded with books. 'Get those back onto the shelves as quickly as you can. Phoebe is looking up something for a visitor.'

Sure enough after an hour the library filled up with ladies from the WI, intent on finding something pleasant to read, and Emma, intent on doing her best, was surprised when Miss Johnson sent Phoebe to the doors to put up the 'Closed' sign and usher the dawdlers out.

Emma was on her knees, collecting up some books someone

had dropped on the floor, when there was a sudden commotion at the door and the man from the baker's shop strode in.

Miss Johnson looked up. She said severely, 'We are closed, Doctor,' but she smiled as she spoke.

'*Rupert Bear*—have you a copy? The bookshop's closed and small William next door won't go to sleep until he's read to. It must be *Rupert Bear*.' He smiled at Miss Johnson, and Emma, watching from the floor, could see Miss Johnson melting under it.

'Emma, fetch *Rupert Bear* from the last shelf in the children's section.'

As Emma got to her feet he turned and looked at her.

'Well, well,' he said softly, and his stare was just as intent as it had been in the baker's shop.

She found it disturbing, so that when she came back with the book she said tartly, 'May I have your library ticket?'

'Have I got one? Even if I knew where it was I wouldn't have stopped to get it, not with small William bawling his head off.'

He took the book from her, thanked Miss Johnson and was off.

Emma set the books neatly in their places and hoped that someone would say something. It was Phoebe who spoke.

'The poor man. I bet he's had a busy day, and now he's got to spend his evening reading to a small boy. As though he hadn't enough on his plate...'

Miss Johnson said repressively, 'He is clearly devoted to children. Emma, make a note that the book hasn't been checked out. Dr van Dyke will return it in due course.'

Well, reflected Emma, at least I know who he is. And on the way home, as she and Phoebe walked as far as the main street she asked, 'Is he the only doctor here?'

'Lord, no. There's three of them at the medical practice, and he's not permanent, just taken over from Dr Finn for a few months.'

Why had he stared so, and why had he said, 'Well, well,' in that satisfied voice? wondered Emma, saying goodnight and going back home through the quiet town.

It wouldn't be quiet for much longer. Visitors were beginning to trickle in, most of them coming ashore from their yachts, mingling with those who came regularly early in the season, to walk the coastal paths and spend leisurely days strolling through the town. More restaurants had opened, the ice cream parlour had opened its doors, and the little coastal ferry had begun its regular trips.

Emma was pleased to see that her mother was already starting to enjoy what social life there was. She played bridge regularly with Mrs Craig and her friends, met them for coffee and occasionally did some shopping. But her gentle complaints made it clear that life in a small, off-the-beaten-track town was something she was bravely enduring, and whenever Emma pointed out that there was little chance of them ever leaving the cottage, Mrs Dawson dissolved into gentle tears.

'You should have married Derek,' she said tearfully. 'We could have lived comfortably at his house. It was large enough for me to have had my own apartment...'

A remark Emma found hard to answer.

As for Emma, she hadn't much time to repine; there was the cottage to clean, the washing and the ironing, all the small household chores which she had never had to do... At first her mother had said that she would do all the shopping, but, being unused to doing this on an economical scale, it had proved quite disastrous to the household purse, so Emma had added that to her other chores. Not that she minded. She was soon on friendly terms with the shopkeepers and there was a certain satisfaction in buying groceries with a strict eye on economy instead of lifting the phone and giving the order Mrs Dawson had penned each week with a serene disregard for expense...

And Miss Johnson had unbent very slightly, pleased to find that Emma really enjoyed her work at the library. She had even had a chat about her own taste in books, deploring the lack of interest in most of the borrowers for what she called a 'good class of book'. As for Phoebe, who did her work in a cheerful slapdash fashion, Emma liked her and listened sympathetically whenever Phoebe found the time to tell her of her numerous boyfriends.

But Mrs Brooke-Tigh didn't unbend. Emma was doing a menial's job, therefore she was treated as such; she checked the cottages with an eagle eye but beyond a distant nod had nothing to say. Emma didn't mind the cleaning but she did not like Mrs Brooke-Tigh; once the season was over she would look around for another job, something where she might meet friendly people. In a bar? she wondered, having very little idea of what that would be like. But at least there would be people and she might meet someone.

Did Dr van Dyke go into pubs? she wondered. Probably not. He wouldn't have time. She thought about him, rather wistfully, from time to time, when she was tired and lonely for the company of someone her own age. The only way she would get to know him was to get ill. And she never got ill...

Spring was sliding into early summer; at the weekends the narrow streets were filled by visiting yachtsmen and family parties driving down for a breath of sea air and a meal at one of the pubs. And with them, one Sunday, came Derek.

Mrs Dawson was going out to lunch with one of her bridge friends, persuaded that Emma didn't mind being on her own. 'We will go to evensong together,' said her mother, 'but it is such a treat to have luncheon with people I like, dear, and I knew you wouldn't mind.'

She peered at herself in the mirror. 'Is this hat all right? I really need some new clothes.'

'You look very smart, Mother, and the hat's just right. Have a lovely lunch. I'll have tea ready around four o'clock.'

Alone, Emma went into the tiny courtyard beyond the kitchen and saw to the tubs of tulips and the wallflowers growing against the wall. She would have an early lunch and go for a walk—a long walk. North Sands, perhaps, and if the little kiosk by the beach there was open she would have a cup of coffee. She went back into the cottage as someone banged the door knocker.

Derek stood there, dressed very correctly in a blazer and cords,

Italian silk tie and beautifully polished shoes. For a split second Emma had a vivid mental picture of an elderly sweater and uncombed hair.

'What on earth are you doing here?' she wanted to know with a regrettable lack of delight.

Derek gave her a kind smile. He was a worthy young man with pleasant manners and had become accustomed to being liked and respected.

He said now, 'I've surprised you...'

'Indeed you have.' Emma added reluctantly. 'You'd better come in.'

Derek looked around him. 'A nice little place—rather different from Richmond, though. Has your mother settled down?'

'Yes. Why are you here?'

'I wanted to see you, Emma. To talk. If you would change into a dress we could have lunch—I'm staying at the other end of the town.'

'We can talk here. I'll make cheese sandwiches...'

'My dear girl, you deserve more than a cheese sandwich. We can talk over lunch at the hotel.'

'What about?'

'Something which will please you...'

Perhaps something they hadn't known anything about had been salvaged from her father's estate... She said slowly, 'Very well. You'll have to wait while I change, though, and I must be back before four o'clock. Mother's out to lunch.'

While she changed out of trousers and a cotton top into something suitable to accompany Derek's elegance, she wondered what he had come to tell her. Mr Trump had hinted when they had left their home that eventually there might be a little more money. Perhaps Derek had brought it with him.

When she went downstairs he was standing by the window, watching the people strolling along the path.

'Of course you can't possibly stay here. This poky little place—nothing to do all day.'

She didn't bother to answer him, and he said impatiently, 'We shall have to walk; I left the car at the hotel.'

They walked, saying little. 'I can't think why you can't tell me whatever it is at once,' said Emma.

'In good time.' They got out of the road onto the narrow pavement to allow a car to creep past. Dr van Dyke was sitting in it. If he saw her he gave no sign.

The hotel was full. They had drinks in the bar and were given a table overlooking the estuary, but Derek ignored the magnificent view while he aired his knowledge with the wine waiter.

I should be enjoying myself, reflected Emma, and I'm not.

Derek talked about his work, mutual friends she had known, the new owner of her old home.

Emma polished off the last of her trifle. 'Are you staying here on holiday?'

'No, I must return tomorrow.'

'Then you'd better tell me whatever it is.' She glanced at the clock. 'It's half past two...'

He gave a little laugh. 'Can't get rid of me soon enough, Emma?'

He put his hand over hers on the table. 'Dear Emma, I have given much thought to this. The scandal of your father's bankruptcy has died down; there are no debts, no need for people to rake over cold ashes. There is no likelihood of it hindering my career. I have come to ask you to marry me. I know you have no money and a difficult social position, but I flatter myself that I can provide both of these for my wife. In a few years the whole unfortunate matter will be forgotten. I have the deepest regard for you and you will, I know, make me an excellent wife.'

Emma had listened to this speech without moving or uttering a sound. She was so angry that she felt as though she would explode or burst into flames. She got to her feet, a well brought up young woman who had been reared to good manners and politeness whatever the circumstances.

'Get stuffed,' said Emma, and walked out of the restaurant, through the bar and swing doors and into the car park.

She was white with rage and shaking, and heedless of where she was walking. Which was why she bumped into Dr van Dyke's massive chest.

She stared up into his placid face. 'The worm, the miserable rat,' she raged. 'Him and his precious career...'

The doctor said soothingly, 'This rat, is he still in the hotel? You don't wish to meet him again?'

'If I were a man I'd knock him down...' She sniffed and gulped and two tears slid down her cheeks.

'Then perhaps it would be a good idea if you were to sit in my car for a time—in case he comes looking for you. And, if you would like to, tell me what has upset you.'

He took her arm and walked her to the car. He popped her inside and got in beside her. 'Have a good cry if you want to, and then I'll drive you home.'

He gave her a large handkerchief and sat patiently while she sniffed and snuffled and presently blew her nose and mopped her face. He didn't look at her, he was watching a man—presumably the rat—walking up and down the car park, looking around him. Presently he went back into the hotel and the doctor said, 'He's a snappy dresser, your rat.'

She sat up straight. 'He's gone? He didn't see me?'

'No.' The doctor settled back comfortably. 'What has he done to upset you? It must have been something very upsetting to cause you to leave Sunday lunch at this hotel.'

'I'd finished,' said Emma, 'and it's kind of you to ask but it's—it's...'

'None of my business. Quite right, it isn't. I'll drive you home. Where do you live?'

'The end cottage along Victoria Quay. But I can walk. It is at the end of Main Street and you can't drive there.'

He didn't answer but backed the car and turned and went out of the car park and drove up the narrow road to the back of the town. It was a very long way round and he had to park by the pub.

As he stopped Emma said, 'Thank you. I hope I haven't spoilt your afternoon.'

It would hardly do to tell her that he was enjoying every minute of it. 'I'll walk along with you, just in case the rat has got there first.'

'Do you think he has? I mean, I don't suppose he'll want to se me again.' She sniffed. 'I certainly don't want to see him.'

The doctor got out of the car and opened her door. It was a splendid car, she noticed, a dark blue Rolls-Royce, taking up almost all the space before the pub.

'You have a nice car,' said Emma, feeling that she owed him something more than thanks. And then blushed because it had been a silly thing to say. Walking beside him, she reflected that although she had wanted to meet him she could have wished for other circumstances.

Her mother wasn't home and Emma heaved a sigh of relief. Explaining to her mother would be better done later on.

The doctor took the key from her and opened the door, then stood looking at her. Mindful of her manners she asked, 'Would you like a cup of tea? Or perhaps you want to go back to the hotel—someone waiting for you...?'

She was beginning to realise that he never answered a question unless he wanted to, and when he said quietly that he would like a cup of tea she led the way into the cottage.

'Do sit down,' said Emma. 'I'll put the kettle on.' And at the same time run a comb through her mop of hair and make sure that her face didn't look too frightful...

It was tear-stained and pale and in need of powder and lipstick, but that couldn't be helped. She put the kettle on, laid a tray, found the cake tin and made the tea. When she went back into the sitting room he was standing in front of a watercolour of her old home.

'Your home?' he wanted to know.

'Until a month or so ago. Do you take milk and sugar?'

He sat down and took the cup and saucer she was offering him. 'Do you want to talk about the—er—rat? None of my business, of course, but doctors are the next best thing to priests when one wishes to give vent to strong feelings.'

Emma offered cake. 'You have been very kind, and I'm so grateful. But there's nothing—that is, he'll go back to London and I can forget him.'

'Of course. Do you enjoy your work at the library?'

She was instantly and unreasonably disappointed that he hadn't shown more interest or concern. She said stiffly, 'Yes, very much. Miss Johnson tells me that you don't live here, that you are filling in for another doctor?'

'Yes, I shall be sorry to leave…'

'Not yet?'

His heavy-lidded eyes gleamed. 'No, no. I'm looking forward to the summer here.' He put down his cup and saucer. 'Thank you for the tea. If you're sure there is nothing more I can do for you, I'll be off.'

Well, he had no reason to stay, thought Emma. She was hardly scintillating company. Probably there was someone—a girl—waiting impatiently at the hotel for him.

'I hope I haven't hindered you.'

'Not in the least.'

She stood in the doorway watching him walking away, back to his car. He must think her a tiresome hysterical woman, because that was how she had behaved. And all the fault of Derek. She swallowed rage at the thought of him and went back to clear away the tea tray and lay it anew for her mother.

Mrs Dawson had had a pleasant day; she began to tell Emma about it as she came into the cottage, and it wasn't until she had had her tea and paused for breath that she noticed Emma's puffy lids and lightly pink nose.

'Emma, you've been crying. Whatever for? You never cry. You're not ill?'

'Derek came,' said Emma.

Before she could utter another word her mother cried, 'There— I knew he would. He's changed his mind, he wants to marry you—splendid; we can leave here and go back to Richmond…'

'I would not marry Derek if he was the last man on earth,' said Emma roundly. 'He said things—most unkind things—about Father...'

'You never refused him?'

'Yes, I did. He took me to lunch and I left him at the table. I met one of the doctors from the health centre and he brought me home. Derek is a rat and a worm, and if he comes here again I shall throw something at him.'

'You must be out of your mind, Emma. Your future—our future—thrown away for no reason at all. Even if Derek upset you by speaking unkindly of your father, I'm sure he had no intention of wounding you.'

'I'm not going to marry Derek, Mother, and I hope I never set eyes on him again.'

And Emma, usually soft-hearted over her mother's whims and wishes, wouldn't discuss it any more, despite that lady's tears and gentle complaints that the miserable life she was forced to lead would send her to an early grave.

She declared that she had a headache when they got back from evensong, and retired to bed with a supper tray and a hot water bottle.

Emma pottered about downstairs, wondering if she was being selfish and ungrateful. But, even if she were, Derek was still a worm and she couldn't think how she had ever thought of marrying him.

Mrs Dawson maintained her gentle air of patient suffering for the rest of the following week, until Emma left the house on Saturday morning to clean the cottage. The week's tenants had had a large family of children and she welcomed the prospect of hard work. As indeed it was; the little place looked as though it had been hit by a cyclone. It would take all her time to get it pristine for the next family.

She set to with a will and was in the kitchen, giving everything a final wipe-down, when the cottage door opened and Mrs Brooke-Tigh came in, and with her Dr van Dyke and a pretty woman of about Emma's own age.

Mrs Brooke-Tigh ignored her. 'You're so lucky,' she declared loudly, 'that I had this last-minute cancellation. Take a quick look round and see if it will suit. The next party are due here in half an hour but the girl's almost finished.'

'The girl', scarlet-faced, had turned her back but then had to turn round again. 'Miss Dawson,' said Dr van Dyke, 'what a pleasant surprise. This is my sister, who plans to come for a week with her children.'

He turned to the woman beside him. 'Wibeke, this is Emma Dawson; she lives here.'

Emma wiped a soapy hand on her pinny and shook hands, wishing herself anywhere else but there, and listened to Wibeke saying how pleased she was to meet her while Mrs Brooke-Tigh, at a loss for words for once, tapped an impatient foot.

Presently she led them away to see round the cottage, and when they were on the point of leaving Mrs Brooke-Tigh said loudly, 'I'll be back presently to pay you, Emma. Leave the cleaning things at my back door as you go.'

The perfect finish for a beastly week, thought Emma, grinding her splendid teeth.

And Mrs Brooke-Tigh hardly improved matters when she paid Emma.

'It doesn't do to be too familiar with the tenants,' she pointed out. 'I hardly think it necessary to tell you that. Don't be late on Wednesday.'

Emma, who was never late, bade her good afternoon in a spine-chilling voice and went home.

It would have been very satisfying to have tossed the bucket and mop at Mrs Brooke-Tigh and never returned, but with the bucket and mop there would have gone sixty pounds, not forgetting the tips left on the dressing table. She would have to put up with Mrs Brooke-Tigh until the season ended, and in the meantime she would keep her ears open for another job. That might mean going to Kingsbridge every day, since so many of the shops and hotels closed for the winter at Salcombe.

Too soon to start worrying, Emma told herself as she laid out some of the sixty pounds on a chicken for Sunday lunch and one of the rich creamy cakes from the patisserie which her mother enjoyed.

To make up for her horrid Saturday, Sunday was nice, warm and sunny so that she was able to wear a jersey dress, slightly out of date but elegant, and of a pleasing shade of blue. After matins, while her mother chatted with friends, a pleasant young man with an engaging smile introduced himself as Mrs Craig's son.

'Here for a few days,' he told her, and, 'I don't know a soul. Do take pity on me and show me round.'

He was friendly and she readily agreed. 'Though I have part time jobs...'

'When are you free? What about tomorrow morning?'

'I must do the shopping...'

'Splendid, I'll come with you and carry the basket. We could have coffee. Where shall I meet you?'

'At the bakery at the bottom of Main Street, about ten o'clock?'

'Right, I'll look forward to that. The name's Brian, by the way.'

'Emma,' said Emma. 'Your mother is waiting and so's mine.'

'Such a nice boy,' said her mother over lunch, and added, 'He is twenty-three, just qualified as a solicitor. He's rather young, of course...' She caught Emma's eye. 'It is a great pity that you sent Derek away.'

Emma quite liked shopping, and she enjoyed it even more with Brian to carry her basket and talk light-heartedly about anything which caught his eye. They lingered over coffee and then went back through the town to collect sausages from the butcher. His shop was next to one of the restaurants in the town and Brian paused outside it.

'This looks worth a visit. Have dinner with me one evening, Emma?'

'Not on Tuesday or Thursday; I work at the library.'

'Wednesday? Shall we meet here, inside, at half past seven.'

'I'd like that, thank you.' She smiled at him. 'Thank you for the coffee; I've enjoyed my morning.'

Miss Johnson was grumpy on Tuesday evening and Mrs Brooke-Tigh was more than usually high-handed the following day. She couldn't find fault with Emma's work, but somehow she managed to give the impression that it wasn't satisfactory. Which made the prospect of an evening out with Brian very inviting. Emma put on the jersey dress once more and went along to the restaurant.

Brian was waiting for her, obviously glad to see her, and sat her down at the small table, ordering drinks.

In reply to her enquiry as to what he thought of the town he smiled wryly. 'It's a charming little place, but after London's bright lights... What do you do with yourself all day long?'

'Me? Well, there's the library and the shopping, and all the chores, and we're beginning to know more people now.'

'You don't get bored? My mother likes living here; it's a splendid place for elderly widows: nice hotels, bridge, coffee, reading a good book in the sun, gossiping—but you are rather young for that.'

'I've been coming here ever since I was a small girl. It's a kind of a second home, although most of the people I knew have left the town. But I'm quite content.'

They went to their table and ate lobster and a complicated ice cream pudding, and finished a bottle of white wine between them, lingering over their coffee until Emma said, 'I really must go home. Mother insisted that she would wait up for me and she sleeps badly.'

'I'm going back on Friday. But I'm told there's a good pub at Hope Cove. Will you have lunch with me there? I'll pick you up around twelve-thirty?'

'Thank you, that would be nice. If you like walking we could go along the beach if the tide's out.'

'Splendid. I'll walk you back.'

They parted at the cottage door in a friendly fashion, though

Emma was aware that he only sought her company because he was bored and didn't know anyone else...

Her mother was in her dressing gown, eager for an account of her evening.

'You'll go out with him again if he asks you?' she enquired eagerly.

'I'm having lunch with him on Friday.' Emma yawned and kicked off her best shoes. 'He's going back to London; I think he is bored here.'

'Mrs Craig was telling me that she wishes he would settle down...'

'Well, he won't here; that's a certainty.' Emma kissed her mother goodnight and went to bed, aware that her mother had hoped for more than a casual friendship with Brian.

He is still a boy, thought Emma sleepily, and allowed her thoughts to turn to Dr van Dyke who, she suspected, was very much a man.

Miss Johnson was still grumpy on Thursday evening, but since it was pay day Emma forgave her. Besides, she was kept busy by people wanting books for the weekend. She felt quite light-hearted as she went home, her wages in her purse, planning something tasty for the weekend which wouldn't make too large a hole in the housekeeping.

Friday was warm and sunny, and she was out early to do the weekend shopping for there would be no time on Saturday. Her mother was going out to lunch with one of her new-found friends and Emma raced around, getting everything ready for cooking the supper and, just in case Brian wanted to come back for tea, she laid a tea tray.

He came promptly and they walked through the town to the car park. He drove up the road bordering the estuary onto the main road and then turned off to Hope Cove. The road was narrow now, running through fields, with a glimpse of the sea. When they reached the tiny village and parked by the pub there were already a number of cars there.

The pub was dark and oak-beamed and low-ceilinged inside, and already quite full.

Brian looked around him. 'I like this place—full of atmosphere and plenty of life. What shall we eat?'

They had crab sandwiches, and he had a beer and Emma a glass of white wine, and since there was no hurry they sat over the food while he told her of his work.

'Of course I could never leave London,' he told her. 'I've a flat overlooking the river and any number of friends and a good job. I shall have to come and see Mother from time to time, but a week is about as much as I can stand.' He added, 'Don't you want to escape, Emma?'

'Me? Where to?'

'Mother told me that you lived in Richmond. You must have had friends...'

'My father went bankrupt,' she said quietly. 'Yes, we had friends—fair-weather friends. And we're happy here. Mother has made several new friends, so she goes out quite a lot, and I'm happy.' She went on, 'If you've finished, shall we walk along the cliff path for a while? The view is lovely...'

She hadn't been quite truthful, she reflected, but she sensed that Brian was a young man who didn't like to be made uneasy. He would go back to his flat and his friends, assuring himself that her life was just what she wanted.

They drove back to Salcombe presently, parked the car at the hotel and walked back through the town.

Outside the bakery Emma stopped. 'Don't come any further,' she suggested. 'If you are going back today I expect you want to see your mother before you go. I enjoyed lunch; Hope Cove is a delightful little place. I hope you have a good journey back home.'

'I'll leave within the hour; it's quite a long trip. I'll be glad to get back. Life's a bit slow here, isn't it? I wish we could have seen more of each other, but I expect you'll still be here if and when I come again.'

'Oh, I expect so.' She offered a hand and he took it and kissed her cheek.

Dr van Dyke, coming round the corner, stopped short, wished them a cheerful hello and gave Emma a look to send the colour into her cheeks. It said all too clearly that she hadn't wasted much time in finding someone to take Derek's place.

He went into the baker's, and she bade a final hasty goodbye to Brian and almost ran to the cottage. The doctor would think... She didn't go too deeply into what he would think; she hoped that she wouldn't see him again for a very long time.

It was a brilliant morning on Saturday, and already warm when she got to Mrs Brooke-Tigh's house, collected her cleaning brushes and cloths and started on her chores. From a bedroom window she watched Mrs Brooke-Tigh go down the lane, swinging her beach bag. On Saturday mornings she went to the hotel at the other end of the town, which had a swimming pool and a delightful terrace where one could laze for hours. The moment she was out of sight the girl in the other cottage crossed over and came upstairs.

'Thought I'd let you know I've given in my notice. She's furious; she'll never get anyone by Wednesday. Wouldn't hurt her to do a bit of housework herself. Mind she doesn't expect you to take on any more work.'

Emma was stripping beds. 'I don't see how she can...'

'She'll think of something. I'd better get on, I suppose. Bye.'

Mrs Brooke-Tigh came back earlier than usual; Emma was setting the tea tray ready for the next tenants when she walked in.

'That girl's leaving,' she told Emma without preamble. 'She never was much good but at least she was a pair of hands. I'll never get anyone else at such short notice. We will have to manage as best we can. I shall notify the next two weeks' tenants that they can't come in until six o'clock. If you come at nine o'clock and work until six you can do both cottages. I'll pay you another fifteen pounds a day—thirty pounds a week more.'

Emma didn't answer at once. The money would be useful... 'I'm willing to do that for the next week and, if I must, the second week. But no longer than that.'

Mrs Brooke-Tigh sniffed. 'I should have thought that you

would have jumped at the chance of more money.' She would have said more, but the look Emma gave her left the words dying on her tongue. Instead she said ungraciously, 'Well, all right, I'll agree to that.' She turned to go. 'Bring your stuff over and I'll pay you.'

There was a car outside the door as she left. It appeared to be full of small children, and a friendly young woman, the one who had been with the doctor, got out. 'I say, hello, how nice to meet you again. We're here for a week so we must get to know each other.' She smiled. 'Where's that woman who runs the place?'

'I'll fetch her,' said Emma, 'and I'd love to see you again.'

CHAPTER THREE

IT WAS quite late in the evening when the phone rang. 'It's me, Wibeke Wolff. There wasn't time to talk so I got that woman to give me your phone number. I do know who you are, Roele told me, so please forgive me for ringing you up. I don't know anyone here. Roele's only free occasionally, and I wondered if you would show me the best places to take the children. A beach where they can be safe in the water? If you would like, could we go somewhere tomorrow? I'll get a picnic organised. This is awful cheek...'

'I'd love a picnic,' said Emma. 'There are some lovely beaches but we don't need to go far tomorrow; there's South Sands only a few minutes in a car. Would that do for a start?'

'It sounds ideal. You're sure you don't mind?'

'No, of course not. Where shall I meet you?'

'Here at this cottage? About ten o'clock? I thought we might come back about three o'clock. You're sure I'm not spoiling your day?'

'No, I'm looking forward to it. And I'll be there in the morning.'

'Who was that, Emma?' Her mother looked hopeful. 'Someone you have met taking you out for lunch?'

'A picnic. Mrs Wibeke Wolff with three children; we're having a picnic lunch at South Sands tomorrow.'

'Oh, well, I suppose it's a change for you. I shall be out in the afternoon; I'll make a sandwich or something for my lunch.'

Emma took this remark for what it was worth. Her mother had no intention of doing any such thing. She said cheerfully, 'I'll leave lunch all ready for you, Mother, and cook supper after we've been to church. Unless you want to go to Matins?'

'You know I need my rest in the morning. Just bring me a cup of tea and I'll manage my own breakfast.'

'If you want to,' said Emma briskly. 'There'll be breakfast as usual in the morning, but if you would rather get up later and cook something?'

'No, no, I'll come down in my dressing gown. I don't have much strength in the morning, but then of course I have always been delicate.'

Emma, her head full of the morrow's picnic, wasn't listening.

Sunday was another glorious morning. Emma got into a cotton dress and sandals, found a straw hat and a swimsuit, got breakfast for her gently complaining parent and made her way through the still quiet streets to the holiday cottages.

Wibeke was loading the car and waved a greeting. As Emma reached her she said, 'I've got the children inside. Everyone here seems to be asleep and they're noisy.'

Emma glanced at Mrs Brooke-Tigh's house. There was no sign of life there and the curtains were still drawn. A good thing, since she didn't approve of the cleaners mixing with the tenants. Emma said, 'Hello, it's going to be a warm day; the beach will be pretty crowded.'

'The children will love that.' Wibeke opened the door and they piled out. 'Hetty, George and Rosie,' said Wibeke as Emma shook hands with them. They were three small excited kids, bursting with impatience to get their day on the beach started. Without waste of time they crowded into the back of the car and, with Emma beside her, Wibeke drove through the town and along the coast road. It was a short drive.

'It's really only a short walk away,' said Emma as they began the business of parking the car and unloading the children and picnic basket, the buckets and spades, the swimsuits...

The beach was full but not crowded. They settled against some rocks and got into their swimsuits, and Wibeke and the children raced to the water's edge while Emma guarded their belongings. It was pleasant sitting there, for the sun was warm but not yet hot enough to be uncomfortable, and there was no one near by. This, she reflected, was the first day out she had had since they'd come to Salcombe. She didn't count Derek or Brian, for she hadn't been at ease with either of them, but Wibeke and the children were friendly and undemanding; she had only just met them and yet she felt that she had known Wibeke for years. Of course they would all be gone in a week, but still she would have pleasant memories...

They came trooping back and Wibeke said, 'It's your turn now. A pity we can't all go together. Do you suppose we might? There's no one very close and we could see our belongings easily...'

'Let's wait and see if the beach fills up.'

The water was chilly, but within seconds Emma was swimming strongly away from the beach and then idling on her back until the thought of Wibeke coping with three small children sent her back again.

Time passed, as it always did when one was happy, far too quickly. They built sandcastles, dug holes and filled them with buckets of water, and went swimming again. This time Wibeke stayed on the beach.

Wibeke was peering into the picnic basket when Dr van Dyke joined her.

'Roele, how lovely. Have you come to lunch? You're wearing all the wrong clothes.'

'I've been to see a patient and I've another call to make; no one is going to take advice from a man in swimming trunks.' He was watching the children and Emma prancing around at the water's edge, her magnificent shape enhanced by her simple swimsuit, her bright hair tied up untidily on the top of her head.

'She's rather gorgeous, isn't she?' Wibeke peeped at her brother. 'She should be out in the fashionable world, with a string of boyfriends and lovely clothes.'

'Never.'

The doctor spoke so emphatically that she stared at him, and then smiled.

'Why, Roele...'

But by then the bathing party were within a few feet of them, and while the children rushed at their uncle Emma hung back, taken by surprise, feeling suddenly shy.

'Hello,' said the doctor easily. 'I see you've been landed with these tiresome brats—sandcastles and looking for crabs and digging holes—you'll be exhausted. Don't let them bully you.' He got up, the children clinging to him. 'I must go—have a lovely day and don't get too much sun.'

He hadn't really looked at her, she reflected, just a casual smile and a wave as he went. She had been silly to feel shy.

By mid-afternoon the children were tired, and they left the now crowded beach and drove back to the cottage.

'Come in and have a cup of tea,' begged Wibeke, but Emma shook her head.

'It's been a lovely day but I really must go home. If you would like me to babysit one evening I'll do that gladly. It'll give you a change to go out if you want to.'

'Would you really? That would be great. What are you doing tomorrow?'

'Shopping, washing, ironing, household chores—but would you all like to come to tea? We're right by the water and there's lots for the children to see.'

'We'd like that. Where exactly do you live?'

Emma told her, bade the sleepy children goodbye, and went home.

Her mother was there, complaining in her gentle voice that it had been far too warm at the hotel, where she had had tea with Mrs Craig. 'I'm not sure that I have the energy to go to evensong.'

'You'll feel better when I've made another cup of tea—China, with a slice of lemon.'

'You enjoyed your day?' asked her mother.

'Very much. The sea's a bit chilly but it was lovely to swim... I've invited Mrs Wolff and the children to tea tomorrow. You might enjoy meeting them.'

'Small children? Emma, dear, you know how quickly I get a headache if there's too much noise, and children are so noisy.'

'You'd like Wibeke—Mrs Wolff...'

'Shall I? How did you meet?'

Emma had glossed over her second job; her mother would have been horrified to know that she was doing someone else's housework. 'Oh,' she said vaguely, 'she is staying for a week in a rented cottage.'

There was no need to say more for her mother had lost interest.

As it turned out, the tea party was a success. Wibeke was a lively talker, full of the light-hearted gossip Mrs Dawson enjoyed, and willing to discuss the latest fashions, the newest plays and films, who was marrying whom and who was getting divorced. When she and the children had gone, Mrs Dawson pronounced her to be a very nice young woman.

'Obviously married well and leading a pleasant social life.' She looked reproachfully at Emma as she spoke. 'Just as you would have if you hadn't been so foolish about Derek.' And when Emma didn't reply she added, 'I must say the children were quiet.'

Well, of course they were, reflected Emma, who had made it her business to keep them occupied—first with a good tea and then with a visit to her bedroom, where they had been allowed to open cupboards and drawers, try on her hats and shoes while George took the books from her bookshelf and piled them in neat heaps. For a three-year-old he was a bright child, so she had hugged him and told him that he was a clever boy, and that had led to hugs for the little girls, too. She felt a stab of envy of Wibeke...

The doctor called on his sister in the late evening.

She gave him a drink and sat down opposite him in the little living room.

'We all went to Emma's cottage and had tea. Have you met her mother? Darling, she's a ball and chain round Emma's neck. Charming, small and dainty and wistful, harping on about having to live here after an obviously comfortable life at Richmond. Told me that Emma had chosen to reject some man or other who wanted to marry her.'

The doctor smiled. 'Ah, yes, the rat...'

Wibeke sat up. 'You know about him? Have you met him?'

'I happened to be handy at the time. He would never have done for Emma.'

'Perhaps she will meet a man here, though she doesn't have much of a social life. Not that she says much; it's what she doesn't say...'

'Quite. Is Harry coming down on Saturday to see you back home?'

This was a change of conversation not to be ignored. 'Yes, bless him. He'll take George and most of the luggage, and I'll have the girls. We plan to leave quite early.' She peeped at the doctor. 'Before Emma starts her cleaning.'

And if she had expected an answer to that, she didn't get it.

When Emma got to the cottages in the morning there was a good deal of bustle. The children, reluctant to go, were being stowed into their mother's car, and Wibeke was fastening George into his seat behind his father, who was packing in the luggage.

'We're off,' cried Wibeke as soon as she saw Emma. 'This is Harry. Come and say hello and goodbye!'

Which Emma did, uncaring of the fact that she would be late starting her day's cleaning and sorry to see them go. She had liked Wibeke and Wibeke had liked her; they could have been friends...

The little lane seemed very quiet when they had driven away, as Emma fetched her bucket and brushes and started work.

It was a scramble to be finished by six o'clock, and the second lot of tenants drove up as she closed the door. She had managed to get one cottage ready in time for the early arrival of its occupants, but she told herself that, despite the extra money, one more week of doing two persons' work was all she intended to do.

She told Mrs Brooke-Tigh that when she stowed away her cleaning things.

'You young women are all the same,' said Mrs Brooke-Tigh

nastily. 'Do as little as you can get away with for as much as possible.'

'Well,' said Emma sweetly, 'if you cleaned two of the cottages you would only need to find one young woman.'

Mrs Brooke-Tigh gave her a look of horrified indignation. Emma didn't give her a chance to reply but wished her good evening and went home. She was tired and, not only that, she was dispirited; the future, as far as she could see, was uninviting. The pleasant hours she had spent with Wibeke and the children had made that clear.

As though that wasn't bad enough, she was met by her mother's excited admission that she had seen the most charming dress at the boutique. 'Such a sweet colour, palest blue—you know how that suits me, dear—I just had to have it. I've not had anything new for months. When your dear father was alive he never grudged me anything.'

Emma took off her shoes from her aching feet. 'Mother, Father had money; we haven't—only just enough to keep us going. How much was the dress?'

Her mother pouted. 'I knew you'd make a fuss.' She began to weep tears of self-pity. 'And to think that everything could have been so different if only you hadn't sent Derek away.'

Too tired to argue, Emma went to the kitchen to start the supper, and while she cooked it she drank a mug of very strong tea—a bottle of brandy would have been nice, or champagne. In fact anything which would drown her feeling of frustration. Something would have to be done, but what? Her mother had made up her mind to be unhappy at Salcombe; she had always taken it for granted that anything she wanted she could have and she had made no attempt to understand that that was no longer possible. If only something would happen...

She was coming out of the bakery on Monday morning when she met Dr van Dyke going in. He wasted no time on polite greetings. 'The very person I wanted to see. Wait while I get my pasties.'

Outside the shop, Emma asked, 'Why do you fetch pasties? Haven't you got a housekeeper or someone to look after you?'

'Yes, yes, of course I have, but when I have a visit at one of the outlying farms I take my lunch with me. Don't waste time asking silly questions. One of my partners is unexpectedly short of a receptionist and general dogsbody. No time to go to an agency or advertise. He's a bit desperate. Would you care to take on the job, Monday to Friday, until he can get things sorted out? Half past eight until eleven o'clock, then five in the afternoon until half past six.'

She stood gaping at him. 'You really mean it? Would I really do?'

'I don't see why not; you seem a sensible girl. Oh, and there's no evening surgery on Tuesdays and Thursdays.'

'So I could still work at the library?'

'Yes. Come up to the surgery after eleven o'clock and see Dr Walters. Talk it over with him.'

He nodded goodbye and strode away. Emma watched him go, not quite believing any of it but knowing that after eleven o'clock she would be at the surgery, doing her best to look like a suitable applicant for the post of receptionist.

She did the rest of the shopping in a hopeful haze, hurried home to tidy her unruly hair and get into her less scruffy sandals, told her mother that she would be back for lunch and made her way through the town.

The surgery was at the back of the town, away from the main street. It was pleasantly situated in a quiet street, and even if the surgery hours were over it was still busy. Bidden to wait, since Dr Walters was seeing his last patient, Emma sat down in the waiting room and whiled away ten minutes or so leafing through out-of-date copies of country magazines, at the same time rehearsing the kind of replies she might be expected to give. Since she had no idea of the questions she would be asked, it was a fruitless occupation.

The moment she entered Dr Walters's surgery she knew that she need not have worried. He was a small middle-aged man, with the kind of trustful face which made women want to mother him. He was also a very good doctor, though untidy, and forgetful of anything which wasn't connected with his work or his patients. His desk was an untidy mass of papers, patients' notes, various forms and a pile of unopened letters.

He got up as she went in, dislodging papers and knocking over a small pot full of pens.

'Miss Dawson.' He came round the desk to shake hands. 'Dr van Dyke told me that you might consider helping out—my receptionist and secretary, Mrs Crump, had to leave at a moment's notice—her daughter has had an accident. She will return, of course, but I need help until she does.'

He waved Emma to a chair and went back behind the desk. 'Have you any experience of this type of work?'

'None at all—' there was no point in pretending otherwise '—but I can answer the telephone, file papers, sort out the post, make appointments and usher patients in and out.'

Dr Walters peered at her over his old-fashioned spectacles. 'You're honest. Shall we give it a trial? I'm desperate for help with the paperwork. I can't pay you the usual salary because you aren't trained. Could we settle for—let me see...' He named a sum which made Emma blink.

'I'm not worth that much,' she told him, 'but I'd like the job.'

'It's yours until Mrs Crump gets back. If after a week I think that you don't deserve the money I'll reduce it. No references— Dr van Dyke seems to know enough about you. Start tomorrow? Half past eight? We'll see how we get on.'

For all his mild appearance, Emma reflected, he certainly knew his own mind.

The next few months were the happiest Emma had spent since her father died. She sorted patients' notes from letters, and letters from the endless junk mail, she kept the doctor's desk tidy, and saw that the day's patients were clearly listed and laid on his blotter where he couldn't possibly mislay the list, she answered the phone and booked patients in and out. She didn't attempt to

do any of Mrs Crump's skilled jobs, and she had no doubt that
that lady would have a great deal of work to deal with when she
returned, but she did her best and Dr Walters, once he realised
her limitations, made no complaint.

And in all that time she barely glimpsed Dr van Dyke. A brief
good morning if they should meet at the surgery, a wave of the
hand if she passed him on her way home... She told herself that
there was no reason for him to do more than acknowledge her,
but all the same she was disappointed.

All the wrong men like me, she thought crossly, and when I
do meet a man I would like to know better he ignores me.

The season was at its height when Mrs Dawson received an
invitation to go and stay with an elderly couple who had been
friendly with her and her husband before his death. The friendship
had cooled, but now it seemed that sufficient time had glossed
over the unfortunate circumstances following his death and they
expressed themselves delighted at the prospect of a visit from her.

'So kind,' declared Mrs Dawson. 'Of course I shall accept!
How delightful it will be to go back to the old life, even if it is
only for a few weeks. You will be able to manage on your own,
won't you, Emma? You are so seldom home these days, and
although I'm sure you don't mean to neglect me I am sometimes
lonely. There is so little to do,' she added peevishly.

There were several answers to that, but Emma uttered none of
them.

'I shall be perfectly all right, Mother. You'll enjoy the change,
won't you? When do they want you to go? We must see about
travelling. Someone will meet you at Paddington?'

'Yes, I couldn't possibly manage on my own. I shall need some
new clothes...'

Emma thought of the small nest egg at the bank. 'I'm sure we
can manage something; you have some pretty dresses...'

'Last year's,' snapped her mother. 'Everyone will recognise
them.' She added, 'After all, you take half my pension each
week.'

They mustn't quarrel, thought Emma. 'You will have all of it while you are away,' she pointed out gently, 'and we'll put our heads together about some new clothes for you.'

'I must say that since your father died, Emma, you have become very bossy and mean. I suppose it's the result of living here in this poky little cottage with no social life.'

'Now I'm working at the medical centre I haven't much time to be sociable. And, Mother, we couldn't manage unless I had a job. When do you plan to go?'

'On Friday. I'll collect my pension on Thursday; that will give me a little money in my purse. I want to go to the boutique tomorrow and see if there is anything that I can afford.' She looked at Emma. 'How much money can I spend?'

When Emma told her, she said, 'Not nearly enough, but I suppose I'll have to manage.'

A most unsatisfactory conversation, thought Emma, lying in bed and doing sums in her head that night. Mrs Crump wasn't going to stay at home for ever. Sooner or later she would lose her job, and with summer coming to an end so would the kind of jobs she could apply for. Of course she could live more cheaply when her mother had gone, but once summer was over there would be the cottage to keep warm and lighted.

She shook up her pillows again, determined to think of something else. And that wasn't at all satisfactory, for all she could think about was the complete lack of interest in her envinced by Dr van Dyke.

Mrs Dawson spent a good deal more money than Emma had bargained for. There had been such a splendid choice, her mother enthused, and really the prices were so reasonable it would have been foolish to ignore such bargains. At least she was happy getting ready for her visit, talking about nothing else.

Emma, tidying books on the library shelves, listening to Phoebe's cheerful gossip, thought about her day with Dr Walters. He had been untidier than usual, and his morning patients had taken longer than usual too. It had been almost one o'clock before she had been ready to leave, and then she had discovered his scribbled note asking her to return for an hour that afternoon as he had arranged to see a patient privately.

She had hurried home, got lunch and rushed to the shops with her Mother's wispy voice echoing in her ears; there was so much to tell her about the letter she had received from her friends and Emma couldn't be bothered to stay and listen. Emma, racing in and out of the butcher, the greengrocer and the bakery, prayed for patience…!

Getting her mother away on time, properly packed and the journey made as easy as possible, hadn't been the problem she had feared. Mrs Craig had offered to drive her mother to Totnes to catch the train, and the prospect of leaving Salcombe had changed her from a disgruntled woman to a charming lady who, having got what she wanted, was prepared to be nice to everyone. All the same Emma, who loved her mother, missed her.

Life became more leisurely as there was less of everything to do: meals didn't need to be on time, the cottage, with only her in it, was easy to keep clean and tidy, and it no longer mattered if she needed to stay late at the surgery.

Her mother was happy too; she had met several old friends, all of whom wanted her to visit them. 'I shan't be home yet,' she told Emma gleefully. Emma, relieved to know that her mother was once more living the life she enjoyed, permitted herself to forget the worries of the forthcoming winter. The summer was sliding gently into autumn, and although there were still plenty of visitors very soon now the shops would close for the winter. And still there was no news of Mrs Crump's return…

Her mother had been gone for two weeks when Dr Walters, sipping coffee after the morning surgery, began tossing the papers on his desk all over the place. He found what he wanted, a letter, and he put on his glasses.

'News, Emma. I have heard from Mrs Crump. She at last sees her way clear to returning to work.' He glanced at the letter. 'In a week's time. That brings us to Friday, which is most convenient for there is no surgery on Saturday, so you will be able to leave after Friday evening surgery.'

He beamed at her across the desk. 'I must say I shall be sorry to see you go; you have been of great help to me. I'm sure I don't know how I would have managed without you. You will be glad to be free again, no doubt?'

'Yes,' said Emma steadily, 'that will be nice, Dr Walters, although I have enjoyed working here for you. I expect Mrs Crump will be delighted to come back to work and you will be equally pleased to have her.'

'Indeed, I shall.' He put down his cup. 'I must be off. I'll leave you to clear up and I'll see you this evening.'

Emma set about putting the place to rights, her thoughts chaotic. She should have been prepared for the news but she had been lulled by several weeks of silence from Mrs Crump so that leaving had become a comfortably vague event which she didn't need to be worried about just yet. She would have to set about finding another job, for her hours at the library would hardly keep body and soul together.

She finished her chores and left the medical centre just as Dr van Dyke got out of his car. For once he stopped to speak to her.

'Rather late leaving, aren't you? Not being overworked, are you?'

'No, no, thank you.' She tried to think of something casual to say, but her mind was blank and at any moment now she was going to burst into tears.

'I must hurry,' she told him, and almost ran down the road.

He stood watching her fast retreating back, frowning; he had been careful to avoid her during the past months, aware that she attracted him and just as aware that he would be returning to Holland within a few weeks and that to allow the attraction to grow would be foolhardy. Perhaps it was a good thing that she showed no signs of even liking him.

He went along to his surgery and forgot about her. But later that evening he allowed his thoughts to return to her, smiling a little at her rage at the hotel and then again at the quite different Emma, playing with the children on the sands.

* * *

Back at the cottage, Emma gave way to her feelings. The situation called for a good cry, not a gentle flow of tears easily wiped away with a dainty hanky and a few sighs. She sat bawling her eyes out, her face awash, sniffing and snuffling and wiping away the tears with her hands, catching her breath like a child. It was a great relief, and presently she found a hanky and mopped her face and felt better. It was something which she had known would happen, and she told herself that it wasn't the end of the world; she would soon find another job—probably not as well paid, but enough to live on. It was a good thing that her mother was away…

She washed her sodden face, tidied her hair and made a sandwich and a pot of tea, and, not wishing to show her red nose and puffy lids to the outside world, spent the afternoon doing the ironing. By the time it was necessary to go back to work she was almost herself again, fortified by yet more tea and careful repairs to her face.

There were a lot of patients, and Dr Walters was far too busy to do more than glance at her. Confident that she looked exactly as usual, she ushered patients in and out, found notes and made herself generally useful. Only to come face to face with Dr van Dyke.

She tried sidling past him and found her arm gently held.

'So you will be leaving us, Emma. Dr Walters is sorry to see you go, but I dare say you will be glad of more leisure?'

'Oh, I shall, I shall… I can't stop. Dr Walters wants some notes.'

He took his hand away and she skipped off to hide behind a cupboard door until he had gone. The less she saw of him the better, she told herself, and knew that that wasn't true. But he would be gone in a few weeks and she would forget him.

The week went too rapidly, and her last day came. She said goodbye to everyone—everyone except Dr van Dyke, who had gone across the estuary to East Portlemouth to deliver a baby.

'You're bound to see him around the town before he leaves,' observed Dr Walters. 'We shall miss him, but of course he wants to go back to his own practice, and naturally we shall all be glad

to see Dr Finn back again. Probably he will bring back a number
of new ideas from the States.'

There was a letter from her mother when she got home; she
wouldn't be coming home for the next week or so, she wrote.

*And Alice Riddley—remember her, my old schoolfriend—has
made an exciting suggestion to me, but I will let you know more
about that later, when we have discussed it thoroughly. I'm sure
you are enjoying yourself without your tiresome old mother to
look after. Make lots of young friends, Emma, and buy yourself
some pretty dresses. You can afford them now that I'm not at
home to buy food for.*

Emma folded the letter carefully. Why was it that her mother
always made her feel guilty? As for new clothes, every penny
would need to be hoarded until she had more work. She would
start looking on Monday...

Mrs Craig stopped her after church on Sunday. 'I have had a
letter from your mother; she hints at all kinds of exciting happen-
ings for the future. Do you know what she means, dear?'

'No, I've no idea, Mrs Craig. She mentioned that she would
have something to tell me later, but I've no idea what it is. She
won't be coming home for another week or two.'

'You're not lonely, Emma?'

'Not a bit; the days are never long enough...'

A pity she couldn't say the same of the nights. Why is it, she
wondered, that one's brain is needle-sharp around three o'clock
in the morning, allowing one to make impossible plans, do complicated mental arithmetic and see the future in a pessimistic light?

She started her job-hunting on the Monday. The season was
coming to an end, temporary jobs would finish very soon, and
since so many of the shops would shut until the spring there was
no question of them taking on more staff. The holiday cottages

to rent would lock their doors and the few for winter-letting were maintained by their owners.

After several days Emma realised that she would have to go to Kingsbridge and find work there. It would mean a daily bus ride, and not much leisure, but if she could find something full-time that would see them through the winter. There was a large supermarket there which sounded promising...

She had seen nothing of Dr van Dyke. Perhaps he had already left, she wondered, and found the thought depressed her. He might not have liked her but she would have liked to have known him better. And he had been very kind about Derek.

She went to the library on Thursday evening, and as they packed up Miss Johnson called her over. 'After this week we shall be closing down the evening session and I'm afraid there won't be enough work for you to continue, Emma. We shall be sorry to let you go but there wouldn't be anything for you to do. If you would come on Tuesday evening and help us go through the shelves and generally tidy up...'

Emma found her voice. It didn't sound quite like hers but at least it was steady. 'I shall miss working here. Perhaps I could come back next year? And of course I'll come on Tuesday.' She said goodnight, called a cheerful greeting to Phoebe and went home.

This was something she hadn't foreseen. The money from the library wasn't enough to live on, but it would have helped to eke out her savings until she was working again. This time she didn't cry; she hadn't time for that. She would have to plan for the next few weeks, pay one or two outstanding bills, think up some cheap menus. At least she had only herself to think about.

She was getting into bed much later when she heard a faint whine. It sounded as though it was coming from the front garden and she went downstairs to have a look, opening the door cautiously, forgetful that she was in her nightie and with bare feet.

There was a very small dog peering at her through the closed gate, and she went at once to open it. The cottage next door was empty of visitors so there was no one about. The dog crept past her and slid into the cottage, its tail between its legs, shivering.

Emma fetched a bowl of bread and milk and watched the little beast wolf it down. It was woefully thin, its coat bedraggled, and there was a cut over one eye. There was no question of sending it on its way. She fetched an old towel and rubbed the skinny little body while the dog shivered and shook under her gentle hands.

'More bread and milk?' said Emma. 'And a good night's sleep. Tomorrow I shall give you a good wash. I always wanted a dog and it seems I'm meant to have one.'

She carried him upstairs to bed then, wrapped in a towel, and he fell asleep before she had turned out the light. She went to sleep too, quite forgetful of the fact that she was out of work and, worse, was never going to see Dr van Dyke again.

CHAPTER FOUR

IT WAS raining when she woke up in the early morning and the little dog was still asleep, wrapped in the towel. But he opened frightened eyes the moment she moved and cowered away from her hand.

'My poor dear,' said Emma. 'Don't be frightened. You're going to live here and turn into a handsome dog, and in any case this is no weather to turn you out into the street.'

He pricked up his ears at her voice and wagged a wispy tail, and presently, rendered bold by the promise of breakfast, went cautiously downstairs with her.

She had intended job-hunting directly after breakfast, but that would have to wait for a while. Full of a good breakfast, the dog accepted her efforts to clean him up, sitting on his towel in the little kitchen, being washed and dried and gently brushed. When she had finished he looked more like a dog, and cautiously licked her hand as she cleaned the wound over his eye. By that time it was mid-morning and he was ready for another meal...

Emma found an old blanket, arranged it in one of the chairs, and with the aid of a biscuit urged him into it.

'I'm going out,' she told him. 'You need food and so do I.'

A marrow bone was added to the sausages for her own lunch, suitable dog food and dog biscuits and, in one of the small shops which sold everything, a collar and lead. She went back in the rain and found him asleep, but he instantly awoke when she went in, cowering down into the blanket.

She gave him another biscuit and told him that he was a brave boy, then fastened the collar round his scrawny neck and went into the garden with him and waited patiently while he pottered among the flowerbeds and then sped back indoors.

'Time for another meal,' said Emma, and opened a tin. Since

he was still so frightened and cowed she stayed home for the rest of the day, and was rewarded by the lessening of his cringing fear and his obvious pleasure in his food. By bedtime he was quite ready to go upstairs with her and curl up on her feet in bed, anxious to please, looking at her with large brown eyes.

'Tomorrow,' she told him, 'I must go looking for work, but you'll be safe here and we will go for a little walk together and you'll learn to be a dog again. I have no doubt that before long you will be a very handsome dog.'

The rain had stopped by morning. The dog went timidly into the garden, ate his breakfast and settled down on his blanket.

'I won't be long,' Emma told him, and went into the town to buy the local paper. There weren't many jobs going, and the two she went after had already been taken. She went home dispirited, to be instantly cheered by the dog's delight at seeing her again.

'Something will turn up,' she told him, watching him eat a splendid dinner. 'You'll bring me luck. You must have a name...' She considered that for a minute or two. 'Percy,' she told him.

She took him for a short walk later, trotting beside her on his lead, but he was quickly tired so she picked him up and carried him home.

And it seemed as though he *was* bringing her luck for there were two jobs in the newsagent's window the next day. She wrote down their addresses and went home to write to them. She wasn't sure what a 'general assistant' in one of the hotel's kitchens might mean, but the hotel would be open all winter. And the second job was part-time at an antiques shop at the end of an alley leading off Main Street. She was tempted to call there instead of writing, but that might lessen her chances of getting the job.

She posted her letters, saw to Percy's needs, had her supper and went to bed, confident that the morning would bring good news.

It brought another letter from her mother, a lengthy one, and Emma wondered at her Mother's opening words. 'At last you will be free to live your own life, Emma.'

Emma put down her teacup and started to read and when she

had read it, she read it again. Her mother and her old schoolfriend had come to a decision; they would share life together.

We shall live at the cottage, but since she has a car we can go to Richmond, where she will keep her flat, whenever we want a change. I'm sure you will agree with me that this is an excellent idea, and since I shall be providing a home for her she will pay all expenses. So, Emma, you will be free to do whatever you like. Of course we shall love to see you as often as you like to come. Such a pity that there are only two bedrooms, but when we go to Richmond you can use the cottage.

Emma drank her cooling tea. She had no job, she had received her very last pay from Miss Johnson, and now, it seemed, she was to have no home.

'Well, things can't get worse,' said Emma, and offered the toast which she no longer wanted to Percy. 'So things will get better. I'll advertise in the paper for a live-in job where dogs are welcome.'

Brave words! But Emma was sensible and practical as well. There was work for anyone who wanted it; it was just a question of finding it. Since her mother now didn't intend to return for another week or so she had all the time in the world to go looking for it.

There were no replies to her two letters, but there was still time for their answers. She didn't give up her search, though, and filled in her days with turning Percy into a well-groomed, well-fed dog. He would never be handsome, and the scar over his eye had left a bald patch, but she considered that he was a credit to her. More than that, he helped her to get through the disappointing days.

She had written to her mother, and it had been a difficult letter to write. That her mother had had no intention of upsetting her was obvious, but circumstances had arisen which would make it possible for her to live in comfort with a congenial companion and she had brushed aside any obstacles which might stand in her way. She had had no difficulty in persuading herself that Emma would be glad to be independent and she had written cheerfully to that effect, unconcerned as to how Emma would achieve that independence.

It might take a little time, Emma had pointed out, before she could find work which would pay her enough to give her her independence, but no doubt that was something which had been considered in their plans and in any case Salcombe was still full of visitors. Which wasn't quite true, but Emma had felt justified in saying so. The longer her mother delayed coming back to Salcombe the better were her chances of getting a job.

The days went by. She went to Kingsbridge by bus and spent the day searching out agencies and scanning the adverts in the newspaper shops, and finally she tried the supermarket. No chance of work, she was told roundly. They were shedding seasonal staff, and if a vacancy occurred it would go to someone local.

It was early evening by the time she got back and Percy was waiting impatiently. She fed him and took him for a walk, and went to get her own supper. Almost another week, she reflected. Unless something turns up tomorrow I shall have to write to Mother and tell her I can't leave until I can find a job...

She wasn't hungry; Percy gobbled up most of her supper and went back to sleep on his blanket and she sat down to peruse the local paper. Work was getting scarce now that the season was almost over and there was nothing there for her. She sat in the darkening evening, doing nothing—for once her cheerful optimism had left her.

Someone knocking on the door roused her and Percy gave a small squeaky bark, although he didn't get off the blanket.

Dr van Dyke was on the doorstep.

Emma was conscious of the delight and relief she felt surge through her person at the sight of him—like finding a familiar tree in a wood in which she had been lost. She stood there looking at him, saying nothing at all.

When he asked, 'May I come in?' she found her tongue.

'Yes, of course. Did you want to see me about something?'

He followed her into the living room and closed the door. He said coolly, 'No, I was walking this way and it seemed a good idea to call and see how you are getting on.' His eye fell on Percy. He lifted an eyebrow. 'Yours?'

'Yes. His name is Percy.'

He bent to stroke Percy's untidy head. 'Your mother is not home?'

'Mother's away, staying with friends in Richmond. Won't you sit down? Would you like a cup of coffee?'

She must match his coolness with her own, she thought, and sat down composedly, facing him, forgetful of the table-lamp which highlighted her face.

'What is the matter, Emma?'

The question was unexpected, and she said far too quickly, 'The matter? Why, nothing. Have you been busy at the medical centre?'

'No more than usual. I asked you what is the matter, Emma?'

He sounded kind and friendly in an impersonal way, but he watched her from under his heavy-lidded eyes. The weeks without a regular sight of her carroty topknot and their occasional brief meetings had made it plain to him that the strong attraction he felt for her had become something beyond his control; he had fallen in love with her.

He smiled at her now and she looked away quickly. 'Oh, it's nothing. I'm a bit disappointed at not finding another job, and the library doesn't want me now that summer's over...'

When he remained silent, she said with barely concealed ill-humour, 'I'll make some coffee.'

'You have no work, no money and you are lonely.'

She said waspishly, 'You've put it very clearly, and now, you know, I think you should go...'

'You will feel better if you talk to someone, and I am here, am I not? What is more, I have the added advantage of leaving Salcombe in the very near future. After all, I am a good listener; that is something which my profession has taught me—and you need a pair of ears.'

'Well, there is nothing to tell you,' said Emma rather defiantly, and burst into tears.

Dr van Dyke, by a great effort of will-power, stayed sitting in his chair. Much as he would have liked to take her into his arms, now was not the moment to show more than friendly sympathy, but presently he leaned across and stuffed his handkerchief into her hand and watched while she mopped her face, and blew her nose in an effort to return to her normal sensible manner. But her voice was a bit wobbly and she was twisting his handkerchief into a travesty of its snowy perfection.

'Well,' began Emma, and it all came tumbling out—not always in the right order, so that he had to sort out the details for himself. And when at last she had finished she muttered, 'Sorry I've made such a fool of myself. I do think it would be better if you went now; I am so ashamed of being such a cry-baby.'

Already at the back of the doctor's clever head a vague plan was taking shape. Far-fetched, almost for certain to be rejected by Emma, yet it was the obvious answer. To leave her to the uncertainties of her mother's plans, workless and more or less penniless... It was something he would think over later, but for now he said cheerfully, 'I'll go if you want me to, but I think a cup of coffee would be nice first.'

She jumped up. 'Of course. I'm sorry. It won't take long.'

She went into the kitchen and laid a tray, and was putting the last few biscuits in the tin onto a plate when he followed, the dog at his heels.

'This is a charming little house. I've often admired it from the outside, and it's even nicer indoors. I like kitchens, don't you?' He glanced round him. She had left a cupboard door open and it looked empty; she was very likely not having quite enough to eat. He carried the tray back to the living room and sat for another half an hour, talking about nothing in particular, feeding a delighted Percy with some of his biscuit, taking care not to look at Emma's tearstained face.

'Wibeke wanted to know how you were,' he told her. 'They

enjoyed their holiday here. The children have all got chicken pox now; she's thankful that they're all having it at the same time.'

'They were dears, the children,' said Emma, and smiled at last. 'They must be such fun.'

'They are.' He got up to go. 'Have dinner with me tomorrow evening and we'll talk about them. Eight o'clock? Shall we see if the Gallery has any lobsters?' And when she hesitated, he added, 'I'm not asking you because I'm sorry for you, Emma, but a meal and a pleasant talk is a comfortable way to end an evening.' He glanced at Percy. 'I dare say we might be allowed to hide him under the table—the manager owes me; I stitched up his cut hand late one night.'

He didn't wait for her to answer.

As she closed the door she decided that it would be most ungracious to refuse his invitation since he had been so kind.

She went to bed and slept soundly and set off once more on her fruitless search for work in the morning, to return home to the pleasant prospect of dinner with Dr van Dyke.

Aware that she had hardly looked her best on the previous evening, she took pains with her appearance. The evenings were cool now, so she got into a dress and jacket in a soft uncrushable material. It was a subdued silvery green which made the most of her hair, which she had twisted into an old-fashioned bun at the nape of her neck. 'Out-of-date but respectable,' she told Percy, who was sitting on the bed watching her dressing.

Dr van Dyke was waiting for her, studying the board outside the restaurant. His 'Hello,' was briskly friendly. 'I see we're in luck; there's lobster on the menu.'

'Hello,' said Emma breathlessly. 'I've brought Percy—you said...'

'All arranged. Let's go in; I'm famished.'

The lobster was delicious, served simply on a bed of lettuce with a Caesar salad. They talked as they ate, unhurriedly. The place was almost empty and would close for the winter in a few days' time. Peach Melba followed, and a pot of coffee which was renewed while they talked. As for Percy, sitting silently under the table, he had a bowl of water and, quite contrary to the house rules, a plate of biscuits.

It was well after ten o'clock when they left. Walking back to the cottage, Dr van Dyke glanced at Emma in the semi-darkness of the little quay. His plans had become reality. It was now a question of convincing Emma that they were both practical and sensible. No hint of his feelings for her must be allowed to show. This would be a businesslike arrangement with no strings attached. Now it was merely a matter of waiting for the right moment.

He unlocked the cottage door, switched on the lights, bade Percy goodnight and listened gravely to her little speech of thanks.

'It is I who thank you, Emma. Lobster is something one should never eat alone and I have much enjoyed your company.'

'I've never been compared with a lobster before,' said Emma tartly.

'I wouldn't presume to compare you with anyone or anything, Emma. Sleep soundly.'

'Oh, I will.' As he turned away she asked, 'When do you go back to Holland?'

'Very soon now. Goodnight, Emma.'

Not a very satisfactory answer.

The doctor had kindly Fate on his side; two evenings later the lifeboat was called out to go to the aid of a yacht off Prawle Point. He had just sat down to his supper when the maroon sounded and within ten minutes he was in oilskins and heavy boots, putting to sea with the rest of the crew. It was a stormy evening, will squalls of heavy rain and a strong wind. This was something he would miss, he reflected, taking up his station. When he had first come to Salcombe a crew member had fallen ill; he had volunteered to take his place and been accepted as a man who could be useful when the need arose.

Two hours later they were back in harbour, the yacht in tow, its crew led away to the Harbour Master's office for warm drinks and plans for the night. Half an hour later the doctor said goodnight and went out into the narrow lane behind the boat house. He glanced along Victoria Quay as he reached it and then lengthened his stride. Emma and Percy were just turning into the cottage gate.

She was at the door when he reached the cottage.

She saw him then, and waited at the door until he reached her, took the key from her hand, opened the door and switched on the light. She saw him clearly then: wet hair, an old pullover.

'What's happened?' she asked, and then 'You were in the lifeboat...?'

'Yes, I was on the way home when I saw you both.'

'I went up to the boat house to see if there was anything I could do. You're all safe?' When he nodded, she added, 'Would you like a hot drink? Cocoa?'

That was a drink he associated with his childhood, gulped down under Nanny's sharp eye. 'That would be most welcome. The weather's pretty rough outside the estuary.'

The little room looked cosy and smelled strongly of furniture polish. Indeed, looking round him, he could see that everything gleamed as though waiting for a special occasion, and in one corner there was a small box neatly packed with books.

Emma came back presently, with the cocoa and a tin of biscuits, and he studied her face narrowly as he got up. She looked sad, but not tearfully so, and there was a kind of quiet acceptance in her face. He had seen that look many times before on a patient's face when they had been confronted with a doubtful future.

He sipped his cocoa, pronounced it delicious, and asked, carefully casual, 'Have you heard from your mother? She plans to return soon?'

'They will be coming next week—on Wednesday.'

'And you? You have plans?'

'I'll find a job.'

'For some time now,' said the doctor casually, 'I have been badgered by my secretary in Holland to find someone to give her a helping hand. She does have too much to do, and when I return there will be even more work. It has occurred to me that perhaps you would consider working for her? It is rather a menial job: filing letters and running errands and dealing with phone calls if she is engaged. She is a fierce lady but she has a heart of gold. She speaks English, of course. The money won't be much but there's a room in the house where she lives which I think you could afford.' He added, 'A temporary measure, of course, just to tide you over.'

'You're offering me a job in Holland? When?'

'As from the middle of next week. Should you consider accepting, we could leave on the day your mother returns here, so that you could spend some time with her. I plan to go over to Holland on the late-night ferry from Harwich. We wouldn't need to leave here before five o'clock.'

'I can't,' said Emma. 'I won't leave Percy.'

'He can come with us; there's time to deal with the formalities. Do you have a passport? And do you drive a car?'

'Yes, to both.' She put down her mug. 'You do mean it, don't you?'

He said evenly, 'Yes, I mean it, Emma. You would be doing Juffrouw Smit a good turn and save me hunting around for someone when I get home.'

'Where do you live?'

'Near Amsterdam. My rooms are in the city, as are the hospitals where I work. You would live in Amsterdam itself.'

He put down his mug, lifted a somnolent Percy off his knee and got up.

'It's late. Think about it and let me know in the morning.' And as she went to open the door he said again, 'The cocoa was so delicious.' He smiled down at her bewildered face. 'Sleep well.'

And strangely enough she did, and woke in the morning with her mind made up. Here was her opportunity to make a life for herself. Moreover, it meant that she would still see Dr van Dyke from time to time. He was kind and thoughtful, he liked dogs and children, and he had offered her a job...

'It's a pity that I don't appeal to him as a woman,' said Emma to Percy. 'It's my hair, of course, and bawling my eyes out all over him.'

She would have to let him know and without waste of time. But first she made sure that she had her passport, and then she sat down to tot up her money. She would leave half of it in the bank and take the rest with her; she might not be paid for a month and she would have to live until then.

It wasn't much but it would give her security, and she would arrange with the bank that her mother could use the money there. She would have to bear in mind that her mother and her friend might agree to part later on, in which case she would have to return. But there was no point in thinking about that; her mother had been quite positive about her plans and made it clear that Emma had no part in them.

The doctor's surgeries would be over by eleven o'clock; she went to the medical centre and waited until the last patient had gone and then knocked on Dr van Dyke's door. He was sitting at his desk but he got up as she went in.

'Emma—sit down.' When she did, he sat back in his chair again. 'And what have you decided?'

'When I went to bed last night,' said Emma carefully, 'I decided to make up my mind this morning—think about it before I went to sleep. Only I went to sleep first, and when I woke up this morning my mind had made itself up. If you think I could do the job you offered me, I'd like to accept.'

'Good. Now, as to details: you will work from eight o'clock in the morning until five in the afternoon. An hour and a half for lunch at noon, half an hour for tea at half past three. You must be prepared to turn your hand to anything which Juffrouw Smit or I ask of you. You will be free on Saturday and Sunday, although if the occasion should arise you might need to work on either of those two days. You will be paid weekly.' He named a sum in guilders and then changed it into English pounds. It seemed a generous amount, and when she looked questioningly at him, he said, 'It's the going rate for a job such as yours, and

you will earn it. Juffrouw Smit expects the best. Do you still want
to come?'

He was friendly, but he was brisk too. This was a businesslike
meeting, she reminded herself. She said quietly, 'Yes, I still want
to come. If you will tell me where to go and when...'

'You will go over to Holland with me. You will need your
passport, of course, not too much luggage—and Percy. You will
perhaps let your mother know that we will leave in the late afternoon on Wednesday, so that she can arrange to be here before
you leave? You are quite sure that is what she wants?'

'Yes. She—she has never been happy living here with me, but
I think she will settle down with her friend. They like the same
things: bridge and driving around the country and being able to
go back to Richmond when they want to. And if it doesn't turn
out as they hoped, then I'll come back here...'

'Just so,' agreed the doctor. If he had a hand in it that would
be the last thing his darling Emma would do.

He said smoothly, 'Shall we settle some of the details? I'll see
about Percy and arrange the journey. I'll come down to the cottage
at five o'clock on Wednesday. It will be quite a long drive and
we shan't get to Amsterdam until well after midnight. Will you
have much luggage?'

'A case and a shoulder bag.'

Going home presently, she thought how coolly businesslike he
had been. Since he was to be her employer, perhaps that was a
good thing. She took Percy for a brisk walk and set about the task
of sorting out her clothes. She wouldn't need much; she doubted
if she would have much social life...

Her tweed jacket and skirt, the cashmere twin-set, a grey jersey
dress which she thought might do for her work, another skirt—
jersey again because it could be squeezed into a corner without
creasing—blouses and a thin sweater, and, as a concession to the
social life she didn't expect, a sapphire-blue dress which could be
folded into almost nothing and remained bandbox-fresh. 'Shoes,'
said Emma to a watchful Percy. 'And I'll wear my winter coat

and cram in a raincoat, gloves, handbag, undies and dressing gown...'

She laid everything out on the bed in her mother's bedroom and, being a sensible girl, sat down and wrote out all the things she had to do before Wednesday.

There was a letter from her mother in the morning. She and Mrs Riddley would arrive during the morning on Wednesday.

We shall spend the night on the way, and get to you in good time for coffee. Just a light lunch will do because we shall eat out in the evening. I expect you have arranged everything; I'm sure that by now you must have found just the kind of job you would like. Far be it from me to stand in the way of your ambition...

Emma put down the letter. She loved her mother, and she hoped that her mother loved her, but that lady had a way of twisting circumstances to suit herself, ignoring the fact that those same circumstances might not suit anyone else. Emma had known that since she was a small girl and had accepted it; her mother had been a very pretty woman, and charming, and Emma had grown up taking it for granted that she must be shielded from worry or unpleasantness. There had been little of either until her father had died, and she didn't blame her mother for wishing her former carefree life to continue.

She went the next day to say goodbye to Miss Johnson and Phoebe. Miss Johnson wished her well and told her to be sure and visit the splendid museums in Amsterdam, and Phoebe looked at her with envy.

'Lucky you, going to work for Dr van Dyke. What wouldn't I give to be in your shoes? Going for keeps or coming back here later?'

'I'm not going for keeps,' said Emma, 'and I dare say I'll come back later on.'

She met Mrs Craig the next day.

'My dear Emma, the very person I want to see. I had a card from your mother. How excited you must be. It's good news that she is going to stay in Salcombe—bringing a friend with her, she tells me.' She gave a little laugh. 'The cottage is rather small for three of you...'

'I won't be here,' said Emma. 'I'm going to work for Dr van Dyke when he goes back to Amsterdam. At least, I shall be working with his secretary. I'm to have lodgings with her. I've been working at the medical centre and I liked the work. It would have been difficult fitting three of us into the cottage, as you say.'

'Your mother will miss you.'

'Her friend is delighted to take my place—they have known each other since schooldays. She's very much looking forward to being here and meeting you and Mother's other friends.'

Mrs Craig studied Emma's face. There was no sign of worry or annoyance on it, all the same she didn't sound quite right.

Emma bade her a cheerful goodbye and hurried home to take Percy for his walk. He was becoming quite handsome, with a gleaming coat, melting brown eyes and a long feathery tail. Only his ears were on the large side, and she suspected that he wasn't going to grow much larger. She had told him that he was going to live in another country with her and he had wagged his tail in a pleased fashion. This was only to be expected, considering the doubtful life he had been leading in Salcombe.

Her mother and Mrs Riddley arrived in a flurry of greetings and embracing and gentle grumbling because they'd had to leave the car by the pub and there was no one to carry their luggage.

'Do find someone, darling,' said Mrs Dawson plaintively. 'And I quite forgot to ask you to find someone to clean the place for us.'

Emma accepted the car keys. 'Well, it's a bit late for me to do anything about that now,' she said cheerfully, 'but there are plenty of adverts in the newsagent's. I'll see what I can do about your luggage. Don't let Percy out of the gate, will you?'

'Such an ugly little dog,' said Mrs Riddley. 'But of course you'll take him with you?'

'Yes,' said Emma. 'We shall be gone this afternoon.'

She didn't like Mrs Riddley. Emma had heard of her from her mother from time to time but they had never met, though she could quite see that she would be an ideal companion for her mother. Another one skimming over the surface of life, making light of anything serious or unpleasant, being fashionable and excellent company; her mother would be happy with her.

The odd-job man at the pub helped with the luggage and Emma lugged it upstairs. She left the two ladies to begin their unpacking while she got the lunch, and over that meal she listened to their plans and intentions.

'We two old ladies intend to keep each other company while you go off and enjoy yourself. You're only young once, Emma. How wise of you to decide to see something of the world.'

Just as though I had planned the whole thing, reflected Emma. She felt bitterly hurt at her mother's bland acceptance of her leaving home, and felt as guilty as though she had actually arranged the whole thing herself. But there was no doubt that her mother was happy; she had convinced herself that Emma was pleasing herself, and beyond saying that it was so fortunate that Emma was going to work for someone she already knew she didn't want to know about the job itself.

After lunch Mrs Dawson said, 'You must tell me what you have done about the bank account. Dear Alice will see to the bills, since she is living here rent-free, but I must contribute towards the housekeeping, I suppose, and that will leave me almost penniless.'

'There's an account in your name at the bank. I've put in all the money I've earned except for the last two weeks' wages. I don't know what expenses I'll have until I've been in Amsterdam for a while and I won't get paid until the end of the month.'

'A good salary? You'll be able to help me out if I get short, darling?'

'Don't depend on that, mother. I shan't be earning much and I'll have to pay for food and lodgings.'

Her mother pouted. 'Oh, well, I suppose I'll just have to manage as best I can. Your father would turn in his grave, Emma…'

Emma didn't speak because she was swallowing tears. But presently she said, 'I must take Percy for a walk. I'll prepare tea when I come back.'

She took quite a long walk: round the end of Victoria Quay and round the back of the town and back through the main street. She wasn't sure when she would see it again, with its small shops and the friendly people in them. She waved to the butcher as she went past, and even the cross-faced woman at the bakery smiled.

They had finished their tea and Emma had washed up and put everything ready for the morning when Dr van Dyke came.

She introduced him, and she could see that the two ladies were impressed. He looked—she sought for words—respectable, and he said all the right things. But he didn't waste time; he told her that they must leave and made his goodbyes with the beautiful manners which her mother and Mrs Riddley obviously admired.

And then it was her turn to make her farewells, sent on her way with cheerful hopes that she would have a lovely time and to be sure and send a card when she had time. 'And don't forget your poor old mother,' said Mrs Dawson in a wispier voice than usual—which sent Emma out of the door feeling that she was an uncaring daughter deserting her mother.

She walked beside the doctor, with Percy on his lead, and he took her case and shoulder bag. He didn't look at her, and it wasn't until she was in the car beside him that she muttered, 'I feel an absolute heel…'

He still didn't look at her. 'Your mother is a charming lady, Emma, but you mustn't believe all she says. She was merely uttering a remark which she felt suited the occasion. She will be very happy with her friend—I believe that and so must you—far happier than living with you; you must see that for yourself. You may love each other dearly but you are as unlike as chalk from cheese.'

Emma sniffed; she had no intention of crying although she felt like it.

His large comforting hand covered hers for a moment. 'You must believe me; she will be happy and so will you.'

CHAPTER FIVE

EMMA sat beside the doctor, watching the quiet Devon country-side flash past as he made for the A38 and Exeter. He had told her that everything would be all right and she had to believe him, although she was beset by doubts. Juffrouw Smit might dislike her on sight; she might not be able to cope with the work. She would have to acquire at least a smattering of Dutch—and would she be able to live on her wages?

And over and above all that there was the unhappy thought that somehow or other she must make a success of the job, stay there until she had experience and some money saved before she could return to England. And what then? Her mother would be glad to see her as long as she didn't upset her life. Perhaps she would never be able to go back to the cottage at Salcombe...

'Stop worrying,' said Dr van Dyke. 'Take each day as it comes, and when you have found your feet you can make your plans. And I promise you that if you are unhappy in Amsterdam then I will see that you get back to England.'

'You're very kind,' said Emma. 'It's silly of me to fuss, and actually I'm rather looking forward to working for your Juffrouw Smit.'

He began to talk then, a gentle meandering conversation which required few answers on her part but which somehow soothed her. By the time they had bypassed Exeter, left the A30 and joined the A303, she actually felt quite light-hearted.

At the doctor's speed it didn't take long to reach the M25 and take the road to Harwich, but first they stopped at Fleet, parked the car, took Percy for a run and went to the café for coffee and sandwiches.

'We can get something else on board,' said the doctor, 'and of course there will be someone waiting for us when we get home.'

'In Amsterdam? Not at Juffrouw Smit's house?'

'No, no, I wouldn't dare to disturb her night's sleep. I live a few miles outside the city. You'll spend the night at my house and go to Juffrouw Smit in the morning.' He glanced at his watch and sent the great car surging forward. 'We are almost at Harwich. You're not tired?'

'No. I've enjoyed the trip; it's a lovely car.' She peered over her shoulder. 'Percy's asleep.'

They were very nearly the last on board the ferry. The doctor drove on, tucked Percy under one arm and ushered Emma to a seat.

'Make yourself comfortable. It's a short crossing—about three and a half hours. It may be a bit choppy but it is most convenient with the car, and the catamaran is as steady as an ordinary ferry.'

'I'm not nervous.'

'Coffee and a brandy, I think, and something to eat. I'll order while you trot off...'

How nicely put, thought Emma, making a beeline for the ladies'.

They ate their sandwiches, drank their coffee and brandy, and presently the doctor got some papers out of his briefcase. 'You don't mind if I do some work?'

She shook her head, nicely drowsy from the brandy, and, with her arms wrapped round a sleeping Percy, presently she slept too.

The doctor's hand on her arm woke her. 'We're about to dock. Better give me Percy.'

It was dark and chilly and she could see very little of her surroundings.

'Not long now,' said Dr van Dyke, and swept the car onto a lighted highway. After a few minutes there were no houses, just the road ahead of them, and Emma closed her eyes again.

When she woke she could see the lights of Amsterdam, but before they reached the outskirts the doctor took an exit road and plunged into the darkness of the countryside. But not for long, for there were a few trees, and then a house or two, and then a village—nice old houses lining the narrow road. She glimpsed a church—closed now, of course—and a tall iron railing, before he turned the car between brick pillars, along a short straight drive and stopped before the house.

'You had better go straight to bed. I'll see to Percy.' He got out of the car, lifted Percy off the back seat, opened her door and urged her out.

She stood a minute, looking around her, for a moment wide awake. The house was large and square, with white walls and a steep gabled roof. The massive door was open and there were lights in some of the windows.

'Is this your home?' asked Emma.

'Yes.' He sounded impatient, so she trod up the steps to the door beside him and went into the hall. It was large and square, with doors on all sides and a vast expanse of black and white tiled floor. There was a rather grand staircase curving up one wall, and a chandelier which cast brilliant light over everything. She saw all that in one rapid glance before the doctor at her elbow said, 'This is my housekeeper, Mevrouw Kulk—Katje, this is Miss Emma Dawson.' And when they had shaken hands, he spoke to Katje in Dutch.

Mevrouw Kulk was tall, stout and dignified, but she had a cheerful smiling face. She was answering the doctor when a door at the back of the hall opened and a middle-aged man came towards them.

He went to the doctor and shook hands, saying something in an apologetic voice. The doctor laughed and turned to Emma. 'This is Kulk. He and his wife run my home. He is apologising because he wasn't here to greet us. He was shutting my dog into the kitchen.'

Emma shook hands and looked anxiously at Percy, standing obediently by the doctor's feet. 'Shall I take him with me? He'll only need a minute or two outside...'

'Go with Mevrouw Kulk. She will show you your room, bring you a hot drink and see you safely into bed. I'll see to Percy and she will bring him up when you're in bed. He'd better be with you tonight.'

Mevrouw Kulk smiled and nodded and beckoned, and the doctor said briskly, 'Sleep well, Emma. Breakfast at half past eight, before I take you to Juffrouw Smit.'

Emma followed the housekeeper upstairs. I'm twenty-seven, she thought sleepily, and he's ordering me around as though I were a child. But she was too tired to bother about that.

The stairs opened onto a gallery with doors on every side. Mevrouw Kulk opened one and ushered Emma inside.

Emma had an instant impression of warmth and light. The mahogany bed had a soft pink quilt, matching the curtains at the window. There was a small table, with a triple mirror on it and a slender-legged stool before it, and on either side of the bed there was a small table bearing pink-shaded lamps. A lovely room, but surely not one in which Percy would be allowed to sleep?

The housekeeper turned down the coverlet. 'Bed,' she said firmly, and smiled and nodded and went away.

Emma kicked off her shoes and dug her feet into the soft white carpet. Someone had already brought her luggage to her room. She found a nightie and, since it seemed the only thing to do, had a quick shower in the small, splendidly equipped bathroom next door. She got into bed just in time; Mevrouw Kulk was back again, this time with Percy prancing beside her and a blanket over one arm, which she spread at the end of the bed. She nodded and smiled once more, to return within a minute with a small tray, containing hot milk and a plate of biscuits.

'Dr van Dyke says, "Eat, drink and sleep!"'

She patted Emma's shoulder in a motherly fashion and went away again.

So Emma drank the milk, shared the biscuits with Percy, put her head on the pillow and slept—to be wakened in the morning by a buxom girl with a tea tray. There was a note on the tray: *Let Percy go with Anneke; she can take him for a run in the garden.*

Breakfast was at half past eight and it was already eight o'clock. She showered and dressed, wishing she had more time to take pains with her face and hair, and went downstairs, wondering where she should go.

Kulk was in the hall. His 'Good morning, Miss', was uttered in a fatherly fashion as he opened a door and invited her to go past him into the room beyond. This was a small room with a bright fire burning in the steel fireplace, its windows open onto the gardens beyond. There was a round table set for breakfast, a scattering of comfortable chairs, bookshelves overflowing with books, and small tables just where they were needed. The walls were panelled and the ceiling was a magnificent example of strap work.

Emma rotated slowly as the doctor came in from the garden. There was a mastiff beside him and, trotting as close as he could get, Percy.

His good morning was brisk. 'Percy and Prince are the best of friends, as you can see. You slept well? Shall we have breakfast?'

Emma had bent to stroke Percy. 'What a beautiful dog you have.' She held out a fist and Prince came close and breathed gently over it, then went back to stand by his master. Kulk came in then, with a loaded tray, and the doctor sent the dogs outside into the garden while they ate.

Emma was hungry. It seemed a long time since she had sat down to a decent meal, and as if he had read her thoughts Dr van Dyke observed, 'I do apologise for depriving you of a meal yesterday. You must allow me to make up for that once you have settled in.'

An invitation to dinner, thought Emma, loading marmalade onto toast. What a good thing I brought that dress. But all she said was, 'That would be very nice,' in a non-committal voice. It might be one of those half-meant, vague invitations exchanged so often amongst friends and acquaintances when she lived in Richmond, which never materialised. But no one had expected them to anyway.

Given no more than a few minutes in which to collect her things and thank the Kulks for their kindness, she was urged into the car, her luggage put in the boot, and Percy, waiting on the doorstep, was put on the back seat. Since the doctor had nothing to say, she held her tongue. She knew him well enough by now to understand that if there was nothing she should know she should be quiet.

Amsterdam was surprisingly close: first the modern outskirts and then the real Amsterdam—narrow streets and gabled houses leaning against each other lining the canals.

The doctor stopped before a row of old redbrick houses with imposing fronts.

'I shall be a few minutes,' he told her, before he got out and went inside one of the houses, which gave her time to look around her. There were several brass plates beside the door; this would be his consulting rooms, then. Very stylish, thought Emma.

He got back into the car presently. 'My consulting rooms,' he told her. 'You will work here with Juffrouw Smit.'

He swung the car down a narrow lane with small houses on either side of it and stopped again before one of them. He helped her out, scooped up Percy and rang the old-fashioned bell. The door was opened immediately by a lady who could have been a close relation of Miss Johnson: the same stiff hairstyle, white blouse and cardigan and sensible skirt, the same severe expression. Emma felt a surge of relief; it was like meeting an old friend...

'Good morning, Doctor, and I presume, Miss Dawson?' Her eyes fastened on Percy. 'And the little dog. Come in. Will you have coffee? You have an appointment at ten o'clock, Doctor...'

'How nice to see you again, Smitty. I must go to the hospital first, so I had better get along. Bring Emma round with you, will you? Give her some idea of her work. She can settle in this afternoon.' He smiled down at Emma. 'Juffrouw Smit, this is Emma Dawson. I'm sure she will be an apt pupil.' And when the two women had shaken hands, he said, 'I'll be off.'

Juffrouw Smit shut the door behind his vast back. 'Coffee first, then a quick look at your room before we go round to the doctor's rooms. We will speak English, but once you have found your feet you must learn a little Dutch.'

She led the way out of the tiny hall into a small sitting room, rather too full of old-fashioned furniture but very cosy. 'Sit down. I'll fetch the coffee.'

When it was poured Emma said, 'Did you know that I had Percy?'

'Yes, Dr van Dyke told me. I have a small garden with a very high wall and I shall leave the kitchen door open for him. He will be alone, but not for long, for I come home for my meals and if there are no patients you can slip back for a few minutes. He will be happy?'

'He was a stray, and I've had to leave him alone from time to time, but I'm sure he'll be happy. You don't mind?'

'Not at all. Drink your coffee, then come and see your room. The doctor took your luggage up before he went.'

It was a small low-ceilinged room, overlooking the lane, very clean and cheerful, with simple furniture and a bed against one wall.

'My room is at the back of the house and there is a bathroom between. And if you should wish to be alone there is a small room beside the kitchen.'

Emma looked out of the window, trying to find a suitable way of asking about the rent; Juffrouw Smit wasn't like the usual landlady.

It was her companion who said briskly, 'Dr van Dyke is paying me for your room and board; that is why your wages are small.'

'Oh, thank you. Your English is so perfect, Juffrouw Smit— have you lived in England?'

'For several years some time ago. You will find that most people here speak English, although we appreciate foreigners speaking our language.'

Of course I'm a foreigner, reflected Emma, although I don't feel like one.

They settled Percy on a blanket in the kitchen, with the door open into the neat garden, and walked to the doctor's rooms. Two or three minutes brought them to the imposing door and across the equally imposing hall to another door with his name on it.

Juffrouw Smit had a key and led the way into a short hallway which opened into a well-furnished waiting room—comfortable chairs, small tables with magazines, bowls of flowers and a desk in one corner.

'Through here,' said Juffrouw Smit, and opened the door by the desk. 'This is where we keep patients' notes, the account book, business letters and so on.' She shut the door, swept Emma across the room and opened another door. 'Dr van Dyke's consulting room. The door over there leads to the examination room.'

She led the way out again. 'This last door is where we make tea and coffee, and here is a cloakroom.'

Emma took it all in, rather overwhelmed. She had never thought of the doctor as being well-known and obviously wealthy. She thought of the understated luxury of his consulting room and remembered his rather bare little room at the medical centre in Salcombe. His lovely house, too. He had never given her an in-kling—but then, why should he? She had come over here to work and as such would hardly be expected to take a deep interest in his personal life. He had, of course, got one; she wished she knew more about it.

'Sit here, by my desk,' said Juffrouw Smit, 'and watch care-fully. You must learn the routine before you will be any use to me.'

Emma, obediently making herself unobtrusive, reflected that Juffrouw Smit was every bit as severe as Miss Johnson.

The first person to arrive was Dr van Dyke, crossing to his own room with a brief nod, and five minutes later an imposing matron who replied graciously to Juffrouw Smit's greeting and ignored Emma. She was followed at suitable intervals by a fat man with a red face, a thin lady looking frightened, and lastly a sulky teen-ager with a fierce-looking parent.

When they had gone, Juffrouw Smit said, 'This is a typical morning. Dr van Dyke goes next to one or other of the hospitals where he is a consultant, and returns here around mid-afternoon, when he will see more patients. Very occasionally he sees patients in the evening. Now, if you will make the coffee and take him a cup, we will have ours and I will explain your work to you.'

'Do I knock?' asked Emma, cup and saucer in hand.

'Yes, and no need to speak unless he does.'

She knocked and went in. He was sitting at his desk, writing, and he didn't look up. She put the coffee on his desk and went out again, vaguely disappointed. He could at least have lifted his head and smiled...

She and Juffrouw Smit had their coffee and she took the cups back to the little cubbyhole. When she got back it was to see the doctor's back disappearing through the door.

'Now,' said Juffrouw Smit, 'listen carefully...'

Her tasks were simple: fetching and carrying, making coffee, answering the phone if Juffrouw Smit was unable to do so with the quickly learned words *'een ogenblik'*, which it seemed was a polite way of saying 'hold on'. She must see that the doctor's desk was exactly as he liked it each morning, tidy the newspapers and magazines, and, once she felt at ease with these jobs, she was expected to find and file away patients' notes and sort the post.

'Many small tasks,' observed Juffrouw Smit, 'of which I shall be relieved so that I can attend to the administration—the paper-work.'

They went back to her house for their lunch, and then Emma took Percy for a quick run before they went back to the consulting rooms and another afternoon of patients. The doctor, coming and going, did no more than nod as he went, with a brief, 'Settling in?' not waiting for an answer.

Quite a nice day, thought Emma, curling up in bed that night. Under Juffrouw Smit's severe exterior, she felt sure lurked a nice middle-aged lady who would one day become a friend. And the work, so far, wasn't beyond her. She had a pleasant room, and enough to eat, and Percy had been made welcome. The niggardly thought that the doctor seemed to have forgotten all about her she dismissed. Any fanciful ideas in that direction were to be es-chewed at once...

The next day went well, despite the fact that the patients

seemed endless. Excepting for a brief lunch there was no respite, so that when the last patient had gone, soon after five o'clock, and Juffrouw Smit told her to get her coat and go to the post office with a pile of letters, she was glad to do so.

It was an early dusk, and chilly, but it was lovely to be out of doors after the warmth of the waiting room. The post office was five minutes' walk away; Emma went over the little bridge at the end of the street, turned left and followed the canal. The post office was on the corner, facing a busy main road thick with traffic, trams and people. She would have liked to have lingered, taken a quick look around, but that would have to wait until she was free tomorrow. She hurried back and found Juffrouw Smit still at her desk, with no sign of the doctor.

'Take the key,' said Juffrouw Smit, 'and go to my house. Perhaps you would put everything ready for our meal? *Zuurkool* and potatoes and a smoked sausage. Put them all on a very low gas and feed Percy. I shall be another ten minutes. While I cook our meal you can take him for his walk.'

So Emma went back to the little house, to be greeted by a delighted Percy and deal with the saucepans and wait for Juffrouw Smit.

Juffrouw Smit was sitting opposite the doctor's desk, listening to him.

'Yes,' she told him, 'Miss Dawson—who wishes to be called Emma—has settled in without fuss. A sensible girl with nice manners, and quick to grasp what is wanted of her.' Juffrouw Smit fixed the doctor with a sharp eye. 'Do you wish me to train her to take my place, doctor?'

'Take your place? Smitty, you surely don't want to retire? There are years ahead of you. You surely never supposed that that was in my mind? I cannot imagine being without you. No, no, I will explain…'

Which he did, though giving away none of his true feelings, but as Juffrouw Smit got up to go and reached the door she turned to look at him.

'You wish to marry Emma, Doctor?'

He glanced up from the papers he was turning over. 'That is my intention, Smitty.'

The smile he gave her warmed her spinster's heart.

Emma, unaware of the future planned for her, took Percy for a brisk walk, noting the names of the streets as she went. The ranks of tall old houses all looked rather alike, and so did the canals. As she went back she passed the consulting rooms and saw the lights were still on. She hoped the doctor wasn't sitting there working when he should be at home with that magnificent dog. Kulk should be offering him a stiff drink after his day's work while Mevrouw Kulk cooked him a delicious meal. It would be nice to see the house again, but she doubted if she would.

That evening she listened to Juffrouw Smit's suggestions—clearly to be taken most seriously—concerning her washing and ironing, the time of the day when she might consider the bathroom to be hers, and the household chores she was expected to do—which weren't many, for a stout woman came twice each week to clean. Emma must keep her room clean and tidy, and help with the cooking and tidying of the kitchen.

Armed with a Dutch dictionary, and a phrasebook Juffrouw Smit gave her, Emma spent a good deal of her evening in the small room beside the kitchen. Only just before bedtime did she join Juffrouw Smit in the sitting room for a last cup of coffee before saying goodnight. They talked a little then, and watched the news, before she let Percy into the garden prior to taking him upstairs with her.

For the moment Emma was content; it was all new to her and it would be several weeks before she would feel anything other than a lodger. A day out tomorrow—Saturday—she decided. She would get a map of the city and find her way around at her leisure, and on Sunday she would go to church—there would surely be an English Church? And she would write letters in the little room, out of Juffrouw Smit's way.

She had written home once already, a brief letter telling her mother of her safe arrival, with the address and phone number. She would buy postcards too, and send them to Phoebe and Miss Johnson and Mrs Craig. And find a bookshop...

She went to bed with a head full of cheerful plans. Juffrouw Smit had listened to them and nodded and offered a street map, and told her where she would find the English church. She had observed that she herself would be spending Saturday with a cousin and on Sunday would be going to her own church in the morning.

'So you must feel free to spend your days as you wish, Emma. You have a key, and I hope you will do as you wish and treat my house as your home.'

Emma told herself that she was a very lucky girl; she had a job, a home, and Percy—and, as well as that, her mother was once more happy.

She helped to wash up and tidy the little house in the morning and then went to her room to get her jacket and her handbag. When she went downstairs Percy was in the hall waiting for her. So were Juffrouw Smit and Dr van Dyke.

His good morning was genial. 'If you feel like a walk I thought I might show you some of Amsterdam. It can be a little confusing to a stranger...'

She stared up at him. 'Thank you, but I wouldn't dream of wasting your time. I have a street map...'

'Oh, but I'm much easier to understand than a street map.' He smiled at her. 'The canals can be very confusing, don't you agree, Smitty?'

'Oh, undoubtedly, Doctor. And it will be much quicker for Emma to find her way around once she has been guided by someone who knows the city.' She said briskly to Emma, 'You have your key?'

Emma nodded, trying to think of something to say which wouldn't sound rude; she was having her day arranged for her, and although it would be delightful to spend it with the doctor she couldn't help but feel that he was performing a charitable act prompted by good manners. To refuse wasn't possible; rudeness was something she had been brought up to avoid at all costs, so she said quietly, 'You're very kind. May I bring Percy?'

'Of course. He'll be company for Prince.'

They bade Juffrouw Smit goodbye and went out into the street. The Rolls was there, with Prince in the driver's seat, and Emma came to a halt.

'I was going to explore Amsterdam...'

'So we will, but first we will go back to my place and have coffee, and leave Prince and Percy in Kulk's charge; neither of them would enjoy sightseeing, you know.'

This statement was uttered in such a reasonable voice that there was no answer...besides, it was obvious when they reached his house that Percy was delighted to be handed over to the care of Kulk and Prince's fatherly company.

She was ushered into the room where they had had breakfast and the dogs rushed out into the garden as Kulk came in with the coffee tray. Emma, pouring coffee from the silver pot into paper-thin cups, allowed herself to enjoy the quiet luxury of the doctor's household. A pity, she thought as she nibbled a wafer-thin biscuit, that she couldn't see behind the ornate double doors on the other side of the hall. It was a large house, and doubtless full of lovely furniture...

She made polite small talk, encouraged by the doctor's grave replies, but it was a relief when he suggested that she might like to tidy herself before they went back to Amsterdam.

He parked the Rolls outside his consulting rooms. 'I shall show you the lay-out of the city,' he told her, 'so that you are familiar with the main streets. We shall walk first to the station. Think of it as the centre of a spider's web. The main streets radiate from it and the canals encircle it. Always carry Juffrouw Smit's address with you, and my telephone number, and keep to the main streets until you know your way around.'

He walked her briskly to the station, then down Damrak to Damrak Square, where he allowed her a moment to view the royal palace and the memorial before taking her through Kalverstraat, lined with shops, to the Leidesgracht, into the Herengracht and into Vizelstraat back towards the Dam Square.

He took her to lunch then, in a large hotel close to the flower market and the Mint, and Emma, her appetite sharpened by their lengthy walking, ate smoked eel—which she hadn't expected to like but which turned out to be simply delicious—followed by sole *meunière* with a salad and a dessert of profiteroles and whipped cream. Pouring coffee, she said in her sensible way, 'That was a lovely lunch. Thank you!'

'Good. Now I will show you where the museums are, and the churches, the Town Hall, the hospitals and the post office and banks.'

So off they went once more. It was hardly a social outing, reflected Emma, conscious that her feet were beginning to ache, excepting for the lunch, of course. On the other hand it was going to make finding her way around the city much easier.

It was four o'clock when he said finally, 'You would like a cup of tea,' and ushered her to a small elegant café. She sank into a chair and eased her feet out of her shoes, drank the tea and ate a mountainous pastry swimming in cream and then pushed her feet back into her shoes once again.

It was a relief to find that they were only a short walk from Juffrouw Smit's house, and when they were in sight of it the doctor said, 'I've tired you out. Go indoors; I'll fetch Percy.'

If her feet hadn't been hurting so much perhaps she might have demurred. As it was she went thankfully into the house and he went at once. 'Fifteen minutes,' he told her, and was gone.

She had her shoes off and her slippers on, her outdoor things put away and everything ready for coffee by the time he returned with Percy.

She opened the door to him, embraced Percy and politely offered coffee.

The doctor stood looking at her. The bright overhead light in the little hall had turned her fiery head into a rich glow, and the long walk had given her a splendid colour. The temptation to gather her into his arms and kiss her was great, but he resisted it, well aware that this wasn't the time or the place.

'Would you like coffee?' asked Emma.

'I've an appointment,' he told her. 'I do hope I haven't tired you too much?'

'No, no. I've enjoyed every minute of it—and it will be so helpful now that I've a good idea of the city. It was a lovely day. Thank you very much.'

He smiled, then bade her goodbye and went away.

It seemed very quiet in the little house when he had gone. She made dark coffee, fed Percy and thought about her day. Being with the doctor had been delightful, for he was a good companion and she felt quite at ease in his company, but she doubted if there would be many occasions such as today. He had felt it his duty, no doubt, to make her familiar with Amsterdam, since she had had no chance to do anything about it herself, and probably he felt responsible about her since she was in his employ. And that was something she must never forget, for all his friendliness.

Juffrouw Smit had said that she would be late home, so Emma got her own supper presently, and wrote a letter to her mother. She had plenty to write about, and she had only just finished it when Juffrouw Smit came back. They sat together for an hour over coffee, exchanging news of their day until bedtime.

Tomorrow, thought Emma sleepily, curling up in her bed, I shall go to church, have lunch somewhere and explore. The quicker she felt at home in Amsterdam the better.

She found the little church in the Beguine Court, which the doctor had told her about, and after the service wandered around looking at the charming little houses surrounding it before going in search of a small café.

Much refreshed by a *kaas broodje* and coffee, she found her way to the station, bought a timetable with an eye to future expeditions, and then boarded a sightseeing boat to tour the canals.

The boat was full, mostly with Americans and English, and the guide kept up a running commentary as they went from one canal to the other. It gave her a splendid back-to-front view of the city, with the lovely old houses backing onto the canals, some with high-walled gardens, some of their windows almost at water level. If she had had the time she would have gone round again for a second time, but it was almost four o'clock and she intended to have tea before she went back to Juffrouw Smit.

She found the café where the doctor had taken her, and, reckless of the prices, had tea and an enormous confection of cream and meringue and chocolate. Then, well satisfied with her day, she went back to Juffrouw Smit's little house.

They spent a pleasant evening together, talking about nothing much while Juffrouw Smit knitted a complicated pattern with enviable ease. Beyond hoping that she had enjoyed her day she asked no questions as to what Emma had done with it, nor did she vouchsafe any information as to her own day. Emma sensed that although they liked each other they would never become friendly enough to exchange personal feelings. But it was enough that they could live together in harmony.

The days went smoothly enough. As the week progressed Emma found herself taking on more and more of the trivial jobs at the consulting rooms, so that Juffrouw Smit could spend more time at her desk, dealing with the computer, the e-mails and the fax machine. For all her staid appearance, there was nothing lacking in her modern skills.

These were things Emma supposed she would have to master if she wished to make a career for herself, but first she supposed that she must learn at least a smattering of the Dutch language. She must ask Juffrouw Smit if there were evening classes. But for the moment it was enough that she had a roof over her head, a job and her wages.

Towards the end of the week she had a letter from her mother. Mrs Dawson was happy—something she had never been with her, thought Emma wistfully, but it was good to know that she was finding life fun again. She and Alice, she wrote, had settled in well. They had found a woman to look after the place, and they had joined a bridge club. They had coffee with Mrs Craig and various friends each morning, and the boutique had such lovely clothes for the winter. At the end of the letter Mrs Dawson hoped that Emma had settled in happily and was getting to know some young people and having fun. *You really must learn to enjoy life more, darling!* She didn't ask about Emma's work.

Emma, stifling hurt feelings, was glad that her mother was once again living the kind of life she had always enjoyed. She wrote back cheerfully.

Otherwise she spent her evenings poring over the Dutch dictionary, and replied with a cool politeness to the doctor's brief greetings as he came and went each day.

She had been there almost a month when she decided that she could afford to buy a winter coat. She had learned her way around Amsterdam by now, and there were side streets where there were little dress shops where one might pick up a bargain...

Her pay packet crackling nicely in her pocket, she was getting out the case sheets for the day's patients when the doctor came out of his room. He put a letter on the desk and turned to go back.

'Please see that your letters are addressed to Juffrouw Smit's house and not to my rooms,' he observed pleasantly, and had gone again before Emma could utter an apology.

She picked up the letter. It looked official, typewritten and sent by the overnight express mail. She opened it slowly—had she left an unpaid bill? Or was it something to do with the bank?

She began to read.

CHAPTER SIX

IT WAS from Mr Trump. This would be a severe shock to her, he wrote, but her mother and her friend Mrs Riddley had died instantly in a car crash while making a short visit to friends at Richmond. Fortunately, someone who knew them had phoned him at once and he was dealing with the tragic matter. He had not known how to reach her on the phone but begged her to ring him as soon as possible. It was a kind letter and he assured her of his support and assistance.

She read it through again, standing in the cubbyhole, until Juffrouw Smit's voice, a little impatient, penetrated the blankness of her mind. Would she take the doctor's coffee in at once, or he would have no time to drink it before the first patient arrived.

She made the coffee, filled his cup and carried cup and saucer across to his door, knocked and went in. As she set them down on his desk he looked up, saw her ashen face and promptly got up to take her in his arms.

'Emma, what's wrong? Are you ill?' He remembered the letter. 'Bad news?'

She didn't trust herself to speak but fished the letter out of her pocket. Still with one arm round her, he read it.

'My poor dear girl. What shocking news.' He sat her down in the chair facing his desk and pressed the button which would light the discreet red light on Juffrouw Smit's desk. When that lady came, he said, 'Smitty, Emma has had bad news from England. Will you bring her some brandy, then delay my first patient if she comes on time?'

When she brought the brandy he explained in Dutch, and then asked, 'Is Nurse here yet?'

'Any minute now.'

'She must cope here while you take Emma back to your house.

Stay with her for as long as you need to, get her a hot drink and try to get her to lie down.' Then, in English, he said, 'Drink this, Emma. Juffrouw Smit will take you back to her house in a moment. Leave the letter with me. I will telephone Mr Trump and discover all I can, then let you know what is best to be done.'

'I must go...'

'Of course. Don't worry about that. I'll arrange everything. Now, drink the rest of the brandy like a good girl.'

A little colour had crept into her cheeks and he took her hands in his.

'Do as Juffrouw Smit suggests and wait until I come, Emma.' His quiet voice pierced her numb senses, firm and comforting, letting her know that he would do everything he could to help her. She gave him a small bleak smile and went with Juffrouw Smit.

There were five minutes before his patient would arrive, and the doctor spent them sitting at his desk. By the time she was ushered in by the nurse he knew exactly what had to be done.

Emma, like an obedient child, did just what Juffrouw Smit bade her do: drank the tea she was offered and lay down on her bed with a blanket tucked around her. She was aware that Juffrouw Smit was talking to her in a quiet, comforting voice, sitting by the bed holding her hand. Presently, she told herself, she would think what must be done, but somehow her thoughts slid away to nothing...

She had no idea how long she had been lying there when Dr van Dyke came in.

Juffrouw Smit slipped away and he sat down in her chair and took Emma's hand in his. She opened her eyes and looked at him, and then sat up in bed as the realisation of what had occurred penetrated her shock.

'Mother,' she said, and burst into tears...

The doctor sat on the bed beside her and took her in his arms again and let her cry until she was exhausted. When she had finally come to a stop, he mopped her face and said, 'There's my

brave girl—and you must stay brave, Emma. I shall take you over
to England this evening. We shall go to Mr Trump's house, where
you will stay for a few days. He will help you and advise you
and make all the necessary arrangements. So, now I want you to
come downstairs and eat something and pack a bag. We shall
leave here as soon after five o'clock as possible.'

She peered at him through puffy eyelids. 'Am I not to come
back here?'

'Of course you're coming back. I shall come over and fetch
you. But we will talk about that later. Just take enough with you
for five or six days. I'm going to take Percy with me now; he
will stay with Prince and Kulk until you come back.'

'Did you phone Mr Trump? I'm sorry to give you so much
trouble…'

'Yes, I rang him and he is expecting you to stay. Don't worry,
Emma, he will explain everything to you this evening.'

'But you can't leave here—your patients, the hospital…'

'Leave that to me.' He gave her a reassuring pat on the shoulder. 'I'm going now. Be ready for me shortly after five o'clock.'

For Emma the day was endless. She packed her overnight bag,
did her best to swallow the food Juffrouw Smit offered her and
tried to think sensibly about the immediate future. But time and
again her thoughts reverted to her mother and the awful suddenness of it all. She wanted desperately to know exactly what had
happened. Perhaps she wouldn't feel so grief-stricken once she
knew that. She knew it was useless, but she longed to run from
the house and go back to England without wasting a moment.

But five o'clock came at last and she stood ready to leave the
moment the doctor came for her. She neither knew or cared how
she got to Mr Trump; the doctor had said he would see to everything and she had thought no more about it.

When she had been waiting for ten minutes he finally came,
but her nerves were on edge and when Juffrouw Smit offered him
coffee and something to eat she could have screamed at the delay.

He took a quick look at her tense face, declined the offer and
picked up her case. He was tired and hungry, for he had spent

time arranging their journey as well as doing his hospital round and then leaving his registrar to deal with anything urgent.

Emma bade a hasty goodbye to Juffrouw Smit and made for the door, impatiently listening to the doctor telling his secretary that he would be there in the morning for his patients. He spoke in Dutch, but as far as Emma was concerned it could have been any language under the sun; if only they could start their journey...

She wondered from where they would get a ferry—and surely it would be far into the night before they got to Mr Trump's house?

As though he had read her thoughts, Dr van Dyke said, 'Just a short drive. There's a plane waiting for us at Schipol; we will be at Heathrow in an hour or so.'

She hardly noticed anything of their journey; she was deeply thankful that she would be back in England so quickly, and at any other time she would have been thrilled and delighted at the speed with which they travelled, but now all she could think of was to get to Mr Trump as quickly as possible.

It seemed perfectly natural that a car should be waiting at Heathrow. She had thanked the pilot when they left the plane and hardly noticed the ease with which they went from it to the car.

The doctor, who had had very little to say on their journey, asked now, 'You know where Mr Trump lives? I have his address but I am not familiar with Richmond.'

Half an hour later they were sitting in Mr Trump's drawing room, drinking coffee while his wife plied them with sandwiches. To her offer of a bed for the night the doctor gave a grateful refusal. 'I've arranged to fly back at eleven o'clock; I have appointments I cannot break in the morning.'

The quiet normality of Mr Trump's home had restored some of Emma's habitual calm. 'But you can't,' she declared. 'You'll be tired. Surely there is someone who could take over for you...?'

She wished she hadn't said that; he had gone to a great deal of trouble to get her to Mr Trump but of course he wanted to get back to his home and his practice as soon as possible. She had disrupted his day most dreadfully.

She said quickly, 'I'm sorry. Of course you know what is best. I'm very grateful—I can never thank you enough... Of course you must go back home as quickly as possible.'

The doctor got up to go. 'I shall be back for your mother's funeral, Emma.' He took her hands in his. 'Mr Trump will take care of everything for you.' He bent and kissed her cheek. 'Be a brave girl, my dear.'

He shook hands with Mrs Trump and went out of the room with Mr Trump. The two men had talked on the phone at some length during the day, and now the doctor said, 'I will arrange things so that I can get here for the funeral and stay for several days. It is very good of you to have Emma to stay.'

'My wife and I are very fond of her, and we have always thought that she had less fun out of life than most girls. She was splendid when her father died. There's Salcombe to decide about, of course.'

'If you think it a good idea I'll drive her there.'

'That might be a very good idea. I'm grateful to you for getting her here so quickly.'

They shook hands and the doctor drove back to Heathrow and was flown back to Schipol, to get thankfully into his car and take himself home. Tomorrow he would get his plans made so that he could go back to England for as long as Emma needed him.

Mr Trump vetoed Emma's request for an account of her mother's death. 'You are tired,' he told her. 'Go to bed and sleep—for I'm sure that you will, whatever you think. In the morning we will sit quietly and I will tell you all that I know. I can promise you that your mother and her friend died instantly; they would have known nothing.'

Emma, worn out by grief and the nightmare day, went to her bed and fell at once into exhausted sleep.

Facing her as she sat opposite him in his study the next morning, Mr Trump saw that she was composed and capable of listening to what he had to say. 'I will tell you exactly what happened, and then we must discuss what arrangements you will wish to be made...'

It was almost a week later, on the evening before her mother's funeral, that Emma went into Mr Trump's drawing room and found Dr van Dyke there.

He got up and went to her at once and took her hands in his.

'Emma—how are you? Mr Trump tells me that you have been such a help to him...'

'Have you come...? That is, will you be here tomorrow?'

'Yes. Mr Trump and I have talked it over and he agrees with me that, if you agree, I should drive you down to Salcombe after the funeral. You will have several matters to deal with there.'

'Oh, would you do that? Thank you.' She found her hands were still in his and withdrew them gently. 'But you will want to get back to Holland...'

'No, no. I don't need to return for several days. Ample time in which you can attend to matters.' He smiled down at her. 'When everything is settled to your satisfaction, I'll take you back to Amsterdam.'

Mrs Trump bustled in then. 'Had your little chat?' she asked comfortably. 'I'll bring in the tea tray; I'm sure we could all do with a cup.'

The doctor went after tea, saying that he would be back in the morning. The funeral was to be at eleven o'clock and he proposed driving Emma down to Salcombe shortly afterwards. From what Mr Trump had told him there would be small debts to pay in the town, and an interview with the bank manager.

'I suspect,' Mr Trump had said thoughtfully, 'that there is no money—indeed, there may be an overdraft. Of course, the bank were not able to tell me this on the phone, but I feel I should warn you.'

'Will you let me know if there is any difficulty? You may count on me to deal with any.'

Mr Trump had given him a sharp glance. 'I don't think that

Emma would like to be in your debt, even though you have proved yourself to be such a good friend.'

The doctor had only smiled.

It was a grey afternoon by the time he drove away from Mr Trump's house with a silent Emma beside him. The funeral had been quiet; there were no close relatives to attend, although there had been friends who had known her mother when she had lived at Richmond. They had been kind to Emma, saying all the right things but careful not to ask as to her future. It had only been the Trumps who'd wished her a warm goodbye, with the assurance that she was to come and stay with them whenever she felt like it. And Mr Trump had added that she could count on him for advice and help in any way.

There was no will; her mother had delayed making one, declaring that making a will was a morbid thing to do, and he had explained that there might be very little money.

'The cottage will be yours, of course, and I'll see to that for you, and its contents, but I know of nothing else. You will need to see your bank manager... Ask him to get in touch with me if there are any difficulties.'

So Emma had a lot to think about, but the first muddle of her thoughts must be sorted out, so it was a relief when the doctor said cheerfully, 'Do you want to talk? Perhaps you would rather have your thoughts?'

'I've had them all week,' said Emma bleakly, 'and they've got me nowhere.'

'Then think them out loud; perhaps I can help?'

'You've done so much already. I can never repay you.' All the same she went on, 'I've forgotten to do so much. The cottage— I should have written to Mrs Pike, who used to clean it for us— and asked her to go and turn on the water and the electricity; it's always turned off when there is nobody there...'

'That's been dealt with,' he told her, 'and there will be food in the fridge and the beds made.'

'Oh, did Mrs Trump think of it? She's been so kind.'

He didn't correct her. 'So that's one problem settled. What's next?'

Slowly, all her doubts and fears came tumbling out, but she stopped short at her biggest fear: her own future. The doctor hadn't said any more about her going back to Amsterdam and she could hardly blame him; she had been enough trouble to him. But if, as Mr Trump had hinted, there wasn't much money in the bank, she would have to find work quickly. 'What about Percy?' she asked suddenly.

'I left him in splendid spirits. He and Prince are devoted; he even climbs into Prince's basket and sleeps with him. They may not look alike but they are obviously soul mates.'

It was on the tip of her tongue to observe that they would miss each other when Percy came back to England, but she stopped herself in time; the doctor might think she was trying, in a roundabout way, to find out if he intended to employ her. Instead she said, 'I must see to things at the cottage.' A task she dreaded— sorting out her mother's possessions, her clothes, looking through her papers.

'Only after you have seen your bank manager and Mr Trump has advised you.'

He gave her a quick sideways glance. 'Mr Trump told me how splendidly you coped when your father died; you will cope splendidly now, Emma.'

They were on the A303 by now, going fast through an early dusk, but as a roadside service station came into sight he slowed.

'Tea, don't you think? We still have quite a way to go.'

Over tea and toasted teacakes she asked him anxiously, 'You don't have to drive back this evening, do you? And won't you be too late for the evening ferry? I didn't think—I'm sorry I've made things so difficult for you.'

'Not at all. I'm staying at Salcombe until you've got things settled as you want them.'

'Staying in Salcombe? But it might be days...'

'Don't worry, I've taken a week or so off.' He smiled at her across the table—such a kind smile that her heart gave a happy little skip; he would be there, helpful and self-assured, knowing what had to be done and how to do it. She smiled widely at him. 'Oh, how very nice—and how kind of you. It will be all the quicker with two, won't it?'

He agreed gravely and passed his cup for more tea, and Emma, feeling happier than she had done for days, bit with something like an appetite into her toasted teacake.

It was a dark evening by the time he parked the Rolls by the pub, took out her case and his own, and went with her to the cottage. He took the key from her and opened the door, switched on the lights and ushered her inside.

There were logs ready to light in the small fireplace, and he put a match to them before she had closed the door, and although the little room was chilly it was cheerful.

'While you put the kettle on,' he said briskly, 'I'll take the cases up. Which was your room?'

'On the left... Cases? But there's only my overnight bag—the case is in the car.'

He was halfway up the narrow stairs. 'I'll have the other room.' He looked over his shoulder at her surprised face. 'Did you really suppose that I would dump your things and leave you on your own?'

'Well,' said Emma, 'I don't think I'd thought about it.' She paused. 'No, that's not true. I've been dreading being alone here. I thought you would have booked a room in one of the hotels and driven back in the morning.'

'You must think me a very poor-spirited friend. But now we've cleared the matter up, go and make the tea; while we drink it we will decide what we will cook for supper.'

She took off her coat and went into the kitchen. She put the kettle on and got a teapot and mugs, then peered into the fridge. There was milk there, eggs and butter, bacon and a small loaf of bread.

'There's bacon and eggs and bread and butter,' she told him as he came into the kitchen, and he saw with relief that the shadow of sorrow had lifted from her face. She was pale and tired and unhappy, but the sharpness of her grief had been melted away by familiar surroundings and his matter-of-fact acceptance of events. Without thinking about it, she had accepted his company as a perfectly natural thing. Which was what he had hoped for.

She cooked their supper presently, while he laid the table, and when they had washed up they sat by the fire talking. There were plans to be made but he wouldn't allow her to get too serious about them. Beyond agreeing with her that seeing the bank manager was something which needed to be done as soon as possible, he began to discuss what groceries they would need to buy and the necessity of visiting Mrs Pike.

It was only much later, when she was in bed and on the edge of sleep, that she remembered that if she was to stay in Salcombe she wouldn't need that lady's services. And tomorrow, she promised herself, she would ask the doctor if he still wished to employ *her*.

She was awakened by his cheerful bellow urging her to come down to the kitchen and have her early-morning tea. She had slept all night, and although at the moment of waking she had felt a remembering grief, it was no longer an unbearable ache. She dragged on her dressing gown and went downstairs, and found the doctor, in a vast pullover, with his hair uncombed and a bristly chin, pouring the tea into mugs. His good morning was cheerfully impersonal. 'I can see you've slept well. While you drink your tea I'll go and shave.'

'Have you been up long? I didn't hear you.'

'Proof that you slept well; your shower is the noisiest I've ever come across. While you cook breakfast I'll go and get some rolls; they should be hot from the oven.'

It was a cold bright morning when, after breakfast, they walked through the town to the bank. At its door Emma said hesitantly, 'Would you mind coming with me? I'm sure there's nothing I can't understand or deal with, but just in case there's something...'

The manager received them gravely, uttering the established

condolences, enquiring after Emma's health, and acknowledging
the doctor's presence with a thoughtful look. He opened the folder
on his desk and coughed.

'I'm afraid that what I have to tell you is of a rather disturbing
nature, although I am sure we can come to some decision together.
There was a small sum of money in your joint account with your
mother to which you added before you went to Holland. Not a
great deal of money, but sufficient to give your mother a modicum
of security. She had her pension, of course, and she gave me to
understand that she had no need to contribute to household expenses so that the pension was an adequate amount for her personal needs. Unfortunately she spent her money freely, and when
the account was empty persuaded me to allow her an overdraft,
assuring me that you would repay it. In short, she spent a good
deal more than the overdraft and there are a number of debts
outstanding.'

Emma asked in a small shocked voice, 'But what could she
have spent the money on? Her pension was enough for clothes
and spending money—there was a few hundred in our account.
Are you sure?'

'Quite sure. I'm sorry, Miss Dawson, but I was assured by your
mother that there were funds she could call upon, and since I have
known your parents for a number of years I saw no reason to
question that.'

'Besides the bank, do you know to whom she owed money?'

'I hold a number of cheques which the bank have refused to
pay. It would be quite in order for you to have them and settle
them personally. I suggest that I should open an account here in
your name so that you can settle the accounts at your convenience.'

'But I haven't...' began Emma, but was stopped by Dr van
Dyke's calm voice.

'That is sound advice, Emma. Allow Mr Ansty to open a new
account in your name, and perhaps he would be good enough to
tell me how much is needed to cover any payments.' When Emma

opened her mouth to protest, he said, 'No, Emma, allow me to deal with this for the moment.'

There was something in his voice which stopped her saying anything more. Only she gave a little gasp when Mr Ansty told the doctor how much was needed to cover the debts and the overdraft. After that she didn't listen while the two men dealt with it, for her mind was wholly occupied with the ways and means of paying back so vast a sum. How on earth was she going to do it?

It wasn't until they were out on the street again that she stopped suddenly.

'I must be mad—whatever have I let you do? We must go back and tell him that you've changed your mind.'

The doctor said nothing, but whisked her into the nearby patisserie and ordered coffee.

'Didn't you hear what I said?' hissed Emma.

'Yes, I did. And when we get back to the cottage I will explain everything to you. Now, drink your coffee like a good girl and we will do the shopping.'

He sounded matter-of-fact, and quite unworried, and that served to calm her down a little. All the same, going in and out of the shops buying their lunch and supper, and listening politely to sympathetic condolences, at the back of her mind was the uneasy feeling that she wasn't quite sure what was happening...

There was a message on the answerphone from Mr Trump when they returned to the cottage. Mrs Riddley's niece would be driving down to Salcombe on the following day to collect her aunt's possessions. She hoped that Miss Dawson had left everything untouched so that she could check for herself that everything was as it should be.

'Well, really,' exclaimed Emma crossly. 'Does she suppose I'd take anything which wasn't Mother's?' She sliced bread with a good deal of unnecessary energy. 'And do I have to stay here all day waiting for her?'

'Very likely. And I must go to the medical centre tomorrow. What's for lunch?'

'Welsh Rarebit. I must go and see Mrs Pike and Miss Johnson...' She was buttering toast. 'And you are going to explain to me about paying the bills.'

He had intended to explain a good deal more than that, but as they finished their meal there was a knock on the door and there was Mrs Craig standing on the doorstep, expecting to be asked in.

'I heard you were here.' She looked at Dr van Dyke, 'With the doctor. I had to come to see you to express my sympathy and have a little chat. I saw your mother frequently, you know, and I'm sure you would wish to know what a happy life she was leading. Such a sad thing to happen, and you so far from her at the time, although I hear that she died instantly.'

Mrs Craig settled herself comfortably in a chair. 'I would have gone to the funeral if it had been here, but of course she wished to be buried with her husband.'

She doesn't mean to be unkind, thought Emma, sitting rigid in her chair, but if she doesn't go soon I shall scream.

It was the doctor who came to the rescue. 'You are the very person we wanted to see,' he told Mrs Craig. 'May I come back with you to the hotel? There is someone there I believe had dealings with Mrs Dawson, and it would make it so much easier if you could introduce me. I'm sure you must know her...'

Mrs Craig got up at once. 'Of course, Doctor. I'm so delighted to be of help. I've lived here for some time now and know almost everyone here. Emma, you will forgive me if I don't stay, for I'm sure Dr van Dyke is anxious to settle his business.'

Emma was left alone, to cry her eyes out in peace, so that when the doctor came back she was tolerably cheerful again, in the kitchen getting their tea.

'There were one or two small bills at the hotel,' he told her. 'I've settled them.' He didn't tell her that he had telephoned Mr Trump, paid a visit to the rector and talked at length with Kulk.

When she suggested again that they had to talk about his arrangements with the bank he brushed it aside. 'You have had enough to think about today,' he told her. 'We will get a meal at the pub and not be too late in bed, for we don't know how early this niece will arrive.'

They ate fresh-caught fish and a mountain of chips, and since there was no one else in the little dining room behind the bar the landlord came and talked to them while they ate, gathering up their plates when they had finished and promising them apple pie and cream.

The doctor kept up a casual flow of talk during their meal, urged her to have a brandy with her coffee and walked her briskly back to the cottage. She was pleasantly sleepy by now, and needed no urging to go to her bed. Tomorrow they would have that talk, and once Mrs Riddley's niece had taken her aunt's things she would pack away her mother's possessions. That left only Mrs Pike to see...

She woke in the small hours and sat up in bed, struck by a sudden thought. What a fool I am, she reflected. I can sell the cottage and pay back the money. I must tell him in the morning.

She fell asleep again, satisfied that the problem was solved.

They had barely finished breakfast when Mrs Riddley's niece arrived. Emma disliked her on sight; she was a youngish woman, fashionably thin, expensively dressed and skilfully made-up.

She answered Emma's polite greeting with a curt nod. 'You're Emma Dawson? I haven't much time; I intend to drive back as soon as possible.' She went past Emma into the cottage. 'I hope you haven't touched any of my aunt's possessions...'

Emma said quietly, 'No. I'm sorry that Mrs Riddley died.'

The doctor, at the kitchen sink, rattled a few plates.

'Someone else is here?'

'A friend who brought me back to England. Would you like coffee, or would you prefer to go straight to your aunt's room?'

'Oh, I'll get her stuff packed up first. Which room is it?'

'I'll show you, and when you are ready perhaps you will look around the cottage and make sure that there is nothing you have overlooked?'

'Certainly I shall.' She closed the door firmly in Emma's face.

The doctor was drying plates with the air of one who had been doing it all his life. He lifted an eyebrow at Emma as she went into the kitchen.

'Keep a sharp eye on her; she might filch the spoons!'

Emma, a bit put out, giggled, feeling suddenly light-hearted.

After a while the niece came downstairs. 'I've packed up my aunt's things. There are several dresses and hats too old to bother with. I dare say you can take them to a charity shop.'

She looked at the doctor, all at once smiling.

'Dr van Dyke—this is Miss or is it Mrs Riddley?' said Emma. 'And actually I think you should take everything with you.'

'Oh, undoubtedly,' said the doctor smoothly. 'One needs to be careful about these matters. I'll fetch a plastic sack and you can bundle everything in it.'

'Would you like coffee?' asked Emma. 'And then you must go round the cottage.'

Miss Riddley refused coffee. 'I left the car at the end of the quay...'

'I'll carry your bags to it,' offered the doctor. 'We will let Mr Trump know that you have been and removed everything of your aunt's.' He stood up. 'Shall we go? I dare say you are anxious to get back home?'

Chilling good manners, thought Emma, watching Miss Riddley mince along on her high heels beside the doctor. He looks very nice from the back, reflected Emma, and then she thought, I'll tell him about selling the cottage and how I'll pay back his money, and then he can go back to Amsterdam and not feel he has to do anything more for me. Of course there's Percy. Perhaps he wouldn't mind giving me a lift back so that I can bring Percy back here...

Much taken with this half-witted idea, she went upstairs to make quite sure that Mrs Riddley's possessions had really gone.

There was no sign of the doctor when she went back downstairs and she remembered that he had intended to go to the medical centre. She had her coffee and started on a task she had been putting off: going through the desk her mother had used and clearing out the papers in it. It was something which had to be done, and it seemed likely that now everything was more or less settled the doctor would wish to return to Holland. That was something else she must talk to him about without delay. She had been living in a kind of limbo, doing what he suggested, not allowing herself to think too much about the future, but it was time she faced up to that.

She finished clearing the desk and set the table for lunch, which would be cheese and pickles and the rolls he had fetched early that morning—there was to be no lingering over lunch, she decided. There was too much to talk about.

But she wasn't to have her wish. The doctor came in briskly, observed that he had seen the niece drive away and then gone to see his former colleagues, then added as a kind of afterthought, 'What do you call me, Emma?'

'Call you? Why, Dr van Dyke.'

'My name is Roele.'

'Yes, I know, but I can't call you that; I've been working for you. Which reminds me...'

He gave her no chance to continue. 'Yes, you can.' He sat back in his chair and smiled at her. 'Will you marry me, Emma?'

She put the roll she was buttering back on her plate, staring at him.

'Why?' she asked.

He was amused, but all he said was, 'A sensible question. I am thirty-six, Emma. I need a wife to run my home, entertain my friends and—er—support me.'

'But Kulk runs your home beautifully and your friends might not like me. Besides, you don't need supporting. Indeed, you've been supporting me.' She added politely, 'Thank you for asking me. I've had a very good idea this morning. I shall sell the cottage and then I can pay you back all that money you gave the bank.'

'And?'

'Then I'll get a job.'

'For such a sensible girl you have some odd ideas, Emma. What job? And where will you live? And how will you pay the rent and feed yourself on the kind of wages you are able to earn?'

'Well, I must say,' said Emma crossly, 'I thought you'd be pleased to be free to go back home.' She frowned. 'This is a very strange conversation.'

'Indeed it is. Shall we start again. Will you marry me, Emma?'

CHAPTER SEVEN

SHE stared at him across the table. 'But you don't—that is, you can't possibly be in love with me...'

'I have made no mention of love, or falling in love, Emma. Indeed, a happy marriage is as likely to be the result of compatibility, a real liking for each other, and the slow growing of deep affection which would surely follow. Sound bases on which to build. Whereas all too often marrying on impulse whilst in the throes of a love which so often turns into infatuation turns into disaster.'

He smiled at her. 'Do I sound like an elder brother giving you advice? I don't mean to; I'm only trying to make the situation clear to you without pretending to a romance that doesn't exist.'

'And if I should say yes?'

'We will marry as soon as possible and go back to Amsterdam. You will, of course, keep this cottage. We both like Salcombe, don't we? And it would be nice to keep a foot in the door here.'

'Have you ever been in love?' asked Emma. If he was surprised at her question he didn't show it.

'Oh, countless times. Young men do, you know, it's all part of growing up. And you?'

'Oh, yes. With film stars and the music master at school and my best friend's brother—only they went to live abroad and I forgot about him. And of course there was Derek, but I didn't love him—only got used to him. Mother liked him and he was always very attentive—until Father died and he discovered that he was bankrupt and it would damage his career if he married me. Would I damage *your* career?'

He answered her with perfect gravity. 'No. Indeed, I suppose it would be a great advantage to me. A married man always seems so much more reliable!'

'You might meet someone and fall in love... So might I...'

'There is that possibility, but remember that I am no longer an impetuous youth and you, if I may say so, have reached the age of reason.'

'I'm twenty-seven,' snapped Emma, 'and if you suppose that I'm a staid spinster you're mistaken.'

'No, no, I wouldn't imagine anything of the sort. I merely meant to imply that we are both of us ideally suited to be man and wife.'

'You're not asking me because you are sorry for me?'

His, 'Good Lord, no,' had a satisfyingly genuine ring to it. All the same she frowned.

'Ought we to wait and think about it?'

'For my part, I've done my thinking, but by all means take all the time you need, Emma. I'll go back to Amsterdam in a while, and you can make up your mind at your leisure.'

This was a prospect she didn't fancy; to be here in the cottage on her own and Roele not there to advise her... But of course she couldn't ask his advice about marrying him, could she?

'You don't know anything about me...'

'On the contrary, I know that you are capable, sensible, have similar tastes and interests to mine, you are a good listener, have the ability to face up to life, and, as a bonus, you are a very attractive young woman. And let me make it quite clear to you that I do not wish for or expect you to strive for a romantic attachment until such time as you feel ready for it.'

'Just friends to start with?'

'You see what I mean? Sensible and matter-of-fact. Just friends—good friends.'

'There's another thing. I think you must be comfortably off, but I want you to know that I'm not marrying you for your money.'

Roele gave a small inward sigh of relief. His darling Emma was going to marry him, and sooner or later would learn to love him. In the meantime he had more than enough love for them both. He said firmly, 'I know you aren't, and, yes, I do have rather a lot of money. It will be nice to share it with someone.'

His smile was warm and friendly and utterly reassuring. 'Will you marry me, Emma?'

'Yes, I will. I like you very much and I know that I would miss you very much if you were to go away, and—and when you're not here I feel a bit lost. Only I hope I won't be a disappointment to you.' She looked at him with a question in her eyes. 'You would tell me?'

'Yes, I promise you that I will.' He leaned across the table and took one of her hands in his. 'Would you object to getting married by special licence as soon as possible? Here in Salcombe? And we'll return to Amsterdam as soon as possible afterwards.'

'I still have Mother's things to pack up...'

'Then start on that while I go and see Mrs Pike and talk to the rector.'

'Does it take a long time to get a special licence?'

'It should be in the post tomorrow morning; all we need to do is fix a time and a day.'

'Just us?'

'Well, I think Dr Walters might like to be at the church, and what about Miss Johnson and Mrs Craig?'

'Oh, witnesses. Of course. All right. And now everything is settled we had better get started.'

She got up and began to clear the table, but he took the dishes out of her hands and put his hands on her shoulders. 'How very unromantic of me to propose to you over the remnants of a meal. I must make up for that...' He bent and kissed her gently. 'We shall be happy, Emma, I promise you...'

His kiss sent a glow of warmth through her; she was honest enough to admit that she enjoyed it, and for the first time since her mother's death she felt a surge of content and happiness.

As soon as he had gone in search of the rector and Mrs Pike she went to her mother's room and began the sad task of packing up her clothes.

The cupboards and drawers were stuffed full. In the short time in which Emma had been away Mrs Dawson had indeed spent a good deal of money on dresses, hats and shoes—most of them hardly worn. They would have to go to a charity shop.

She picked out one or two of the more sober garments in case Mrs Pike might like to have them, bundled everything else in sacks and then opened her mother's jewel box. There was a pearl necklace, rings and brooches and earrings. They were hers now, Emma supposed. She closed the box. She would wear the pearls on her wedding day but the rest she would put away until an occasion when she might need to wear them.

She wept a little as she thought of her mother and father. I'm an orphan, she thought, drowning in sudden self-pity, until her sensible self took over again and she reminded herself that she was going to get married to a man she liked very much and go and live in a splendid house and share his life. And she was going to make a success of it too.

Roele came back then, with the news that the rector would marry them in two days' time at ten o'clock in the morning, if she was agreeable to that. And as for Mrs Pike, he had arranged for her to go to the cottage once a week and keep it in good order. 'For of course we shall come here from time to time, even if it is only for a few days. Now, what do you want me to do with your mother's clothes?' he asked.

She had been crying, poor girl. The quicker the cottage was empty of things which would remind her of her grief the better.

'There are three sacks full. Could you take them to the charity shop? The nearest one is in Kingsbridge.'

'A good idea. Get your hat and coat; we'll both go. I'll take them along to the car while you get ready.'

By the time she had done that, and tidied her face and hair, she looked quite cheerful again. As they drove the few miles to Kingsbridge he kept up a steady flow of cheerful remarks, so that by the time they reached the shop and handed everything over she was quite ready to go to a tea room at the bottom of the high street and linger over tea and hot buttered crumpets.

* * *

They were married two days later, on a morning of tearing wind and persistent rain, despite which a surprising number of people came to the church to see them wed. Dr Walters and his colleagues, Miss Johnson and Phoebe, Mrs Craig and Mrs Pike, several members of the lifeboat crew, even the cross-looking baker's wife.

They gathered round when the simple ceremony was over, offering good wishes and waving goodbyes as they got into the Rolls. They drove through the little town and on to the road to Exeter on the first stage of their journey back to Holland.

They had had an early breakfast. Roele had taken the luggage to the car and locked the cottage door with the cheerful remark that they would be back in the spring, and then popped her into the car and driven to the church without giving Emma time to feel regret or sadness. And now he kept up a steady flow of talk: the unexpected pleasure of seeing friends and acquaintances at the church, the stormy weather, the pleasure of seeing Prince and Percy again.

'You won't see much of me for a few days,' he told her. 'I'll have a backlog of work, but that will give you time to get used to the house and do some shopping. I should warn you that the nearer we get to Christmas the more social life there will be. Which will give you a chance to meet my friends.'

'Oh, do you have a lot of friends and go out a great deal?'

'Plenty of friends, yes. And I do have a social life, but a very moderate one.'

They were on the A303, driving into worsening weather. As they approached Middle Wallop Roele said, 'We will stop for lunch.' He turned to smile at her. 'Breakfast seems a long time ago. There's rather a nice place where we can get a meal.'

He took a side-turning and stopped before a handsome manor house on the edge of a village. After the gloomy skies and heavy rain its comfortable warmth was welcoming. Emma, led away by a pleasant waitress, returned to find that Roele was sitting at the bar.

'I hope you're hungry; I am.' The bartender put two champagne cocktails before them. 'To our future together, Emma.'

It was probably the champagne which gave her such a pleasureable feeling of excitement.

They lunched on sauté mushrooms, duckling and orange sauce and bread and butter pudding and a pot of delicious coffee. Looking out at the wild weather, Emma felt very reluctant to leave.

'I'll phone from the car,' Roele told her. 'I doubt if the Harwich Ferry will be running in this weather. If that's the case, we'll make for Dover.'

It was the case; the Harwich Ferry was cancelled. But the Dover ferries were still running, so the doctor drove on to the M25 and presently took the Dover road.

It was well into the afternoon now, and already getting dark with no sign of the weather improving. Emma, sitting in the car, waiting to go on board the ferry, looked at the rough seas and hoped for the best.

On board, she drank the tea she was offered and opened the magazine Roele had bought her. They should be home by midnight, he assured her. It was a long drive to Amsterdam, but the roads were good and fast and Kulk would be waiting for them. She smiled and nodded and tried not to notice the heaving deck. They were halfway across when she put the magazine down.

'I'm going to be sick,' said Emma.

The doctor took a quick look at her white face, heaved her gently to her feet and led her away. And she, feeling truly awful, wouldn't have cared if he had thrown her overboard.

Instead he dealt with things with an impersonal kindness which made it less awful than it was, finally gently washing her face and settling her in her seat again with an arm round her. He made her drink the brandy the steward brought, then tucked her head onto his shoulder. 'Go to sleep,' he told her, 'we are nearly there. Once we're on land you'll be quite yourself again. My poor girl, I should never have brought you—we should have stayed until tomorrow.'

Emma mumbled into his coat, feeling better already. 'That wouldn't have done; you told me that you had an appointment tomorrow.' She hiccoughed as a result of the brandy, and closed her eyes. She was quite safe with Roele's arm around her, and not only safe but happy.

He was right, of course, once on dry land she was quite herself again. It was dark night now, the rain lashing down, blown hither and thither by the wind, but the road was good and almost empty of traffic. Roele drove fast, relaxed behind the wheel of the big car, not saying much, only telling her from time to time where they were—along the coast to Ostend and then inland onto the E40. He turned off again onto the motorway to Antwerp, and then over the border into Holland to Utrecht and finally the outskirts of Amsterdam.

But before they reached the city the doctor turned off to go to his home, driving slowly now along the narrow road until he reached the village and a moment later drew up before his front door. There were lights shining out from the downstairs windows and the front door opened wide to reveal more light, with Kulk and Mevrouw Kulk standing there.

The doctor got out, opened Emma's door and swept her into the house through the rain and wind, to be greeted by handshaking and beaming smiles and a rush of excited talk. She was borne away by Mevrouw Kulk to have her coat taken, and ushered into the cloakroom at the back of the hall. She was tired and very hungry, and the prospect of bed was enticing, but she washed her face to wake herself up, tidied her hair and went back in to the hall.

Kulk was bringing in their luggage and Roele had gone out again to put the car in the garage. She stood for a moment, feeling uncertain. But only for a moment, for Mevrouw Kulk appeared through a door behind the staircase. With her was Percy, and close on his heels Prince.

Emma was kneeling on the floor, her arms round the two dogs, when the doctor came back. He threw his coat onto a chair, received the lavish affection offered by Prince and Percy and helped her to her feet.

'Welcome home, Emma. Mevrouw Kulk has a meal ready. You must be hungry—and longing for your bed. Sleep for as long as you like in the morning; I shall be away all day until early evening, forgive me for that, but the Kulks will look after you.'

He took her hand and led her through an arched double door into a room with a high-plastered ceiling and long windows. The walls were white and hung with paintings in heavy gilt frames, and the furniture matched the room—a rectangular mahogany table ringed by ribband-backed chairs, a massive sideboard bearing a display of silver, and a wide fireplace surmounted by an elaborate chimneypiece.

'This is a beautiful room,' said Emma, forgetting her tiredness for a moment as Roele sat her down at the table, where two places had been laid. Despite the lateness of the hour, she noted, silver and crystal gleamed on the lace tablemats and there were fresh flowers in a Delft blue bowl. And their supper, when it came, was delicious: beef bouillon, a creamy golden soufflé and finally a fruit tart, the pastry light as a feather.

'And, since it is our wedding day, champagne is obligatory,' said the doctor. He smiled at her across the table. 'You were a beautiful bride, Emma.'

She gaped at him. 'In last year's suit and the only hat I could find in the town?'

'And still a beautiful bride. An unusual wedding day, perhaps, but I have enjoyed every minute of it.'

'Really? Well, yes, I suppose I have too—not the ferry, though!'

'I'm sorry about that too, but at least you will never forget your wedding day.' He studied her tired face. 'You would like to go to bed, wouldn't you? No coffee; it might keep you awake. Mevrouw Kulk shall take you to your room.' He got up and walked to the door with her, and bent and kissed her cheek. 'Sleep well, Emma.' After a pause, he added, 'I'll see to Percy.'

Already half asleep, she followed Mevrouw Kulk up the wide staircase, along a gallery and into a softly lit bedroom.

'I must explore it in the morning,' muttered Emma as Mevrouw Kulk drew curtains and opened doors and cupboards, switched on another bedside light and patted the turned-down coverlet before beaming with a *'wel te rusten'* as she went away.

Emma cleaned her teeth, washed her face, tore off her clothes and got into bed—to fall asleep instantly.

When she woke there was a sturdy young girl drawing back the curtains to reveal a dull morning. She sat up in bed and ventured a *'Goeden morgen'* with such success that the girl answered with a flood of Dutch.

Emma tried again. 'I don't understand' had been one of first useful phrases she had learnt. The girl smiled, picked up the tray she had set on the table under the window and brought it to the bed. Emma, struggling to find the words she wanted, was relieved to see a note propped up against the teapot. Roele in an almost unreadable scrawl, wished her good morning, recommended that she ate a good breakfast and then took the dogs for a walk, and said he would be home at about six o'clock.

Emma drank her tea, read the note again and got up. The bathroom held every incentive to linger, with its deep bath and shelves loaded with towels, soap and everything else she could possibly want, but she resisted its luxury after a pleasurable time lying in a scented bath and dressed once more in the suit. Nicely made up, and with her hair in its usual topknot, she went downstairs.

Kulk was hovering in the hall to wish her good morning and lead her to the small room where she had breakfasted on her earlier visit. The table had been drawn near the brisk fire and Prince and Percy were waiting for her.

This was her home, she reflected as Kulk set a coffee pot down before her, moved the toast rack a little nearer and asked her if she would prefer bacon and eggs, scrambled eggs, or perhaps an omelette...

And I actually belong here, thought Emma, devouring the scrambled eggs with appetite and deciding that toast and marmalade would be nice, with another cup of coffee. She handed out morsels of toast to both dogs, and when Kulk came to see if there was anything else she would like she asked, 'The doctor, did he leave very early?'

His English was good, although the accent was pronounced. 'At half past seven, *mevrouw*. I understand he has a number of patients to see before going to the hospital, where he has a clinic and ward rounds.'

'You have been with the doctor for a long time?'

'I taught him to ride a bicycle, *mevrouw*, when I was a house-man at his parents' home. When they retired to a quiet life I came as his houseman and my wife as his cook.'

Emma set down her coffee cup. 'Kulk, this is all strange to me. I would be glad if you will help me...'

'With the greatest pleasure, *mevrouw*. Katje and I will do everything to assist you in any way. If you have finished your breakfast you might like to come to the kitchen and we will explain the running of the household to you. Katje speaks no English but I will translate, for you will wish to order the meals and inspect the linen and cutlery as well as the stores she keeps.'

'Thank you, Kulk. I should like to know as much as possible, but I have no intention of taking over.' She hesitated; Kulk was an old family servant and to be trusted. She said carefully, 'You see, Kulk, the doctor and I married without waiting for an engagement. I have recently lost my mother and I had no reason to stay in England.'

'Katje and I are happy that the doctor is happily married, *mevrouw*. For a long time we have wished that, and now we are delighted to welcome you and serve you as we serve him.'

That sounded incredibly old-fashioned, but she had no doubt that it was spoken in all sincerity. 'Thank you—and Katje. May I call her that? I know that I—we are going to be very happy here. I'll come with you now, shall I? May Prince and Percy come, too?'

'Of course, *mevrouw*.'

He led the way into the hall, through a door beside the staircase and along a short passage which led to the kitchen. This was a large room, with windows overlooking the grounds behind the house. It was old-fashioned at first glance, but as well as the vast wooden dresser against one wall and the scrubbed table at its centre there was an Aga flanked by glass-fronted cupboards and shelves gleaming with shining saucepans. There was a deep butler's sink under one window and a dishwasher beside it, and on either side of the Aga were two Windsor armchairs, each with a cat curled up on its cushion.

'The cats!' exclaimed Kulk. 'Perhaps you do not care for them...?'

'Oh, but I do—and what a lovely kitchen.'

Mevrouw Kulk wasn't there, but she had heard them for she called something to Kulk from an open door in one wall. She came a moment later, holding a bowl of eggs. She put them down, wished Emma good day and offered a chair.

Emma sat at the table, listening to Kulk talking to his wife, trying to understand what was being said. But presently she gave up. As soon as possible she would take lessons; her smattering of the language wouldn't be of much use if she were to join in Roele's social life. Besides, she would want to shop; he had never mentioned her clothes, but she was quite sure that as his wife she would be expected to dress with some style.

Mevrouw Kulk interrupted her thoughts, standing beside her with a pad and a pencil.

'Dinner for tonight,' said Kulk. 'Is there something you would wish for? Katje has it planned, but perhaps you would wish for other things.'

'No, no, of course not. But I'd like to know what we are to have...'

She left the kitchen after an hour with a good idea of the day's routine kept by the Kulks. There was a girl to help—she who had brought her early-morning tea, Bridgette—and a gardener, and once or twice a year local women came in from the village to help with the bi-annual cleaning of the house. 'If there is to be a social occasion,' explained Kulk, 'then we get extra help.'

Obviously it was a well-run house which needed no help from her.

She put on a coat and went into the grounds with the dogs. There was a terrace behind the house, with steps leading down to a formal garden, and beyond that a great stretch of lovingly laid out shrubs and ornamental trees, and narrow stone paths with unexpected rustic seats and stone statues round every corner. Whoever had planned it had done it with meticulous attention to detail. She wandered round for some time, with Percy and Prince chasing imaginary rabbits and racing back to see if she was still there. It was a beautiful place even on a wintry morning; in summer it would be somewhere where one would want to sit and do nothing.

She went back indoors then and had the coffee Kulk had ready.

If *mevrouw* wished, he suggested, he would show her round the house. But perhaps she would prefer to wait for the doctor?

She thanked him. 'I would rather wait for the doctor to come home, and then we can go round it together, Kulk.'

'Quite right and proper, too,' said Kulk to Katje later, 'and them newlyweds and having plans and so forth. Such a nice young lady he's found for himself. Used to nice living, I can see that, but it must be very strange for her. A bit of help from us from time to time won't come amiss.'

There were books in the small sitting room, as well as newspapers in both Dutch and English. Besides that there was a television, discreetly tucked away in a corner. Emma, not easily bored, had plenty to keep her occupied, but after lunch she sat down by the fire, hemmed in by the dogs, and allowed her thoughts free rein.

It was apparent that Roele was more than just very well off, he had what her old schoolmistress had always referred to as 'background'—a background which, she suspected, stretched back for generations. She must ask him about that—but she must also remember not to plague him with endless questions for the time being. Having worked at his consulting rooms, she was aware of the number of patients he saw each day and the length of his visits to the hospital—more than one hospital, Juffrouw Smit had told her. Only when he had the leisure to talk to her would she question him.

There was a great deal unsaid between them, but she had expected that; they might have married, but they didn't know each other well. At least, she didn't know Roele, and she supposed that he didn't know her as a person. That they liked each other was a solid fact and that they would, in time, have a happy life together was something she didn't doubt. Until then she would be content...

She went upstairs to change into the jersey dress after tea, and when she came downstairs Roele was taking off his coat in the hall, fending off the dogs' delighted greeting. When he saw her he came to the bottom of the stairs and held out a hand.

'How nice to find you here, have you been bored or lonely?'

'Neither. It would be impossible to be lonely with the dogs, and I could never be bored in this house.'

'You have explored?'

'No.'

He was quick to see her hesitate. 'You waited for me? Splendid. We will go round now, and while we are having a drink before dinner you can tell me what you think of it.'

He put an arm round her shoulders and turned her smartly towards the big arched doorway on one side of the hall.

'The drawing room,' he said, and opened the door.

It was a large room, with walls hung with pale green silk between white-painted panels. There were brass sconces between the pillars and a cut-glass chandelier hung from the strapwork ceiling. The three tall windows were curtained in old-rose velvet and the floor was covered by a dark green Aubusson carpet with a floral design at its centre. Above the fireplace was an elaborate Rococo chimneypiece with an enormous mirror.

It was a very grand room, and its furniture reflected its grandeur: William and Mary settees on either side of the fireplace, two Georgian winged armchairs with a Pembroke table between them, a group of armchairs around a veneered rosewood tripod table and a scattering of small tables, each with its own lamp. There were two walnut display cabinets, filled with porcelain and silver, and a long-case clock facing the windows.

Emma stood in the middle of the room, taking it all in. 'What a wonderful room!' She caught sight of the pile of magazines and an open book lying on one of the tables. 'Do you use it often?'

'Oh, yes. It's remarkably cosy with a good fire burning in the winter. Tea round the fire on a Sunday afternoon with a good book and the right music. And for social occasions, of course.'

He crossed to the door and opened it. There was a conservatory beyond, and Emma lingered among the wealth of plants and shrubs before he ushered her through a further door and back into the hall. 'We've seen the dining room, now here is my study.' This proved to be another panelled room, its walls lined with bookshelves and a vast desk under its window.

Emma gazed around, wondering if she would be welcome in it. Probably not, she thought.

'You know the morning room,' said Roele, 'but there's one more room here.' He crossed the hall again and opened a door onto a quite small room, with two easy chairs by a small steel grate and a sofa table standing behind a big sofa under the window. 'My mother always used this room. She wrote her letters here and sat in that chair, knitting and working at her tapestry. I do hope you will make it your own, Emma.'

'Your mother?'

'She and my father live just outside Den Haag now. My father is retired—like me, he was a medical man—and they have a house in the country. We will go and visit them shortly.'

'Do they know that you married me?'

'Of course, and they are delighted to welcome you into the family.'

They were now halfway up the staircase, but she paused, her hand on the carved wood balustrade. 'If I were them,' she declared, letting grammar go to the winds, 'I wouldn't want to welcome me, coming in from nowhere—I might be an adventuress.'

The doctor laughed. 'An adventuress wouldn't have carroty

hair,' he told her. 'Besides, they trust my judgement. Don't worry about them, Emma; they will like you and I think that you will like them.'

He led her across the gallery to the front of the house, opened a door and urged her inside. The room was large, with two tall windows opening out onto a wrought-iron balcony. A four-poster bed faced them, its coverlet in the same satin chintz as the curtains. There was a mahogany dressing table between the windows, with an elaborate carved framed triple mirror on it, a cabinet chest against one wall and a tallboy facing it. On either side of a small round table there were small tub chairs, and at the foot of the bed a Regency chaise longue. It was a beautiful room, and Emma said so.

'You must love your home, Roele,' she said.

'As you will love it too, Emma. We can go through here...' He led the way through a bathroom to a smaller room, simply furnished, and then out into the gallery again to open another door.

Emma lost count of the rooms after a time. When they had inspected those opening onto the gallery there were the side passages, leading to even more rooms, and then a staircase to the floor above.

'The nurseries,' said the doctor, sweeping her in and out of doors. Children's bedrooms, more guest rooms. And then up another staircase. 'Kulk and Katje have rooms here, and Bridgette too, and along here are the attics and a door onto the roof.'

There was a narrow parapet and an iron staircase down to the ground.

'We keep the door locked but the key hangs above it. Kulk has another key and so have I.'

'I had no idea...' began Emma.

He understood her at once. 'It is a large house, but it is also home—our home, Emma. You will learn to love it as I do.'

They went back downstairs and had drinks and a splendid dinner, and shortly afterwards Roele went to his study to work. Emma spent a blissful few hours in the drawing room, examining everything in it. Percy was with her, but Prince had gone with his master. Presently she was joined by the two cats, who wandered in and settled onto one of the settees with the air of welcome guests. That was what was so delightful about the house, reflected Emma, it *was* a home as well.

Roele came back then, asked her if there was anything she would like before going to bed and suggested that she might like to go and see Juffrouw Smit on the following day. 'She would like you to go to her house for lunch. Kulk will drive you in about midday. I shall be at the hospital for most of the day, but I'll call for you at about half past one and bring you back here.'

He smiled at her. 'I shall be free at the weekend and we can be together. You're not too lonely?'

'No, of course not. There's such a lot to see. Tomorrow I had thought I'd walk to the village, but now I'm going to Juffrouw Smit, so I'll go to the village the next day. The days won't be long enough.'

She sounded so convincing that she almost convinced herself, and tried hard not to mind when he made no effort to keep her after she suggested that she should go to bed.

CHAPTER EIGHT

EMMA was relieved to see Juffrouw Smit's severe countenance break into a smile when she arrived for lunch the next day. It could have been an awkward meeting, but somehow her hostess gave the impression that she had expected Dr van Dyke and Emma to marry, and it was something of which she entirely approved.

'The doctor is coming for you at half past one so we do not have much time for a chat, but perhaps you will come again? I am interested to hear of your wedding and the cottage at Salcombe—as you know, the doctor has very little time to chat. A quiet wedding, I expect?'

So Emma sat down and drank very dry sherry and described her wedding; not that there was much to describe, but she made the most of it, enlarged upon their journey back and the awful weather, and, over lunch, described the cottage in detail.

'Perhaps you would like to stay there when you have a holiday? It is a charming little town and the people are friendly—besides, your English is so good.' She added impulsively, 'You were so kind to me when I came here to work for the doctor, and I never thanked you for that. But I do now. I'm glad I did work here, even in such a humble capacity, because now I can understand how hard Roele works.'

'You will be a good wife to him,' pronounced Juffrouw Smit. 'Now, we will have coffee here at the table, for the doctor will be here very shortly and I must go back to work. But you will come again, I hope?'

'Yes, please. There is such a lot I need to know—about the shops and all the everyday things one takes for granted in one's own country.'

Roele was punctual and she was glad that she was ready for

him for, although he was his usual quiet self, she sensed that he was impatient to be back at work. So she shook hands with Juffrouw Smit, thanked her for her lunch without lingering and got into the car.

'I could have found my own way home,' she told him as they drove off.

'So you could, and I'll tell you how best to do that some time.' He smiled at her, thinking that she had called his house home quite unconsciously; they had been married for only a day or so and she was already fitting into his life as though it had been made for her. 'I'll be home earlier today,' he told her. 'We will have tea together and then take the dogs to the village.'

It was a short walk to the village. He took her to see the church, which was small and austere outside but the interior held high carved wood pews and a magnificent pulpit and its walls were covered by black and white marble plaques, many of them from Roele's family. And underfoot there were ancient gravestones, inscribed in flowery Latin. He showed her the front pew under the pulpit, with its red velvet cushions and hassocks. 'This is where we come on Sundays,' he told her.

The village was small, its little houses and cottages having shining windows and spotless paintwork. Here and there were larger houses, set haphazardly between the cottages. There was a small shop too, selling, as far as Emma could see, absolutely everything.

'And yet the village is so close to Amsterdam...'

'Yes, but off the beaten track, and a good many of the people living here are elderly and don't want the hassle of a bus ride to the shops. Come and meet Mevrouw Twist.'

The shop was dark inside, and it smelled of onions and of the smoked sausages hanging from the ceiling, with a whiff of furniture polish and washing powder. The doctor introduced her, bought dog biscuits and listened courteously to Mevrouw Twist's gossip, then shook hands, waited while Emma did the same, and then they went back into the small square.

'Tomorrow we have been asked to the *dominee's* house so that I may introduce you to him and his wife. In the evening at about

six o'clock. We shall drink home made wine and stay for an hour.'
He tucked her arm in his. 'You see, I lead two lives, Emma. I
know everyone in the village but I have friends in Amsterdam,
too.'

They were walking up the drive to the house, the dogs running
ahead.

'Bear with me for a few more days and then we will go shopping. You always look nice, but you will need warm clothes and
some pretty dresses...'

The following evening they walked to the *dominee's* house arm-
in-arm, talking of everyday ordinary events, and Emma realised
that she felt like a wife...

The *dominee* was tall and thin and rather earnest, while his
wife was blonde, wholesomely good-looking and friendly. She
took Emma away to see the baby—a boy, lying sleeping in his
cot. 'Roele is his godfather,' she told Emma. She led the way into
an adjoining room. 'Anna, Sophia and Marijke,' she said and
waved towards the three small girls sitting at the table, school-
books spread around them.

Emma said hello, and their mother blew them a kiss then took
Emma back to the men. The *dominee* gave her a glass of wine,
saying, 'My wife is clever; she makes the wine. This is from
rhubarb.'

He came and sat beside her. 'I am sorry to hear that you have
had a good deal of unhappiness, but now you are married to Roele
you will be happy again.'

'Yes, I know,' said Emma, and knew that that was true.

Walking back presently, she told Roele, 'I liked the *dominee*
and his wife, and the baby and the little girls. Have you known
them for a long time?'

'Years and years. He and I were at school together. Jette is an
old friend too.'

Towards the end of the week Roele told her over dinner, 'I'll
be free until the evening tomorrow. Shall we go shopping?'

Emma, heartily sick of the few clothes she had brought with her, agreed with enthusiasm.

'You will need a winter coat and a good raincoat—get yourself whatever you wear in the winter, and some pretty dresses for the evening and anything else you need.'

'Thank you, but how much may I spend?'

'You can use my account at some of the shops, but at the smaller shops I'll settle the bills as we go. I'll arrange for you to have an allowance as soon as possible, but in the meantime leave the paying to me.'

In bed that night, Emma thought uneasily that she needed a great deal, and that perhaps Roele hadn't realised how much even a basic wardrobe would cost him. But she had stayed awake worrying about that to no purpose; the next morning he drove her to Amsterdam, parked the car and walked her briskly to a street of small fashionable shops. The kind of shop, she saw, which displayed one or two mouthwatering garments in its narrow window with no price ticket in sight.

The doctor stopped before an elegant shop window. 'My sisters go here,' he observed, and ushered her into its dove-grey interior.

The elegant woman who glided towards them took in Emma's out-of-date but expertly tailored suit, the well polished equally out-of-date shoes and handbag, and recognised a good customer.

'Dr van Dyke—you were here with your sister some time ago.'

'Indeed I was. My wife would like some dresses. We shall be entertaining, so something for dinner parties.'

'I have the very thing for *mevrouw*, and so fortunate that a consignment of delightfully pretty outfits arrived only this week. If *mevrouw* will come with me?'

So Emma went behind elegant brocade curtains and had her useful suit and sweater taken from her and replaced by a dark green velvet dress, very plain, with long sleeves and a high neck, and a skirt which just skimmed her knees and showed off her shapely legs to great advantage.

She showed herself rather shyly to Roele, sitting comfortably in a gilt chair reading a newspaper.

'Very nice. Have it.'

'But I'm sure it's very expensive,' hissed Emma.

'Just right for dinner parties; get another one...blue...'

The saleslady had splendid hearing; she had a blue crêpe dress with short sleeves, a low square neck and a wide pleated skirt ready to slip over Emma's head.

When she went back to Roele again, he nodded. 'Very nice, have it, and get a couple of warm dresses...'

Emma, slightly light-headed, allowed herself to be fitted into a soft brown cashmere dress, and then a green jersey dress, a two-piece, and, since Roele approved of them both, she added them to the others. Once more in her old suit, she waited while Roele paid for everything and arranged for them to be sent round to his consulting rooms.

'We will pick them up before we go home,' he told her. 'Now, if I remember rightly there is a place here where they stock Burberry...'

With a short pause for coffee, Emma acquired a raincoat and hat, two tweed skirts she'd admired, a couple of cashmere sweaters and a handful of silk blouses. By then it was time for lunch.

Over lobster thermidor at Thysse and Dikker, she pointed out that she now had a splendid wardrobe—and shouldn't they go home?

'We are by no means finished,' the doctor pointed out. 'You need shoes, a couple of evening dresses, a wrap of some kind for the evening, a winter coat, a hat—for church—and undies. There's a small shop where my sisters always go, not too far away.'

Emma stopped worrying about the cost of everything, for it was obvious that Roele was unmoved by the bills. She bought shoes and slippers and boots, and a brown cashmere coat, and, after much searching, a plain, elegant felt hat with a narrow brim which she set at an angle on her carroty hair—the effect of which made the doctor stare so hard at her that she blushed and asked him if he didn't like it.

'Charming—quite charming!' he told her, and thought how beautiful she looked.

As for the undies, he left her for half an hour, and when he returned the saleswoman handed him a bag the size of which was evidence of her success in finding what she wanted.

He took her to an elegant little café for tea, and then presently drove to his consulting rooms, stowed her shopping in the boot and then drove home. Emma sat beside him, rehearsing the thank-you speech she intended to make once they were indoors. It had been a wonderful day, she reflected, and Roele appeared to have enjoyed it as much as she had. Let there be more days like this one, she prayed silently, doing things together...

She went to her room once they had reached the house, leaving Kulk to bring in the parcels while Roele stood in the hall, looking through the letters on the tray on the console table.

'I'll be down in a minute,' she told him, and flew upstairs to throw off her coat and tidy her hair, add a little lipstick and powder her nose. She was less than five minutes, and when she got downstairs again the doctor was still in his coat, talking to Kulk, who, when he saw her, tactfully slid away.

'Roele, thank you for a lovely day'—began Emma, to be interrupted.

'Delightful, wasn't it? I won't be in for dinner and don't wait up; I shall be late home. I'm glad you enjoyed the day; we must do it again some time.' He crossed the hall to her and bent and kissed her cheek. 'I won't be home until early morning; we can have breakfast together. Sleep well, Emma.'

She conjured up a smile and watched him go, her lovely day in shreds around her; he had probably hated every minute of it, but his beautiful manners had prevented him from showing his wish for the tiresome day to be over. And where was he going now, and with whom?

Emma felt a sudden and unexpected surge of resentment. And she felt ashamed of that, for he had been very patient with her and spent a great deal of money.

She went to find Katje and ask if she might have dinner a little earlier, so that she had time to spend the evening unpacking her clothes and trying them on before she went to bed. She even tried to explain what a splendid day she had had, and Katje nodded encouragingly and Kulk said what a pity it was that the doctor should have to spend the evening out of the house.

He shrugged his shoulders. 'But of course it is his work, *mevrouw*.'

So what right had she to feel so disgruntled? She told herself that she was becoming selfish and thoughtless.

After dinner she told Kulk that she would go to her room and would need nothing further that evening. 'The doctor told me that he would be very late back. Do you usually wait up for him?'

'No, *mevrouw*. Coffee and sandwiches are left ready for him and he lets himself into the house. I'll take Prince and Percy out for their final run, but the doctor doesn't like me to stay up later than midnight.'

Unpacking her new clothes and trying everything on took a long time. Emma was surprised to find that it was midnight by the time the last garment had been carefully hung away. She bathed and got ready for bed and then, on an impulse, went quietly down the stairs. The *stoel* clock in the hall chimed one as she reached it, dimly lit by a wall-light above the console table. She stood for a moment, listening. Perhaps Roele was in his study or the kitchen. But he was in neither. Only Prince and Percy, curled up together, lifted sleepy heads as she went into the kitchen.

There was coffee on the stove and a covered plate on the table. Sandwiches—slivers of ham between thin buttered slices of bread. Emma took one and sat down by the Aga to eat it. She was wearing her new dressing gown, pale pink quilted silk, her feet thrust into matching slippers, and she admired them as she ate. She wasn't sure why she had come down to the kitchen, but it was warm and comfortable and Roele might be glad of company when he got home. She took another bite of sandwich and turned round at the faint sound behind her.

Roele was standing in the doorway. He looked tired, but he was smiling.

'What a delightful surprise to find you here, Emma, eating my sandwiches...'

He came into the kitchen, acknowledging the dogs' sleepy greeting, and sat down opposite her.

'You don't mind? I don't know why I came down. Well, I suppose it was because I thought you might want to talk to someone. But I'll go back to bed if you don't want company.'

'My dear Emma, I am delighted to have company. But are you not tired?'

She was pouring coffee into two mugs and had put the sandwiches within his reach.

'Not a bit.' She sat down and added quietly, 'It was so kind of you to waste a whole day shopping with me. I enjoyed it, but all the while you must have been thinking about your patients and the hospital and wanting to be there.' Before he could speak she added, 'I want to thank you for everything, Roele. All my lovely clothes, and showing me the shops, and lunch and tea...'

It was tempting to tell her then that the day had been a delight for him too, that buying all the clothes she wanted had given him the greatest delight, and that if it were possible he would buy her the most splendid jewels he could find. But it was too soon; she was at ease with him, trusted him, but that was all. It was a strange situation, wooing Emma with a courtship after they were married, but he had no doubt of its success, provided he could possess his soul in patience.

He settled back in his chair and between sandwiches told her about the patient he had driven miles to see that evening: a public figure whose illness needed to be kept secret; even the faintest whisper of it would send the Stock Market into a state of chaos.

'He'll recover?'

'I believe so, and no one will be the wiser.' He ate the last sandwich. 'How satisfying it is to come home to someone and talk.'

Emma took the mugs to the sink. 'Well, that's why we married, wasn't it, to be good companions?'

He got up, too. 'Yes, Emma. Is that thing you're wearing new? It's very pretty.' He kissed her cheek, a cool kiss which she had come to expect. 'Thank you for being here. Now go to bed and sleep. We will see each other at breakfast.'

She smiled at him sleepily, aware that something had happened between them although she had no idea what it was. In bed presently, she thought about it, but she was too sleepy to think clearly—knowing only that remembering the hour in the kitchen gave her a warm glow deep inside her.

She wore one of the cashmere jumpers and a new skirt to breakfast, and felt pleased when he remarked upon them.

'Will you be home for tea?' she asked him.

'I'll do my best. I've a clinic this afternoon, and sometimes we have to run overtime, but I'll be back in good time for dinner. I'll be free on Saturday, as well as Sunday, so we will go and see my mother and father. They are anxious to meet you. They wanted us to stay the night but I thought we might have Sunday to ourselves. We'll go for lunch and stay for tea, and perhaps for dinner. We can take Percy and Prince.' He picked up his letters and came round the table to bend and kiss her. 'Have you any plans for today?'

'I'm to inspect the linen cupboard with Katje and then I'm going for a walk with the dogs.'

'Don't get lost. But if you do say who you are and someone will see you safely home.'

The countryside round the village was quiet, despite the fact that Amsterdam was only a few miles away, and, warmly wrapped in the new winter coat, she and the dogs walked along the narrow brick roads. They met few people, but those she did, greeted her cheerfully. She came to a canal presently, and walked beside it for some distance. The country was very flat, and she could see the village churches dotted here and there in the landscape. They were further away than they appeared to be, however, and so she turned for home.

The walk had given her an appetite, and she ate lunch and then settled down to read by the fire, with the dogs snoozing at her feet. Presently she snoozed off herself, her rather untidy head lolling on the chair cushions.

Which was how Roele found her, sprawled awkwardly, her
shoes kicked off, her mouth slightly open. He sat down opposite
her, watching her until she stretched and woke and sat up.

'Oh, goodness, I fell asleep. Have you been here long?' She
was scrabbling around for her shoes and tucking odd wisps of
hair tidily away. 'I went for a long walk and ate too much lunch.
I'll go and tidy myself and tell Kulk to bring the tea.'

'You are very nice as you are, and Kulk will be here in a few
minutes. Where did you go? As far as the canal?'

Emma decided on the green jersey two-piece for their visit on
Saturday. It was simple, the colour flattered her, and if they stayed
for dinner it would pass muster. Wrapped in her new winter coat,
she got into the car beside Roele, telling herself that she wasn't
at all nervous. He had settled Percy and Prince on the back seat
and now turned to look at her.

'Nervous? Don't be. They are longing to meet you and I believe
that you will like them. They're elderly, but interested in just
about everything. They are enthusiastic gardeners, they love the
theatre and concerts and they still travel. You met Wibeke—and
I have another sister, married with children, living in Limburg,
and a brother. He's a doctor too, not married yet. He's at Leiden.'

Which gave her plenty to think about.

Roele drove down towards Den Haag and turned off to
Wassenaar on the coast north of that city. Wassenaar was so close
to Den Haag that it might be called a suburb, peopled by the well-
to-do. But once past the elegant tree-lined roads and villas there
was the old village, and past that a stretch of fairly open country
bordering the wide sands stretching out to the North Sea. The
doctor turned into a narrow lane with a pleasant rather old-
fashioned lot of houses on either side, and at one of these he
stopped.

Nice, thought Emma, getting out and taking a look. Homely
and solid. As indeed the house was. It was red brick, with shutters
at the windows and an iron balcony above a solid front door. And
the garden, even in winter, was one to linger in.

Not that she was allowed to linger. Roele took her arm and whisked her through the large stout door which a woman was holding open. He flung an arm around her and kissed her plump cheek. 'Klar...' He said something to make her laugh and turned to Emma.

'Klar looks after my mother and father,' he told her. 'She has been with us for even longer than the Kulks.'

Klar shook hands and beamed, and led the way through the hall to a door at its end and opened it. The room beyond was large, with a great many windows giving a view of the garden beyond. There were plants arranged in it, as well as comfortable chairs and tables and an old-fashioned stove at one end of it. It was warm, light and old-fashioned. Children, thought Emma, would love it.

She gave a small sigh of relief as the two people in it came to meet them. Roele, thought Emma, in thirty years' time: a nice old gentleman in elderly tweeds, still handsome, his eyes as bright and searching as his son's. And his mother—she had tried to imagine her without much success, and she had come nowhere near the plump little lady with hair in an old-fashioned bun and a pretty face, unashamedly wrinkled. Her eyes were blue and she was wearing a dress of the same colour, not fashionable, but beautifully made.

'Mother, Father,' said the doctor, 'here is my wife, Emma.'

She had not known such warmth since her father died. She was welcomed as though they had known and loved her all their lives. She swallowed back unexpected tears and was kissed and hugged and made to sit down beside Mevrouw van Dyke, and over coffee and sugary biscuits she listened to her mother-in-law's gentle kind voice.

'You poor child, you have had little happiness for the last year or so, but now Roele will make you happy again. We are so delighted to have you for another daughter. He has taken a long time to find a wife to love and to be loved by her.'

Presently Emma found herself sitting with the old gentleman. 'Roele has told us so much about you; we feel we know you well already. We don't see as much of him as we should like, for he is a busy man. You will know that already. But you must come and see us as often as you wish. Do you drive? Then he will get you a car so that you can be independent of him.'

Emma murmured agreement, not sure that she wanted to be independent. Roele's company wasn't only a pleasure, she had a feeling that she didn't wish to do without it. Surely he didn't want her to be one of those women who had so many interests outside the home that they were hardly ever there?

She caught his eye across the room and had the feeling that he knew just what she was thinking. That made her blush, and that in turn made Mevrouw van Dyke smile.

Lunch was a light-hearted meal, with cheerful talk about the wedding, and afterwards Emma walked round the garden with her father-in-law. Since she was quite knowledgeable about plants, flowers and shrubs, they got on famously.

Later, he told his wife that Roele had married a splendid girl. 'She knows the Latin names of almost everything in the garden but doesn't boast about it. He's met his match!'

His wife knew just what he meant. She said comfortably, 'Yes, dear. He's met his love too.'

It was late when Roele and Emma got home, for they had stayed for dinner and sat talking long after the meal was finished. The house was quiet, for the Kulks had gone to bed, and they went into the kitchen to sit at the table drinking the hot chocolate Katje had left on the Aga, not saying much, sitting in companionable silence. Prince and Percy, curled up together in Prince's basket had given them a sleepy greeting and dozed off again, and Emma yawned.

'A lovely day,' she said, sleepily content—only to have that content shattered a moment later when Roele told her that he was going to Rome in the morning.

Emma swallowed the yawn. 'Rome? Whatever for? For how long?'

In her sudden dismay she didn't see the gleam in the doctor's eyes. There had been more than surprise on her face; his Emma was going to miss him...

'I have been asked to examine a patient who lives there. I shall be gone for four or five days, perhaps longer. It depends upon her condition.'

'A woman?' said Emma, and he hid a smile.

'Yes, a famous one too. In the entertainment world.'

'How interesting,' said Emma tartly, and got to her feet. 'Shall I see you tomorrow before you go?'

'I'll leave here tomorrow about nine o'clock. Shall we have breakfast about eight?'

She nodded. 'I'll leave a note for Katje.' She went to the door and he went with her and opened it, bending to kiss her cheek as she went past him.

'Goodnight, Emma, sleep well.'

Well, I shan't, thought Emma crossly, intent on lying awake and feeling sorry for herself. Leaving her alone in a strange country while he jaunted off to Italy. And who was this patient? Some glamorous film star, bewitchingly beautiful, no doubt, lying back on lacy pillows in her bed, wearing a see-through nightie...

Emma allowed her imagination full rein and cried herself to sleep.

She went down to breakfast feeling quite contrary, wearing a tweed skirt and a cashmere jumper, wishing to look as much unlike the hussy in the nightie as possible. She had dabbed powder on her nose but forgotten her lipstick, and swept her colourful hair onto the top of her head in an untidy bunch.

The doctor thought she looked adorable, but from the look on her face he judged it hardly the time to tell her so. He enquired instead as to whether she had slept well, passed the toast rack and told her that he would phone her that evening.

'What time will you arrive in Rome?'

'Early afternoon.'

'Then you can phone me when you get there.' That sounded like a suspicious wife, so she added hastily, 'That is, if you have the time.'

'I'll ring from the airport.'

The matter settled to her satisfaction, Emma finished her breakfast, remarking upon the weather, the garden, the dogs—anything but his trip to Rome.

When he had gone, with Kulk beside him so that he could drive the Rolls back from Schipol, she took the dogs for a walk. She was beginning to find her way around now. The countryside wasn't dramatic but it was restful, and there was little traffic. She walked a long way, meeting no one and feeling lonely.

Roele phoned after lunch. His voice reassured her that the flight had been uneventful and he was about to be driven into Rome.

'I hope you will find your patient not too ill,' said Emma, 'and that you will have some time to enjoy Rome.'

They had had orgies in ancient Rome, she reminded herself. Did they still have them, and would Roele be tempted to go to one? She wasn't exactly sure what one did at an orgy but there would be bound to be beautiful girls there...

Such thinking wouldn't do at all, she told herself. Her imagination was running away with her again. It was only because she liked Roele so much that she wanted him to take care. It was a pity that she couldn't picture him, calm and assured, bending over the bed of a famous singer who had been struck down by some obscure illness which, so far, no one had diagnosed. The bed of the hospital variety, without a lace pillow in sight, and his patient's wan face as white as the all-enveloping garment she was wearing. And, since she was feeling very ill, the doctor could have been an ogre with two heads for all she cared.

There was plenty to keep Emma occupied during the next few days. The *dominee* called to ask her to go with his wife to Amsterdam to buy the small toys to be handed out to the schoolchildren on Sint Nikolaas Eve, and the following day they had to be wrapped in bright paper and stowed away ready for the party. When Roele phoned Emma told him about it, not taking too long, in case he was anxious to ring off. But it seemed he wasn't, for he wanted to know what else she had done, whether the dogs were behaving themselves and had she taken any long walks?

She wanted very much to ask when he was coming home, but surely he would tell her? She was on the point of bidding him a cheerful goodbye when he said, 'I shall be home tomorrow, Emma.'

Before she could stop herself she said, 'Oh, I'm so glad; I've missed you...'

She hung up then, wishing she hadn't said it.

She went to find Kulk and tell him, and discovered that he already knew. He was to take the car to Schipol to pick up the doctor from the plane landing at three o'clock. And would *mevrouw* like to see Katje about dinner for the following day? The doctor was bound to be hungry...

Emma felt hurt. Roele could have told *her* at what time he would arrive, and she could have gone to Schipol to meet him. But he hadn't wanted her.

For the first time since they had married she wondered if she had made a dreadful mistake. Somehow the close friendship she had felt at Salcombe was dwindling away. Perhaps he was disappointed in her, although she had done her best to be what he wanted. He had said he wanted a friend and a companion, someone who would ease his social life for him and preside at his dinner table when they had guests.

She worried at her thoughts like a dog worrying a bone for the rest of the day, and a good deal of the night. But by the following afternoon she had pulled herself together, deciding she was being silly, imagining things which didn't exist. She put on one of the pretty warm dresses, took pains with her face and subdued her hair into a French pleat. She went downstairs and sat in the drawing room with Prince and Percy and, so as not to look too eager, had a book open on her lap.

She didn't read a word but sat, her ears stretched for the sound of the heavy front door closing, so that the doctor, coming into his house by a side door, caught her unawares.

He stood in the doorway and said, 'Hello, Emma,' in a quiet voice.

She dropped the book and spun round and out of her chair to

meet him. She forgot that she was going to be pleased to see him in a cool friendly way; instead she shot across the room and he came to meet her and take her in his arms.

'Well, what a warm welcome,' he said, smiling down at her. He held her a little way from him. 'And how pretty you look. For my benefit, I hope?'

'No, of course not. Well, yes. I mean, you were coming home...' She saw his slow smile and added hastily, 'Was it a success, your visit?'

'I hope so. An obscure chest condition which might bring an end to the lady's singing career.'

He came and sat down opposite her and Kulk brought in the tea tray. Emma felt a very warm contentment.

It was on the following day that he told her that they had been invited to have drinks at the hospital director's house. 'We have known each other some time now, and he has a charming wife. Will you be ready if I get home around six o'clock.'

'Then I'll tell Katje to have dinner ready at eight?'

'Yes, by all means. I should warn you that this is the beginning of an obligatory social round so that you may meet everyone— my colleagues, their wives, old family friends. I did tell you that I knew a number of people.'

'My Dutch...' began Emma.

'No need to worry; they all speak English. I must rely upon you to deal with invitations, and of course we shall have to invite everyone back again.' He smiled at her. 'You can see why I need a wife!'

For some reason his remark depressed her.

CHAPTER NINE

SHE must look her best, decided Emma, getting ready for the drinks party that evening. She brushed her hair to shining smoothness, took pains with her face and got into the dark green velvet dress. Which, even under her critical gaze, was without fault. And Roele's admiring look clinched the matter.

Although she was by no means unused to social occasions, Emma felt nervous. The director of the hospital was an important person, and she wanted to make a good impression and not let Roele down. But she need not have worried. Their host was a middle-aged, scholarly man who appeared to be on the most friendly terms with Roele, and as for his wife, an imposing lady with a rigid hairstyle and ample proportions, she was kindness itself, taking Emma under her wing and introducing her to several other people there.

Going back home later, Emma asked anxiously, 'Was I all right? I wish I could speak Dutch—your kind of Dutch, not just the odd word.'

'You were a great success, Emma. I have been envied by the men and congratulated by the women and, should you wish, you have a splendid social life ahead of you.'

'Well,' said Emma, 'I like meeting people and going to the theatre and all that sort of thing, but not by myself and not too often. And only if you're there, too.'

'I shall do my best to be on hand, but you will have to go to numerous coffee mornings on your own.'

'I'm going to one in the village tomorrow. A kind of coffee morning the children have got up to raise money for Christmas. All the mothers are going and the *dominee* asked if I would go too. It'll be fun and I can practise my Dutch on the children. I asked Katje to make some biscuits so that I could take something. You don't mind?'

'My dear Emma, of course I don't mind. This is your home in which you may do whatever you like, and I'm glad that you like the village. My mother did a great deal to help the *dominee* and he will be delighted to have your interest.'

The visit to the village was a success; the children accepted Emma's fragmented Dutch in the unsurprised way that children have, and even though she seldom managed to complete a whole articulate sentence no one laughed.

No one laughed at the various coffee mornings she attended either, but then everyone spoke English to her. They were kind to her, these wives of Roele's colleagues, introducing her to an ever-widening circle of acquaintances, concealing their well-bred curiosity about her, making sure that she went to the right shops, dropping hints as to what to wear at the various social functions. Emma took it all in good part, sensing that they wanted to be friends and had no intention of patronising her.

But she didn't allow the social round to swallow her up. She was beginning to understand the running of Roele's house, under Katje's tuition: the ordering of food, the everyday routine, the careful examination of its lovely old furniture, checking for anything that needed expert attention, the checking of the vast linen cupboard. All things which needed to be done without disturbing Roele's busy day.

Besides that, there was the village. She went at least once a week, always with the dogs—to have coffee at the *dominee's* house, to talk to the middle-aged school teacher at the primary school, and join the committee engaged in organising first Sint Nikolaas and then Christmas. Her days were full and she was happy. Though not perfectly happy, for she saw so little of Roele.

It sometimes seemed to her that he was avoiding her. True, they went to a number of dinner parties, and he once took her to the theatre to see a sombre play in Dutch. She hadn't enjoyed it, but sitting by him had made her happy; she saw so little of him...

There was to be a drinks party at the hospital. 'Black tie and those slippery bits and pieces to eat,' Roele had told her. 'Wear something pretty. That green thing with the short skirt. It won't only be hospital staff; there will be the city dignitaries there as well.' He had smiled at her. 'Mother and Father will be there, and quite a few people who know you quite well by now.'

On the evening of the party she went downstairs to the small sitting room and found him already there, immaculate in black tie, standing at the open door into the garden where the dogs were romping.

As she went in he whistled them indoors and closed the French windows, shutting out the cold dark evening.

'Charming,' he said, and crossed the room to her. 'And it's about time we got engaged.'

'But we're already married,' said Emma.

'Ah, yes, but I have always fancied a long engagement, buying the ring and so on.'

Emma laughed. 'Don't be absurd, Roele. You do all that before you marry!'

'So we must do it after, must we not? I cannot offer to buy you a ring, but perhaps you will wear this one? A family heirloom which gets handed down to each successive bride.'

He had a ring in his hand, a glowing sapphire surrounded by diamonds set in a plain gold band. He slipped it onto her finger above her wedding ring.

'There, they go well together.'

Emma held up her hand to admire it. 'It's very beautiful—and it fits.'

'I remembered the size of your wedding ring and had this one altered.'

He was matter-of-fact, rather like someone who was aware of something which had to be done and did it with as little fuss as possible.

I have no reason to feel unhappy, thought Emma. He had given me a gorgeous ring and I'm a very lucky girl. So she thanked him with just the right amount of pleasure, careful not to gush. Sentiment seemed to have no part in his gift.

The party was a grand and dignified affair, with champagne being offered on silver trays by correctly dressed waiters and sedate women in black dresses and white aprons proffering canapés from wide dishes. It wasn't long before Emma became separated from Roele and taken under the wing of the director's wife, handed from one guest to the next. They were all kind to her, and the younger men were flatteringly attentive while the younger women bombarded her with questions about the wedding.

She would have liked Roele to be with her but he was at the far end of the large room, deep in conversation with a group of other men, so she did her best to give light-hearted replies without saying much. Roele was a reserved man and wouldn't want the circumstances of their marriage broadcast. She felt a wave of pleasure, remembering his obvious admiration in the drawing room, and earlier, just before they had gone to greet their host and hostess, he had said softly, 'I'm proud of my wife, Emma.'

The evening was half over when she found herself standing beside an older woman, elegantly dressed and discreetly made up. She had a beaky nose and rather small dark eyes. Emma didn't think she liked her, but since she had made some trivial remark it needed to be answered politely.

'So you are Roele's wife. I am surprised that he has married at last, and to an English girl. I wish you both a happy future. You will find everything strange, no doubt.'

'Well, not really,' said Emma, being polite again but wishing the lady would go away. 'Life here is very much as it is in England, you know.'

'It is perhaps a good thing that he has chosen someone not from his own country. I—we all—thought he was a confirmed bachelor. After all, he was devoted to Veronique. He was a changed man when she went to America. But of course he needs a wife, a domestic background. For a man in his profession that is necessary. I am sure that he has made a very good choice in you.'

The woman was being spiteful and gossipy, thought Emma to herself. She said sweetly, 'I suppose it is natural for people to be curious about our marriage. But everyone I have met so far has been so kind and friendly. I feel quite at home. And I never listen to gossip...'

She was saved from saying more by one of the younger doctors coming to ask her if she would be coming to the hospital ball.

'You must come. Now that Dr van Dyke has you for a partner I don't see how he can make an excuse. He comes and dances once with the director's wife and then goes away again, but now he can dance all night with you. Although he won't get the chance; we shall all want to dance with you!'

'A ball? How lovely. Of course we shall come. When is it to be?'

The beaky-nosed woman said sourly, 'It is an annual event—Roele hasn't done more than put in a token appearance since Veronique went to America.'

'Then we shall have to change that,' said Emma brightly, and was thankful when the young doctor suggested that she might like to go to the buffet with him and have something to eat.

'Mevrouw Weesp is a little—how shall I say?—sour. She is the widow of a former director and now I think she is lonely and not much liked.'

'Poor soul,' said Emma, and forgot her for the moment, for Roele was coming towards her.

'Oh, I'll make myself scarce,' said the young doctor cheerfully.

'Enjoying yourself?' Roele was piling a plate for her with smoked salmon and tiny cheese tartlets. 'You've scored another triumph, Emma.'

'It must be this dress.'

They were joined by some of his friends and their wives and she had no chance to speak to him again.

'A pleasant evening,' observed the doctor later, ushering her into the house and the welcoming flurry of dogs. 'The ball is the next event to which we have to go.'

'That young man I was talking to said you don't stay—only for one dance.' Which reminded her of something.

They had gone to the small sitting room, where Katje had laid out coffee and sandwiches, and she cast down her wrap and kicked off her shoes.

'Someone called Mevrouw Weesp talked to me. Roele, who was Veronique?'

She watched his face become still. 'A girl I once knew. Why do you ask?'

Emma said crossly, 'May I not ask? I'm your wife, aren't I? Husbands and wives don't have secrets from each other.'

'Since you ask, I will tell you. She was—still is—a beautiful woman, and I fell in love with her—oh, ten years ago. She went to America and married there and is now divorced. I met her again last year when I was over there at a seminar.'

'So she wouldn't marry you and you made do with second best. Me.'

'If you think that of me, then perhaps we should discuss the matter when you aren't so uptight.'

'Me? Uptight?' said Emma in a voice which didn't sound quite like her own. 'Of course I'm not. I asked a perfectly civil question about someone you should have told me about ages ago.'

'Why?' he asked slowly. 'It isn't as if you are in love with me, so my past can be of little interest to you. Just as your affair with Derek is of no interest to me.'

Emma exploded. 'Affair with Derek! You know it wasn't an affair… I couldn't bear the sight of him.' She drew a shaky breath, 'But you met her again last year, and she's divorced.'

He was staring at her rather hard. 'Do you mind so much, Emma?'

She was grovelling around for her shoes. 'I don't mind in the least. I'm going to bed.'

In her room she flung her clothes off, got into bed and cried herself to sleep. Even then she didn't realise that she was in love with Roele.

But Roele knew. He knew too that he would have to handle the situation very carefully, and say nothing for a day or so while she realised her feelings for him. He had been patient; he would continue being patient for as long as need be.

Emma went down to breakfast the next morning, half hoping that Roele would have already left the house. But he was there, wishing her good morning in his calm, friendly fashion, passing her the toast, remarking on the mild weather.

'I shall be at the hospital for a good deal of today, but I'll be free to go with you for the St Nikolaas party in the village tomorrow afternoon. Have they got all they want for the children?'

Emma replied suitably, wondering if they were to forget about last night. Well, he might, but I shan't, she reflected, and to make matters worse as he picked up his post, ready to leave, she saw that the top letter bore a USA stamp.

He put a hand on her shoulder as he went, but he didn't give her the light kiss she had come to expect.

She took herself and the dogs for a long walk that morning, and after lunch wrote a long letter to Miss Johnson and a still longer one to Phoebe. After tea Emma went to her room and examined her clothes, finding that it gave her no satisfaction at all; she might just as well wear an old skirt and jumper, for there was no one to see the lovely things she had bought with such pleasure. Wallowing in self-pity, she went downstairs.

Roele was in the small sitting room, stretched out on one of the comfortable armchairs. He was asleep, his tired face relaxed, the lines in it very marked.

Emma, standing there looking at him, knew then.

Her bad temper, uncertainty and bewilderment and self-pity were swept away. She was in love with him—and why hadn't she realised it sooner? She had always loved him, from that first meeting in the bakery shop at Salcombe.

Now they were in a pretty pickle, weren't they? This woman in America, now free to marry him, and he was tied to a wife he had married for all the wrong reasons. She had been feeling sorry for herself when in fact she should be sorry for Roele. He would do nothing about it even if he had given his heart to this other woman, for that was the kind of man he was. So she would have to do something about it. For him to be happy was the one thing which mattered.

He opened his eyes and sat up. 'Hello, I got home earlier than I expected. Have you had a pleasant day?'

'Yes, I took the dogs through the village and along the road by the canal. Would you like tea? Or coffee? Dinner won't be for an hour or so...'

He got to his feet. 'Just time for me to go and see the *dominee* about the Christmas trees...'

So she was alone again, and even if she had wanted to talk to him he hadn't given her the chance.

They talked over dinner, of course, trivialities which didn't give her an opening to say what she wanted to say, and after the meal he told her that he had work to do and went away to his study. He was still there when she opened the door and wished him goodnight. Perhaps that would have been a good moment, but he was engrossed in a sheaf of papers, and although he got to his feet he had the papers in his hand, obviously waiting to get back to them.

Perhaps tomorrow, thought Emma before she slept.

True, he was home early, and went with her to the village, where she helped distribute plates of food and mugs of lemonade. She was aware that he was having a word with everyone there, listening gravely to the elderlies who had come to have a look, laughing with the younger women, admiring their babies, and then finally handing out the prizes. She could see that he was enjoying himself among people that he had known for most of his life, and that they accepted him as one of themselves. Just as they accepted her, she discovered with pleasure and surprise.

There was an hour or more before dinner when they got home. Emma went into the small sitting room and Roele followed her. He shut the door and said quietly, 'I think that we might have a talk, Emma...'

'Yes, but before you start, did you know that Veronique was free to marry again when you married me?'

The doctor hadn't expected that. He answered quietly, 'No, Emma.'

Emma sat down and Percy climbed onto her lap. 'You see,' she observed, 'that is important…'

He said, suddenly harsh, 'It is not of the slightest importance—' The phone stopped him. He picked it up, said savagely, 'Van Dyke,' and listened. 'I'll take the car to Schipol—give me an hour,' he said finally.

He put the phone down. 'I'm going to Vienna. I'm not sure how long I'll be away.' He was halfway to the door. 'Get Kulk to pack a bag, will you?'

He went into his study and shut the door and she went to find Kulk and ask Katje to have sandwiches and coffee ready.

Fifteen minutes later he had gone.

The next day she was to go to a coffee morning one of the doctor's wives was giving. Since it was being held for charity, she knew that she would have to go.

There were familiar faces there, and several of them knew that Roele had gone to Vienna.

'An emergency,' one of the older women told her. 'All a bit hush-hush—a political VIP shot in the chest, and of course Roele's splendid with chests.' She smiled kindly at Emma. 'But you know that already. You've not heard from him yet?'

'No, he left in a tremendous hurry. He'll ring just as soon as he can spare a minute.'

Her companion laid a kindly hand on her arm. 'I know just how anxious you feel, my dear. Even now, after years of being married to a medical man, I still fuss privately if he goes off somewhere. We are all fond of Roele, we older wives. He is still so young, and brilliantly good at his job. We were so relieved when that woman Veronique—you know about her, of course?' Emma nodded. 'When she went off to America. A most beautiful woman, but with a cold, calculating heart, greedy and selfish.'

Emma said lightly, 'Roele tells me that she is divorced now…'

'Well, thank heaven that he found you. We all think that you are exactly the right wife for him.'

She was, she knew now that she was, but did he know it? She

had fitted in very nicely to his life but there was more to it than that...

She was to meet Kulk with the car at the consulting rooms, and she made her way there, passing Juffrouw Smit's house on the way. On impulse, she rang the old-fashioned bell. Juffrouw Smit opened the door, her severe expression softening to a smile.

'Emma, come in. I don't need to go to the consulting rooms until two o'clock and I've just made coffee. You'll have a cup?'

It was more of a command than a query. Emma, awash with coffee already, meekly said that she would love that.

They sat each side of the old-fashioned stove and talked. One didn't gossip with Juffrouw Smit; the weather was discussed, the government torn to shreds, the high price of everything in the shops condemned, and all in a very refined manner, until at last, these subjects exhausted, Emma said, 'May I ask you something, Juffrouw Smit? In the last day or so I have twice been told about someone called Veronique—someone the doctor knew some years ago. I have no wish to pry into his past life, and I know that he would tell me about her, but each time he is about to do so he has to go away in a hurry. If I knew a little more about her it would be easier for me when people talk to me about her.' She looked hopefully at her companion's severe face. 'You do see that, don't you? And you would know about her, because Roele regards you as his right hand.'

Juffrouw Smit's face remained severe, and Emma said in a rather sad voice, 'I dare say you don't wish to talk about it, and I quite understand. I know it isn't important, but I might say the wrong thing. Everyone takes it for granted that I know about her...'

Juffrouw Smit sniffed delicately. 'There is always gossip, and you have probably got the wrong impression from it. I do not feel that it is any business of mine to discuss it with you, Emma. All I will say is that this woman went to America a long time ago and that if the doctor sees fit to tell you about her then he will do so. There is always gossip at these social gatherings, some of it quite unfounded.'

Emma swallowed disappointment. 'I'm sure you're right,' she agreed politely. 'I don't really enjoy coffee mornings and tea parties, but Roele told me to meet as many people as I could so that I would feel at home quickly.' She glanced at her watch. 'I must go. Kulk will be waiting for me. I do hope that I haven't hindered you.'

'No. I'm always glad to see you, Emma. I hope the doctor will be back home soon. You will be going to Wassenaar for Christmas?'

'Yes. All the family will be there. And you? You spend it with family, too?'

'My brother in Utrecht, just for two days, but I shall go again for the New Year.'

At the door she put a hand on Emma's arm. 'You mustn't worry,' she said.

Which was a useless bit of advice, for there was another letter with an American stamp on top of the pile waiting for Roele's return, and, as if that wasn't enough, that evening there was a phone call. It had gone to the consulting rooms and the porter had switched it through to the house, as he always did.

When Emma answered his ring he said gruffly, 'A call from Washington, *mevrouw*. I'm putting it through for you.'

She had understood most of what he had said, but the woman's voice in her ear took her by surprise.

As she was speaking in Dutch, Emma waited until there was a pause in the rather shrill voice.

'I'm sorry, Dr van Dyke is away and I don't speak Dutch. Will you leave a message? He will be back in a few days.'

The voice sounded annoyed, snapping, 'No message.' Then the caller replaced the receiver.

Perhaps whoever it was would ring again, thought Emma. When the porter went off duty he would switch the answering machine on and Juffrouw Smit would check it in the morning as she always did.

Emma got her coat and went into the garden with the dogs. Two letters from America and a phone call within days? They had to be more than coincidence, and surely whoever it was could have at least given their name or a message?

Emma, usually so matter-of-fact and sensible, allowed her imagination to run riot. If only Roele would phone...

He did, just as she had finished dinner. He sounded just as he always did, friendly, unhurried. How was she? What had she done with her day?

She told him, then added, 'There is another letter for you from America, and this evening a—woman—phoned from Washington. She spoke Dutch. She didn't give a name and she wouldn't leave a message.'

He sounded unconcerned. 'Oh, yes. I was expecting a call. I'll get on to Smitty about it. I can't get away for several days, Emma. I hope that when I do get home we shall have a chance to talk. I'm not prepared to go on as we are.'

'Me too. Goodnight, Roele.'

Emma knew what she was going to do. She went and sat down at the little walnut Davenport in the sitting room and began to write a letter. The first attempt was no good, nor was the second, while the third was brief, almost businesslike.

She was going back to Salcombe, she wrote in her rather large writing. She quite realised that their marriage had been a mistake which could luckily be put right. It would have been nice if he had told her himself about Veronique, but luckily she had been told by several people. She quite understood that now Veronique was free he could be happy with his real love.

It would be quite easy, wrote Emma, writing fast and untidily. She would tell everyone that she had to go back and settle some family business and when she had been away for a week or two he could explain.

She didn't pause to consider if he might object to doing this, but signed herself, 'Your friend Emma', before putting the letter in an envelope and into a pocket. She would leave it on his desk in the study when she went.

She sat for a while at the little desk, doodling on the blotting paper, writing his name in various ways, drawing a heart with an arrow piercing it and then adding 'I love you' several times.

'I'm a fool,' said Emma to Percy and Prince, who were watching her anxiously, and she tucked the blotting paper behind the fresh sheets on the pad.

The letter written, she went to her room and packed a small case and her overnight bag. She counted her money and found her passport, then went back to the small sitting room and lifted the phone.

It was too late for a flight, but the overnight ferry from the Hoek didn't leave until midnight. If Kulk drove her in the Rolls she had ample time to get there. There was a helpful girl on the telephone enquiry line, who put her through to the ferry offices, and there was no trouble booking a berth.

Next she went in search of Kulk. She told him she had had an urgent message from England and must get there as soon as possible. 'I've booked on the Hoek ferry. If you'll drop me there, Kulk, I can be ready in less than half an hour.'

'The doctor, *mevrouw*—can you let him know?'

Emma, embarked on her impetuous plan, allowed the lies to flow easily from her ready tongue. 'I couldn't get him, Kulk. He wasn't at any of the places I enquired at. I left a message and I'll phone as soon as I reach England.'

She felt quite sick at the muddle she was weaving, but to get away as quickly as possible was paramount. She had no plan other than that. The future, for the moment, meant nothing to her.

A worried Kulk drove her to the Hoek, saw her safely on board and turned for home, feeling uneasy.

At one o'clock in the morning the ferry was making heavy work of the rough weather, and Emma, longing for sleep, was seasick.

And at one o'clock in the morning the doctor got back home, ruthlessly cutting short the various social occasions and meetings laid on for him now that his patient was on the way to recovery. He hadn't liked the sound of Emma's voice on the phone, and his patience was exhausted. He would shake her until her teeth rattled, and then kiss her...

He frowned as he put his key in the lock of the small side door which he used if he was called out at night. There was a light on in the passage leading to the kitchen, and as he went in Kulk came to meet him.

'*Mijnheer*, you are back. Thank heaven...'

'*Mevrouw?* She's ill? There's been an accident?'

'No, no.' Kulk explained, then added, 'It didn't seem right that she should go off like that at a moment's notice. But she insisted. I've only been back half an hour or so.'

They were in the kitchen and Roele sat down at the table.

'Sit down and tell me exactly what happened,' he begged calmly.

Kulk put a cup of coffee before him. 'Upset, she was. Said she couldn't get you on the phone and in such a hurry to be away.'

The doctor drank his coffee. He said with outward calm, 'I dare say there is a letter...'

He went along to the sitting room and saw the envelope propped up on the Davenport. He sat down to read it. When he had finished he was smiling. This was a tangle easily untangled...

His eye lighted on the screwed-up papers in the wastepaper basket and he smoothed them out and read them too. Emma had written in a good deal of agitation but her meaning was clear. He saw the pristine blotting paper too, and thoughtfully turned it over.

He was a tired man, but his wide smile erased the lines etched on his handsome face.

Kulk came presently, with more coffee and sandwiches.

'Go to bed, Kulk. I shall need you in the morning.'

He drank his coffee, ate the sandwiches, and went to bed himself, to sleep for the last few hours of the night, knowing exactly what he would do.

He was up early, but Kulk was waiting, offering breakfast.

'I am going over to England this morning. I've arranged for a plane from Schipol and I'll fly to Plymouth. This is what I want you to do. Take the car over tomorrow morning and drive to

Salcombe. Let me know when you get there. I shall be at the end cottage on the Victoria Quay. Take an early ferry and get to Salcombe by early afternoon if you can. I'll drive back in time to get the late-evening ferry. I shall have *mevrouw* with me and you can catch up on your sleep in the back of the car.'

Kulk listened gravely. 'Very well, *Mijnheer*. You will need an overnight bag?'

In the kitchen he confided in Katje that whatever it was that had gone wrong was being put right without loss of time.

'And a good thing, too,' said Katje. 'Such a nice young lady she is.'

Emma, her feet once more on dry land, couldn't wait to get to the cottage. It would be quiet there and she would be able to think clearly. It had been borne in upon her that she had acted hastily, and perhaps unwisely, but it was too late to have regrets as she began the tedious journey to Salcombe: first to London, on a train which had no refreshment car, let alone coffee or tea, queuing for a taxi to cross London, then finding that she would have to wait for an hour for a fast train to Totnes.

She had a meal, made up her face, bought magazines which she didn't read and finally got into the train. It left late and stopped every now and then in the middle of nowhere for no apparent reason, so that by the time she reached Exeter and found the train to Totnes she was hard put to it not to scream. But at last she was in Totnes, and getting into a taxi to take her the last twenty miles or so to Salcombe.

It was early evening now, and all she could think of was a large pot of tea and the chance to take off her shoes.

The taxi dropped her off by the pub and she walked the last short distance along the quay to the cottage. She had the key ready in her hand and unlocked the door with a rush of relief, to be taken aback for the moment by the pleasant warmth of the little room. She switched on the light and caught her breath.

Lounging comfortably in one of the armchairs was Roele.

He got to his feet as she stood staring at him. 'There you are, my dear. You must have had a very tiresome journey.'

Emma burst into tears and he took her in his arms and held her close. 'You shouldn't be here,' sobbed Emma. 'I've left you. Don't you understand?'

'One thing at a time,' said the doctor calmly. 'I'm here because I love you and you're here because you love me. Isn't that right?'

Emma gave a watery snort. 'But you don't love me. There's this Veronique...'

He sighed. 'Ten years ago I believed that I loved her; then she went to America and I haven't given her a thought since.'

'You met her last year.'

'At a friend's house—and I hardly remembered her. Just as you don't remember Derek.'

'She rang up...'

'No, she didn't. That was the secretary of someone I know in Washington who wants me to do a series of lectures.'

Emma mopped her face on the handkerchief he offered her. 'Do you really love me?'

He looked down at her tired tearstained face. 'Yes, my darling, I really love you. I fell in love with you at the bakery and from that moment you have taken over my life.'

'Have I? Have I really? Do you know I didn't know that I loved you, even though I know now that it was when I first saw you? You bought a pasty.'

'My darling girl... And that reminds me. There are pasties for our supper.'

'I'm hungry. Can one be so in love and be hungry too?'

'Undoubtedly.' He smiled down at her as he unbuttoned her coat and pulled off her gloves. 'There's a bottle of champagne too.'

Later, replete with pasty, pleasantly muzzy with champagne, Emma asked, 'How do we get home?'

'Kulk is bringing the car; we will drive home tomorrow.'

'Back home,' said Emma, in a voice so full of content that he felt compelled to sweep her into his arms once more.

She peered into his face—such a handsome face, tired now, so that he looked older than he was, but happy...

'I am so very happy,' said Emma, and she kissed him.

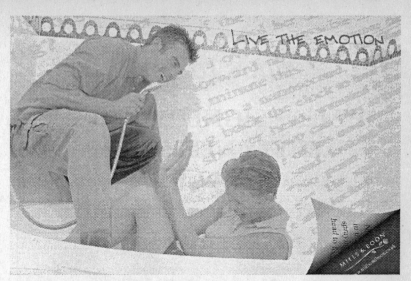
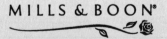

Betty Neels Ultimate Collection
Official Prize Draw Rules

NO PURCHASE NECESSARY

Each book in the Betty Neels Ultimate Collection will contain details for entry into the following prize draw: 4 prizes of a signed Betty Neels book and a weekend break to Amsterdam and 10 prizes of a signed Betty Neels book. No purchase necessary.

To enter the draw, hand print the words "Betty Neels Ultimate Collection Prize Draw", plus your name and address on a postcard. For UK residents please send your postcard entries to: Betty Neels Ultimate Collection Prize Draw, PO Box 236, Croydon, CR9 3RU. For ROI residents please send your postcard to Betty Neels Ultimate Collection Prize Draw, PO Box 4546, Kilcock, County Kildare.

To be eligible all entries must be received by July 31st 2003. No responsibility can be accepted for entries that are lost, delayed or damaged in the post. Proof of postage cannot be accepted as proof of delivery. No correspondence can be entered into and no entry returned. Winners will be determined in a random draw from all eligible entries received. Judges decision is final. One mailed entry per person, per household.

Amsterdam break includes return flights for two, 2 nights accommodation at a 4 star hotel, airport/hotel transfers, insurance and £150 spending money. Holiday must be taken between 1/8/03 and 1/08/04 excluding Bank holidays, Easter and Christmas periods. (Winner has the option of accepting £500 cash in lieu of holiday option.)

All travellers must sign and return a Release of Liability prior to travel and must have a valid 10 year passport. Accommodation and flights are subject to schedule and availability. The Prize Draw is open to residents of the UK and ROI, 18 years of age or older. Employees and immediate family members of Harlequin Mills & Boon Ltd., its affiliates, subsidiaries and all other agencies, entities and persons connected with the use, marketing or conduct of this Prize Draw are not eligible.

Prize winner notification will be made by letter no later than 14 days after the deadline for entry. Limit: one prize per an individual, family or organisation. All applicable laws and regulations apply. If any prize or prize notification is returned as undeliverable, an alternative winner will be drawn from eligible entries. By acceptance of a prize, winner consents to use of his/her name, photograph or other likeness for purpose of advertising, trade and promotion on behalf of Harlequin Mills & Boon Ltd., without further compensation, unless prohibited by law.

For the names of prize winners (available after 31/08/03), send a self-addressed stamped envelope to: For UK residents, Betty Neels Ultimate Collection Prize Draw Winners List, PO Box 236, Croydon, CR9 3RU. For ROI residents, Betty Neels Ultimate Collection Prize Draw Winners List, PO Box 4546, Kilcock, County Kildare.